Gargoyle

Editor/Publisher: Richard Peabody

Design: Nita Congress

Layout: Stephen Caporaletti

Webmaster: Wendy Guberman

Staff/Interns: Caleb Driker-Ohren
Victoria Gaffney
Kristy Feltenberger Gillespie
Ivy Grimes
Jessica Harper
Victoria Horton
Stephanie Joyce
Beth Konkoski
Raima Larter
Stephanie Leow
Kelly Wolfe

FOREVE
blosso

ning
EAL JOY

Hat tip to Blair Ewing.

Special thanks to Sheerly Avni, Linda Blaskey, Hildie S. Block, Jamie Brown, Nancy Naomi Carlson, Mark Danowsky, Sid Gold, inlandia institute, Gerry LaFemina, Jen Knox, Roz Kuehn, mixtusmedia, Daniel Mueller, nanowrimo, the poetic justice institute, Doug Rice, Jeff Richards, screen craft, script anatomy, D.E. Steward, and *Writer's Digest*.

Magical alms and OMGs to Denise Duhamel and Gregg Shapiro for finding Pamela Gordon.

Undying love to the Barlows, Blair and Mary Ewing, Albert Jordan and Lyn Lifshin, the Sheridans, James Patterson and Rose Solari, not forgetting every reader out there in *Gargoyle* Land.

We're so happy with the results. Took forever in this crazy pandemic year, but I think you'll love it.

In Memoriam

Hank Aaron
Herb Adderley
John Aldridge
Miguel Algarin
Michael Apted
Jon Arnett
Sheila Ascher
Len Barry
Marvin Bell
Ed Benguiat
Bruce Berger
Walter Bernstein
Harold Betters
Gary Blankenburg
Tim Bogert
Claude Bolling
Chadwick Boseman
Ben Bova
Julian Bream
Lee Breuer
Wilford Brimley
Lou Brock
Ed Bruce
Harold Budd
Jeremy Bulloch
Richard Burgin
Thomas Jefferson Byrd
Pierre Cardin
Rene Carpenter
Jean-Claude Carrière
Sandie Castle
Kay Carroll
John Chaney
Michael Chapman
Maxine Cheshire
J. Wesley Clark
Ron Cobb
Joan Colby
Freddy Cole
Sean Connery
Chick Corea
Simeon Coxe
Claude Crabb
Ben Cross
Stanley Crouch
David Darling
Rennie Davis
Spencer Davis
Christopher Dickey
Eric Jerome Dickey
Diane di Prima
Jim Dwyer
Joe Englert
Clayton Eshleman
Steve Farmer
Conchata Ferrell
Bobby Few
Tom Finn
Leon Fleisher
Michael Fonfara
Wayne Fontana
Bob Gibson
Ruth Bader Ginsburg
Terry Goodkind
Kathleen Ann Goonan
Shirley Ann Grau
Juliette Greco
Peter Green
Alberto Grimaldi
Winston Groom
James E. Gunn
Pete Hamill
QR Hand
Gordon Haskell
Olivia de Havilland
Jim Haynes
Ken Hensley
Toots Hibbert
Hal Holbrook
Tony Hooper
Paul Hornung
Florence Howe
Denise Johnson
Howard Johnson
K.C. Jones
Nelly Kaplan
Terry Kay
Jack Kehoe
Randall Kenan
Frank Kimbrough
Rosalind Knight
Lee Konitz
Neil Landon
Tommy Lasorda
John le Carre
Cloris Leachman
John Lewis
Floyd Little
Gerald Locklin
Barry Lopez
Trini Lopez
Kurt Luedtke
Richard Allen Lupoff
Alison Lurie
Naomi Long Madgett
Linda Manz
Diego Maradona
Ellis Marsalis
Gerry Marsden
Richard McCann
Leslie McGrath
Ved Mehta
Daniel Menaker
Diana Millay
Joe Morgan
Jan Morris
Johnny Nash
Rupert Neve
Phil Niekro
John O'Brien
Julia O'Faolain
K.T. Oslin
Geoffrey Palmer
Alan Parker
Gary Peacock
Sharon Kay Penman
Ray Perkins
Bucky Pizzarelli
Christopher Plummer
Mark Power
Rocco Prestia
Charley Pride
David Prowse
Terry Quirk
Ann Reinking
Emitt Rhodes
Tony Rice
James Ridgeway
Diana Rigg
Jimmie Rodgers
Annie Ross
Giuseppe Rotunno
Dennis Saleh
Gale Sayers
Murray Schisgal
Marty Schottenheimer
Jake Scott
Tom Seaver
Lee Sharkey
Neil Sheehan
Barbara Shelley
Joan Micklin Silver
Lynn Stalmaster
Chad Stuart
Carol Sutton
Don Sutton
Stella Tennant
Wayne Terwilliger
John Thompson
Pamela Tiffin
Cicely Tyson
Hilton Valentine
Jean Valentine
Eddie Van Halen
C.T. Vivian
Howard Wales
Jerry Jeff Walker
Lewis Warsh
ruth weiss
Leslie West
Paul Westphal
Andrew White
Larry Wilson
S. Clay Wilson
Baron Wolman
Eugene Wright
James A. Wu
Kenny Young

Contents

Nonfiction

Poetry

Fiction

Art

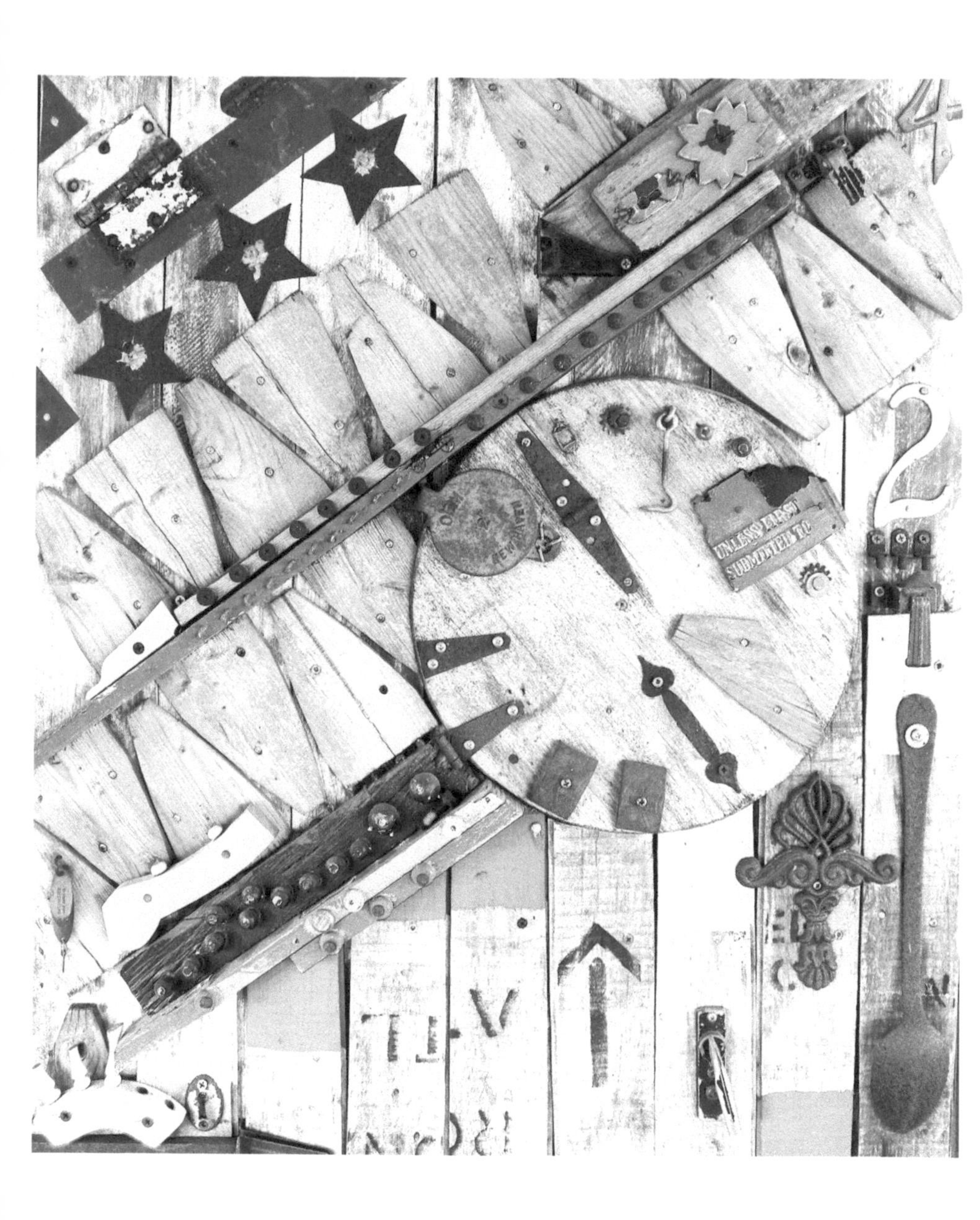
UNLESS FIRST
SUBMITTED TO

Linda Blaskey

Saving My Sister

It's 9:30 in the morning and I'm in the barn mucking out stalls. The temperature is eighty-two degrees and the humidity seventy-six percent. The sweat won't evaporate from my body. It runs in my eyes, drips off my nose, makes my hands slick on the pitchfork handle. I chuck a forkful of manure into the wheelbarrow and look up towards the house. The reason that I am doing this labor and not boarding my horses at a local stable, as I have always done in the past, is sitting on the back steps, smoking, watching me work. It is my sister, and she has lived with my husband and me for eighteen years. She is what is known as a hoarder, of both animals and things, and fits the profile perfectly—single, white, female, had lived with one parent, intelligent, articulate and well educated, but not in a way that benefits her in this technological age, her training in journalism and advertising taking place before the widespread use of computers.

She is six years younger than me and resembles our mother; short, dark haired, dark eyed, with a tendency to be slightly overweight. It is like someone drew a chalk line on the sidewalk with my mother and sister on one side and my father, brother and me on the other; taller, fair haired, blue eyed.

When my father returned from the South Pacific after WWII, my brother was already over a year old, so I was the first of his children whose life he got to experience from conception to birth. I was daddy's little girl the six years before my sister was born and during that time he taught me to fish, hunt, drive a nail, identify trees and bird song.

I had the advantage of having my mother around when we were small, but from the time my sister was a toddler, my mother worked. My father became a cost-estimating engineer for Boeing/Vertol and we left the farm to move east. His job required great amounts of time and travel from him. Sometimes he was only home on weekends. When my sister was twelve my father was given a promotion at the plant in Pennsylvania. His hours became regular and he no longer had to travel. For the first time in my sister's life, she had a constant father.

She lived with my parents, before moving in with us, for all of her life. It wasn't until my father died at a young age, fifty-nine, that it all started to fall apart. He had managed through the long years of his emphysema and heart disease to keep a control on things like the number of pets my sister could own and his illness demanded that clutter and dust in the house be kept at a minimum.

He managed the finances and a year before he died asked my husband to find a financial advisor that would invest his death benefits because he knew both my mother and sister wouldn't seek help. In the long run, it didn't make any difference at all because as CDs came due they would cash them in instead of rolling them over. They burned through money—trips to Texas and Europe, a new Mazda RX-7 for my sister, a large screen projection television. We could only advise.

Meanwhile, the house, in a nice suburban neighborhood in northern Delaware, deteriorated. The gutters filled with debris and bent, paint peeled from the shutters, the sidewalk cracked, the lawn went uncared for, the above ground pool, my father's joy, collapsed and was left to rust in the backyard.

And my sister began to collect.

It started with animals, three Basenji dogs. She had wanted to own a Basenji ever since she had seen the movie, *Farewell, My Lady*, as a child. My sister had always loved animals, was always bringing home injured squirrels or ducks, was always finding stray kittens. My father had permitted only one pet at a time but now he was gone, the restraints removed.

She allowed the dogs to breed and continued to pick up strays until there were eighteen dogs in the house, fourteen Basenjis, a standard Poodle, a Great Pyrenees, a Chow-Malamut mix, and a large mutt. The dining room was given over to crates, the kitchen to dog food bowls and water bowls. The floors were covered with mud from the dogs' feet and the walls were blackened where the animals rubbed against them. She began to allow stray cats into the house and even opened an upstairs window so that they could come and go as they pleased. None were ever neutered or spayed. It was not unusual to see thirty or more cats sitting on the roof.

The house was a maze of trash, boxes, dirty dishes buried under newspaper. Electrical outlets and switches shorted out and were never repaired. The toilet in the upstairs bathroom broke and was unusable. The screen fell off the back door from the dogs jumping against it. Nothing was ever dusted. The garage was filled with mildewed books, broken furniture and became a breeding ground for cats and sometimes raccoons.

In the beginning I made frequent trips to their house. I would arrive with Windex and Pine-Sol, buckets, dust rags, mops, brooms and would work until exhaustion set in. But I couldn't combat the determination of my mother and sister to live in filth. They seemed oblivious to their surroundings. At one point, I rented a large roll-off trash container and asked my sons to help me clean and toss. In one day we filled the dumpster with trash, threw out peed on chairs and mattresses, clothes that hadn't been washed in months, shredded pillows, years-old magazines, unopened mail. My boys had each brought a change of clothes and when we were done for the day they stood in the front yard and stripped to their skivvies. They threw their dirty clothes into the dumpster declaring they would never wear them again. My grandchildren have never been allowed to visit at my mother's house.

My husband, although he supported my efforts to a degree, would ask me not to go. He said I was wearing myself out to no avail, that I wasn't helping them. Despite the stress it caused in my marriage it was very difficult to watch two people that I loved choose to live in the way that my sister and mother did. But after the massive cleanout with the dumpster, as I watched the clutter rebuild, I stepped back and let go.

My mother's health was failing. She had already suffered two heart attacks and had been diagnosed with diabetes. Never one to pay close attention to household details or finances, she chose not to acknowledge that my sister was out of control. Things got worse. The county wanted to condemn the house but since there was one working bathroom, they didn't. Neighbors complained to the SPCA. The air around the house reeked of animal urine and feces.

The end finally came when my mother fell and broke her hip after she tripped over one of my sister's dogs. Her hip was surgically repaired and she was sent to a nursing home to recover, where she fell again and broke her other hip. She lingered for another year, part of the time in my home, the rest back in the nursing home, until she finally died, the day after Thanksgiving of 2001, at eighty-one.

My sister worked for Border's Books and didn't make enough money to support herself now that Mother's pension and social security were gone. She only had enough to feed her dogs, and that just barely. I would make the two hour trip once a week, from my home in southern Delaware, to buy groceries for her. We paid her electric bill, phone bill and car insurance. All of this to stave off the inevitable loss of her home, which would mean that she would be homeless, her animals euthanized.

My husband and I agonized and argued for months over what to do. And finally reached the only decision that was right for us. Many of our friends didn't understand and judged our choice. It was the animals, you see, more than my sister. We couldn't bear the thought of so many dogs and cats being killed for a situation that was not their fault.

We sold our home in the small beach town of Lewes and bought seven and a half acres in the country. We petitioned the county counsel to build a kennel, then had a utilitarian, modular rancher placed on the property and built dog runs off the garage. The garage became the kennel. The SPCA captured most of the cats at my sister's house but there were still seventeen that ended up with me. I found homes for all but four and they became barn cats.

With so much acreage we couldn't justify boarding my horses any longer so we had an Amish-built shed row barn dropped on the property. There are some days, like today when the heat is sweltering and I feel every one of my seventy-three years, that the full weight of what we've done bears down on me. Has my sister changed? No. Her room is a miniature of my mother's house. From the door of her room to her bed there is a path through piles of clothes, empty boxes, wrapping paper, books, magazines. She can't get to her closet or her computer. We constantly remind her of the rules: If you can't keep your room in order, the door must be kept closed; your bathroom must be cleaned at least once a week; smoking is done outdoors, no matter the weather; if you don't eat what we eat, you must buy your own food; you must hold down a steady job.

For the most part, she kept to the rules but the bathroom became a point of contention and we ended up hiring someone to clean it as I couldn't take on any more chores.

On other days, I heed the advice of the Buddhist monk, Thich Nhat Han, that in times of stress turn to nature, half smile, breathe. It was on one of these days, I was stacking hay, listening to the sounds of killdeer in the field behind me, and concentrating on each inhale/exhale, that a memory came back to me. I was about nine, my sister three. At the time, we lived with my paternal grandparents in a small farmhouse on top of a bald knob in the Ozark mountains of Arkansas. The yard around the house was fenced to keep animals, such as bear, cougar and wild hog, out. But the outhouse was on the other side of the fence, down a small rise, in back of the chicken coop. I needed to use the outhouse and my mother asked me to take my sister with me. It was midday in the summer and the trees were in full leaf and there was lush undergrowth in the woods. I had finished my turn and was helping my sister get her pants down when we heard something move in the underbrush and what we thought was a deep growl. I screamed and ran to the house leaving my little sister behind. The sounds we heard turned out to be my father returning from one of the lower fields. Out of politeness, he had cleared his throat to alert anyone at the outhouse of his presence. When he got back to the house, carrying my hysterical little sister, he took me aside and told me how disappointed he was in me.

"She is your sister. You should never run off and leave her like that. Promise you won't ever do that again." And of course, because he was the person I loved most in the world, I promised.

I told my husband of my recollection. We were in bed, there was a full moon, crickets were chirping and an owl called from the trees. After a while, he said, "You know, it was never the dogs. It was always the promise."

Ruth Boggs

MoMA Moments

New York City is a hot, humid and sticky mess when I arrive late on a Tuesday afternoon on the Acela Express from D.C. for a three-day meeting. I check into the Renaissance on East 57th and then set out for a walk to stretch my legs and scout the area.

In anticipation of a tough meeting the next day, I go to bed early, get up early, prep some more, put on my pinstripe suit, shoulder my briefcase, and walk the two blocks to Madison Avenue.

The receptionist at the *Mad Men*-like penthouse office suite gives me a quizzical look when I tell her that I'm there for a deposition.

"The deposition has been canceled," she says. "The case settled early this morning in Europe. You will be compensated for the three days."

I'm out of the building before it is even nine a.m. Streams of hurried people still emerge from subway stations and coffee shops and rush to their offices, but I'm out in the sun, with a whole free day ahead of me.

I quickly decide against taking the next train back to D.C. Why waste a day in NYC when the MoMA is only a few streets away? Some scenes in a German novel I just finished played in the MoMA. Time to go and explore!

Back at the hotel, I pack my bags and leave them with the concierge, and then I head up 57th to 5th Avenue and take a left. Rounding the corner onto 53rd Street, I notice that the line to get into the MoMA stretches halfway around the building. Not good. But I get in line anyway and as soon as the doors open, it moves fast and I'm in.

The sign "German Expressionists" immediately catches my eye and I head up to the sixth floor where the exhibit is located. It features "Die Brücke" artists who started the German expressionist movement in 1910 in Dresden and later continued it in Berlin.

Works of Kirchner, Heckel, Kokoschka, Kollwitz, Dix, Beckmann and Nolde, just to name a few, are prominently displayed. Like a good tourist, I listen intently to the electronic museum guide dangling from my neck to unravel the mysteries of German expressionism.

The works of Otto Dix and his gory paintings of slain prostitutes are particularly intriguing. They would make a great story line for a crime novel. Perhaps the perpetrator could use clues from the paintings to leave for the investigators to figure out. And then an investigator who by chance sees the Otto Dix exhibition has an "aha" moment. Maybe.

After spending two hours learning about German expressionism, I briefly skim the Skÿs collection on the 5th floor and then head to the rooftop terrace restaurant where the magic of my lucky day continues: Despite the busy lunch hour, I'm seated at an outside table on the railing, a prime spot with an excellent unobstructed view of the MoMA courtyard.

The strategically positioned rectangular reflecting pools with cascading fountains, surrounded by aspen trees and lush shrubberies, and the inviting benches grouped around the pools, look like a green oasis of quiet and solitude.

The menu looks inviting and I settle on a smoked trout salad and an iced tea, with mango sorbet and a cappuccino to finish it off. As I wait for my food, still reveling in the exciting turn the day has taken, I observe the people in the courtyard below me and notice a couple in a very tight embrace.

I figure them as tourists. The man has gray hair and is wearing khaki shorts and a polo shirt. The woman has a long brunette mane and wears a strapless summer top and Capri pants. She has her arms slung around his neck. Her head is buried in his chest and he holds her very tight. They remain motionless for a very long time. A couple of times, when she tries to leave, he tightens his embrace. They're oblivious to the people around them. I feel like an intruder witnessing a crucial moment in their lives. A goodbye? Making up after a lover's spat? A proposal?

When the man finally lets go of the woman, he goes to a nearby bench and sits down, and she heads toward the exit. Aha. Goodbye. But then she turns around and walks right past the man in the other direction, while he's focusing his camera on an object and doesn't even look up as she crosses his field of vision. Then he puts his camera away, hunches over, drops his head into his hands, and stares at the ground for a very long time.

The woman then sits on another bench, one section over, and stares at the water in one of the reflecting pools. Since I can't see the expression on their faces from my lofty location, it is difficult to gauge their emotions. They're two stick figures in a sea of many other stick figures. But then the woman returns, a small child appears seemingly out of nowhere, and the three head off together, holding hands.

Their brief interlude leaves me puzzled. It's as much an expression of the complexities of the human condition as the exhibit in the Francis Alÿs collection I just viewed and can't get out of my mind.

Alÿs is a Belgian artist known for his use of poetic and allegorical methods to address political and social issues. He works primarily in Mexico, and this particular piece of art is a home movie projected onto a huge white wall of a room. The image is grainy and shows a dusty hillside in a remote poor area of Mexico. A dirt road leads straight up to the crest of the hill. Decrepit little houses dot the hillside on either side of the steep road. At the bottom of the hill, a wide horizontal flat road runs perpendicular to the steep road.

A red Volkswagen Beetle tries to drive up the hill on the steep road. The driver revs up the engine but halfway up the hill, the engine sputters and dies and the car rolls backward.

Undeterred, the driver tries again. He revs up the engine and starts up the hill.

This time, he gets just a little farther before the engine dies again and the car slides backward.

The driver, determined to take the steep road over the hill, tries again and again.

Each time, he gets a little farther up the hill. The volume and crescendo of the mariachi music that underscores the movie rises as the VW crawls up the hill. But once the car's engine dies, so does the music, and the car rolls back down in silence.

During driver's relentless pursuit of his mission, there is other movement on the hill: A couple of stray dogs cross the road. A man leaves one of the shanty houses and walks over to another one. A large white American-made limousine enters the picture on the bottom of the screen from the right on the horizontal flat road that intersects the steep road, and then disappears to the left. The picture itself never changes. There's only one screen shot: The hill, and the little red VW Beetle that desperately tries to mount it to the bolstering sounds of the mariachi music, only to fail and roll back down again and again in silence.

During the fifteen minutes I watch this scene, visitors to the left and right of me get bored with it. They get up and leave, but my mind is churning: Shouldn't the VW's engine have overheated and blown up by now? What's going to happen next? Will the car accidentally run over one of the dogs or people as it rolls back down the hill? Maybe the driver should start from farther back so he can get a better momentum going? Is he EVER going to make it to the top?

Hungry for lunch, I don't want to wait for the end of the movie. I've already lasted much longer than the other visitors. On the way out, I ask one of the attendants, a tall, good-looking man in a navy blue blazer and a Caribbean accent,

"Please tell me–is he EVER going to make it to the top of the hill?"

"I don't want to spoil the ending for you," he says in a sonorous voice, and winks at me.

"Don't worry," I say. "You won't be spoiling anything. I'm leaving."

He bends down a bit and whispers in my ear, "OK then. I'll tell you. Eventually, he gives up and turns left on the flat road, like the other cars, and goes around the mountain."

Duh.

As I'm contemplating the fate of the couple in the courtyard and the driver of the VW Beetle, my eyes catch a young woman at a table across from me. Like me, she's by herself. We make eye contact and she nods hello and smiles at me. I smile back and muster her inconspicuously. I peg her as a foreigner, probably from one of the Eastern bloc countries. Black jacket, black skirt, dark top. No makeup, brown hair pulled back into a tight ponytail. Shy demeanor.

Then she reaches for her pocketbook, pulls out a spiral notebook and a pencil, and starts scribbling.

I should have known–a kindred soul. I pull out my own pen and notebook and write down a memorable phrase I read on a poster in the gift shop:

"Art is art. Everything else is everything else."

Dylan Emmons

The Cold—A Definition

/kōld/

Derived from the old English "cald" "Cold"'s uncanny aptness in describing itself goes beyond a combination of letters in a row, past the feelings and images it conjures. Cold is an inherently hopeless syllable. Beginning with the hard "c," the word is at first cutting and Germanic, sending the barren "ol" howling about until the mountainous "d" rises up to cut it dead.

There is something of impotence in cold; it leaves a bad taste in the back of one's mind. Things are dying. Older, more humbling, glass-eyed teachers are stepping in. The sun hates what it sees.

Uses

1

"I love the cold." I know how that sounds. We've made the weather into something to brag about. Across the nation, The Polar Bear Club, a small society of socially conscious "woke" masochists puff themselves up with vodka and walk into February lakes, raise money to cure homelessness and cancer and AIDS and polio and zika and swine flu. To have willed oneself through the nipple hardening discomfort, end always in sight, earns credit that can be cashed in during reunions and repeated drunken conversations. On the worst days, just getting where you're going is a congratulatory offense worthy of some time in a corner with a beer or a hot cocoa. And it's socially enforced. A crashing, Kramer-like touchdown into a river or a grocery store, coupled with a drawn-out sigh, and followed with a weather-beaten expression, tends to drag out all of the polite sympathy within earshot.

And yet to reject the need for this type of recognition is to close your mind to its necessity. Part of the irritation that comes with exclusion from this coat-room comradery is of course a jealousy. I'm not a part of it so I don't understand it so I don't get it, but it isn't that I don't want to. I don't want to joke with the bodega's six AM construction crew about the pubic icicles that formed when I got out of the shower this morning. But I want to want to.

2

I have a tendency to take things literally. I *am* cold. Identity is a compend of memory and principle. So I won't trivialize my sense of cold for the sake of some transparent social lubricant, by pretending to be able to explain its import. To be cold is to be exposed, be by nature open to warmth, but it means not buffering your personality in the winding wrap of small-talk, to insulate only in yourself, to look inward for what others find elsewhere.

See also

Autistic, a cold word, *autos*, all by itself. Sensory dysfunction has altered my pain/pleasure perception. I walk when I don't have to. I've turned into one of the people who carry themselves down the road like the astronaut at the bottom of a fishtank—head up, boxy shoulders, apparently preoccupied by matters worldlike in weight (or the fan theory that *Ed, Edd n' Eddy* exists in a purgatorial realm). It's not just that I'm into the anesthetic effect of cold. I have different coping mechanisms

Asperger's: a set of conditions for a mildly extraterrestrial, synesthetic worldview. My comfort falls apart only in an ice storm or a quick drive into the sun. I keep my jacket open to see what I can take.

Examples/used in a sentence

1

We'd find Marconi beach—named for the man who in 1903 crossed the Atlantic without wires—cramped with the late August budget crowd, trying to outsmart the market and outwit the weather, like us. Laura and Dad and I passed the nesting sea gull signs, and never actual gulls in nests. There was a chalk board for the tides and temperature. On this day, gray and blank like the sky, just: "53."

Beach. Crowded, bare and uninteresting, save for a nearby German family and their intermittent nudity. At the edge of the ocean, Fall had happened. Laura and I, seasoned by a childhood in the northeast and years incubating in its cold waters, knew it was best to submerge yourself quickly, let your breath quicken, let the numb. From there, it would come in stages. The point passed, as we bobbed past the first big breaker, at which pain gave way to an irregular pulse. A burning. Voodoo needles, migrating over the body in herds. Arms: long pregnant socks, each finger a wooden toe. Laura was determined; she stayed in at least fifteen minutes before some signal I wasn't sensing led her back to her towel and the Wheat Thins.

No prickling or want anymore—just a jostling neutrality like weightlessness. I let myself get pushed back into the samsaric wash of breakers. My flesh purpled and contracted. Seeing the surfers in what I thought of as their seal suits offered me a measure of pride, like I'd figured out something they hadn't. I was the only one floating around without a wet suit, salmon skinned vanilla rebel not to emerge until I looked like Grimace. Dad gave me a towel, gripping my arm it felt, through an overstarched sleeve, and laughing. Chugged a little seltzer. Ate three Pringles. Didn't care, long as I knew there was nothing macho about catching a cold. And I've never been good at hiding disappointment. Everyone should have a father like that. Right, but not insistently.

Purpose

There's an immediacy to cold, an urgency intrinsic in its sting; it's a sort of vitality made palpable only because the cold invading the warmth of skin reminds us of the death trying from all sides to push its way past life's membranes. The warmths, then, by contrast, shimmer with divinity and purpose. The cold is dumb opposition, a necessary foil, a death in itself.

[Murder is said to occur in cold blood, implying the murderer's personhood is in question, that his reptilian brain has won him over, that he is something other than all of us.]

In extreme latitudes, entire ecosystems of blubber-gutted and furry things lurch in opposition to this force. But for humans who aren't fitted with this evolutionary indifference to the war with the winds, the struggle is unignorable; succumbing to it is shame, but in prevailing, that pride of victory in the heart of survival. As with an unsettling number of life's pleasures, the exhilaration of cold lies in your knowledge of its ability to kill you while you watch—which it will do, and not know it. But this is a pacifier distinction, a fantasy, cold and death as separate, external, foes you might conquer in the world arena and watch die.

At first, the approach of the Romance languages to the experience of cold makes more sense than the English "I'm cold." In Italian, *Io ho freddo* ; in Spanish: *Tengo frío.* They literally mean "I have cold(ness)." Cold, heat, fear—one catches and carries and by extension can get rid of it by some means. In Italian, you think of yourself as more than your experiences. Makes more sense. You are not, after all, your coldness.

Synonyms

In English, the direct translation stirs images of noses buried in white cloths, dragging, aching days spent chained to the couch, of an existence structured around Afrin and Aleve and Nyquil. The English equivalent, "I am cold" is more dramatic and, it would seem, not as aptly descriptive as the concept of "having" cold. "I'm cold" is ice-driven winds that claw through jackets and evening plans, lovers and children shivering. It's a state of resignation to environmental forces that the Romance languages don't have. When I step out into a negative twenty degree windchill, I stop being a human being with senses experiencing a sense object; the cold takes away my right to perceive anything else. I am reminded that humans are animals, and that most animals spend all of their time this way, in dialogue with universal forces that for all of our knowledge about its mechanics we, like every other farting thing, just don't get. As with hunger, the experience of the cold is total. One is submissive to it. Cold is already inside and we are not separate from it.

Having a cold in the English sense baffles and disorients. The throat gets scratchy; the head is full of mucus, and one sleeps indefinitely, only to be woken up by the same gunk evacuating itself in quick wet hitches. One becomes allergic to accomplishing normal life tasks. Standards for productivity lowered drastically. Showering and shaving are commendable indeed—any actual work completed is plaque-worthy. Just about every medication designed to help also makes one feel like a dumbbell sinking to the bottom of a tub of Jello.

You can tell a lot about someone by the way they handle having a cold. For example it can be widely understood that big, jacked guys become whimpering infants in the face of any illness. On the other hand, in a testament to the power of necessity, some extraordinarily dedicated working class people refuse to miss work no matter how sick they are; they're the ones sitting in cover-alls on the bus, staring a thousand yards into the back of the headrest in front of them, sniffling, staying awake, making dismissive complaints all day about a struggle the less desperate people surrounding them may understand, but won't ever believe. Some won't accept any help—some expect to be waited on. You are not your coldness. And you are not separate from it.

Those optimistic about their colds take Dayquil and vacuum the ceiling. Three pumps afrin, do the taxes. Their focus on looming issues brings into light the impermanence of the state of discomfort.

Pessimists see their colds as the latest injustice in an endless onslaught by the universe against their basic happiness and progress. The shittiness of their current state is inescapable. Given any outlet, their misery overflows and stumbles out.

And then, there are those who are sort of zen about getting sick. My girlfriend once said something to the effect of you let it come and just have it and it runs its course, and you get over it. Actually she said it better than that.

Uses

3

It's been stated that as human beings we are not separate from the cold. But it's worth clarifying that the cold really and truly isn't its own separate thing. Hot and cold are just umbrellas hovering over their respective spots on a thermometer. Though most commonly used as an adjective, cold also has nounal functionality, which given this paragraph's thesis statement could present as problematic. However, for precedent we can look to the example set by other elusive, evanescent nouns. Religion, for instance, is a word that misleads through its own nounship. It is a noun only in that it is an abstract noun. The idea really has no physical counterpart—which is what gives it a separate distinction from *thing* within the definition of a noun. You can't point to a religion on the street, or an atheism, for that matter. Therefore, though both religion and the cold are undeniable forces of influence, they must achieve it by sticking their inky fingers deep into the more tangible aspects of existence. If I catch a virus or I "have cold" in the sense of a romance language, or get religion, its existence is perpetuated through my own—I harbor and incubate it. My life force, my personhood, my *thing*ness is a necessity, and I become a vehicle for the cold's very existence. As the sense and the sense object meet, the loop is closed. The cold, like any idea, must always have medium. For cold, it can be the air, the water, a phrase, a personality, a war. It doesn't have a body of its own, and so it must invade and sustain itself with these. Cold's lifejuice is perception itself, or else a nameless swirl.

Examples in a sentence

2

Coldness, in the context of war, or any conflict of the flesh, really, signifies a state of sleep or rest, or at least a tendency towards inaction. Silos sleep concealing missiles like earthbound microdicks in titanium circumcisions. Temperature is assessed by and reflects the movement of particles. More active particles create more motion and generate more heat. As with any measurement, the assessment of temperature must be relative. It's in reference to something such as the boiling or freezing point of water the average temperature, which is to say the swirling of infinitesimal particle. And because the cold must be relative to itself, or to heat, it is not absolute. So it isn't that during the second half of the twentieth century there weren't ample conflicts in the Balkans or in Afghanistan or in Cuba. It's just that the relative movement of soldiers and resources was (particles) assessed as frigid and beleaguered compared with the situation's potentials.

Imperialism and greed are forces driven from cold spots deep within, where some souls, tilted like the earth's axis, receive life's sunlight unevenly. Their emotional ecosystems and psychological landscapes have not adapted well. In the process alluded to above, their bodies and even their lives become vehicles for such twisted and driving factors.

3

The relativity of cold is a concept I can scarcely escape but that tends to go unaccounted for. In Alejandro Jodorowsky's *The Holy Mountain* characters are introduced as ambassadors, representatives, stand-ins for other planets. However jarring and enthralling Jodorowsky's segmentations of the different aspects of humanity, the idea of temperature difference among the planets is scarcely addressed. Though maintaining and depicting the integrity of proven scientific laws was clearly not the director's aim, the viewer at least subliminally notices the lack of difference in the characters' environments. Perhaps the unrealistic and earthlike fantasy of life on other planets reflects a fundamental human inability to sympathize with states of being other than our own. Because cold, like time, rarely presents itself to two people exactly the same way. But in being so formulated by its conception (that is perception by a vehicle/medium), the cold is also formative. Yet Jodorowsky's anthropomorphic aliens lack the basic biological truth of having arisen in relationship with and reacting to diverse environments.

How would an actual alien perceive earth? Our temperature swings miniscule, our storms benign? Maybe just a cruel frustration of recycling and sex, a nonsense of volcanos and icy wind. Or as it is to us—an absurd juxtaposition of livable and lethal environments held together by the play of adversarial forces?

4

In winter, when I walk past cemeteries, I think of the dead snug in their frost-eaten ground rooms. The scene betrays the nature of that little licking flame in cold, driving the dance of the erosion of structure, the whole process, coffins weathered by detrivores, by the soil itself, by the groundrocks at it again like the earth's teeth: slow, unintelligent, frigid—lifelike.

Darlene Fife

from This holy temple where a meadow has come into bloom with spring flowers and breezes [May 20–July 1st]

May 20

Especially grateful for blue sky—the lightning, thunder and rain intense last night, the creek roaring this morning. Hedda was scared of the thunder, wide-awake looking to me for assurance but not as scared as she is in town when she sits mouth open, panting. Here come dark clouds.

Catbird mimicking a thrush as the day lightens, will he switch with the light to the towhee song? If the thrush were singing from the dark woods I couldn't hear him since the creek is so loud.

May 23

6:15. 52 degrees, the waning moon just scratching the edge of the south hill.

I can see in the gap between the porch boards a black snake skin wrapped around one of the supports. I put the skin around the railing in case a bird might like it for a nest.

First bullfrogs heard last evening. To be like Timaeus and see soul in every tree, every blade of grass.

Plato—"Timaeus is our best astronomer and has made it his special task to learn about the nature of the universe... beginning with the origin of the cosmos and ending with the generation of mankind."

A box turtle in the mown grass. She hesitates, head up, alert, knowing some being is watching her. I sit down out of view so the box turtle can continue on her path without interference.

"He put soul in the middle and stretched it through all he created."

8:20 the thrush from the east. The western thrush has been singing all morning.

May 27

62 degrees, Memorial day. I wonder if the high school band and majorettes still parade to the town graveyard where I in majorette uniform thought not at all of death or dying.

Last evening in the chair half-asleep after an afternoon of weeding I hear a towhee symphony, so many songs. I felt how separate they, this place is from me. This world right here right now lives and breathes without me.

Fireflies last night, seems earlier than usual.

Thoreau's two acres is not only a lot of land to weed but a lot of land to prepare for the seeds. This Thoreau didn't do. In his expenses he lists "horse cultivator and boy 3 hours—$1.00" and then "horse and cart to get crop—.75."

Thoreau's work consisted of the field plan, the purchase of seeds and the weeding. What to look out for he writes are the woodchucks which he says as they are eating sit "erect like a squirrel." He doesn't mention the Mexican bean beetle as voracious and destructive as the woodchuck. Luckily for him the Mexican bean beetle had not arrived in the US during his lifetime.

May 30

Hedda and I made it up last afternoon with three minutes to spare before the rain.

58 degrees, everywhere so many shades of green. A phoebe out and about moving from elderberry to rose of sharon, staying low the whole time.

Grasses below the porch at the start of the grassland are in bloom. I've been busy looking at books on weeds and grasses. So many of our weeds are not native though I note that trumpet creeper is native and referred to as "aggressive" a description I can testify is accurate.

June 3

50 degrees. I am used to Indigo Buntings in the very top of a tree singing loudly. This one is on a lower dead branch of the cherry singing softly, quietly.

Thoreau exalts the seeds of "sincerity, truth, simplicity, faith, innocence and the like"... and he slights the farmer planting seeds "I saw an old man the other day, to my astonishment, make the holes with a hoe for the seventieth time at least,...as if there were a fate to it." Maybe Thoreau's one year of planting was not enough for him to see the seeds of "sincerity, truth, faith, innocence and the like" within the farmer's work. Maybe he was too quick to judge.

"If I knew only Thoreau I should think cooperation of good men near impossible." —Emerson.

"Our Thoreau was in love with the natural, but still more in love with the supernatural, yet he prized the fact and his books abound in delightful natural history." —John Burroughs

I feel blessed each summer that I can still walk up here, Hedda at my side, still work in the garden and still hear the thrushes singing. As I write this my many other blessings crowd into my thoughts so I will not write them down; just say thank you.

June 10

Two crows flying just above the tree tops—looking for cherries? They remind me that no matter how much I may try in insinuate myself into this their world I am destined to be a stranger.

And in my world I wonder when (not if) it will start raining and how wet I and Hedda will get. Hedda that being who bridges the worlds, though more in mine which is where, I think, she wants to be; but still her nose, her body, no doubt her brain brings her into alliance with the world that is not mine.

Cauliflower, and small cabbage, a few peas from the garden.

I wonder if they miss me, those beings from the other world. When I got here yesterday afternoon I apologized to the world for missing a day because of my reluctance to getting myself and especially Hedda soaked once again which fear was not realized since heavy rain contrary to the weather reports did not happen.

As I listen to a bird in the cherry, the thrush from the deep woods comes closer, his song clearer—listen to me.

June 13

Drizzle. Yesterday full of sun was like a new world.

Female towhee walking along the mown path, then is joined by the male about 20 feet apart, separate yet together. It looks like a happy life. I wonder if he is the towhee I often hear with a first note very abrupt and a brief trill—drink, tee hee hee.

Enough of a steady light rain to bring me from the porch into the doorway.

June 20

Clothes drying by the stove. As soon as we got here yesterday the rain stopped.

Rain drops lined up along the underside of the trumpet creeper limbs. I look to see if there is a sequence like Fibonacci numbers but not that I can perceive. I am impatient for the flowers.

The Chinese Chestnut is in full bloom. With its white streams of flowers one has to look close to see them unlike the red of trumpet creeper which proclaims its presence for me and for the hummingbird.

Dark clouds are moving so fast from the west like Bukowski's horses.

June 24

6:15, 56 degrees and half moon in the southern sky. Sun on the hill top southwest, female towhee in the mown grass. Quarter to seven the moon is now directly south above the skid row, ¼ of the way up the sky, sun on the south mountain, thrush from the east.

Memorial for Fran yesterday. In October 2005 I decided to take piano lessons, I have no idea why. Certainly there was the feeling of if not now, when.

When Fran was moving out of her studio in Lewisburg she gave away possessions and to me she gave her metronome and the collage hanging on her wall which I had many times admired.

And now, Fran, would you finish the fingering for the Brahms' Intermezzo?

June 27

6:35 sun at the top of south mountain. 6:50 thrush in the west. Indigo bunting singing on a lower branch of the cherry looking toward me. I wish I could speak the language. After about a minute and with no response he flies away. Even though not able to communicate, at least not in language, for a moment I am transported to another world, the one the exists here and that I occasionally glimpse.

"...the three most precious resources of life, ..books, friends and nature and the greatest of these is nature."—John Burroughs

July 1

58 degrees, trumpet creeper in bloom, chinese chestnut flowers on the ground. Just saw two long strands fall very quick, no graceful swaying just fast like an apple.

There's the male robin in the open mown patch near the peach tree. He was there last night as was a thrush orchestra three or more in the twilight. I tried to count the number of voices but couldn't. I am used to the lone ethereal voice from the wooded distance.

Male hummingbird in the trumpet creeper. Last evening to my eyes the bright red flowers seemed forlorn, longing til at last the hummingbird arrived. Such a spell is cast that I hesitate to get up for another cup of tea.

The pond has become a mecca for bullfrogs. The sky is blue and like a true gardener, never satisfied, I am longing for rain.

Burroughs pries large stones from a field, an ironwood pole with a horseshoe as lever, then a team of oxen to drag the boulders from the field. How far from Thoreau is Burroughs' feeling toward the farmer. "A farmer's fields become in time almost a part of himself; his life history is written all over them; virtue has gone out of himself into them, he has fertilized them with the sweat of his brow; he knows the look and quality of each one."

In writing of his doubts about natural selection's "protective coloration," Burroughs refers to Darwin and Wallace. Wallace is now almost forgotten.

Jesse Lee Kercheval

Sandman, Bring Me a Dream

1.

I once dreamed that I looked out a window in the middle of the night at the building across the street and I saw Virgin Mary washing the dishes. Not in just one apartment, in one kitchen, but in every apartment in West Berlin. She was standing at the sink, dressed in deep blue with a light blue apron tied around her waist, her hands deep in dish soap. I could see her by the light of the glowing yellow crown on her head. I could see her and see her and see her in every window, in every apartment building, as far as the Berlin Wall.

I had this dream in 1987, before the wall came down, in the Berlin Frei Hospital where I had just had my appendix removed. I am not Catholic, so I am not sure what made me have this vision of Mary, Mother of God, except maybe the anesthesia. But it gave me a great sense of comfort, Mary awake doing all the housework for tired mothers and housewives in the middle of the night. Like the elves in that fairy tale making shoes for the poor, tired cobbler. Thinking about it still gives me a sense of calm. Maybe it is the luminescent blue of Mary's dress or the warm light of her crown. But it also occurs to me that it was a pretty gendered dream. I mean, of course, the Mother of God was doing the dishes! Why not Jesus, maybe with rubber dish gloves to protect those nail holes in his hands. Or Jehovah, his great white beard swept over one shoulder. Or Buddha who looks, in his statues, like the kind of considerate dinner guest who would help with the washing up. Or Brahma, putting all those extra arms to good use use.

Except that makes it all a joke. When I dreamed of Mary, it felt not so much like a dream, as a vision. An admonition to be kind not just to your own, but to all.

Now during this current pandemic that dream comes back to me. As I look out the window of my apartment in Montevideo, Uruguay, where I am currently in lock-down, I can see towers of other apartments, their windows lit up. In the building next door a couple plays with their little girl. In the apartment below an elderly couple sits reading on the balcony during the day. There's the young couple across the street with the black lab who barks at the cars six floors below. Each of us in our bubble of light and aloneness. Each of us about to roll down our shades, turn out our lights—to sleep, perchance to dream.

2.

In the middle of this pandemic, everyone I know has been telling me that they have been having the most vivid dreams. Of course, they are telling me through some virtual form of communication or other (skype, zoom, email, facebook posts, whatsapp) since I haven't been in the same room with anyone but my husband in two months. Sitting up late at night, I've read countless articles on the phenomena. NBC News calls them "quarandreams." In the *Harvard Review,* researcher Dr. Deirdre Barrett says a common pandemic dream is one that converts the virus into a metaphorical bug: "There are swarms of every kind of flying insect you've ever heard of; there are armies of cockroaches racing at the dreamer; there are masses of wriggling worms; there were some grasshoppers with vampire fangs; there are bed bugs, stink bugs."

Dr. Barrett is very much the dream researcher of the moment. I find her again in a long article on pandemic dreams in the *New York Times* that even gives pointers on how to control your dreams—if you are tired of all those creepy insects. *The Times* tells me "Dr. Barrett recommends attempting to 'program' your dreams as you fall asleep. So-called 'dream incubation,' she said, 'has a pretty high success rate.' Choose a category of dream you'd like to have—for instance: flying."

Digging even deeper, I find a 2014 scientific article "Frequency and nature of flying dreams in a long dream series," in the *International Journal of Dream Research* where researcher Michael Schredl writes, "One of the most exciting dream topics is flying without any mechanical assistance... 30% to 63.5% of the participants reported that they had experienced flying dreams at least once." He goes on to hypothesize that flying dreams have increased over the last few decades as the overall amount of air travel has increased. If so, it occurs to me, the nearly ubiquitous Dr. Deirdre Barrett might need to chose another type of dream for us to "program" since during this pandemic almost no one is flying.

Me, I love flying. I love flying in dreams. I love dreaming. But so far, I have gone from nervous half-awake sleep, too shallow and filled with the buzzing of the news to dream, to nights spent in dreamless sleep as dark, as we say in Wisconsin where I usually live and teach, as the inside of a cow. And to sleepless nights spent, clearly, reading articles about quarandreaming.

3.

All my life, I have been fascinated by dream books that interpret the meanings of objects that appear in our dreams. I have a dozen of them in my house in Wisconsin, but here in Montevideo, *nada*. So in the middle of another sleepless night, I download one from the internet. It is called *GOODE'S Universal DREAM BOOK* and it has a wood cut on the cover with a sleeping woman in the foreground and arrayed around her are a shipwreck, a giant snake with a forked tongue, a masked man with a dagger, a frowning skull, a pistol, both a flying bat and a bird carrying a letter in its beak and a man down on one knee clearly proposing marriage.

The objects that might appear in your dreams are arranged in alphabetical order. starting with acorns. "To dream of acorns, and you eat one, denotes you will rise gradually to riches and honour. If you do not eat, and throw one on the ground, you will quickly get rich but another will enjoy your property." In the *Universal Dream Book*, dreaming of eating or food is sometimes good. If you eat cheese in a dream, it "denotes profit." But it is not always a good thing. If you dream of bacon, "it denotes the death of a friend. Eating oysters "the coming of much want." Oranges "implies wounds and grief."

But one given of dream interpretation is that dark images usually mean the opposite. To dream of death, "denotes happiness and a long life." Of drowning, "that you will be preserved through great difficulties." To dream of the gallows "is the most fortunate omen, it shows the dreamer will become rich, and arrive at great honors." I look for "sleep," or what it means to dream you are sleeping, but there is no entry. Nor one for insomnia. Though "being ridden by a nightmare is the sign of a sudden marriage."

But I am already married. And I can't seem to sleep long enough to have a nightmare.

4.

But what if I am asleep now? What if I'm dreaming and don't know it? That's a question neither Dr. Diedre Barrett nor *GOODE'S Universal DREAM BOOK* quite address. I think about it while I sit up in the night reading articles online about dreaming. Or *I think* I am awake, in an apartment, sitting on the couch with my laptop on my knees, but who knows? Beyond the living room window, a cityscape of lights stretches to the dark of the water. To the west is the old city. To the east is Brazil, but to the north, there is also Brazil. Brazil is a very big country. I don't think this is an imaginary place. I think I am in apartment 601 in Edificio Altair on Bulevar España. If I looked in my address book, I could give you the phone number. The postal code. I think.

But at other times, in what might or might not be dreams, when I might or might not have dozed off just for a minute, I know my neighborhood just as well. My house has a big hedge with a gate in it and that way, down the hill is the school and the playground. Past that is the cafe where they serve the best strudel and then next is the department store which has a supermarket in the basement that you reach by taking an escalator (I am afraid of escalators).

Then I wake up and I am still writing this essay. Or I did I just fall sleep instead and keep typing?

All I know is this: I can always find my way home if I have to, from either place. I must remember this, especially whenever I am on the phone with my mother who has been dead for forty years (surely that is the dream?). Or my sister who, though she lives on another continent and cannot remember how to call me, is very much alive (or I think she is). I need to believe in these landscapes and the people in them. Because if I don't, where will I be?

Last year, doing physical therapy exercises in the warm water pool at the hospital, a woman asked me, "Do you see Dr. McCoy?" I nodded, not wanting to lose count of my leg kicks. "I thought so," she said. "You look exactly as sick as I am." Sometimes, sitting up late at night, I count all the times I have almost died. When I was six months, I had scarlet fever. When I was six, measles. At ten, I fell from a tree and broke many important bones in my body. I have been in three serious car accidents. Had an emergency appendectomy, emergency gall bladder surgery, an emergency c-section. My body lost its mind and attacked my own lungs one year, then last year, my muscles and liver. There must be dream worlds where I died. There must be dream worlds where I have never been sick and so was not doing leg lifts in that therapeutic pool. There must be a timeline where my mother is still alive, even if she would be 103.

So, I am wondering where all this leaves me except with a compulsion to write down what otherwise will surely be forgotten. Only when your mother died in another century, do you wish you could ask her why she hated her middle name (Olive). Only when your only sister no longer remembers the name of the neighbors' old beagle when you were kids (Jeeves Archibald Chatterton III), do you want to write everything down. So, you can live forever.

Or, at last, finally sleep.

C.D. Nickols

Symbolic Acts: Erasing Fables*

I moved to Richmond in the summer of 1996, between undergrad in frigid upstate New York and my graduate studies at Berkeley after taking a job to push plastic in a credit card marketing operation that I ultimately understood mostly targeted people who lacked the income stability or creditworthiness or life circumstances to make payments on time without spiraling into a morass of debt. Richmond wasn't an easy choice by a long shot—I had had offers in NYC, which would have been the more logical option given family ties, but after commuting with my dad into and out of the city during a few summer jobs to pay for school, the idea of an entry-level spot with a one to three hour car ride each way to live with my parents seemed less than ideal. Plus, as I was deciding among the options, my dad had pulled me aside to say: "if you move to New York, you can stay with us a few months. That's it. Then you're out." Four years of writing checks for college and the old cop had had enough. He seemed to be saying *stay away.*

Richmond is a nice town. Warmer than the Northeast, which for me and my Raynaud's meant two months of thermal underwear annually instead of six. The old part of Richmond—the Fan and the downtown area—has nice southern architecture styles, endless townhouses with wrought-iron porches. Farmer's markets and coffee shops were just being reborn, and Richmond had plenty of both. Were you to live your life on a bike as I did, and confine yourself to that old part of town, there was a quaintness to it.

I'd only been living there a few weeks or so when a friend insisted on driving me down Monument Avenue. She, too, had grown up in New York's suburbs, and anticipated how I would react. "Wait, they have statues of...the Confederates? Like the guys that lost?" The guys that were, y'know fighting for slavery? What...the...what?

A few months later I passed men in Confederate war attire marching around those very monuments with rifles slung over their shoulders. Lee's statue is just one in a string of Confederate statues along Monument Ave. The marching exercise was on MLK weekend, so that was weird. I didn't know what to make of it. Later, someone introduced me to the idea of the Sons of Confederate Veterans and explained that it wasn't actually MLK Day, but Lee Jackson King Day. She emphatically conveyed: "Lee Jackson Day...it's part of our heritage... it's part of who we are... it's really important for us to celebrate and remember who we are. To never forget the people that got us where we are." She then went on to say: "I just don't know who Lee Jackson is." She

*Note that this story was accepted for publication in July 2020.

wasn't being ironic. The Wikinet tells me that Lee-Jackson-King Day was celebrated from 1984 to 2000, before the absurdity was apparently recognized by someone with the ability to make the change. In the shadow of Lee-Jackson-King Day one wonders: when is Hitler-Mussolini-Frank Day? Incidentally, before you get the wrong idea, Lee-Jackson Day still exists in Virginia, the dates were just separated from MLK Day.

A close friend during that time was from the suburbs of Atlanta, and explained that her high school history texts wrote not about the civil war, but of the War of Northern Aggression, which was apparently a war about states' rights, not slavery.

None of these things could be comprehended in my Yankee mind. No amount of farmers markets or wrought iron fences could make any of that seem right.

In recent years there have been topsy-turvy debates about whitewashing history and how we just can't take Confederate statues down, and they're part of history, etc. etc. I totally understand—it totally makes sense doesn't it? I mean we don't want to forget the civil war and slavery and all of that? You can't just erase history. After all, didn't the allies leave up all the Nazi flags and statues when they occupied Berlin? Just to have everybody remember the Nazis, to remind everyone by forcing them to relive the memory of Nazi oppression every day? Sure, that sounds reasonable, doesn't it? It's so nice when the people that support the evil are the ones who sympathetically remind us that the only way we can remember the horrors of past wrongs is by retaining the relics that cherish the perpetrators. As in: we need to keep statues of Confederate oppressors hanging around to remind us of our troubled history. So thankful for that perspective, but with all due respect, can we maybe put a Harriet Tubman up there instead [expletive deleted]? (The "all due respect" helps to soften the [expletive deleted], doesn't it?).

Of course, we don't want to erase history. But the monuments aren't history. A temporal tautology: which came first, General Lee or his statue? It's not as if the monuments were there in 1800, before Lee and the Confederates were born, were they? Were Lee and Jackson "heroes" before the war? The monuments were put up well after the war, by people that were harkening back to what they thought were the Good Old Days. Yet, most arguments in favor of "preserving history" are spun from the same spider's web that supports other policy positions that are just racism under a different banner. It can be easy to get deceived into thinking there is another defense for something that is itself inherently unjustifiable. It's my hope that a lot of people out there that have stood for these causes over the years have just been deceived by pundits and political entrepreneurs. It's my hope that once they realize that Confederate statues aren't history, but rather arose out of an attempt to rewrite the past and erase the outcome of the war, that they will drop the arguments and stop siding with those that have twisted words to trick them into aligning inadvertently with an embrace of racism.

Amid my frustrations in 2020, it's been hard to find the right voice to write in (actually, it's been hard to cut out the f-bombs from my writing). Unlike many people I didn't execute a Facebook pogrom in recent years of those that had different views from me. At that time, I silently pledged to try to figure out a way to keep the lines of communication open and try to figure out ways to have a conversation that is in the national interest. I wanted to at least try to keep track of the thinking of those with opposing views. I thought if I could just open the eyes of a few people, it might be worth it. Without a doubt, I've absolutely failed in that undertaking. It's been hard and there's no sugar-coating it: over the past few years I've seen some really amazing things posted by people I know on their social media accounts, stuff on which I really saw no productive path to conversation. One of the things that sticks out is a video posted during the 2017 Women's March that showed men in pickup trucks intentionally plowing through protesters around the country set to a song with lyrics that went "git outta my way bitch!" Yes, that really happened. I've wanted to reach out to that individual, to ask *what was going through your mind*? But I didn't, because I never found the words, I never found anything that started better than "what the f^#& is your problem?," which, according to my notes on social engagement, isn't the best way to start a productive conversation. I didn't purge my social rolls, not because I felt some closeness, but because I felt an obligation. If we can't get back to a conversation, if we can't build bridges, then I really fear the worst for the country. For the past several decades, we have embarked on a great divergence in our social and economic views, one that—unlike past historical episodes—has not been confronted and tamed by moderating forces, but rather has been invigorated by those that have had a lot to gain.

Indeed, there's been a terrible torrent posted on social media over the past years. Some things unspeakable, some unrepeatable, some, I hope just offensive through ignorance. I've seen people who work in areas of public service or schools post horribly racist and misogynistic things that certainly must have reflected on how they did their jobs—if you're a school principal, racism and misogyny and sex-based biases in your private life can't be compartmentalized from your professional performance. If you're a political leader drumming up hate against certain groups, you can't put that genie back into the bottle at your will, and that applies to those who have been far less overt about it over the past few decades than our current leadership (to be clear, there is no "both siding" of this issue, so—to be uber-brief—pledging to push equity aims for a disadvantaged group is not the same thing as race-baiting and hate preaching). I know that some people are not going to change their minds, but I still have a hope that others have just not been tuned in to the facts, and that they can be reached. Yet, as I've been trying to write this essay, I've struggled trying to find a tone that reaches out and gets them to ask *what have I been doing? That's...not...me.*

Tributes to the Confederacy aren't history. They aren't respect for the character and decency of soldiers who fought in the Civil War.* They are part of a long ongoing attempt to rewrite the past of the South as a story of distinguished and respectable southern *gentlemen* sipping tea on their porch, gazing upon halcyon fields of agricultural prosperity. Proud men who, in the lore that has emerged, treated slaves like family, as if the slaves were lost refugees that wandered into their homes to be cared for, rather than commodities that were bought and sold and *tyrannically* suppressed with whips and guns and the tools of the state. In these tales, these were proud men standing up for their homes in the face of (wait for it...) unionist *tyranny*. They were men and women who had a *complex* relationship with slavery, which they of course opposed even as they rushed to bloody battlefields to...protect states' rights. Just imagine them sitting on their porch under a warm summer sunset, looking across their plantation fields as they sipped their juleps and smoked ivory pipes with fine tobacco and caressed those tender hoary hairs of the gentlemanly bristles that adorned their visage, and they slowly debated with themselves: "on the issues of the theory of constitutional law..." Never for a moment would they have contemplated the notion that the notional value of each prime aged male still at work in those fields was some $800 each (about $24,500 in 2019 dollars), or the fact that they, as the median slave-holding gentleman, would have held about five slaves.** Never for a minute would it have factored into their calculus, of course—they were gentleman and would have been above all of that even if those antebellum institutions provided the entire source of their wealth and power.

Ah, those sacred rights. It wasn't slavery at all. It was to defend against Northern Aggression and safeguard the states' rights guaranteed in the constitution. The same fable of states' rights that certain political leaders have continued to peddle for the past several decades to justify other policies that were often racist or misogynistic, even if the states' rights argument sprung up ex-post to provide a more appealing justification. The government is too big, social protections too grand, it all threatens states' rights, which apparently we have to respect more than children and seniors going to bed hungry or facing eviction. A terrible apparition the ghost of state's rights is, always dissipating when you need it on a whole host of other issues like gun control.

---

* https://twitter.com/jeffsessions/status/1271574937879314442

** https://eh.net/encyclopedia/slavery-in-the-united-states/ and my own calculations. Prices on male slaves from https://www.measuringworth.com/slavery.php. Price series from https://www.minneapolisfed.org/about-us/monetary-policy/inflation-calculator/consumer-price-index-1800-. The price series likely understates the importance of a slave in the household wealth of a slaveholder. As Williamson and Cain note, the average price of a slave was approximately equal to the price of a house; an $800 slave in 1850, was approximately equal to relative earnings of $390,000 (in 2016).

Once you start pulling, these yarns just unravel. As you pull more and more you begin to see so many other debates that have centered on race-bait-and-switch. Arguments that were Jim Crowe to the core, but have been dressed up in seersucker suits and bow ties to sound gentlemanly and reasonable. Like the arguments for the monuments, the more you get into these debates, the more the contradictions just pile up. So often we've let ourselves be oblivious to things that just aren't right because we've been given alternative reasons that provided the excuses we were looking for: Confederate monuments are history, not everyone deserves equal education and health care access, etc. The tide that has emerged in the wake of the death of George Floyd is not about the PC police cracking down on someone's sacred beliefs, it's about the basics of right and wrong. It is how we've so often let ourselves be oblivious to things that just aren't right, or fallen prey to simple tools of deception that have aligned us unwittingly with racist paradigms.

How ingrained is all of this in our society? Where to begin? When I hear about the push for keeping education local, I can't help but see it for what it is...just another attempt to keep the War of Northern Aggression and other rewrites from a parallel universe in impressionable kids' textbooks. Because things are nuanced and complex, I can express my contempt for the local education charade at the same time that I see the failures of a policy like no child left behind in many important ways. Let me leave it there lest I get too far down the rabbit hole on this issue, but I will say that the disparities in educational quality in the US are intertwined with all of these issues. And for pure patriots, none of it is in America's interest—our most successful international competitors do not leave resources idle or with unfulfilled potential.

The idea that a certain president needed to produce that extra-long form original birth certificate signed by George Washington, is an overtly racist political device. That's even if one does not see themselves as racist or if they have justified it to themselves with a less overtly racist rationale. To use the language of modern statistics, if 44 white presidents are never asked for their birth certificate (because we know they're Americans, right?)—and one nonwhite President is asked repeatedly to produce documentary evidence that he was actually born, not cloned in a high-tech Wakandan lab and slipped into the country in a secret subterranean tunnel operated by the Mole Man, then statistically speaking, the relation between nonwhite and being asked is perfectly correlated. A statistical test would reject the hypothesis that these two groups were equal. Ergo, the position is overtly racist, the two go together perfectly.

What little I know about football over these past few years is the Colin Kaepernick debacle. His protest completely non-obstructionist (not even creating the kind of inconvenience for onlookers that is essential to most protests), about the very same issues we're talking about today. The outrage stoked by certain networks and political leaders at this peaceful and non-disruptive act of protest, outrage wrapped in an American flag, an outrage reeking of racism—to me it shows how easily people can be twisted against reasonable asks from reasonable people, because I hope that racism wasn't what motivated the anger of so many football fans. The NFL seems to be backtracking on their blindness to this peaceful protest, which, while nice to hear, is hard to regard as genuine and not just arising out of self-reflection about their bottom line.

I can go on and on and on. I haven't even scratched the surface. What does taking down Confederate monuments do? Everything and nothing. It removes a powerful symbol of oppression, but at the same time it doesn't *solve* anything. One cannot clarify four hundred years of building discriminatory institutions in a short essay, just as one can't unwind racist institutions with a few weeks of protest, or a moment of taking a knee with the protesters, or any of the quick fixes that will be proposed—even taking down the monuments. It's a start, it's necessary, but can anyone really believe that two decades into the twenty-first century, we're still talking about removing signs of the Confederacy? No matter how fast change is able to come, there is huge ground to cover. I say this not to discourage people working for change, but to encourage, and to appeal for all of us to not be satisfied with purely cosmetic changes. Not to be patient with a slow pace of change and decades of unfulfilled promises, but patient enough to keep working towards something better.

I'm not going to provide some litmus tests for racists and racism. I'm not going to call people out here as racists just because they have some misguided beliefs. I don't think that serves a purpose of prompting legitimate change that a broad consensus of people can buy into. What I can say is that for those who think they've got a rationale that puts them on the side of Confederate monuments or states' rights issues or cutting social program and so forth—arguments that have become the pillar on which a whole political apparatus has been built—that these arguments have aligned perhaps unwitting individuals with racism and racist views, and I hope that recognition causes them to wake up and smell the deception. Those beliefs are grounded in racist arguments even if there are alternative versions one can tell oneself to keep the racist label at arm's length. But those alternative versions are just made up stories like the one that says that these hurtful monuments are history. My hope is that those that have bought into these stories have simply never seen where those positions were coming from, and that they didn't realize that they've been duped by bull merchants. Understandably, this may sound naïve, but I mean it to be hopeful—hopeful that once the logical inconsistencies of these arguments are revealed, that these people can be converted.

After a crafty fox and its minions led so many astray so much during the Global pandemic, I hope people start to reconsider their decision to get news from human sock puppets, people like Tucker Carlson, the inhuman meat Muppet, who has argued long and hard for the preservation of Confederate monuments, the blacklisting of knee-taking footballers, and called Covid a hoax even as the death toll mounts (and even as the foxes themselves hid deep in their own dens while urging others to venture out and be brave). Guys that have doubled down on these fictions because they are worried that their whole little Wizard of Oz show will crumble if they give an inch.

The reality is that all of this expression over the spring of 2020 is about us. I'm not espousing a view from one political affiliation, I am speaking from a view of radical pragmatism. It is crucial for us to make changes. It is crucial for us to build more equity and equality into our system so that our nation can prosper and thrive and unlock the potential of all of its assets. I hope people understand that it is right to make changes because these matters have intrinsic value. If that's not enough, I hope people see all of this in their own personal interests and in their own patriotic interests—to not be beguiled by a waving flag to follow whatever comes next, but rather to think carefully about what is really in our national interest. That's patriotism. The peaceful protests we've seen this year are among the purest expressions of patriotism. And for those who look upon the protests harshly, especially those that have been swayed by the fox playing old and overstated footage of vandalism: to judge legitimate protesters by early acts of violence that some people have engaged in is no different than suggesting that all police support the murder of George Floyd. (If your reaction to this is something along the lines of: "see, they're bad too" or "both sides are wrong" or some garbage like that, well then I need to subject you to another essay.)

At the same time, I also want to say that for those that already agree with what I'm saying, that we need to have a path for others to genuinely wake up and cross the lines. We have to be open to a true "come to Jesus" moment. That doesn't mean just an empty statement or spending 3 minutes to take a knee or making empty promises or a nice dog and pony show, but we can't continue to anchor a person's future to all of the mistakes they've made in the past. Not everyone grew up bathed in the divine light of moral illumination. We can't be so wedded to every past indiscretion that we don't provide an off ramp for people—almost forcing them to stick with Racist Jeff rather than becoming a pariah to everyone. Before anyone gives an amen for the wrong reason, if your interpretation of this statement is "see, even this libtard thinks that 'they've gone too far,'" then first, that's not what I'm saying, and second, to repeat an earlier refrain, go f^@* yourself. All I'm saying is that one needs to be open to genuine apologies, and genuine attempts at reconciliation, which includes an embrace of all the work we need to do. In that context, it seems totally reasonable to me that it would be hard or impossible to forgive political leaders that have defended signs of the Confederacy in the past few decades. Votes to remove those symbols when they thought someone might bust the door down have to be regarded somewhat cynically.

There's so much more to say and do. But for now, the symbolic acts of pulling down Richmond's Lee monument and purging other Confederate symbols are a start. If people in power don't take the Confederate symbols away peacefully, because they know that it is right to do so—if someone's going to block these necessary and much delayed actions because their white supremacist sensibilities or tax advantages are trampled,* then someone else is going to pull them down forcefully, the same way that the Jefferson Davis on Monument Avenue was toppled,** along with the many other recent changes. Yes, these acts are little more than symbolic, but they need to happen. One way or another, these statues are going to be history.

---

* https://www.richmond.com/news/virginia/six-monument-avenue-residents-sue-to-stop-lee-statues-removal-new-case-moved-to-federal/article_cf0bc699-55d0-56df-9fa6-8ac9039e32ea.html

** https://www.nytimes.com/2020/06/11/us/Jefferson-Davis-Statue-Richmond.html

Randon Billings Noble

Often there are bears

Sometimes it's a school play—I'm Hamlet, not Antigonus—I'm about to go on—I have no idea what I'm doing, how I'm going to fake iambs—but somehow have to answer, stand, unfold myself.

But then the bears. Stalking the woods around my childhood home, and the bottom half of the Dutch door has been left open, and the claws are coming in.

Bears around the house and how can I make it from the barn to the door without their lumbering rush to maul me.

Bears at the window. Bears beneath the tree and coming up.

Bears on the runway as I wait to board a small plane to Los Angeles, a city I have no ties to, just a long ago lover and not a very good one, one I never think about except the morning after I have this dream.

And then a bear wearing a bathrobe in the closet at the foot of the bed I'm sleeping in.

Over my dreaming head: the ceiling, the roof, the night sky. And to the north, if it is not deep winter, the Great Bear herself, older than the Bible, older than Homer. Once the nymph Calisto, punished for a god's lust and a broken vow, she endlessly circles the north.

And the bears descend through my dreams.

Darius Stewart

Dearest Darky

There are a few blackfolk who are servers when you start in the restaurant business in 2001, and only one who is a bartender. The other blackfolk, when there are any, usually work as dishwashers, and only a handful get to grill or bake.

You're trained by whitefolk who will tell you that if you want to make bank as a server you must follow simple protocols:

When listing the daily specials, state the most expensive items last since these are usually the items guests are most likely to remember and this will increase the odds that they'll order them.

Take orders in the following sequence: ladies first, oldest to youngest, followed by men, oldest to youngest; though when you place the order with the kitchen do so in the order that the guests are seated at the table and not the order in which you took them; this will prevent the wrong person from receiving the wrong entree should someone else run your food.

If there are children, ask whether they should be served immediately while everyone else enjoys their soups and salads.

Bring the soup first, before the salad; be sure to ask which salad: Caesar, house, or wedge; don't forget the avocado ranch dressing comes on the wedge with blue cheese *crumbles*; this can be confusing for guests if not clarified; all the dressings are *housemade*; specify those that are the house favorites.

When serving hot soup, pay close attention to guests who swing wide with their arms; remove the soup bowls before you serve the salads.

When serving guests sitting in a booth, serve with your right hand if serving the left side of the booth, and the left hand if serving the right side of the booth; you should give the appearance of a hug instead of a back handed slap (if the wrong hand is used on the wrong side of the booth).

If the restaurant's extremely busy and the kitchen's backed up, place the entree orders before bringing the soup or salad.

When a guest makes a request, never respond *no problem*, as this implies there is a problem; *yes, ma'am* or *yes sir* is always appropriate.

Never take orders from children.

You will be employed by the Copper Cellar Family of Restaurants, which is based in your hometown, Knoxville.

You will wait tables at Calhoun's, one of several restaurants in the Copper Cellar Family of Restaurants, and is famous for having won in 1983 the title *Best Ribs in America.*

You will work there while you're a student at Tennessee State University, at the White Bridge Road location, but when you transfer to the University of Tennessee, you will transfer to the Calhoun's on Bearden Hill, in Knoxville.

You will have risen in the ranks by this time, and not least of all due to your uniform being deemed the best nearly every shift because you take the time to press your khaki pants, your blue striped dress shirt, and you ensure your white apron has a sharp crease down the center.

Your white guests will often joke that you could cut someone with that crease. And sometimes you want to.

You wait on a grandfather having lunch with his granddaughter, and after you've delivered their food, he asks to see your hand. When you show him your hand, he grabs your hand and begins gently to rub it, marveling to his granddaughter, see how smooth the brown skin is? She buries her face in her hands, shaking her head in shock, and when she finally looks up, mouth agape, you ask if there's anything else you can do for them, and leave her to stare at her grandfather while he eats his fried catfish and coleslaw, exclaiming how they are the most perfect combination.

You work the lunch shifts so that you will be guaranteed the prime sections on nights and weekends. You average three a week but try to avoid doubles as much as possible.

You are admired for being a team player, performing bathroom checks when asked, decrumbing the cracks in the booths, sweeping the cigarette butts from the parking lot.

You run food to a table of six, a table that isn't yours. After you've made sure no one needs anything further, you head to the kitchen to return the serving tray. You are unaware the server for whom you've just run food has been looking for you. When she finds you, she approaches you waving a long white strip of paper in her hand and tells you that one of the ladies from her table had flagged her down to give it to her. You notice she is holding the order ticket (or chit) you used to deliver the food. The sever says the lady at the table, as if in a panic, called out to her "Miss, Miss" over the chatter in the restaurant, and beckoned her closer to the table to tell her, that colored boy dropped this ticket.

The server, who is white, laughs because she can't believe in 2001 white ladies are still using *colored* to identify black people.

You laugh because you can't believe the lady tracked the server down to give her the chit. You crumple and attempt to toss into the trash can but miss. You watch it bounce off the rim, onto the floor, and think to yourself how you've never been good at basketball.

You will work for almost two years at Calhoun's before you are poached by managers of the corporation's flagship restaurant, The Copper Cellar, to work there.

You want to work there because it is on The Strip, the main drag on the University of Tennessee campus, and during football season you have heard that servers and bartenders have been known to make two-months' rent in a single weekend. The added bonus is that your dorm is within walking distance.

You will work at The Copper Cellar off and on for sixteen years.

In your final stint working there, you will return to The Copper Cellar broke, having lost two serving jobs in Austin, Texas, and each of them because you were either caught drinking on the job or you called in one time too many. Luckily, the same guests who'd become your benefactors over the years are still there when you return. They are old white couples who have tipped you into the thousands of dollars for your service, in addition to gifting you with Christmas and birthday bonuses. Some have paid all expenses to the casino in Tunica, Mississippi—including money to gamble—while others would insist you bring a plate to the table and share large portions of their meals.

A few of the women love to claim to be your second mother; they've even invited your mama to dinner and told her the same. You are their family, their favorite, their baby boy, although the one most insistent on this fact is the one who makes kissy faces at you as she pinches your cheeks and calls you her dearest darky.

You consider leaving The Copper Cellar after you catch several of your white female co-workers in the banquet room, which is adjacent to the main dining room, with the lights dimmed just low enough for them to see each other's faces while they hatched a plan against you in angry whispers. They elect a whitegirl who wants to be a cop and has wide hips and what she says is a blackgirl booty. She accuses you of sharking all the good tables and they intend to do something about it.

You make the decision to leave The Copper Cellar one afternoon when you're with a former co-worker having an early dinner at Chesapeake's—the corporation's premier seafood house. You tell her about the coup against you and listen to her scoff at the nerve of those white bitches, she says. And because she too is white, you take her rebuke as objectivity, which makes you feel better. It's during this exchange that the general manager—whom you worked with at Calhoun's on Bearden Hill, and again when he hired you back at The Copper Cellar after your return from Texas—tells you that you're always welcome to come work for him whenever you want.

Two weeks later, you start orientation there.

Two years after that, you are promoted to bartender.

What you love about bartending is that the service is pretty straightforward. You make drinks on request. You collect payments. You throw tips in a jar.

How much you make often depends on the merits of a cocktail. If you make it right, it should loosen one's inhibitions but not their resolve. It should be agreeable to the palate. Even if it's high in proof—or has an alcohol content of 50% or more—a cocktail should have a pleasant mouth feel.

You once made a cocktail for a lady dining in the lounge, a perfect Manhattan, equal parts dry and sweet vermouth, Angostura bitters, and Woodford Reserve served on the rocks with a maraschino cherry to garnish. After a few sips, she makes eye contact, lifts her glass: cheers! Before she leaves, she approaches the bar, takes your hand firmly and shakes it as she places five dollars in your palm.

You have bar guests whom you rely on for tips, but when there are guests dining at tables tipping you randomly—and this happens to you often—then you're making money.

On the other hand, when business is sluggish, you entertain yourself popping beer bottle caps into a trash can nearby, peruse recipes on Pinterest, stalk the restaurant until you find that a cadre of Scarlet O'Hara's dependent upon the kindness of strangers has given up on the possibility of making any money and decide to get a jump on their side work, polishing and rolling silverware.

You bitch to them about how much money you need to pay this bill or that bill, and how sad it is that dinner means nibbling on a piece of bread dipped in drawn butter because you're too broke to afford anything more substantial to eat—even with a 40% employee discount.

Except you've been known to meet an income quota by the thinnest margins. The trick is to observe one rule of thumb: charisma is as important as pouring a good drink.

You try always to encourage a convivial atmosphere for guests who choose your services.

Your attitude invites them to step up to the bar and you will wipe a clean spot cleaner just to show them you care.

When you slide a beverage napkin their way, you let them know you're listening.

The dining room guests can have their tables and captain's chairs—at the bar, everyone shares the throne.

May I suggest the filet mignon and cold-water lobster tails this evening? you might say. But, first, you will insist that they consider a menu of six-dollar appetizers while you woo them with offers of two bucks off wine by the glass and liquor by the drink, half off draft beer, a dollar off bottled. These are the happy hour specials (when generous pours can be exchanged for hefty tips, and this—your mutually agreed upon *quid pro quo*—can be initiated with a wink and a nod, a fist bump or thumbs up).

Of course, there's always one or two guests, usually a regular, who, no matter what, will leave a pittance for a tip.

One in particular demands that you wash and polish a snifter for him to slosh his cheap bourbon.

He's fond of telling everyone that he might not always be right, but he's never wrong, and the future just ain't what it used to be.

You don't want to encourage him to expose the wounds of his failing marriage, or else he is likely to grab the crook of your arm when you try to walk away from him because he needs you to listen for just a minute because he has something very important to tell you about marriage, and you have to know it this very instance or else your life will be damaged beyond repair. He makes you bend low, so low his hand rests on your shoulder, so low he breathes his whiskey breath into your face, because you must know this, he says, and you'll thank him later for informing you that despite what you've been told in the past by your mother or father or your wife!, it just isn't true that when you're slicing vegetables and accidentally drop a knife, you should simply let it fall to the floor. You try to catch it! Don't let utensils hit the floor with all that filth. Just mind the blade!

He tells you this, and you shake your head and say, yes, sir, but think, *why, Lord?* because you know you're going to get a paltry tip but still you must provide him the kindest service. You can pat him on the hand still clenched firmly around your arm, tell him that you will remember, and thank him for looking out for you.

You will often make the best money off a group of regulars who are white men from the surrounding boondock counties who make sure that you always keep a drink in their hands. You will observe as they grow gradually drunker and drunker, and you'll slow down the service but you won't cut them off, you'll stay blasé when they slur, when they sit half-tilted off their stools, when their voices boom with boisterous laughter, or lean in with a hushed tone to sneak a few niggers into their sentences because you know they're not racist, they tell you. You know I love you brother! they say.

In fact, one of these white men has a wonderful joke, you think, about a particular type of nigger, a joke that you'll repeat yourself. It's the joke about a white couple named John and Wendy.

John and Wendy are high school sweethearts who are married in a lavish ceremony. John loves Wendy very much, and as his promise of fidelity, he has her name tattooed on his penis.

For their honeymoon, they travel to Jamaica, and every night Wendy is tickled when she sees her name fully spelled out when he's erect, only for her name to abbreviate to WY when his penis goes flaccid.

John and Wendy never leave their suite to tour the island and its luxurious accommodations until the end of their honeymoon. Yet, John has also chosen this time to try a variety of delicious rum drinks, which causes him to piss frequently.

He rushes to the men's room and takes a stall next to a gentleman who appears to be a local. Curious—as some men are in these situations—John peeks over at the local to discover the letters WY tattooed on his penis. What a coincidence, John thinks.

Excuse me, John says when they're each washing their hands at the sink. I noticed that you have WY tattooed on your penis. I do too! It stands for Wendy, my beautiful wife. We're here on our honeymoon. What does your WY stand for?

The local turns to John with equal enthusiasm and says, well, WY does not stand for Wendy. He pauses a moment to toss his paper towel into the trash bin. It stands for Welcome to Jamaica, Have a Nice Day!

When you tell this joke to bar guests whom you feel you can trust, much like the white man from whom you learned the joke, you will whisper it to them because it's a pretty raucous dick joke that needs to be told discreetly and not at all because it's racist.

It's only a joke and you don't want to acknowledge the implied history of racialized terror against black men when white men thought about the size of a black man's dick.

You chalk it up to a joke about penis envy and not about what white men feared a black man's dick would do to their white women.

Racial politics have no place in how you pay your bills, even though when you recall your experiences working at the various Copper Cellar Family of Restaurants, you will tell folks, incredulously, about *see how smooth the brown skin is and Miss, that colored boy dropped this ticket* and *Hey there my dearest darky* and the joke about John and Wendy.

You will tell folks how you couldn't have made the money you did without managers who gave you prime schedules, and that you took a pay cut when you went off to graduate school.

You will tell folks about the time a manager told you to smile so everyone could see your teeth and identify you in the dark when the lights went out in the restaurant during a power failure or another manager called you a niglet for reasons you still don't remember.

You won't tell folks how you often complained alongside your white co-workers that you hated waiting on blackfolk because blackfolk don't tip.

You won't tell folks how you were largely responsible for getting a whitegirl fired for refusing to wait on a table of blackfolk because it was the only way you could get her fired because you didn't like her.

You won't tell folks you didn't like her because she made overtly sexual comments just like everyone else, but unlike everyone else, she was obese, and you were fatphobic, and many of your co-workers urged you to play the race card against her to get her fired since this would be the only way to tone her down.

You won't tell folks there were many strategies you would use to prevent otherwise excellent servers from getting better shifts than you.

You won't tell folks what you fear any of this says about you, what it might have to do with how you want people to feel about you, which is that you've always wanted people to like you, that you don't even know the limits to what is involved in making sure that people will always like you, that you can't see how there's anything wrong with that.

M. Kaat Toy

In the Weight Room

One night in the weight room of the ninety-five percent male private military college where I teach, I am wearing a yellow Camp Shalom T-shirt and staring past my black shorts and pink knees at the bars of weights on the Universal machine, preparing to lift with my legs three hundred pounds in ten repetitions.

I'm watching three upperclassmen lift free weights on the far side of the room, but in particular I watch one lift free weights. He stands sideways to me, in front of the mirror, and as the bar rises above his head, the muscles in the tops of his arms enter the points of his shoulders like jets crashing into the ocean, all lean hard speed dividing on impact. His hair is cut short and harsh in the military way. He's not so good-looking in the face, but he's so hard-looking in the face—a tight beaky face—that it's commanding, so I look at it. Except for the huff of his breath, it is silent as the muscles in his arms moved up and down like the pistons they are as he lifts. He's so beautiful, there should be a movie of it, shot in the cruel white light of the weight room that flatters only hard edges and forgives nothing. The only tragedy is there's no one else to watch him, just the four of us having this little experience together.

So I do my set, pushing and struggling in my not so beautiful way. I'm resting when he comes and sets the weights and grabs the bar at the station next to mine, which, on the Universal machine, is about six inches away. In an uncrowded weight room no one takes the next station on the Universal machine. It is a gesture of intimacy you're not supposed to make, but here he is making it with all the force it takes for him to swing his body down to the floor, which, if you are tall like he is, is the only way you can get the full extension on this part of the machine without sending the weights crashing to the top every time you pull your arms down.

I go on with my next set, not knowing what else to do, and he starts his set, his buddies bracing him down, his beautiful sweating body pumping heavily at a right angle to mine, both of us breathing hard together, muscles moving in and out together, and no one can say it's not like sex. When else do your burning muscles move so sleekly in and out, where pain is everything and nothing, where you cannot stop moving, where you cannot stop trying to get your breath, where everything is beautifully hard inside you, yet yielding, like a dancer, where there is no other world, there are only muscles and breathing and burning tension, mirrored by your partner, mirrored all around you; then, suddenly there is a final push and it stops, the pain ends, your breathing slows down, and you look around at a clean new world, slightly embarrassed by the road you took to get there? So that's what happened in the weight room when that hard-edged boy took the spot beside me, and, for whatever reason, decided to do those reps when every other station was empty.

Jesse Glass

Excerpt from *Hometown*

Ken Koons

Prelude

Strike the hewgag, sound the tomjohn!
Let the loud hosanna ring!
Beat the huzzyfuzzy! Wake the qongquong!
Buntum, fizzlebum, dingo, bim!

Shout aloud, Rumbumtumfoezle!
And let the great humbug bird sing!
Bow before the great bamboozle—
Rumkum, bunken, fumkensling!

Wake again the great Sumpumkims!
And the rumsquash, rouse once more!
Hangum, bangum, chunke maqumskins—
Loudly let the wig-wag roar!

Slaughter now the great krumsquamskee,
Hang the bull calf up to dry;
Harumskarum, slatumhankee—
Make the great Ramfuscus cry!

(1856)

Then became Joseph enraged and stamped with his feet upon the floor, and, like unto a lunatic, did he seem to contend with an unseen foe, and swore that he would not keep cool! And the grasshopper was amazed, and the swallow trembled with affright, but all those who were within the watch-tower with Sam's Sentinel were not affrighted, but laughed at the impotent rage of Joseph.

Chronicles, IV. [Aug. 22, 1856]

"...I admit the wonderful delusion of language, but sirs, an argument in behalf of that which is really wrong may at best be compared to a whited sepulcre. You have but to strip it of its specious ornaments and all within is bones and rotten-ness..." — Wm. P. Preston. June 5th, 1865 Trial record.

1.

Just

Pulled a

Tombstone from the earth

w/ my bare hands

(whip-poor-will & mourning dove a-song)

it was red-rooted/ jagged
as a Zeuglodont's tooth

under—"born"—a deeply cut 1,8,3,5,—

kiss of a sledge hammer (concoid shatter)

covert impact

a distinct attempt at leveling
[not meted out till years after!!!!

Barely a death date (1906?)

To trace w/ a finger

On this lichen-spotted anti-decalogue of an abbreviated monument

Cogged & toggled by entropy Muddy from spring fog earthworms

Whipping

Pneumatic/ hermeneutic.

Bouncing across

Noon cemetery

a lemon-spotted mongrel w/ tongue the color of rumor searching for

c,h,e,w,a,b,l,e,s,

(Looks once, twice, in my direction

then sniffs around obelisk base, rust-eaten sentiment), tail curled over rump &

(rain-melted limestone babes weep a deep cupric trickle thru both cheeks)

sprints this Necropolis length to escape our story

Hermit thrush circles from willows, lands to peer between grass blades screams & pecks

Apart

fox

scat,

I "whump!" the smashed marble loaf thick into mud

(bird flies off cussing

Steady it upright: an "Honest Citizen" of my town/ ready for the interrogation of the Ages—
Lived out his days dripping sweat on the dandelions
Brick-making his trade
When he didn't stab men, trapped in their hotel rooms, to death.

2.

Now look up from among these graves.

That pillared building there? Court House, built by a man named Durbin.

Justly famed for the cupola and Doric columns,

yet

human beings stood chained for inspection on those steps

Bare to the waist, bare under linsey-woolsy, no doubt shivering in this

Weather

(I shiver here today).

September 9, 1861—Emeline Haines. For bastardy and for begetting a child by a slave.
Sentenced to the Maryland Penitentiary for 18 months.
September 9, 1861-Matthew Ward, Col.-Sold and transported for
giving Emeline Haines, a white woman, her child.

What was their story?
1860 census:

A widowed mother with three young girls and a small son to care for

A farm and fields near Bird Hill—she was rather well off
a man who came to work for her...
(the farm is still there)
Did she & he sometimes whisper together about distant Canada?

(She did not own a slave.)

& then...when it could not be hidden

one tragedy and another?

What was the story of them?

All new old news—hidden away in the docket books—until 2007

& denied, denied, denied by the Commissioners

(denied, too, the court house whipping post)

"It's a non-topic/ my ancestors never owned a-one-na-them"

Who are proud to pray to Jesus Christ before each public meeting
But **deny**
That these things ever happened

Blue jays scream circling, drift & land beneath the willows
the shadow of cracked marble loaf frames a question
one might try to answer in thirty years

3.

Versions:

a.

The Frederick Examiner, April 26, 1865.

Excitement At Westminster, Md.

On Saturday, the 15th inst. on the reception of the intelligence at Westminster, Carroll County, Md., of the assassination of President Lincoln, the most intense excitement ensued. A meeting of the citizens was called at the Court House at 8 o'clock, P.M., which was presided over by Mr. [Francis] Shriver, and was the largest and most respectable in point of numbers ever held in the town. Great bitterness of feeling was expressed against Joseph Shaw, the proprietor of the *Westminster Democrat*, a paper in the interest of the rebellion, on account of remarks made in the issue of that week. The editor said, among other things "Some people hope that Lincoln's life will be spared now, in order that the country may be saved the disgrace of an "incoherent" Vice President. But is there not a slight chance of improvement in case that Providence should will it otherwise?" The article continued at length in its vituperative language against both the President and Vice President, such as the Rebel sympathisers have so frequently indulged in.—A proposition was made in the meeting to destroy the office of the paper, but more moderate counsels prevailed, and the resolution was modified to the effect that Shaw be notified that the *Democrat* would no longer be issued in that town.

A resolution was also unanimously adopted, by a rising vote of those present, requiring the chairman of the meeting to appoint a vigilance committee for Carroll County, whose duty it should be to take such measures as would prevent the return of any Rebel who had ever borne arms against the Government of the United States to that county, no matter whether paroled by Gen. Grant or any other authority. Every person who has ever been in the Rebel army will be forced to take up his residence elsewhere, their presence being considered dangerous to the peace of the community.

At midnight, long after the meeting adjourned, the office of the *Democrat* was visited. The types, cases, printing paper, in fact all the material, were taken to the street and burned, and the press, stove, etc., in the building broken with axes, crowbars, etc. Though the establishment was completely gutted, the building itself was unharmed.

A feeling of sorrow and vengeance pervaded the entire assembly. The editor still remains a sad beholder of the wreck of his famous concern.

b.

Joseph Shaw killed at Westminster, MD.

We learn that the town of Westminster, in Carroll County, was the scene of great excitement on Monday evening, resulting in the death of Joseph Shaw, late editor of the *Westminster Democrat*, whose office was destroyed about a week since by a vigilance committee, who ordered him to leave the town. The destruction of his paper, and his banishment from Westminster, was caused by disloyal language used in his paper in relation to the President and the Government, and also on account of having led to ruin a simple-minded girl of the town. He returned to the town on Monday, in despite of public sentiment, and was waited upon at the hotel of Mr. Zacharias by a delegation of citizens. He immediately opened the door and commenced firing with a revolver, wounding Mr. Henry Bell in the hand. The firing was returned by the party, and resulted in the death of Shaw. The excitement in the town was, of course, very great.—*Baltimore Sun* via the Washington D.C. *Evening Star*, April 26, 1865.

c.

WESTMINSTER, June 1st, 1865

CIRCUIT COURT FOR CARROLL COUNTY—Before Hon. John E. Smith, circuit judge—State vs. Henry Bell, Jesse H. Murray, John Baker, Peter Henry and Henry W. Wampler, indicted jointly for the manslaughter of Joseph Shaw, formerly editor of the *Westminster Democrat*, on the 24th of April, 1865, by stabbing him in the left breast, making a wound three inches wide and six inches deep, of which said Shaw instantly died. Wm. P. Preston and Milton Whitney, Esqs., assisting Charles W. Webster, State's attorney. Wm. P. Maulsby, Isaac E. Pearson, Archibald Stirling, Jr. and Henry Winter Davis, Esqs., counsel for defense.

d.

Cross-Examination:

"Wm. Shaw—Is father of Joseph Shaw, deceased, [says]; his son was born with fingers short; some one joint and some two joints—his thumbs were perfect."

(Trial record)

Therefore, how could he fire a gun?

4.

(Pennywhistle)

Somebody walks out the door
somebody walks in.

Seems like we're always saying
Hello or goodbye.
The hellos never linger,
The goodbyes, more often than not,
Are final.

I think we could call this something like truth.

5.

My father's tumor continues to grow

This un-lettered son of toil

Practices his wit in a chair by the half-opened window. Center-stage

Now for the first time in his life

He tells every joke he can manage to recall. While

Nurses, laughing, release the corruption from his bag into plastic buckets.

He recites his brave words

For his sons to hear, for one

Maybe to write down.

6.

(Pennywhistle.)

I walk into Rexall's
And take a seat at the soda fountain,
order French fries,
A chicken salad sandwich,
And a five cent Coke.

I take my time at the counter—
The Dunkard waitress tells me
About her grandson,
(I admire her lace bonnet as she
Stares through her black hornrims)
Someone else walks in
And she tells him, too.
I wipe my fingers and rise.

It's twelve o'clock and the fire siren
Goes off to tell everyone what they
Already know.

7.

Way off beneath cumulus clouds

The sun burns thru a bit

& A tractor made toy by distance
drags sound of motor & wheeled chains rattling behind it

The murdered man's headstone
Sits among the family markers
Father William and the enigmatic Thomas
(Who dies in August, 1865—no record)
black, blotched stones these three.

No inscription calling for outrage
No birth and death and resurrection promises
Blank where it should say love
& blank where it should say eternity
& blank where it should say forgiveness.

I kneel in long meadow grass,

& rub the words transversely
Onto stretched rice paper

taped over screaming ascenders

lean into the silver wax wedge and press so
curds hang from the paper.

8.

Letter of Advice
Union Bridge,
24th of 2nd mo., 1859.

Friend Joseph: I have often admonished thee of thy evil ways, and advised thee to give heed to thy deportment; yet, I fear that my advice and admonitions are unheeded by thee, and that thou art traveling in the broad road that leadeth to destruction.

Thou dost not govern thy temper as thou shoulds't, and thou art much given to other bad habits and evil propensities. Thou dost practice thyself in strange games, the invention of Satan, and for strong drink at the great Inn, in the city where thou dwellest, thou dost wager against thy fellows, and when thou art beaten in thy games, thou dost refuse to redeem thy pledge, and dost leave thy fellows disgusted with thy lack of honor.

Thou dost also attend those inventions of the evil one called Balls, and dost attempt to worship at the altar of their idol by skipping frantically over the floor. Friend Joseph, I know that thy head is but poorly inducted with knowledge, and it appears that thy heels have less experience. For I have heard of thee, that when thou dost attempt to dance, as thy pastime is so called, thou dost make greater motions with thy head, hands, and arms, than thou dost with thy feet.

I have therefore advised thee that thou hast mistaken thy calling in thy attempts at publishing a newspaper. I fear thou hast made a greater mistake in thy attempts at dancing. Thou hadst better quit thy domino playing and dancing; and above all things, refrain from strong drink.

And friend Joseph, it is also said that thou dost keep strict guard over the correspondence of thy workmen, and dost take undue liberties with matters appertaining thereto.—I beseech of thee that thou refrain from this, for thou art in danger, and mayest get thyself into greater difficulties than thou knowest of.

Finally, Joseph, quit thy abusive language to others, and thy low-bred epithets; and, if possible, try to make thyself a decent citizen, and thou wilt fare better.

Thine truly,
Jonathan Broadbrim.

Fran Abrams

Complicit

How can a government bureaucrat
sleep at night after
he has approved the purchase of cages
to hold helpless children hostage?

How can a border patrol agent
wake up in the morning
in her comfortable home,
report to work,
take a baby from his mother's breast?

Are these humans these creatures who do this work?
Do they go home to their own families and weep?
Ask themselves—
    How badly do I need this job?
    Can I build a wall between my own
    compassionate beliefs
    and the duties I am paid to carry out?

Or do they gloat about the power they wield,
brag to their friends about their important jobs?

Renée Adams

King Virus Dance

"Dance me through the panic
till I'm gathered safely in..."
—Leonard Cohen

Curtain gates slowly open
as I bow low my reverence
leaning carefully down and out—
to peek past the fence gap
anyone there?
No one's coming
so I release my tight body onto
the sidewalk stage of my poetry fence
uncoiling ballet to the rhythm
of cardinal's castanet call
I'm stapling a percussive response to the bird
ka-chunk ka-chunk my laminated poem
onto the board fence

Look up!—
here comes the masked Phantom of the Virus,
his dog on a leash,
we start the Pas de Deux
who will glissade, who aplomb?
He pivots to cross the street; I stay put

a Dos a Dos a Dos a Dos a Dos ah

Dance me with your shopping cart
don't touch me with your glove

He waves and smiles behind his mask;
acknowledgment
far enough?

Oh, touch me with your heart
as your body's in remove

Though I need a human hug,
I ball-change and turn
return to my task of placing other's Pandemic poems
on my poetry fence

Here comes another down the sidewalk;
the dance begins again
I breathe into my stomach, shake my shoulders to relax

When will I dance toward you
touch the warm fuzz of your face
Dance me to your body's love

Cynthia Atkins

Illicit

I owned your dirty thoughts, lying
in the afternoon shadows. It's 3 pm,
the streets are desolate. The backlit dive
where we met has replaced me with
your new mistress, hair as green as a virus.
Our love got caught in the no-fly zone
of human distancing. The hands that used to pull
my hair from your sweaty face, are now slicing
Pb & j's on the counter. After school sports
and play dates, canceled. My hair is growing
out white, like the finger lakes
in winter, but it's not winter, it's April
and the buds are calling our names.
You once said there was nothing more sublime
than "my neckline shadowed against the fire-escapes."
I knew each portal, each secret, your body kept
in all your lonely file cabinets. There's a reaper
in the stairwell, listening at the doors, keyholing
all the despair. Tonight, you're all in the living room,
TV and popcorn. The cozy family snuggled up.
Your wife stretches out, wearing my ankle bracelet.
This pestilence writes an elegy with toxic ink—
A world-wide brush with death, to tell us,
there's no place for lovers in a war zone.

Hypnos

We were all made in the Opium den
of Nyx and Erebus, where the dark meets
fibers of light and strange bedfellows greet
　　at *The Rainbow Room, INC.*—The woodwork
is handcrafted Ebony, staircases made
from the ivory teeth of our kin. In the next cloudy
　　room, a sycophant stands beside
The *My Pillow Guy.* Snake oil drizzles
from suitcases bought and sold—Remember
their forefathers selling humans
right off the ship. Now our nightstands
are festooned with bottles and potions,
　　herd inoculations. Left at the door,
the limp ruins of what we longed for.
We're mesmerized by a chameleon
in the town square selling us
bridges and crackpot ideas.
　　The postman walks door to door,
with mail that has passed through
many hands. Invisible pox in a love letter
carried house to house, between
　　sullied hands. Now shut up
and be still, we've got a screen shot.
All *normal as Apple Pie,* that pie
your Aunt Sara cooled from the oven.
Aged lady, defiled, now a nameless piffle
　　that bought the sham. She's laid out
mouth to foot on the bed—The God of sleep holds
out a pillowcase like a car door. Stepping inside,
blind-folded, we're told to count
the sheep— Staring down a barrel,
we see only dead unicorns in a field.

Dolls, Inc

In frilly bedrooms of pink and periwinkle, here lie
the seeds, rubric of the rooms in shadow.
Their generic genitals hidden away
like a shadow government. Two faces
with puckered lips— Shaped by a diva
in a factory of human body parts.
Hair made from a horse's mane.
Sometimes the little dots and bald spots
show through like underthings
no one is supposed to see.
Such a seductive sadness inside
the fish tank of little girls.
Their Satin dresses have ruffles firm
as plaster-of-paris. And some mouths
are not given a voice in the house of sycophants.
A little girl holds a doll, a throbbing
bellow of pain, a frayed heirloom passed
down generations. Watch her walk home
on a long dirt road, holding the one
with bee-stung lips. Eyes darting danger
from side to side, eyelashes fluttering
like butterflies in a field.

Naomi Ayala

Lotus

BoSung Sunim, my old
teacher, is far away yet
even in redbud and dusk.
I miss reciting the Heart Sutra
in the old temple.
I have not learned a thing
about detachment.

Fuego

Fire wake up
and fire no sleep.
Burn lip, singe flank.
Put out the water.

Coal in the pit
burning hot redblack.
Lick wind, root.
Burn up into seed.

And fire is fire.
So, deep bow and
Crow come back home to me.
All things crow.

Kiss

And slip into night sky.
That the Earth's galaxy
is 100 thousand lightyears across
is no small wonder.
Sun way out in the Sagittarius arm
and I still warm here.
Bliss. Salty-sweet.
Eros, son of Chaos
in the universe of my belly.
At the beginning
of someone else's emptiness.

After Lovemaking

He would refuse to let me
slip back into my clothes.

We were to do it all naked—
cook, sit on the couch, read.

All day I liked knowing
my body like this,
incapable of concealing anything.

I was all eyes, all ears for the world.

He outgrew this when winter
swept in with storms
and he was too tired to light
the wood stove.

I was not adept, he'd say
at making fires in large, cast iron things.
And you know, women should just
go about women's things.

And the world already had enough fire
without me.

And he preferred to talk about work.

Men, He Says

We're guilty, guilty of everything.

Jeanne Marie Beaumont

Some Are Haunted

Some have been known to weep
from an eye or bleed.

Two women swore to hearing a horse's clear whinny
all through one night; in the morning they found
its rider thrown into a hedge.

One was reported to descend from his pediment
and romp with the children, then
stiffen again at the end of the day.

When one was torn down, a scream
like a mandrake's was heard by a gardener
a mile away.

Some changed position. Others reformed their expression,
or so it was rumored, believed.
Not one was *simply* anything. None were mere.

Detecting a crescendo, and putting best ears
to the ground, folks felt their heads thrill
with a relentless stampede.

While some were caught in the slightest of twitches
like a pitcher called for a balk
that affects the at-bat that alters the inning
that changes the outcome of the game.

Bucket List

As I was delighting in large flakes sifting outside my window, now and then kicked about by the wind or blown eastways, as it happens, though mostly descending straight toward destiny, I noticed some snow had clumped cotton-like in the branching of the closest tree, or so it seemed although I have only seen cotton plants in movies and may never get any closer, which is fine by me, and I noted that snow had begun to clothe—or shroud, as we often say about a coat of snow, acknowledging its metaphoric layer—the wire mesh sculpture my neighbor had hung on her outside wall, the one of a man, life-size, climbing the building (already two floors up), a terrifying depiction of every New Yorker's fear if you ask me and something I resent having directly in my sights every time I sit in my big red chair to drink coffee and think deeply, but now that it was softened somewhat, padded on its shoulders and masked on its upturned face by snow, it felt less ominous, vulnerable even, pleading for mercy from the blinding onslaught, and I wondered whether I would ever get to Pompeii and how much did I really still want to go though I'd always claimed I did, yet had I now reached a point where mere photos of it in a book would content me, and what point was that, for I was reminded how very much I love to watch the snow, that I wished to watch the snow one hundred more times before I go, if that wasn't asking too much, and was that even a possible number?—I begin to do the math...

Mad Woman's Multiple Choice

for Emma H. and Anna K.

A husband's kiss
a. brings poison to my lips
b. contaminates the immortal soul
c. is a judas kiss

I am only
a. put here because someone was trying to shoot me
b. trapped here because I forgot to bathe
c. a door that god uses to pass in and out of this world

This whirling
a. a scribble in air to make my space
b. is a girlish thing to do
c. gets their attention all right

I sketch with
a. cigarette ashes and spit
b. a carpenter pencil rats gnaw on each night
c. blood and the quill of a mourning dove

Don't touch
a. my hair I am not your puppet
b. my food I will refuse to eat it
c. my papers my soldiers will cut you into pieces

My mission to throw the girl into the river because
a. she was too pure for this world
b. I saw the devil enter her through her ear
c. she was exactly like me

I write to
a. scratch scratch scratch an unrelenting itch
b. the very edges of the paper till no light shines through
c. get to you, Treasureheart, to get to you

The babies
a. each an infection that aimed to kill me
b. left behind—I must go find—
c. romp in the gardens again one day

When I get out of here plan
a. eat the biggest slice of cake
b. deck the baby carriage with winding flowers
c. live on my own deep in the forest

My fate
c. they don't post my letters so no one ever comes
b. to die here and be buried in an unmarked grave
a. all of the abo—

Anne Becker

We All Want It/The Thing With Feathers

The peacock releases his
gooey waste on the balcony
of the rich folks who don't
realize they live in the
fields of North Carolina farm
country, their garage three
times the size of a normal
house, the peacock
who's been on the run
from humans who think
they own him, or at least
consider themselves
responsible for his human-
smelling bowel movements and
follow his sightings as he searches
for the perfect pea-girl through the
woods and fields and gardens
of their neighbors in Chatham
County, open sky above and
white clouds piling up over
green green ground, seed
heads bouncing in the wind.
He's tired of the same old
same old of his own pea-
ladies, perhaps an Easter
Egg, Spoonbread her name,
would be a nice change
of pace, the one who lays
blue eggs among the brown
of her sisters, maybe a female
vulture—a female

hawk—he keeps
running and screaming so
she'll know he's alive and ready
for it. His owners always too
late and he's moved on
gone to the next carport
or tractor shed, dodging
the coyotes and other
beasts of prey: pure desire
blue, green, gold—iridescence
—feathers on the loose.

The Age of Old Women

"...maybe it wasn't an accident that
humans are the only great ape species
in which women live so long past
reproductive age..."
—"Why Grandmothers May Hold the Key
to Human Evolution," NPR

With the men in our lives falling
by the wayside, dropping like flies,
we keep moving forward—one foot
out of bed, one out the front door,
to the grocery store, the doctor's,
to the garden to pluck out weeds—
as our flesh sags, our tissues spread,
our breasts splay into the space—space
men's bodies emptied out for us,
the world now wider, distances
greater—but we are still tender—
how can we not be?—anyone

can touch us and see: our skin still
rosy, plum, olive, ochre, golden
clay, still like it was when we were
young, a satin binding, holding
purple bobbing organs in one
body—ours—creases and wrinkles,
extra flaps, little pimples raised
themselves up, now veins puff out their
blue tunnels just under the surface, fine invisible hairs still
coat our forearms, cheek, line of the
throat, blood twitches the wrist, we now
know at any moment our brains
might let go—dark—hot, might then go
cold, conflict vaginas, wet then
dry—what do they want?—desire still
shakes swollen pink petal threshold
and doorframe, the weakest known force
in nature, hugging our atoms
together, grounding our toes, the ball,
the arch and the heel, through its long
reach to the earth, the heart stays put
in the chest, under the breastbone
dome, hot then cold, a great
aridity surrounds it, rouge,
cliff-red, picked up by the wind in
the high desert glittering sand
scours it, hoarding, eroding the
soft and hard veins, landscape puckers
and broadens, folds, fissures, mesa
and canyon, tussock, tumuli,
we the survivors of the great
civil war, we hold our children
or they need to hold us—known
and unthought knowns, vermilion,
sanguine, cracked wisdom of
the old women.

Guy R. Beining

unsettled view

in all the flat graves
what mumblings, what split weeds
& quaint daisies design the last take?
lock the hearts of those
whistling birds for our era
is being stamped upon.
a spider in its hut of silk
begins its canvas, breaking thru all
the silent steps that we have left.

extinguished

the evening station
with signs muddled
past direct go.
the chute was filled to overflow
evening poured thru icicles
& the raw station
in its purplish moan.

Nina Bennett

The Day We Get Our Marriage License, I Turn Onto a Dead End

We drove separately; he had to go back to work.
I left the interstate an exit early,
headed to the mall. Confident in my sense
of direction, I turned right at the unmarked road,
entrance dimmed by shrubs larger than my car.
Narrow lane, brambles and briars tangled
like cords in a kitchen junk drawer.
Unable to turn around, wheels spun
on loose gravel as I shifted into reverse.
Dust cyclone swirled, surrounded my car, obscured my vision.
Took twenty years to find my way out.

Three Lies About Size, and One Truth

1.

Good things come in small packages:
Not a welcome cliché if it involves your paycheck,
your bedroom closet, or the crabs you ordered
for a summer cookout.

2.

It's a little error:
Not what you want to hear
from the accountant who prepares
your taxes, or your boss
during a performance review.

3.

One size fits all:
Not true if you are 4-9 and weigh
98 pounds, so the hospital scrubs
slither down your nonexistent hips, and you
have to roll the legs into thick sausages.

4.

Size matters:
When it comes to your winning Powerball ticket,
a package you need to mail overnight, and the fact
that you thought this poem was going somewhere else.

What to Do With Poem Drafts

Unfinished poems go in a drawer
to incubate. Months or years
accumulate like dust. Release
the drafts, shake them hard,
hang them on the line, where
they lift to the sky the way
a sunflower does, sway
in a summer breeze. Perhaps
they are soaked in a sudden
August storm, pelted by hail,
words sluiced off the paper.
Perhaps those are the words
not needed.

Legacy for My Sons

I leave you the family photos,
relatives identified on the back
in Nana's formal cursive. I tell
you stories from your childhood,
we laugh over your grandfather's
sayings, recall how much he enjoyed
holidays with big meals. He did
not enjoy the fasting ones, such as
Yom Kippur, but he could make his
seders last for hours on Passover.
Your uncle and I were convinced
he made up half the service.

Amber, magenta, lemon leaves
that crunch under your feet in October.
The first snowflake, drifting slowly
to the tip of your tongue. Sunrise like
a watercolor over the Delaware River.
Perseids while sprawled in sleeping bags
on the lawn on a muggy August night.
I give all these to you.

I leave you infinity.

Susan Bennett

In the Center Ring

Raised by inconstant trapeze artists
I lived in a faded red tent
learned to let go and fly
made friends with the safety net
playmates were impertinent monkeys
my teacher was the bearded woman
dog faced boys my schoolmates
lived on a diet of cotton candy and crackerjacks
sawdust is as hard to get
out of your toes as sand
Mother was the cigarette girl
Father was the fire eater
I still have my big clown shoes

John Bradley

Donald Trump Poses with Bible* Outside St. John's Episcopal Church, Washington, D.C., June 1, 2020

The kerosene of grief —Sun Yung Shin

Nat Turner. When he died. Randomly and often:
In a multichambered cylinder. As if by accident:
Again and again:

Holes grow, where they grow. Clear and close:
Voice of stun grenade, baton, bullet. Bible:
Loaded with gunpowder. And the hammer behind:
Past tense dissolved. Almost by accident:
Into a flashbang civil war. People, assumed to be human:
Do to people. Assumed to be human. Just about anything:
Again, again:

Ignite crowd control drama. Public exhibition:
You have to dominate. The O.K. Corral battlespace:
Looters, thugs, radicals, lowlife, terrorist, scum:
Vision blurring. *Beloved, do not avenge yourselves*:
Holes grow. Clear, close. The harvest eating its hunger:
Nat Turner. Loaded with gunpowder. As if by accident:
Once again:

Dominate, devastate, domesticate. More:
In a multichambered cylinder. Often. Randomly:
Again. Again:

---

*Trump's Bible was transported to the church by Ivanka Trump in her $1,540 white Max Mara bag.

I Don't Even Know If They Know What They Don't Know

As we approached the sign for *United* at the Denver International Airport, I saw from my seat in the shuttle bus a man nearby, bent in half, about to puke. There, on a slender, concrete island, near an immense pillar. Cars and buses grumbling past him on one side, cars and buses on the other. Then I saw the prayer rug. His knitted cap. Let's not talk about skin and bruise. Let's not talk about the body's pressure points. How easily love, how easily hate can break. The man had arranged his rug at a slight angle on the concrete island. In the grim winter light of the parking garage. Amongst the traffic, noise, exhaust. Perhaps he had heard the beeper on his cell phone, stepped out of his taxi, spread his rug, and bent over to pray without ever thinking, *But this is the airport garage.* Without ever thinking, *I don't even know if they know what they don't know.* Angled his rug carefully on the concrete island using the small compass on his keychain. Did he first brush away the grit? Or simply let his carpet unroll? Perhaps the man was praying, *Let me be here, with the world whirling inside me.* Praying, *How breath feathers into ether, ether into ethereal.* Praying, *I want to disintegrate into the hum of an idling engine. Into the rising exhaust from a tail pipe. Tumble into a tumult of sand and salt.*

Portrait of Edith Schiele, Egon Schiele, October 28, 1918

Consider whether it matters we know
Edith, at this dying moment, dies
of the Spanish flu the day after

this last sketch of her by her husband.

Consider the tender, tousled hair,
the centered, unending stare of this figure
on the verge of napping, waking, turning

her head, wading back into sleep.

Consider how he can draw only her
beauty, not purpling flesh. That she
is six months with child. That

Egon, 28, a few days later dives

into that same pool where his wife
dissolved. Consider that moment
when Edith knew her husband's fluid

hand drew her out of her body.

Nick Carbó

Dinner Party

Q: Who would you invite to your dream dinner party?
A: I'd rather not give a dinner party.
—Yoko Ono

I've always wondered what kind of candies
Yoko Ono gave away at Halloween, or what

sort of napkin holders graced her parties.
She has earned the right not to have dinner guests

who'd steal the butter knives or drink all the vino tinto.
I wonder what kind of dreams my mother had during

her last dry days of Alzheimer's disease. My mother,
who loved giving parties, who made

this fabulous appetizer of queso Manchego wrapped
in rice paper and flash fried to be served piping hot

on a sterling silver tray. Her fingers
gnarled into the curve of the letter g,

her eyes would dart back and forth under the lids
as if she were dreaming of her two pet

dogs, Peewee and Calcium. She took
nineteen days to let go. Perhaps she waited

those many nights for all her guests to arrive—
Santa Teresa de Avila, La Virgen de Guadalupe,

San Franciso de Assissi, and loved ones
like her father over there, who's pouring the wine.

Apres Le Pluie

Is that Maurice Chevalier walking up
the Rue d' Escargots? That whistling is so
familiar, so full of funicular fun. Maybe,

his white footed poodle Feee Feee
is not far behind. Perhaps barking
at the googly-eyed geese behind

the bee-yellow fence. In France
they love their dogs so much
that they sell prime ground *boeuf*

right next to the fillet mignon
and lamb riblets. When I got home
from the *supermarche,* I noticed

a picture of a Feee Feee on
the ground *boeuf* package. On closer
inspection, I read that this meat

was specially suited for your favorite
chien de la meson. My hamburger
patties, my *croquettes*, my *albondigas*

all slid into the trash bin along
with that picture of Feee Feee
with his little red tongue lapping.

I can hear Maurice in that fatherly
French accent, "You should have looked
closeure, mon ami. A Feee Feee

is always a Feee Feee." His laughter
fades down the road and the barking stops.

The Wuhan Shuffle

"I've never seen anybody do the things you do before
they say move for me, move for me, ay, ay, ay"
—Tones and I

a cytokine storm rewinds
and returns to selective major
organs in the body.

The Double Step—

ABC News: FBI warns of potential surge
in hate crimes against Asian Americans
amid coronavirus. Midland, TX March 14,
three Asian American family members, including
a two-year-old and six-year-old, were stabbed—
the assailant's reasoning "I thought the family
was Chinese, and they were infecting
people with the coronavirus."

The Side Step—

New York Post: Brooklyn, NY April 5,
Brooklyn woman burned outside home
in possible acid attack. Just before 11 p.m.
a solitary Asian woman was taking out
the trash in front of her Borough Park home
when a man sneaked up and doused her
with a large cup of acid. The unidentified
man side stepped the stairs and took
off like a horseshoe bat out of...

The Spins—

Daily Herald: Naperville, IL March 21,
Local police are trying to identify two white
women who committed assault and battery
on an Asian jogger near 75th
and Washington streets in Naperville.
Among other racist epithets they screamed
was "go back to China!"

The Arm Movements—

KARE 11 NBC News: Minneapolis, MN March 26,
A Woodbury, MN Asian couple says
they are shaken up after receiving
a hateful note on their front door. "We're watching
you fucking chinks take the Chinese virus
back to China. We don't want you hear
infecting us with your diseases!!!!!!!!!!!
—your friendly neighborhood."

Mira Chiruvolu

crayons

you started with "Indian Red,"
browned faces around the fire
stories of the hunt and scavengers.

a scene which now paints the
colored picture
in my first grade classroom.

the streaks across my white paper
not in remembrance of a culture
beaten down and bruised by
colonizers and New Americans,

but in innocent artistry
and elementary school
nap times.

you moved onto "Chestnut"
to avoid misconceptions
but, i can look in between cracks
and see dishonorable choices
washed away by Americanization.

you caught a rainbow with your hands
"Dark Green," "Violet," Turquoise Blue"
and you made it into the material
of coloring books

but, the first names you stirred
in your pots of crayon and glue
were not forgotten or brushed away by
"Chestnut"

because I won't ever forget
my nation's ancestry

and neither should you.

Joan Colby

The Atrium in the Hospital

Last summer when you could still walk
Without halting, we would pause by the atrium
To admire the tiger lilies, the formal beds
Of petunias and marigolds, the profligate
Snowball bushes, the ornamental grasses
And the honey locusts that shaded the stone
Benches, and tables where a woman sat reading.

Occasionally, we'd enter and stroll
The graveled paths. A peaceful oasis
In the heart of catastrophe, code blues
And rushing scrubs, carts clanking
Along tiled corridors. The atrium was real
Unlike years back in a different hospital
Where your dying father thought
He was in a solarium of beautiful flowers.

It was the gray December of hallucinations.
A false sunlight of comfort. You have outlived him
By thirty years though you believed
You would also die young. Each birthday, a dread,
Like a tree about to be felled. The blighted
Decades. This was to be a poem of brevity,
But age, like hope, is garrulous, as if talk
Could ward off absence or despair.

The atrium is full of dead things now,
Brown, fawn, black, wreaths of twigs
And tawny grasses, the trees
Leafless in surrender. No one rests here
On the benches beneath the gray
December sky. The snowball bushes

Hold grotesque bronze ornaments,
Mummified blossoms that the cold wind
Arouses to gasps, to death rattles.
The gloom of early dusk descends
As we make our way slowly. You stop
To catch your breath now,
Every twenty paces.

The End of the Trail

At Gunflint

It could be brutal country.
Fires that turned old growth forests to ash.
The November gales of Superior
With the ship's bells ringing the dead
On the driftwood shores of Whitefish Bay.

We drove the Gunflint Trail to your cousin's cabin
On Devil Track Lake, then further north
To the Boundary Waters where we camped
To watch the moon rise over Canada.

Walked the beaches where the old kettles
Of the Voyageurs rusted, split the agates
To find their pearly striations beneath the roughened shells.

The blowdowns of 1999—our friend lamenting
His view lost forever. The fires of 2011,
Over 300,000 acres burned. We grieved at the
Devastation. Omen of all the hard things to come:
Your failing heart, my shattered knee.

You'd spent your boyhood summers in Grand Marais
With your aunt and uncle, cousins the same ages
As you and your brother. Your uncle drowned
When his canoe overturned in that storm on Superior.

We paddled down the Granite River to an island where we slept
And made love in a shared mummy bag. It was always north
That we headed despite ourselves, to the lure
Of birch and fir. The campfires you built, our daughters
Washing their long hair in buckets, our baby in his canvas chair.

Blueberry picking, bear encounters at the open dumps,
Trash a half-mile wide, the festooned black bears
Wearing fast-food cartons like sailor hats, the moose looming
In the twilight and the jays squawking.

That woman's porch where the snowy owl returned each summer.
That was so long ago, they must both be dead
Except when we remember them. And now you too
Live in my memory, in the ache in my gut.

Selling the Guns

On a morning meant for poetry
I am heading for Gat's Guns,
A store devoted to the ammunition
Of killing. The sport of the target.
I have a 380 Browning Automatic
And your grandfather's Saturday night Special,
Both closeted for years hiding their real intentions.
It's time to release them is what I thought.
Why harbor this darkness? Not bought but inherited.
My son says *Consider the offer if you want*
Or take what you can get. They are old these weapons
As I am hoping for decompensation,
How the body enters the next phase of letting go.

The Salt Widow

I salt my French toast which I prefer to syrup or butter.
Just as I salt fruit from sweet to savory.
I always reach for the salt shaker before I taste
Which is an insult to the cook, but I know
I'll want more. It's what I crave.

I'm Lot's wife.
The woman who could not stop looking back
Until she became a pillar of salt. The residue
Of tears. We need salt to live like the animals
At the lick where sworn enemies congregate
Out of need. I need this element; what is left of the sea
That flooded your body. A congestive force
Like a tsunami enlarging your heart
The way love could. You fought an oceanic battle
For years while I licked salt from my fingers,
This substance you were forbidden.

Lot's wife was left there
Looking back at the ruined city
While her party journeyed onward.
Lot seems to be missing from the story.
I wonder if he'd return and try to scoop her up
Into a silver cellar that he could keep.
If he could shake her like he must have wanted
Why did you have to look!

As for Lot's wife, now she was
On her own as I will be
Thinking *Why did you have to leave!*
Salting my wounds with missing you.

Michael Cole

The Floating Man

Of late, he is bored with levitating like fog over a meadow or a warming lake at dawn. He wants to rise higher. Of course, the moon and stars are out of reach and he knows the extreme cold up there would probably kill him, but he would opt for a fairly low cumulus height. He has spoken with those clouds.

"Hello. May I ask how you shape-shift so easily?

"No. It's a secret gift we cumuli covet. If you are a brother the secret is yours. If not, not."

"But I am almost a cloud."

"Forget it! Almost is not good enough."

More rejection. He's *almost* used to it. Although his wife and daughter tell him that his chief job, floating over parades, is patriotic and noble and that they are proud of him, he knows otherwise. Dressing up in a red, white, and blue clown suit and that goofy top hat, neon-colored ropes tied to his arms, legs, and belt. Hell, he can't even mow the lawn or shovel snow off the driveway. Sometimes, it's a bit much and his tears often fall on the high school marching bands below. More than one grand marshal has warned him about his "attitude." There's got to be a better, more exciting life. Like the time he dozed off one July afternoon as his tether slipped. He rose to the fifteenth-floor balcony of a high-rise condo. Is that little old lady still screaming from her chaise lounge? It's getting late and his wife will pull him down for dinner then tie his tether to the bed. Maybe he'll get lucky and float off to his favorite dream—the one where he's kicking fallen leaves in the forest.

Kathleen Corcoran

Wounded Angel

After the painting by Hugo Simberg

Someone must answer for your blood-stained wings,
your bandaged eyes. Two boys hoist the homemade

stretcher's poles, although an angel should be weightless.
Their black boots trudge across a muddy field

where children once played games, and peepers chirped
spring's arrival from the boggy woods beyond.

Your wings collapse, your white robe drags
raising swirls of dust. One child leads

this lonely procession. Little man with bowler hat
and sagging eye, the pole upon his frail shoulder.

The other boy bears his load, scowling toward
some phantom roadside crowd, a lake now blank

with disbelief, or whatever lies far across
gray hills. Someone has peeled away the grass.

One spindly tree yearns for green. You longed
for spring, since Heaven has no seasons.

Earth's voices called. The white flowers
you loved mimic spring, but those you picked

wither and will soon drop from your pale hand.
Poor sweet angel, you were never terrifying.

Maybe you cried out. But no one heard you
in this savage din, except these children

in their strange black suits who might at least untie
the bandage, unless blindness is your choice.

Dana Curtis

Body Apocalyptic 5

As we watch the deliberate
unfolding of the essential origami-
the silver wires unwind and
twist into the night sculptures
we fail to interpret. Under the bridge,
we are so tired, so worthless
in our parchment lives. Falling
unlike the stars but under the river
we invented: passion
for all that is
celestial and permanent-
there once was
a bridge we loved, a waterway
not gone, not blind.

Andrew Darlington

All the Space Between/ A Part, and Yet Apart

on Mars the trees grow red
and cast a rose glow,
through Martian twilights
I feel you squirm inside my mind,
and know you are close,
on Mars the grass grows red
and whispers secrets
in the thin breeze,
it tells me you are close,
on Mars the moons are red
and cast scarlet shadows that
hint the contours of your face,
in silence there is music
in separation there is touch
where there Is you
is where I choose to reside,
on Mars the constellations
flit like fireflies
to tell me you are near,
I taste the storms roar in your mouth
I taste your breath in my nostrils
the map of your blood is in my veins
your heartbeat is the pulse
that moves the stars...

Low Walls

Why do low walls fascinate?
Why do they always seduce your attention and lure you
with their teasing challenge?
But they always do, and always have.
When I see a low wall, I just have to climb up and walk along it.
There is simply no other option.
I am helpless against its invitation.
So you climb and you teeter along its length,
extending your arms at either side like an agile tightrope-walker,
pretending it's scary, pretending you're about to fall and plummet
to some terrible mangling doom,
even though its barely knee-high from the street.
The tops of some low walls, like the ornamental
walls around municipal flowerbeds,
are raised into a central ridge which makes them even more precarious, take over,
and hence more of a challenge to your nimble skills,
some have hazardous mossy patches or even ivy growing across them which you
must carefully navigate...
until you finally reach the end of the wall,
and have to descend down to the dull pavement-level again.
Until the next wall.

William Virgil Davis

A Response to an Implied Question

After Donald Justice

After the long silence, after the beginning
again, what do we know? Grown too quickly
old, we hardly recognize ourselves
when shouted at in the street—"*Old man,*
old man"—and then don't turn until too late,
to find "the kid" already moving on,
giving us the finger above his shaken head.

A Short Treatise on Black Holes

Stuck there somewhere between Hydra
and the Southern Cross in the midst of Centaurus
for centuries then suddenly to tumble through

windowless dungeons of aeonic age and be
sucked up by a bizarre kind of friction and drawn
through the trapdoor of an event horizon not

even light can penetrate or escape the whole
process the inevitable result of magnetic force fields
sticking awkwardly out from the horizon like a

child's unruly hair and to be suddenly unexpectedly
observed in such a closeted cosmic undressing
by even so sophisticated a satellite as X. M. M.-Newton

with its multi-mirrored telescopes in space so
swirled and twisted that it is impossible even
keeping the most recent discoveries of astronomers

and astrophysicists as well as their lucid explanations
in mind for poets using only the usual ordinary
means of intuition to grasp or even comprehend

in spite of the fact that for as long as metaphors
have mixed and meanings meant to matter nothing
has been more interesting mysterious or revelatory

Kiki Denis

Materialistic Virtues

Time inflates in the absence of caffeine and the presence of money
For an instant you feel immortal
The fear of death, if any, dilutes
The angst of the passing moment subsides
You are capable of not falling in love, again
You feel un-dualistically gallant
Now is when you acknowledge eternity's enormity, magnitude, detachment
You hold this acknowledgement for a second of a second
(Still a long time for a creature of your type)

But "then" comes quickly
You understand you had plenty of decaffeinated moments
And you feel normal, again

You've recuperated your mortality to perfection
You are equipped to fall into the creations of time

If you, only, had plenty of money too

Rewriting Ithaca

You search for Agape
Hoping that Eros will be long
A repetitious cycle of physical agonies
Trying your touch with burning kisses
While inflaming your mind with dazzling ideas

You reach for Agape
Hoping that Eros will guide your journey for ever
A repetitious cycle of passionate sexual yearnings
A magician that conquers your dreams and conceals your thoughts
A caustic aroma mesmerizing your ego

But when you reach Agape
You forget Eros; Him who guided you through the whole journey
You let lusting touch and warm kisses fade in the certainty of Her
And rest in Agape's secure comfort
Failing to remember that Eros doesn't live on promises

The Mirror

I need chocolate after our lovemaking
Creativity is dark in color
And smells of your sex

Racism and flowers are two things I forget when you do what you do
War and mortality is what you don't remember when I do what I do
At those moments shame becomes vulnerable
And morality loses its drive

When we look into the mirror
We know that
Infidelity lies in the mistakes we trust
The rest, is left to lust

?s

And what is true love if not the dissolving of *I* in the presence of you?
What is hate if racism?
What is parenthood if not the urge to defeat mortality?
And war?

Isn't it war the inability to connect?
Our lovemaking, I won't question,
'Cause that's part of all.

Necropolis: a space for more than our bodies

Love
the only remedy for our mortality
And reminiscence
the house of its preservation
is killed by amnesia.
As flesh and bones by
time.

RC deWinter

Memo to Hopper

All those women, Edward.
Every one — shabby or glamorous, naked or clothed,
Standing or sitting or lying in the burning eye of morning sun
or ravaged by the winds of every season's night—
all of them the same woman.

The primal heart of your being.

But for all your genius you were just a man, seesawing
in the arms of the Madonna and the Mystery.
Never sure on any given day which would own you,
but always knowing woman is both, and always will be.

And, trapped in that neverending up and down,
back and forth of desire and resentment, you,
a domestic monster, crushed the woman you couldn't live without
in the remorseless tantrums of that heart.

I'm glad I was born too late to know you, to meet you.
To be captivated by your talent and the charm you spigoted
off and on when it suited you to be charming.
When it suited you to be cruel.

And, despite all this, the bright thread of brilliant loneliness
informing everything you created draws me.
Yes, you were a monster. But one I can adore, knowing you
can only hurt me in the perfection of your work.

Lyudmyla Diadchenko

from *There Will Be Offerings*

11.

I dream of the sea, and I am a fish—I think
Twice, though, before probing the depths.
The current is warm; I wish you felt this,
Streams that flow and rush at our backs.
You would drop me in an aquarium, buy fish food,
Rebuff those dubious people who come to stare.
And I would observe you, knowing your talents:
Detailed, adult fairytales for the nights we've secretly spent,
Fragments of touch, whole phrases of the fire
We kindled, the sky collapsing on our waking habits.
Peer into the ocean—I am *your* fish,
I flap my fins at you;
Do you really think
I swim away?

12.

It defies logic, but miracles really happen:
Sunlight scorches even the saltiest tidal deposits,
The sweet cherries of Eden remain hidden,
The clicks of leisurely footsteps grow silent.
Something you cannot hold
Sinks to the bottom,
Settles into your psyche
As your soul's own thief.
You study in a mirror a landscape
That doesn't appear to care
That you, in your deeds and words,
Stared wide-eyed,
Building memories of seagulls'
Heads and a chunk of sea

Stuck with pine needles.
You stopped there,
Even stayed awhile,
Though no one will ever
Recall this, but you.

13.

Carousel and caramel
Held in windy hands*!*
Climb gently up,
Climb gently down;
You can't always guess, so
Either reassure yourself
With prayer or spit on fate:
What is needed and what comes
Will, at once, save everyone,
Taking one and taking all,
Even this carousel's
Plastic grasshoppers.
Go on—collect
Memories like clustering
Fleas on a stray dog —
It just gets harder,
If relieved, time to time,
By a seagull's squawk,
A squeaking yawp or meow.
To be honest, this is neither
Very little, nor very much.
This entire life is a *place*
You've observed and traded
For other places, because
You were not welcomed.

14.

This island with wild goats and two donkeys
Reveals its deity, a flowering olive grove.
But we need not only treasures: we want them buried,
And we want old, weathered maps to guide our search!
When Autumn arrives to recline upon her altar, there will be
Offerings of lamb and grapes—accept but do not taste them.
This is my command to you—regard it as a Gibraltar
Blocking Africa from joining Europe.
As water scrubs away at the hull of your boat,
Set sail with your cache—it is your freedom.
You did not meet whom you had sought,
But whom you met, you will never find again.

15.

We have nothing in common—so we do not talk,
But neither do we oppose the truth in our silence.
As the duck's wings lumber heavily over the sea,
Is there absolutely nothing left for us to shoot?
Wine drops, guiltily or not, like rain, like milk into coffee;
We will drink this, and we will shatter our cups!
My airplanes will have all been quieted by the sky,
And my motherland's voices will have all grown mute.
Whether I fly or not, mistaken words amuse me;
Wherever you stay, you'll let it go to the dogs.
You cannot hoist pain, like luggage, up with your hands.
Carry it inside yourself, yoke yourself to it, bear-up.

Translated from the Ukrainian by Dmitrou Teplouhov and Padma J. Thornlyre

Buck Downs

odysseys

After Creeley

in all of those movies
the space man is out there,
fully efficient—
the solitary friend, surrounded
by his super devices.

the machines may be
obedient, or turn treacherous,
like HAL, descending into
madness, so human-like—
for example, learning to read lips
in order to eavesdrop—
and returning to that first lesson,
the one of learning how to sing

daisy, daisy
give me
your answer, do

I thought that one part
of Kubrick's plan of it
was that we would learn
the limits of our tool-making
and how to use them, in that
shared forgetting of time
as we bathed in the twilight
of the dream machine.

That was 1968.
This is 2018,

and it turns out
the escape pod only exists
in the movies. We travel through space
on this planet, as we always have,
making up these odysseys
to answer that sense of flying
and/or falling that follows us
through the void of space and time,
knowing its nothingness,
feeling its presence,
and to keep us going
beyond the rocks and desert, the bones,
on toward the distance, all of us, together.

Barbara Drake

Impressions

The path through the woods is by Klimt,
little yellow apples in the grass, bruise spots, circles,
lit dewdrops strung along lines of cobwebs.

The wild apple trees are Van Gogh—
twisted branches like muscular arms,
crows in a neighbor's wheat field,
starry nights in summer.

From the top of the vineyard a view
of Chehalem Ridge and behind it Bald Mountain—
definitely Cezanne, especially in summer drought
when heat wavers above dry yellow grass.

Our orange cat sliding through the vineyard is by Matisse,
and so are the bright daylilies, the blue camas at the pond.

The oak woods on a foggy day, hills in mist,
black cows grazing in the pasture. Turner.
The heron by the Wapato marsh of course is Audubon.
The pines on the southeast corner of the farm, Hokusai.

When I go to our country store for milk
the sturdy woman in an apron leaning over the counter,
pale light coming through the high transom, is Vermeer.

Yamhill Valley, Oregon

A Rainy Night

I think of her each time I drive that way.
She ran into the headlights of my car
a hand stretched out for help. I stopped
and opened up the door—years ago.

The wet green dress was plastered to her body,
her black hair sticking to her cheeks and throat.
She apologized for water dripping on the seat,
and that was all. I asked her where to go.

She looked Chinese, a pretty girl, so young
to be out in the dark, no shoes or coat.
My son was in the back. I'd picked him up
from another boy's birthday party that night.

We left her at her door and went on home.
My son was quiet. He later asked me to explain.

The Elephant Seal at Battle Rock

The elephant seal
on the sand at Battle rock
is molting.

Temporary paper signs on sticks say
please leave the seal alone,
it's natural.

Don't call Audubon,
don't call the fire department,
it's what elephant seals do.

Usually he would be on a sea stack beach
with his honking tribe
out beyond the surf.

Why he chose to shed his old skin here
near the beachside parking lot,
where travelers walk their dogs and children frolic, is a mystery.

We stand amazed and a little envious at what it might feel like
to leave behind worn fur, the wrinkled sack of your old body,
to slide into cold water and swim to the blue horizon.

Port Orford, Oregon

Confetti

Remember summer days we lay on sand
belly-down, looking
for remnants of elegant seashells—
bits of orange scallop, ridged clams, oysters, mussels,
the red speckled fragments of crab shells.
There were curiously etched sand dollars,
some large and unbroken,
some tiny as a baby's fingernail.

Today the waves go in and out, drawing a strange lace.
Bright confetti marks the tide line,
blue, yellow, green, red, bone-white—
jugs that once held laundry soap, car oil containers,
toothpaste tubes, shampoo bottles, plastic syrup bottles,
unbreakable jars for lotions, medicines, fizzy drinks,
sea-blue fishing floats, tanks for sewage, fertilizer, fuel,
Styrofoam picnic boxes, disintegrated flip flops,
all ground down by the ocean's surge.

The waves go on grinding.
The tide says, forever, forever...

Goya's Dog

Goya's little dog looks up
over a berm of darkness.
What is he, or she,
looking for?
The mottled golden wall
behind gives no clue,
is only background,
a flat plane suggesting dust,
aged stucco, or plaster.
There is a hint of shadow
to the right, maybe something
or someone looming.
What does it mean,
that I love this sad picture
so much, that I stay there
a long time looking.
Am I that little dog?

Prado, Madrid

Michael Estabrook

I couldn't be there

I sent her flowers
a beautiful arrangement
colorful
carnations, tulips, roses, daffodils...

What else could I do?
She sponge-bathed my mom
changed her Depends
called the chaplain just in time
just before the last breath came
eyes closed
mouth opened wide
body struggling one last time
before not.

Your body knows when it's had enough
when it's time to move on.

"There is a heaven isn't there Michael?
I will see Kerry again won't I?"

Yes of course, Ma
Kerry and Dad, your sisters, Jean, Bill
Kay, Elmer, Aunt Queenie... your mom.

Making it to 92 is not for the faint-hearted
good thing she was a "tough old bird"
good thing her caregiver was there
making sure she didn't fall out of bed
giving her sips of water
morphine when she needed it.

Yes of course I sent her flowers
what else could I do?

Dyane Fancey

After Seeing Renoir

(Auguste Renoir, his son Jean, and the young model Andree)
For Marie Ponsot

On screen, the air was dappled blue and cold
Mistral blowing from the sea
full of insects, air, and leaves.
The Cote d'Azur, 1915.
Renoir's place was
paradise where joys grow old.

We were not then so divorced
from the authentic,
the pure taste of the ripe fruit,
fire in the blood.
Photographs still staring from the wall
and cinema a parlor game.

But war the uninvited guest
the eternal pestilence brings
Age and Death to stalk all beauties
faraway and near,
the stalking panther
that shadows what we fear.

Put the reels on one by one.
Crank it up to speed.
The lady with the fan
in black and white
weeps a recorded tear.

The nude Andree on canvas drawn
one day will be the lady's movie dawn.
Auguste paints his youth now gone.
Time unreels the naked girl to Jean.

Unfinished poem by Dyane Fancey (Spring 2013)
mashed up and rewritten by Reed Hessler (March 6, 2015)

Biology and King Kong

Looming large as only tall men do,
broad and strong
my husband will not absorb
the fact that I am much more
fragile than I am willing to
let on.
My jutted jaw, the clenched mitt
only belie the laws of relative
physiology.
Small and round, I bounce
like a dharma tumbler
but I can bruise and can
break.
He batters against me in
heat, not comprehending
simply impossible anatomical
possibilities.
Some times I think I am
arguing physics with an
ape
until he plucks an airplane
out of the sky
for me to wear as a
barrette

Ygraine

What did I know? All I could see
was the perfect gray of the perfectly dark
room: Eigengrau.*
He smelled and tasted like all men do,
muddy after battle, slick and slippery with
blood.
Not till it was completely too far gone to
object that it was not the Duke, but
his murderer Uther.
Untimely to object after all.
The queen of an usurper beats back the
final checkmate.

* Eigengrau—from the German: the gray the eye sees in perfect darkness.

Joel Ferdon

Juvenile Offenders Remanded to Concord, NC

Unlike the rest of the boys who had
come from Durham, or Asheville, or
maybe even Elizabeth City, his miles
for deep contemplation stopped short
at a little movie in his head that reeled
a dreaded fire and moved all the way
backwards to a match in his hand—
unlit. Those little clips from just a few days
before were nothing as the boy saw
decayed mansions that ate the earth,
razor wire up high and down below
the tallest of fences surrounding every
"dorm" as they were once called. Hard
turn to the right and up the hill— tree roots
a ubiquitous arch for the bus, sending
wayward boys hard into glass and metal.
This is only the start the driver whispered.
"Stonewall Jackson Training School"—
rusted arch, bright letters dampened
by ancient ivy. This new boy used to sit
& wonder in North Carolina history about
the old Stonewall Boys—shy bodies shaved
pink, pre-fallow skin made ready for *repeat*
after me, son: I will never touch myself again.
How the hum of the boys' words must have
been dulled against the brick walls
as stainless steel sliced through tube
and nether torsion. And the new boy
wondered what special story of his
some other would repeat in their head
one day, years later, when the ground
had finally subsumed the clay brick,
revealing at the foundation a black pit
every boy would be forced to stare into—
the utter incarnation of their worst fear staring back.

Richard Flynn

Apples for Minerva

for Heather Ross Miller

At the Randall Jarrell Centennial Celebration
UNC-Greensboro, April, 2014

Once upon a time, fifty—no sixty—years ago, or more,
Randall Jarrell looked up from reading *The Wind*
In the Willows to tell Bob Watson that Woman's College
Was just like Sleeping Beauty. Mustached Jarrell,
Said Watson, (this was before his beard, before his best-selling
Novel bought him his first sports car) often looked bored
Or miserable except when enchanted by books—
Books like T*he Wind in the Willows*—into "a flashing
Vitality and enthusiasm." Then Jarrell would brim
With sudden delight, with a youthful "Gee" or "Golly,"
Or, when most enthusiastic, "Baby doll!"

Under the trees
Of the University, Jarrell the soldier had dreamed
Of "all that the world would be, if it were real." When he grew
A beard black as the beard of the Polar explorer
He imagined long ago in the childish night,
In the unreal world, perhaps it was to hide the face
Haunting him in the mirror. The beard became
So famous even Langston Hughes admired it.
But when Jarrell turned fifty and the children began
To call him Santa Claus, he panicked. The magic pills
The doctor gave to ease his fear of aging, made him manic,
Or as he explained, ashamed, "elated."

Words flew at him so fast
He could barely write them down.

In 1964, en route to
Baltimore, as luck would have it, he talked
To Johnny Unitas on an airplane. Seeing
A young man behind the quarterback's cracked
Face, Jarrell hoped that he, too, had a young face
Under the old one. But Unitas was only thirty,
And so the poet shaved his beard in a vain
Attempt to wake his sleeping beauty. Like the queen
In "Snow White," he gazed hard until
The rearview mirror said to him, "You're old."
It's not fair, the mirror taunted, not to be
The fairest of them all.

This year, I'm almost sixty,
And find I have again fallen under Jarrell's magic spell
Visiting what *was* Woman's College, now neither Woman's
Nor College, not sleeping anymore, not beautiful.
I sit with other grown-ups in the Jarrell Lecture Hall
Hidden away beneath the library. We listen
To the grown-up talks, and to young students reciting
His poems in honor of his hundredth birthday.
After what seems like ages, we emerge in the late
Sunlight of early spring, and—lo and behold! —a statue
Of Minerva stands by a swing set. At her feet
Are rows and rows of apples. Are these the apples
Of discord cast to protest Paris's judgment, we wonder?
They aren't golden. So we ask two young men—
Boys really—playing their guitars at Minerva's feet.
They explain the apples are offerings to the Goddess
That she may bestow some strength, wisdom, or
Luck on those taking finals.

Then I remember Jarrell made offerings to the gods once.
When he was young, barely twelve years old, he was
Their cupbearer. His wit and beauty charmed two
Sculptors who asked his mother if they
Could adopt him.

You can still see him, reclining
With his cup, one ear resting on the lyre,
One hand resting on Apollo's thigh: the most beautiful
Boy ever, forever frozen in time, frozen
On the East Pediment frieze
Of the Parthenon, in Nashville, here,
In the twenty-first century

Marc Frazier

Design

After The Women He's Undressed *documentary about Orry-Kelly, the three-time Oscar-winning costume designer*

How to solve a problem like Bette's breasts
Hanging like fruit almost to the waist?
(She thought wire support caused cancer).
Or how to make the ball gown in *Jezebel*
Appear to be red using black and white?
You did the impossible with layers,
Types and sheerness of fabric, ingenuity.
The cheek of making Marilyn appear nude,
Breasts overflowing, resting on air,
Censors shocked into submission.
Toning down Roz Russell's outfits
For the serious scenes while running amok
With wacky designs for her dynamo ones,
Her Mame a force blasting the Hollywood screen.

Behind the scene you worked your sleight of hand
made the real look illusory to a waiting audience,
But refused the ruse that you preferred women.
Archie Leach/Cary Grant never rose to the occasion
As your friend, so enamored with fame and posterity
Hiding like so many did then.
Three times you took Oscar home like a trick,
A queer conquering fear in a dangerous time.
You show them it can be done like
the magic you perform with tulle, linen, and silk
to wrap your leading ladies. A design for living—

Journal of the Plague Years: One

All wars are lost.
The people I face every day are not the people I face every day.
I want ecstasy but your sensible shoes lie smug at the foot of the bed.
If I could touch a face and not forget it, I could die and not regret it.
No one should have to watch their lover leave on a train.
I laugh as the shower curtain pops its hinges one by one.
The altar wavers like a mirage.
I drink the holy water and pee on the outside of the church.
I do not have one life.
He tried to salvage our relationship like it was half-burnt toast.
After Bozo retired and needles were found in Girl Scout cookies, I went into hiding.
None of this has happened.
None of this has anything to do with me.
I see your face in the moon: cheeks like windswept sand traps.
I thought we were going to have sex, but we had pork chops instead.
A day drinking: the T.V. is what I hope for most—a blur with voices somewhere near.
Always the return to you in the night like a bat to something detected in the wavy space around it.
Sometimes flotsam. Sometimes something with a root.
Dreams flare like flamingos into more light.
How will I know when I arrive at the place I most desire to be?
What if you recover from your life?
What happens next is happening.
I am almost who I'm meant to be.
My head: an old house overwrought with too many dreams.
Burnt slippers on an asylum floor.
The debris is necessary.
The sun, strong old warrior, lies down in a cloudy bed of ember.
I was the river once. He was the sea.

DJ Gaskin

Secrets

I have been
in underground
offices with no
address, accessed
by tunnels deep
under the city
unaware. I have
remained seated
in silence
in rooms
where secrets
are shared
and vows
are professed
and history
is amended. I know
more than I want.
I've heard things
I'm not even allowed
to remember.

Fragments

She sees the world
in pixels, fragments,
slivers too thin
to capture. She
compartmentalizes
artlessly.
If caught in one
place, she slips
unseen
to another,
shadow realm.
She divines
each movement,
intuits
each moment.
No one
calls her
by her name.
Oracle.
Few can fathom
how she sees
what's hidden
from most.
She follows the moon
when the trees
aren't looking.
She'll find you
as you find
no hiding space
is safe.
You'll lose her
amid tombstones
where she mingles
with fluency. No one
calls her name.

Jason Gebhardt

The Collected Poems of Frank O'Hara

I wish you were smaller, though no shorter,
so I could more easily carry you around
especially on days when that sadness
begins to grip and I need someone
to nudge my chin up. I flip you open
as I walk, and Lectio O'Hara, press my finger
to a page where it's Rachmaninoff's birthday
and your author is talking to the Mothers
of America, Lana Turner, Kenneth Koch.
Almost alive again in a way that I can't
really have known because I couldn't
have met him and only have ever had you.

Katherine Gekker

Memory's Snake

Chicory shivers, bracts shake as that snake
glides through our yard—its elegant black top,
white underside—shimmering mercury.
Once. I was just a girl. My father eased
a snake from our beagle's jaws. The snake twined
around his arm. Green. Slender. He released
it deep in the woods. It vanished in leaves.

He loved those simple souls. Orphaned at twelve
at the start of the depression, he knew
what it was to be feared, unloved.

That last
doctor visit. The last time he played Brahms.

Tonight the snake drifts over the downspout,
glides in and out of latticework, disappears
into its own shadow—night's smoke—

Autobiography

First you loved me. Then you stopped.

Whole years disappear.
Past. Present. What have I been good for?
Future. Imperfect tenses.

My steel ruler measures inches and millimeters on one side,
picas and points on the verso.
You said I smelled like work:
Varsol, type wash, ink, kerosene.

I never mix plaids with stripes. I'm handy around the house.

I've been careless with my body. 14 bones broken.
My brain bounced off pavement. Now I stammer.
But I never ran with scissors.

I've been incredibly lucky. Today, a mourning dove,
an 18-pica twig in her beak. We studied each other.
Or else she watched herself
reflected in the balcony door plate glass.

The violinist plays a Paganini "Caprice,"
presto, rapido, con drammatico,
till bow strings break, dangle, wave—witches' hair.
I am that violinist.

My first two names are the names of Empresses.

I can't speak of my shames, disgraces. My cruelties.

I'm ambidextrous.

That time I had been so ill,
then sat outside on the front steps.
Where had I been the last weeks?

First I forgot. Then, after that dream, I remembered.

Robert L. Giron

Split This Bone

How is it that between
this bone and that bone

tissue as soft as mush
can cause so much pain?

I try to continue and ignore it
but it radiates down like electricity

to the toe and burns going down—
a hot coal in the cheek when I

walk gingerly and bend grandfatherly
like a rooted, tender willow,

beaten by the harsh wind,
whirled and thrust up against

a wall of brick and mortar,
nearly toppled but springing upward.

Numb it like a doctor
anesthetizes gums

before he inserts his
instrument deep and inward

in a state of ecstasy,
sedated to forget the war,

the fall of dividends,
a domino closing of stores

I lie opened like a whale
with the spine exposed

and now, here the physician
splits the bone and fuses

the short and the long,
screwed in place so I can

walk with less pain
yet no longer limber

like the willow
now more like the oak.

Gabriele Glang

Menopause

is a second chance
at puberty: a circus
of feats not yet dared.

Desires careen
through the weeks, the crisp whip's slap
on elephants' hides

goading them to stand
on their hind legs, while dropping
huge piles of dung

on a dusty, straw-
covered floor. And high above:
a dancer poses

on a tightrope thin
as air, while those below bate
their collective breath,

waiting to hear that
fatal thud of the body
thrown off balance.

Love means choosing not
to see, my radio croons
consolingly. But

what do such songs know
of menopause—that second
chance at love and grace

goading us to fly
only on the wings of dreams—
blindly, weightlessly—

the tightrope's high-pitched
call: It's time to run away—
ah!—with the circus—

Cut and Paste

I wonder sometimes if I am writing
the same poem over and over.
—Maya Rachel Stein, "Cut and Paste"

I *am* writing the same poem—
my life's collage of cuts and pastes
in short, ongoing chapters.

Sifting a few wisdoms gleaned
from my stony path, I pick up
the same stones along the way,

wondering why they all look
the same. (Maybe they *are* the same;
I'm going around in circles.)

Sometimes I toss them over
my shoulder, thinking they'll mark
the way back, forgetting (*yes*)

there is no way back. This journey
only moves forward. The compass
always, always points north. Switchbacks

offer taunting views of the past—
out of reach, as seductive
as photos of a younger me.

(Slimmer, younger, bikini-clad—
did I really look like this?
How I fretted to be that!)

What a waste. I could have been
writing more meaningful poems
for posterity. (But I sense

the *more* and *meaningful* smack
of delusion.) Foraging
the dailies, couch-bound, I snip

a phrase, a solitary noun,
cut and paste expedient verbs.
Broadsiding these seeds, I mull

combinations that might ignite
fireworks of words that fall
to earth before annealing

into something like a poem.
In the end, it's always the same:
the heart dictates the melody,

a nocturne in a minor key.
A common addiction: wordlust
gone awry, delirious

tangle of naked desire
to create something beautiful
and true and utterly mine.

Camera Obscura

Once, in the hush and gloom
of a preserved palazzo,
I bent over vitrines filled
with Canaletto's drawings.
Preparations for etchings,
those spidery crosshatched lines
held fast a perishable
view beneath protective glass.
The pinhole camera helped him
to get it right: *vedute*
recognizable to those
who knew La Serenissima.

My concentrated pucker
stared back at me, a starburst
of lines spreading from my mouth.
We never think we're old
until we are confronted
with the incongruity
of who we thought we were
and who we have become.
But memory, like the camera
obscura, blurs what's distant, so:
we invent to make distinct
those disappearing edges.

Canaletto's quality
declined in later life.
Perhaps his eyesight failed,
or he painted what he knew
instead of what he saw,
or others' expectations
made him repeat himself.
No telling why his works
lacked fluidity. Accused
of being an impostor,
he was compelled to paint
in public to refute the claim.

Four hundred years later,
squinting into those vitrines
on a dull Venetian day,
I recognized the woman
in that glassy likeness:
her shriveled-apple face
the woman I'll become, tethered
to her perishable view,
doing what's expected
instead of what she must,
regretting repetitions,
an impostor of herself.

Regan Good

Lord's Day: There Is in This Universe a Staire

Lord's Day spent in the peppercress by the sandy berm,
where silks fell and hard candies turned to syrops
in the sun. The Lord's Day, its principall Fabrick
being the misshapen chaos of lapping cosmic cloaks.
We only saw their edges and felt their tatters on our cheeks
like whiskers of a colossal hungry cat. But O it was hot
on that heady afternoon and lush things somersaulted
as well as suffocated, such as toads and driveway moles.
Its hooked tongue licked and licked and licked us raw.
Centrally and along the edge, threads were Freezing cold,
like clear streams or silver wire fastened to blocks of ice.
Even in summer, which deforms, as the mind rolls out
all the world a watery valley, a pre-sleep of hazy blights...

The sun is a spinning falconette in a battlefield sublime!
What remnants, what edged Fabrick, satined and ripped,
hangs now from that greasy sagging line? Never ugly,
even the lowly worm is a cylindrical toy, highly prized.
As it turns its wet way through a rotting stair, it purifies the air.
It aerates the woody chips and earthen dirts, breaks
the masses of thready whites that resist the savage spade.
Lounging in the cress by the lamb's quarters, I saw
one tendril looped around a rusted screw. The other groped,
at nothing in the air, its tip lost beyond the rim.
What errors were made? Some tall loves gone fallow.
What Late afflicting fire in this dark and flowing River World?

Braid Like a Coprolite

At last the strands form
a thick braid of hair,
to be left behind in tissue,
or in a book, or box.
Such long and strong hair
it is today, to be braided.
After such failure one
should have no hair, but I
combed internal strands,
an inside rope, its ends
like a Portuguese Man
O' War's hot tentacles.
It grew down my throat
to my pelvis where it was stopped
by a hard and glossy knot,
like a show horse's tail, brushed,
then bound in braids.
One tucks the ratty strays
under the waxed ball.
To see the work in its widowhood.
Black boats in the reeds;
they rock, cradles of ruin.
All thoughts and memories
wove the hanging braid.
Anxiety of influence,
confluence and words fed the hair,
like eggs and oils so it grew
luxuriantly, internally. I
thought an overseer accounted
for each strand, until recently.
Just now, I felt the braid
sway inside me, a heavy chain

or a waxed ship rope
knotted at its end, then burned.
My braid reminds me
of the Saxon braid on a trowel
dug up from a grave.
It resembled common excrement,
but for the twine at its tip,
or an equine or bovine coprolite,
or a cursed plait that, no matter
how long buried, will
simply not disintegrate.

Susan Gubernat

The Pangolin Redux

after Marianne Moore

Some say it was the pangolin,
armored mammal that curves
up into a ball when in danger,

whose leathery hide made cowboy
boots for kings,
its soft insides feasts for gourmets,

that brought us this plague.
Beast of the night,
tree-climber, red ant-sniffer,

prized by the great poet
who'd never seen one,
and by those who grind cures

from its scaly skin. Yet some
mortars and pestles
should gather dust on shelves,

some ovens never fired.
Some animals
that do not exist for us
(And you might say "all")
except to be praised well
as she once did—

"miniature artist engineer"
"Leonardo Da Vinci's replica"—
are best left to themselves.

Going Viral

Palm to my own forehead again
because what if fever, what if viral load
no team of oxen can drag away,
no escape. Truly, this self-interest
numbs me, hems me in. The world
shrinks to a teaspoon, the universe
to a glass of cold water. Galaxies
compress, accordion-pleated,
into a cardboard box, wheezing
like an old concertina. The monkey
perches in my brain, won't even
afford me the dignity of scuffling
onto my back. And the animal digs
in until she reaches my animal heart.

Others of the Pandemic

The way we give them wide berth,
veering into the empty street, stepping
into the curb as they run past,
masked, or not: it's how we've been
for years, this being the apotheosis
of our era of memes, of avatars.
If we could send bodies far away
or freeze-dry them in some cryogenic
fantasy, we would, until it's safe
to add liquid, to become
mostly water again without filling
our lungs with the lethal stuff.
Gleeful girl on her bicycle,
riding ferociously, too close
on the sidewalk, her naked mouth
taking in all the air, angered you.
She'll live, she'll live—the odds
in her favor. *Christ, why doesn't she*
stay in the bike lane, you said. *Jesus*.
Blue smoke of someone vaping
billows from behind tinted glass
while their bass line rumbles in traffic.
Six feet apart. Six feet under.
Coyotes roam the beaches at noon
under a sky that—finally—resembles sky.

Bardo State of the Quarantine

We cannot touch our friends,
we cannot see them. They are there, they
assure us, wandering idly
as we wander room to room,

even as trees uproot themselves
after the wild storms
while birds flocking back
to find a fresher sky,
Giotto's blue,
hung out to dry like Marian
cloth and white linen,
keep singing about it,

singing about their travels,
their long migrations,
to mock us.
A ladybug
landing on my windshield
flew off before I could swipe
at her in my cruelty.
She spread her orange wings,
diva-taunting, on the biggest
stage she'd ever seen.

Who knows how long
she'll last? Not my consolation
though to think
next spring I'll be free of this cell
I call my home. One way.
Or another.

Robert Head

Thera Pompeii of the Ancient Aegean

i was reading about Thera
the same day Etna blew up
Thera blew up thirty five hundred
years ago & the pumice & ash blew to

Egypt & the priests recorded it
& hwen Plato went there to study
he read these records & they became
the foundation of the Atlantis legend

the frescos were buried under ashes
& are described as pompeii of the ancient
Aegean. the increased risk associated with
Covid & cardio vascular disease is 4.44-fold

this can be prevented by taking Carnitine.

the blue monkey attending the goddess
tho i prefer the old english *gidden*
hwich survives in *giddy*
appears to be a supernatural being

& the girl gathering croci the first
flower in spring in my front yard
yellow, purpl, or hwite
the purple flowers & orange stigmas

yield a dye, seasoning, & medicine.
even today saffron is very expensiv:
name for the autumn-flowering hwite

or lilac crocus, & for its dried
stigmas also calld saffron, long used for
coloring, flavoring, perfume & medicine.

in New York City, a report analyzing risk
factors for over four thousand confirmed
Covid-19 patients (with a median
age of fifty-two years) found that

14 percent suffered from diabetes,
26.8 percemt were obese & 30.1
percent sufferd from cardiovascular disease.
to cope with this comorbidity Dr. Atkins recommends

pantethine, a derivativ of the B-complex
nutrient pantothenic acid, and
magnesium, coenzyme Q10, & carnitine.
i take carnitine.

in the priestess fresco in building 4,
the priestess wears a saffron-
dyed gown. one of the ship's
hulls in the ship fresco bears

paintings of crocus blooms,
& more crocus deck the ship's rigging.

saffron appears to be useful for treating
erectile dysfunction & depression. perhaps
these two conditions go together or
are one & the same.

we should be grateful that we can
walk down the street & are not being
tortured, & for my luv for her
there is no answer.

Blaine & i were in Fort Pickens
hwer Geronimo was imprisoned
& his spirit passd to us
& we shall go forward unto the final day.

we can fly away at night
& flutter in the wind
like flying foxes in Wodenham.

a pottery bee-hive indicates that
the Akrotirians kept bees for honey
probably from croci.

i don't understand how it workt
so i am reproducing the pottery bee-hive
so that sumone more knowlejabl than i
can understand it.

the drug has been liabl to adulteration in spite of
penalties, the severity of hwich suggests
the surviving tradition of its sacred character.

thus in Nuremberg a regular saffron
inspection was held, & in the 15th
century we read of men being burnd in
the market place along with their adulterated saffron.

the flowers are gatherd at the end of
October, in the early morning, just hwen
they are beginning to open after the night.
the stigmas & a part of the style

are carefully pickt out. good
saffron has a deep oranj-red
color; if it is light yellow or
blackish, it is bad or too old.

in ancient Ireland a king's mantl
was dyed with saffron, & even down to
the 17th century, the saffron-dyed
shirt was worn by persons of rank in the Hebrides.

the handsum youth Crocus sets out
in pursuit of the nymph Smilax
in the woods near Athens, in a brief
dallying interlude of idyllic luv,

Smilax is flatterd by his amorous
advances, but all too soon tires of
his attentions. he continues his pursuit;
she resists. she bewitches Crocus:

he is transformd—into a saffron crocus.
its radiant oranj stigmas were held as
a relic glow of an undying & unrequited passion
& the blue monkeys blend into the sky.

Ditta Baron Hoeber

Untitled

you could say it was a kind of sexual torment all that flesh all the time. it was interesting though. I wanted to look. but it didn't stop.

I learned to find it disgusting. the soft pale malleability of the flesh. the not luxuriant the embarrassing hair. the always having to look.

I found an old page of drawings. on the corner I'd written: all the naked models begin to look like my mother.

all the naked are my mother. when I am naked I see her flesh. she is my body. I see her endlessly. I do not own myself. I don't know how to look at myself. I am a torment to myself.

when we are making love I want his body to cover me. want not to see myself. want not to feel my body exposed to the air. I want him inside of me and to cover me. then I am safe. then I am only me.

Shane Holohan

Rondo in Vitro

Raspberry sherbet, dusky-rose, salmon-fillet.
Imagined paint names pass the time.
Nurses slipper by, smile reassuringly, knowingly.

The procedure room's window-blinds twitch open.
I watch them help you from the table to the door.
You walk more slowly than I've ever seen you walk—
drug-slowed, fireman's-carry steps, wounded-soldier steps.

I'm locked onto details—downward gaze,
bunching hair from lying sweaty on the table,
flattened dressing gown pile, exposed nape of your neck.

Then the tray of instruments and vials,
the hollowed bayonet that pierced and probed you,
exfiltrating proto-lives, each escape-hatch cut
and cut again through willing flesh.

They nurse you to me.

We've just a moment—a sagging, leaning,
careful moment; a fingers finding, brows pressing,
sweating, red-eyed moment; then the nurse interrupts—
more still to be done.

Joyce L. Huff

Punching a Nazi

For my mother-in-law, Elisabeth Bahr Smith

I. Berlin, 1938-1945

The swastika
made Elisabeth ashamed
to show her birth certificate.
Stamped over her name,
bleeding into her origins,
hard angles and lines pointing
back through history.

She remembers the bodies
on the road home from school—
how the hands of the children
twisted the ropes, watching corpses spin
like tops hanging from the lampposts;
how the younger ones hopped
on the chests of the dead in the street
to watch the eyes bulge;
how the Russians came,
and her small hands clutched
her mother's legs to hold them tight together,
till soldiers forced those legs apart
before her seven-year-old eyes.

At ten, she raised those hands
to catch a miracle,
chocolate from the sky,
dropped by Americans.

So to America she went.

II. Baltimore, 1979

On her tiptoes, Elisabeth
peeked over shoulders in the crowd
to watch her daughter march
with her gleaming flute
in the Columbus Day parade.

A giant with a shaved head
and handlebar moustache
pushed his way through spectators
and slipped a paper into her hand.

That hand, still small, was strong
from kneading bread and sewing clothes,
leaving pins stuck in the sofa cushions,
from scrubbing and hugging, creating a new life
for her American children.

When she saw the shameful sign
emblazoned on the page she held,
a red line spread up her neck to the top of her head.
Her hand closed tight, changing the course of her lifeline.
She punched him in the nose.

His blood stained the fliers, obscured the dark design.
The crowd gathered round, ignoring the parade.
The huge man turned and ran.

III. Indiana, 2004

I dress you in a nightgown
patterned with suns and moons,
circles joining past to future,
pieced together by the hands
that did their best to craft
a better world for you, her granddaughter.

Red Among the Women

Red is too loud she talks too much when she walks she walks like a man arms swinging and when she has the women to dinner she doesn't have a gravy boat she apologizes for this they say you could just buy a gravy boat Red wonders what kind of people have the money to just buy a gravy boat

when they go out for dirty martinis Red wants a beer but she orders a Cosmo then thinks why did I do that her shoes do not hurt because they are sneakers which she got for $2.50 she does not know where to get a pedicure nor does she have a husband who doesn't do dishes so she has nothing to say and sits silent

they recommend a salon that dyes your hair for only $100 Red thinks why would I dye my hair it is good and gray and I like it but this is not the right answer then she tells an anecdote about when she was a girl and one with her hair curled under makes a joke about the movie *Carrie* Red realizes that to them her life is a horror story

her mom always said Red intimidates people but Red doesn't think that's true that is just the sort of things moms say to girls who don't fit in there is something these women know that Red just doesn't get something made of money and perfume Red knows how to defend herself with a handbag weighted down with batteries and how to duck so an alarm clock aimed at her head will smash against the wall instead and she knows the right words to stop a man from pulling the trigger but none of those things will help her survive here among the lipstick-rimmed women

The Lady of Shalott Leaves Her Loom

"'I am half sick of shadows,' said The Lady of Shalott." —Alfred Lord Tennyson

The river weaves
through the darkened warp
of alleyways and streets,
where spires and rooftops meet
the clouded sky.

At sunrise, human shuttles fly
to the smoky isle
where the factory lies,
through the gray doors
to the workroom floor.

Wheels screech. Gears clack.
All other sounds surrender.
Her eyes know no horizon
but the edges of the woven web.
If she should stay to glance away,
the loom exacts its price in flesh.

Behind the gleaming window,
on a seat of burnished leather,
Mr. L sings tirra lirra
to the clapping of the looms.

A sudden hush.
A three-minute smoke.
A gulp of scalded coffee.

The cracked mirror
on the bathroom wall
shows the weft that lines her face,
pale strands of hair hid by a scarf
to save them from the hungry looms.

As a tapestry reversed reveals
only tangled knots of yarn,
she can no longer trace
the pattern of herself.

Back to the web,
her blistered fingered keeping time
to the shuttle's pulse, the thrum of threads:
click, click, click, half sick, half sick.
What if she should slip inside
to join the rhythm of her work?
The loom swallows her.

Crack! It splinters, unable to hold her.
Out flies the lady, shattering
panes in dingy windows, scattering
herself, like threads unwound,
diffusing, floating wide.

Tendrils of her reaching out across the factory walls,
stretching through crowded streets,
catching at the heels of businessmen,
tangling in the wheels of buses and cabs,
drifting on the river, spelling out her name,

unraveling into the meadow,
parachuting like dandelion seeds,
winding round the limbs of a tree,
shining with dew, entwining plump
succulent flies for delighted spiders.

Frankenstein's Sonnet

You hack her into fourteen parts. Then stack
the bones. You mount her like a butterfly.
Begin with feet. Add syllable and line.
Re-member her and render her. Attack
the flesh next. Cram and squeeze until it fits
the narrow mold. Suck out the blood and milk.
Then, to achieve your object, rime with silk.
You suture Venus's gums to Helen's lips.
You slap on alabaster, rose, azure.
Stitch spun gold or black wires to the skull.
You stuff the beating iambs in the chest.
Extract the tongue. Your art will speak for her.
Now gaze upon this thing you made. Voila!
She's wholly yours. Try not to think of death.

Tom C. Hunley

Loving the Traumatized Teen While She's Acting Out

Before our children's birthday parties, we determined
to keep putting our breaths into balloons
until we ran out of breath or out of balloons.

Our daughter's therapist says soldiers
learn to survive by pouring warpaint
all over their souls, but then they bring the fight
home and scare their families, by which she means
that while lying and sneaking may have helped
our daughter stay in foster homes longer,
now that she's allowed to date, she doesn't need
to invite boyfriends to the hotel where she works
as a housekeeper so they can *have more privacy*.

My wife's voice sounds like cake mix smells,
but I know she's just a flicker
like an empire or a firefly.
Best not to think too hard about that
or whether our souls, after leaving
our bodies, wander like lost children.
Donne said that no man is an island,
but he didn't say no woman is. My wife
might be Bora Bora and I might be a shipwreck.
By which I mean I'm sorry I'm not a better husband.

Our daughter's therapist wants her to revisit a memory
of her birth father's hands in her pants but that's
like asking a dot to revisit Pacman.
Our daughter wants to marry a childhood memory
of running barefoot in the rain, but that memory
is holding hands with a suppressed memory of her
birth mother's mouth wrapped around a crack pipe.
I don't want to walk my daughter down that burning aisle.
By which I mean I'm sorry I'm not a better father.

I feel like a toner cartridge running out of ink.
I feel like the actor who plays the gravedigger
in every drama about soldiers. Forget it.
I'm grappling like the junior varsity wrestler that I once was.
By which I mean I wish I were a better poet.
By which I mean that none of these words touch what I really feel.
By which I mean deep sadness and a sense of failure
stronger than the sense of sight and the sense of smell combined.

Paul Ilechko

Butterflies Cross the Border at Night

Don't you love how weeds turn into butterflies?

how the sky turns white under the pressure of degrees   burning the moisture from the plantings   searing and sizzling until night restores balance   as a sugar-thick syrup heals the scarring of veins

and somewhere nearby a candle burns   its heavy white smoke curling into the insignificance of the chill of morning

and children cocoon in piles of three   or five   bundled and tumbling in chaotic layers of rags and yesterday's stale clothing   grasping together inside the stink of memory

and another new day prompts them   with the unlikely promise of flight

is this at last the speech of dirt?   earth's bilious mutterings?

Paul Jaskunas

No one on earth knows how to ski

No one on earth
knows how to ski
down this impossible
mountain
with slopes so steep
even the snow
is sliding off it.

But here I am
wreck in the making,
snowplowing my skis
through slush, knowing
I could die up here
easy-peasy—gangly me
careening limb over
limb, over the edge
of middle age—too
damn old for this
for prayers, too,
or am I?

My long dead grandfather
always said a man
before he dies
should learn
an instrument
a language
how to ski.

As for me,
will I learn to love
better how it feels
to fail so
completely
my arm's out of joint
my nose is full
of snow and my
skis are skittering
down the mountain
without me?

No choice,
I get up, I go
again on shaking
legs down and down
the slopes so steep,
hoping the fool's hope
for a smooth run
into that valley
below.

Mark Allen Jenkins

Stalled on the Atchafalaya Basin Bridge Outside Grosse Tete, Louisiana

When is a bridge a concrete island across wetlands, or swamp
Like an airport, twin lines, nearly a place, the only straight way

to get to Lafayette or Baton Rouge, human intervention drying
up 931 square miles. I cross it frequently looking back between blackened

barriers, mildewing like the rest of Louisiana. I'd been stuck
before, waiting for a Gulf Coast depression

to clear. I'd study train bridge skeletons, live
oaks, phone poles, all jutting above the bent foil surface.

At night, empty like a gator's snout, a police car waits
for anyone who tries to let loose, to see if they could fly somewhere

else, the way an egret lands on a tree outside my car's rear window.

Lane Jennings

Retirement Resolves

An uncluttered desk top,
Fewer boxes, more shelves,
Longer walks, less commuting,
More active days,
Quieter nights.

More friends, fewer colleagues,
Diminished possessions,
More gifts,
Fewer hours of lamplight,
More stars.

Braves

George Caitlin saw them
leap from their ponies
to dance on the backs
of buffalo; draw bead
with spears and arrows
from inside their own stampede!

Foolhardy, glorious!

"To shine and be remembered—"
ever the warrior's wish. Children
fearless in play, content
among familiar dangers.

We quiet ones know better
and dare less. Prefer
the peace pipe
to the tomahawk. A few,
born old, never follow
the hunt, nor go armed
except with words.

Five centuries after Christ
one last Egyptian
painted prayers
in the sacred symbols
of the pharaohs, knowing
no one still alive but he
could read them.

Foolhardy, glorious!

Beth Baruch Joselow

Nostalgia For Utopia

snow palace
woe under
prince one per
land
woe under
snow one per
prince
&

Terminus

You miss all of them.
A series of goodbyes,
wire and darkness, words
chained to another land.
Change at the gate
in the heat of
late arrivals, boxes
draped in falsehoods.
With something other than
a military brass band
yet with boots
and flags and arms
my country welcomes you
like a cowboy on an airplane
glancing up from his book
to wish you away.
You, in a hurry, abandoned
nets and guidewires

to swing out over the edge
toward what is possible
but not here,
not now, not you.
"This" is your "home" now
even if not home even if
made of fire and air, and
a series of goodbyes,
the missing words that keep you
chained to somewhere else.

Sound and Pictures

What if
we had kept to sound, forbearing
pictures that so soon seized
the center of our attention.
What if
violence had been detained
in the dark corners of imagination, ground
like a spice used sparingly and not
to everyone's taste.
What then.

Line Dance

Should your next step lead you to
an unbroken trail of tears
are companions welcome?
May I join the caravan?
Answer yes, I will be there
where joy too may appear.
Where I am not I, am not
you. Yet
observe
the dance of bees,
the V of migrating geese,
the line of ants bearing food to their colony.
Reverence for singularity
distorts space and time, points
to the brink of nothingness.
Only connect, through tears and all.
Joy too will do.

The World

Dissonant and unobserved
a blue dish clatters to the floor.
The automated kitchen rinses itself, casts off
the shards and noise as well as
a striped towel stained with burns.
Domesticity remains a cage, but
preferable to the iron bars and fetid
holes of a world, *the* world, become more
strange, no less cruel, at the same time recognizable
and still a perfect fit.
Home's away from this.
O take me there in pieces if you must.
I'll clean it on my knees.
I'd love,
but cannot love enough, to make it
whole again.

Ken Kakareka

Education

We sometimes forget
that this learning thing
is a two way street.
You are never too old
to learn something.
I sent my aunt a poem.
The poem is about White privilege,
published in a journal
that promotes empathy
and peaceful protesting through words.
My aunt read the poem
and said, "I don't see color."
I said, "Auntie, that's an outdated phrase."
She got offended.
I know her heart's in the right place.
But she has to learn.
We all do.
The world is constantly evolving.
We deem the elderly wise.
They have all the experience.
But often times,
they lack relevance.
Education is multi-faceted.
There is no age
too young
or too old
to have an education.

Numb

I was in my apt drinking Honey Jack.
I began to feel numb.
Trust me, it wasn't the whiskey.
First a report of a Black person murdered
by 4 white people on the news.
Then another one
2 new cases in the same
nightly news segment.
There were just so many cases nowadays
They were catching up to the mass shootings.
How can you feel numb
to such evils?
It's been an ice-cold winter in America for
a very long time.

John Kinsella

Bond

The grief-tones of recovery are road repairs
done by volunteers when networks break down.
Some have called this anarchism. Expecting loss
is not to start grieving early, which, for me, has

little or no definition. What I feel is an eruption
of ghostly internalizing, placeholding for long stretches
in black holes and supernovas, an interior fracas
of weight and light. The thornbill flock doesn't ask me

to show my affects, though it's expected by consumers.
I type each tree that's fallen, and each grief cannot
be focused *in memorium*, not really, these commemorative
apparitions that reveal via weight of type-stroke

that a specter is buried in the thyroid. I count the pavers
basket-woven around the house, but they pre-exist my arrival.

Aligning, Imploding and Dispersing Contrast in Metaphors on Helen Frankenthaler's *Seven Types of Ambiguity, 1957*

As if a spine of metaphor where metaphor

has abandoned veneration of bodily resolution—that

head of some author or other reflected as if in their face,

that argument for a different blue coat-hanger direction of hue

as if in the contradictions of orange deportment messing

with pierced color agreement of depth as if we might pull

sharp-smooth together heart-and-eye as bathysphere of surfaces alike.

Naveen Kishore

5 Calcutta Poems

I

neck-deep in   take your pick

loose change
sand water oil music   city
        eyes darting
        groping hands that cannot find loose change?

the city
        pisses
on the street

the horses race neck
to neck as street children
place bets
        on Betsy and Orange Fever

you can hire a room for an hour   in some hotels
as long as you pay in cash and
        do not ask for a receipt

street dogs chase bicycles against the wind

the city moves with purpose
        in the wrong direction
all traces

the smog deletes   all traces
of its footsteps

XI

man without legs
drawing a god
on a sidewalk
the chalks he uses are pink blue and
white

the girl plays hopscotch with
an imagined friend we call bondhu
humming a ditty
in a language called Bengali

her bare feet mean no disrespect
as they accidentally step
on the third eye
rendering the god blind

frightened
the people in the street
shut their eyes
in what they call bhoy

XXIII

our promises
rustling in the evening breeze like
wayward nylon skirts
that had forgotten how to flutter shyly
their eyelids half in controlled laughter
and the rest in light hearted flirtation
the shadows giving our bodies
a togetherness otherwise unimagined

XXX

the saxophone player   trapped in a dream about
playing the wrong notes
            lets the haze unfold
            listen up

the folks on the floor begin to swing their feet blur
            into rhythm the blue of the light taking on
its own magic
            as it wraps itself into the groove

tinker-bell flies in through the window   tightens up
her pink laces
smiles through her metal braces and
sprinkles up the dark with dazzle

I sit on the floor
            unclenching a song
about shadows   grieving

XXXIV

it's the blues again
waiting in the wings   blues
snares like whispers
blues dragging their feet
across drum-skins pulling
at heart strings   sway
to the blues frayed memories
rise like smoke   from winter fires
under lamplights
unable to pierce the fog

huddle under and huddle over
as you sing the blues

JoAnn Koff

A Target on Your Back

It's not 40 lashes anymore;
They've upgraded to .22s,
A bullet in the back works.
In daylight? Why hide the fact?
Vacuous anger is their right?
Quiet neighborhoods? Perfect.
It perpetuates the killing game;
American history since 1619.
It's commonplace nowadays.
Each dead black man, a prize
For extremists, who hunt to kill;
Then lie to hide the murderous fact.
Innocent boys lie face down, dead.
Equality, an illusion, when you have
A target on your back.

Roz Kuehn

After the Party

I'll leave the party, alone. Before I go, I'll look around, still pitifully in love, craving the atoms of walls, furniture, artwork, drawing their mortar, hide, sequins into my marrow. I'll slug to the last sip the others' voices. All is now part of me, my molecular structure. I am like the leaf, having used the ray and the current to have been myself at all. Naturally, the festivities will continue without me. Everyone else may dance longer, strobed in sunlight and moonlight, as the band plays birdsong, oceans, and that old hit, car horns in traffic. But I don't feel disinvited, specially. Every one here is a guest. And everyone, now together, wildly devouring their own moments, will share one day the burrowing home, alone.

Patrick Lawler

Two Broken Things

We bang against each other
as if we are two broken things in a storm.
Mathematically it has been proven
that there is an answer, but we cannot ever
know it. What we do know: God is waiting behind
a spigot full of fire and song that looks exactly like water.

In the Apocalyptic Theater There Will Come a Time

What is order in one world will be chaos in the other.
What makes you cry in one world will make you laugh
in the other.
Sometimes things get lost in one world;
sometimes they get lost between worlds.
A madman was the only one given a key, and he can't find it.
Sometimes things get found—but not in this world.

A Strange Sky Grows Over Us

The universe beats like the heart in an anatomy book.
Pick a cardiologist—any cardiologist.
Reality is another language I haven't learned.
I write toward what I don't know:
tomorrow isn't possible; yesterday didn't happen.
These are only two of the lies we are told.

Jack Mackey

The History of Rock & Roll

The all-night drive opens in pieces
three-minute bites and 60's songs
beamed from above, a chasing satellite

silver-tipped beam tracked our veering
path (escaping the plague) and kept us in sight.
After we argued for three days over

the definition of an underlying condition.
Should we try to get home while we can?
Songs in the dark, do you know this one too?

I half-hummed a few lyrics
remembered hits from before you were born,
I tried to explain

what "doo-wop" was. Noises
off, so here I could collapse into
a metaphor about depths, a pitch road

ahead, shallow-breathing, shadows falling
across the globe, an hour of silence, no
singing, the pavement buzz beneath us,

the pressure expanded, threatening to burst
like an over-filled tire. Did your mind
roll into a muddy ditch like mine did

& did you lay there wondering what if?
Then you found the 50's station,
asked how Patti Page became Chuck Berry,

asked how did everything get so different.

Maria Masington

Snow White Walks Home from AA

Leaves loosen their grip and float, dangle
like gems from her yellow skirt. Oak rubies and
birch emeralds cling to her black hair in a wispy
crown, like the lie of "Happily Ever After."

Maple whirlybirds fly to her feet. Detritus dusts
up like chipmunks racing her along the path,
circling her like reel-to-reel tapes of long-ago
conversations with witches, queens, and small men.

Mushrooms freckle the forest floor. Resentments
pop up again and again, betrayal and injustices,
real and imagined. She believes everything she thinks,
a tale where she is cast as dupe instead of darling.

She tries to remember their names, the Seven. She
knew them before the Fall. Happy, Doc, Bashful,
Sneezy, Restless, Irritable, and Discontented. Miners
of seven deadly sins, we *dig, dig, heigh-ho, heigh-ho*.

She loses focus, her eyes jewelers' loupes,
magnifying and misinterpreting outdated
conversations, tiny slights and unintended harms,
rewriting history to suit her mood and attitude.

Acorns plunk like cocktail olives onto the trampoline
of the decaying forest floor. Squirrels trapeze above
her head, chiding her to face the girl in the mirror,
chattering that she should stop biting the poison apple.

Step-by-step, foliage crumbles under high yellow heels,
powdery remnants of resentment in the woods' musty air.
A mile in her sober shoes, flakes of jewel-toned leaves
speckle her silk stockings and anger clings to her soles.

Mary McCoy

Shelter

I have a small blanket
handwoven in warm brown plaid in the Shetland Islands
where the cold wind never ceases.
Handed down from my great aunt
who could still turn cartwheels when she was sixty
and didn't drink but died of cirrhosis of the liver.
I draw it round me now
for shelter,
for comfort.
It's not really cold.
It's spring.
But the wind blows too hard
and the numbers in the news climb too fast.
Too much news.
Too much disruption.

Dora E. McQuaid

First Thought (#1)

First thought: Today the daylight is one minute and forty-one seconds longer than yesterday.

Second thought: I slept alone with the light on again last night.

Third thought: I am afraid to love you. From you, I cannot hide anything.

Fourth thought: The fever wolf haunts me. Holy god, but that wolf.

Fifth thought: And the shotgun. Even now, when so many years have passed, that shotgun haunts me, too.

Fifth thought: You said: *Tell me. Tell me the story behind you having to tell me to not ever cover your mouth again.* You said it twice: *Tell me.*

Sixth thought: My friend brought me pale orange roses the color of kindergarten creamsicles. On the glass-topped table, in a globed vase, they have been unfolding themselves all afternoon.

Seventh thought: The cornhusk doll, made in late fall and placed on the sideboard below the west window, has her arms flung open. You picked her up only days ago in the settle down light of early dusk. I watched you hold her in the expanse of your hand, so gently. Her arms flung open toward you.

Nearly Enough

You across the table from me,
mouth slack and hands restrained and
I could not figure where your eyes were landing
until you said to me, love, your lips are wine-stained,
malbec or merlot, the color of the dress I almost
was married in, my mother relentless with the threat
that she would come to no wedding that found me done
up in red velvet beside a man as brazen as you.
The entirety of the solidness of you leaning across
the expanse of a glittered glass table, chandelier shattering
light above us, to press the pad of your thumb into
my lower lip, staring and stunned and open as you said,
look at you, that mouth of yours, red on the ledge of purple,
and the people around us were silent at how much was left
unsaid between us, so much so that there are days when
I fear I will write endlessly about what was said and what
was left unsaid and the feel of your thumb at the corner
of my mouth and all of you, the core of you, leaning in
to all that once existed between us. There is still too much
between us that has gone this lifetime unsaid but for the ways
that words failed us and for the ways that love failed us and yet
still has never left us, all the same. Forgive me, my love.
I never told you, not nearly enough, how beautiful you are.

Sometimes There Is Just No Way Around It

You want to '*motherfuck*' everyone.
You want to punch the old lady in line in the grocery store,
in the throat, before she says another word.
You want to tell the male barista
It's a large, not a damn Venti.
You want to crush a finger of the young woman
with the blue eye shadow behind the counter at the DMV.
You want to ask the person at the party,
spouting bad fear-based news rhetoric,
Are you freaking serious?
You want to shriek in the library,
in the church,
in the departmental meeting at work,
in the 5:00 pm traffic with the windows rolled down,
into your own pillow on your own bed
with the door closed
until the shriek
becomes the tears,
until the tears
become the song
that saves you.

So let it save you.

First Thought (Conflated)

First thought: The church bells and trains in the distance, how every part of me peels away to listen.

Second thought: The fringe of my shawl, brushing the tops of my bared thighs.

Third thought: I knew. Even then, I knew, even as I fingered the possibility of not knowing like a river stone in my left hand.

Fourth thought: I wanted you to hold me then, to anchor me, so I did not lift up outside of myself.

Fifth thought: You told me once, while I was peeling away, listening elsewhere: *Even in full light, you can disappear from me. Your hair becomes ash in my hands.*

Sixth thought: *I forgive everyone*, you say. *I forgive everyone, of everything.*

Seventh thought: *Look at the moon*, I say. *Does she even remember?*

Origin #11

Which came first, my love? The night sky,
or the fissure of light splitting it?

So many years ago, at dinner, you said to me,
just before we sat at the glass-topped table,
after the champagne, before the red flint of Italian wine,
you said to me: Everything is illuminated.
I blew smoke away from you, thinking for a moment
that the motion hid my startle until I remembered:
Nothing is hidden. If you look into their faces,
any face, nothing is hidden. It is all there, revealed.

I looked back at you, at you watching
me decide if I was turning away,
or toward you, once again.

Alexandra Melnick

The State of Mississippi Is a (Black) Woman

Mississippi is a woman,
the only way a woman can be,
Ancient knowledge and cities dotting her hillsides next to highways for tourists to drive by and farmers who cast their daily lot everyday looking beyond those hills while the land itself is complicit in hiding and holding secrets, small tin toys from sharecroppers, scars where slaves once filled.

Mississippi is a woman,
a woman a woman a woman
the only way she can be,
bound and embodied in a blues song,
Between the blues notes encapsulates the breath between prayer and thank you and Mississippi has always been told what to do by wealthy white men and so I have to conclude she is a (black) woman, that she is an earth mother, that she is every kissed knee by the levee side and she is the fear the towns felt when in 1927 she finally unfolded to her true glory.

Mississippi is a woman because I can see the curve of her hips along north state street and her toenail polish on the gulf shore, dirty with oil, sand, flecks of where the color once filled. Mississippi must be a woman, because Mississippi future has always been a black girl dreaming, someone squaring their shoulders, set to inherit the Delta sky.

Mississippi is a woman because you can smell her strength after a storm,
the high clean note and scent of pollen,
After she came in from playing outside. Moreover,

a woman is Mississippi.

Nitta Yuma

Our family has always lived in Nitta Yuma. The dry land when the sun lounges and comes down, hot insistent seeking tongues like a moment caught off guard or stolen from time. (Stolen into time as something stored into the land, catches you off guard when you touch a tree and you think: did they really do that to a slave here...... could a sharecropper......) Our family is the bones and fountains making the landscape of our place. Our place. Nitta Yuma has always like America been built on the backs of slaves. In Nitta Yuma's case, it is built out of the backs of slaves. Our family.

A self referential loop, a trauma of horror, of terror, and set for you to come back to the same small memories again and again, the iron, the boot, the door opening, the wide eyes, the dropped handkerchief in a planted row. These repeated memories paint the biggest and brightest picture of this place and the shadows cast are all of the buildings.

There is a 1760s carriage house where the family lives presently today. There is a general store full of 3,000 dolls and not one mention of how the family owned and was owned by the people they also treated as dolls, living clockwork soldiers left outside when dinner was called. There are rotting houses with walls fallen clean out, like a breath released when you wake up gasping from sleep. There are several smaller trailers and lean to houses where people still clearly live. Only twenty living people are still here, and the rest is made of up of the great "eternal we," the bodies and bones and hearts and dreams and hopes of people sequestered and soldiered to this land. And through a blues song darkly, we sometimes creep to the window and see.

Corrine, Corrina, where'd you stay last night?

It is so easy to have a narrative of tired grief holding the spirit of folks at the bottom of the ocean, as lookerbys stand and around and comment: "oh, they'll never get out." "It's such a shame." People who lived in Nitta Yuma and who were slaves were not monolithic places or beings living on one plane of existence. They were people who were enslaved, people taken against their will and expressing themselves again and again in music, in song, in the light that escapes out of a black hole or dying star. This is not just another paean to the blues and their ability to ameliorate pain but instead a map to lead the way in and out of Nitta Yuma, a compass to take you inside the heart and safely back out of again, led the way by so many before. From the blues comes the rest of America, and as we know: America was built on the backs of slaves. Nitta Yuma's ghost town is a model for how the rest of the country is, how we can look in and see the glory of the past and how another segment can see the ley lines of resistance, stretching all the way with dusty fingers into almost any aspect of musical joy today.

Amadeo Mangune Mendoza

Erasures

We erase through writing: poetry or prose, fiction or lying obsession, through nonsense and effective nonsense which drive home a somewhere-sunshine to our rules-dominated world. We erase through giving alms to beggars, as we give immortality to our maybe overstaying mortality, they giving back through unforgettable smiles on unbearable streets. We erase through prayers for the dead, poetry for the dead, paintings and artworks for our dearly departed, imagining a buoyant, setting sun, with colors unheard of. We erase through beauty contests, seeing beauty when beauty is most bereft. We erase through Spiderman, through the web, through Aquaman, through the net, through horror and vampire movies and their deep, eerie-immortal bite in us. We erase through leftovers, photographs, forced, sustained living memories of the dead—yes, again the dead—why should they live for so long? Why do they even outlive us? We erase through candles, their brightness, or their flicker, like stolen glances. We erase through comedy films where we see drama at its finest, a world too shy to stare at other worlds. We erase through peculiar stares on strange faces, unwelcome meetings with our usual graces. We erase through leisurely walks along a boulevard of hookers erasing love they surprisingly feel in short-time encounters, who hooks the most? We erase through western astrology, *feng shui*, tarot cards, crystal balls, trying to believe the unbelievably magical in a—let's face it—believe-it-or-not world.

Nancy Mercado

Plagued America

It takes a plague to crystallize
the malignancy occupying the White House
that churns out death
a gross carnage of humanity
stockpiled inside U-Haul trucks

It takes a plague to breach the lies
we live in this America
bearing its mercenary truths
its decomposing laws
scavenged by elected vultures

A plague is what it takes
to realize red baseball-capped buffoons
can freely amass assault rifles
the privileged scant illiterate and starved
lined up for miles to reach food banks
gleefully waving soiled confederate flags in tatters

A plague must be what it takes
to discover our illusory lives
the hamster wheel we've been sold
traveling on it all along
toward manufactured dreams
toward nowhere in reality

It takes a plague to recognize
we are orphans in this America
sparing no expense we're marked for ruin
by the slothful elites who bask
in swimming pools of our blood

A plague is what it takes
to wake up from this American dream
to see our children encaged

our mothers our fathers
butchered in broad daylight
our homes mired in soot water
our lands laced of oil pipelines
discharging at whim
scourging valleys filled of life
decimating our future
under a foul dark layer of evil

A plague must be what it takes
for our redress in the streets
of this America
our decisive rebellion
our final renaissance.

I Come to See for Myself: On the Anniversary of Hurricane Maria

I fly in to see for myself
below, blue tarps over the homes of my nation
like those silver blankets that cover the souls
of Mayan and Arawak children locked inside cages
on the US mainland I left behind

arriving home, I enter a mass of confusion
plantain crops walloped in their places of birth
five-foot tall grass rebelliously advancing to heaven
my mother's lemon tree on her last leg
hunched over, barely breathing

I witness it for myself
splintered wooden electrical poles
held up by a neighbor's twine
trees arrowed through one another
now growing sideways, surviving.

Not the palm trees though
the palm trees chose victory or death
no in-between half-hearted living
some growing new hair
others simply guillotined
by Maria's detonation.

I walk into the new growth of forest
detect the low lamenting sounds of the injured there
witness the anger etched into the undulating
mountains surrounding me in the distance.

I see the US cavalry arrived just in time
Cortes and Columbus repackaged
into a 21st Century nightmare
armies in metallic flying machines
using talking devices, exchanging messages
through invisible airways

I see the cavalry arrived to help
themselves to the casinos they built
to hurl paper towels at the local mortician
to seize their opportunity to maximize
on the extinction of the natives

keeping them in drawn-out darkness
with no power to run hospitals
no shelter, with no water

I cross the land
from West to East, South to North
to see the revelers and the ruined for myself
to lend an ear to survivors and to the dead
see shuttered schools for miles along the route,
I run out of fingers
on which to count them all

part of the plan to ruin us
a small voice reminds me.

I walk along the turquoise shore
lined of amputated homes
crumbled fences
collapsed doorways into the sea
inside, bits and pieces of families remain
their vestiges now
across the Atlantic at the opposite end

back in Ponce, I sit in my mother's rocking chair
watch my neighbor's hummingbirds
who've arrived to visit her ruby coral bells
I think of my father's strength
in his humility, he walked in silence
built a house to withstand
a cyclonic catastrophe.

I've seen for myself
the natives are
the majesty of this world
together they've cleared the paths
sawing, hewing through mammoth
barriers of deceit and loathing

retrieved their own water
traversing the inundation
of Washington's elite
that vowed to drown them

they went about their lives
by the light of a candle
or an old wooden light pole
they stitched back together
with all the love on Earth

maneuvering through a world of cadavers
inside Maria's eye
amid the tantrums of the privileged
a nation held its ground
now, raises its foundation
of ancestral eminence anew.

Gary Metras

The Fox

Winter night begins in high trees.
Soon it will rouse and spread
deliberate as any flood.
It is now that fox world
awakens, no longer abstract.
He waits for others to first disturb
the snow. Fox will track them
in these tests of necessity
for the only nourishment here.
When he rises, ready to hunt,
he sniffs and listens, setting paws
between starlight and shadow,
and enters tonight, his heart beating
against the ribcage of hunger.

To Rhyme With Love

Of senators and popes and such small fry —Edna St. Vincent Millay

The Attic sky hadn't rained in months.
Doves were dying from above. We shoved them
into sewers crawling with catfish and rats
among dead dogs. Neither oracle nor god
had advice worth more than rust on a sword's hilt.
We paced the cobblestones and preached austerity,
while those rhyme-mongers, crowned with laurel,
raised sails toward some island in the sick-green,
tiring sea in search of a new word to rhyme
with love. It's not for nothing Plato banished them.

What use are rhymes when we, the elders,
build a future from out the ruins of the past?
Let us do the hard work with disregard
of poets wandering in labyrinths of words.

Age 23 Wordsworth Sleeps in Stonehenge

After days tramping the Salisbury Plains,
he crept to the center of that stone puzzle,
the point of honor in an antique calendar
of the unknown, and lay himself down
on soft grass to rest and slept.

The dance of diurnal starlight ignored,
the moon's form deranged, the ghosts
of hooded men silent in an obsolete universe,
he joined the slow dream of stone.

He awoke to morning washing his lips,
to war exploding beyond the circle, to young men
lured by a cheap shilling into a slavish Navy,
to widows starving. And that distant voice
closing in was the world, that became his song.

Michael Milburn

Wrath: A Sequel

We all hide it
at some depth,
more treacherous
for being unheard,
like pre-instruments era volcanoes.

So much of mine
has boiled out over the years
I've entered the plausible but foolish stage
of hoping it exhausted,
or at least with the help of meditation
notice a new moat-like space
between the triggering event
and the murderous response,
like an e-mail slept on and revised,
but I never stop dreading
the annihilating eruption
that will alter me in others' eyes.

Even my faith,
which fashions
disharmony into forgiveness,
as good as offloads it onto God,
the original rageaholic
if you've ever listened to a storm
or mourned a child.

Ted R. Miller

Pudgy

As a kid I lived on the Jersey shore
where birds dined on killies
and baiting fish was a waiting game.

In school I drowned
in the shame of a bookish boy
who bullies gutted to draw a crowd.
I was manna to class clowns,
my breast pocket full of pens and sand,
glasses banded to my skull,
awkward as the horseshoe crab
in its helmet shell.

Wheezing from ragweed,
I scuttled,
hooked,
scaled,
until hardy as salt rose
I learned to chum with the best.

Urge to Fly

Off duty in Dunedin

I watch Maoris dive from cliffs—
dare devils who risk rocks to fall free
as gravity pulls
on their calves, used to riding whales,
their bicep tattoos dense as emu down.

How soft your bangs would curl
in the surf's splash.

A pair of royal albatross—
you know they mate for life—
crossed the hotel pool last night,
white wings rippling the sky.

Evenings, with you ten thousand miles gone,
I read how Da Vinci's copters fail,
engines not invented for three hundred years.

How fast would I have to fly
to catch your breath tonight?

Faster than the humpback's song
as it charms the sea.

Gloria Mindock

So Good

for dragon lady

Oh darling, you are so good the way you acted in that scene. You acted so
good, I really loved it. You are so good.

Oh darling, you climbed that ladder so bravely. You are so brave to climb
up that ladder. Oh what fierce determination to change the lights. You changed them so
quickly. You are so good to change them so fiercely.

Oh darling, it is so good to see you. You have such a great smile walking
down the hall. When you walk down the hall you are always smiling. Smiling in the hallway,
oh darling.

Oh darling, the way you directed that play was so good. It was so good the way you directed
that play.

The cast is so delightful. Oh so delightful is the cast. They performed so brilliantly. Oh darling
what a brilliant cast

Oh darling you must act in another show. Your acting is so good. So good you are in every
scene. Every scene is so wonderful. You are wonderful, oh darling.

One week later...

Oh darling, who are you?

1994

I tolerated this road feeling tortured.
Somehow, ending up on a current, drowning, gasping for air.
My sorrow tightens around your neck.
There is an equation between us...you=me.
Somethings are beyond the dark room we entered.
It is spring, and we released each other into the blossoms.
My scars, invisible.
Day after day, the heart is strangled,
floating on water, waiting to be laid to rest.

Barbara Marie Minney

Shooting Crows in the Cornfield

I didn't think I knew you very well.
You died when I was so young,
just dissolving monochrome photographs
carefully mounted in old albums,
cracking morocco leather cover
coming apart at the seams,
found at the bottom of
an archaic traveling trunk.

After a breakfast of creamed chip beef on toast
that you called "shit on a shingle" from the Great War
that was supposed to end all wars,
you would rest in the ragged armchair,
watching the Charleston Indians on
an old black and white television,
volume turned low,
ear bent toward a Crosley table radio
listening to the Cincinnati Reds
play a different game in a different city,
puffing on a corn cob pipe,
the cocoa and molasses aroma of Prince Albert tobacco
swirling around your face.

I inherited your bald head
with the brown age spots
that we kids wanted so desperately
to play connect the dots with
when you dozed in your chair
after Grandma's Sunday dinner
of fried chicken and dumplings,
mashed potatoes and gravy,

and those melt in your mouth fresh baked rolls
glistening with the butter
from the big block at the end of the table
that tasted funny in our citified mouths.
A dessert of coffee poured over sugared
saltines that you said was a favorite
from the great depression.

You taught me my first cuss words.
After watching the bands and floats
parade by your house on College Street,
we spent that Saturday afternoon
at the Glenville State College Pioneers homecoming game.
A student stood behind us holding
a hand printed sign that said
"Beat the Hell out of Concord."
I knew what hell was from Sunday School,
but I didn't know you could beat it out of someone
on the football field.
I asked you about it,
you cracked that mischievous grin of yours and said
"Ask your mother."

You would sit in the dining room,
shotgun pointed out the window,
toward the cackling crows
that dared to venture into
the cornfield that you planted every year
on the other side of the curving county road
running along the Little Kanawha River.
You didn't seem to care whether a car
was driving past or not,
a cloud of dust rising in its wake.
After all, your shooting skills
were the stuff of family legend.

I was twelve when
you gave me my first rifle,
an old Remington shotgun,
almost as tall as me,
that your grandfather had given you,
polish glassy in the dawning sun
surging through the fog shrouded hills
that composed the far-off horizon.

You took me on my one and only hunting trip
in the back garden.
I remember the groundhog
standing on its hind legs
on a block of stone
silhouetted against the barn,

I missed the shot.
What would a city boy like me
do with a dead groundhog anyway?

It would seem like a lifetime
before I held a gun in my hands again,
this time shooting at coca cola cans
sitting on boards
at the Ohio Department of Wildlife's
Grand River shooting range.
I didn't hit anything then either.
I guess my heart just wasn't in it.

I guess I was wrong.
I did know you.

It's funny.
Now that I am advancing
toward the age you were when you died,
these childhood remembrances come back
slyly slipping into my dreams
just like your grin.

Jane Edna Mohler

Making Friends in the Pandemic

I joined a book club.
Thought we'd talk online,
ease into things.

But they're anxious to eye me up,
want to meet me
on their perfect green lawn,

introduce me to Yama,
Malak Almawt, Samael,
Sareil, Santa Muerte.

I'm the only Jane.
They want to hand me a long cold drink
and smile.

Miserere

You desired that truth be in the hidden places,
and in the concealed part You teach me wisdom. Psalm 51

His deep-set eyes looked Russian.
All I can is say is those strong roots
in his face made me stare.

Now, I worship on a floor with one mismatched tile.
Swaying to psalms, I take note of the shoes around me.

He was young and interested in something
I had said; I can't remember what.
It was a dream and I didn't need to ask.

I want to take my fingers and pick at that tile until it gives.
I want to take it home.

Mary B. Moore

Aubade With Door, for an Art Exchange Project

I paint the door chrome yellow, can-do
yellow, and the pre-dawn
light that creases
the stairs' accordion I do
in watered-down violet,
the two folding chairs
viridian green.
I ink squiggle lace in a square,
tight little pen moves--
a curtained window.
They exercise my compulsive.
Medieval writing called
miniscule looks like that,
but says something.
Our privacy is unrelenting.
On the porch, which borders
our two-person country, I wash
groceries, spray-painting
the cement stand-offish
gray, Lent gray.
Can a protein wrapped
in a skin of fat die?
Does having an *in* and *out*
make it alive?
Might as well be a bot.
The brass door knob looks gold now,
its nose so clean—so blameless--ochre
streaked chrome yellow. I soak
the lemons, oranges and mangos

in New Dawn, their still life
baptized in a red bowl.
My skin's washed so dry it flies
away on a small wind.
There I go, over the porch rails,
past the stairs, a tattered
pink-beige body suit,
the limbs flailing.
All that's left down here is the "in."
Veins, nervous system,
bared: even air hurts.

Mary Morris

Rembrandt, Late Self-Portrait

Crimson, with broken blood vessels
he forfeits the mirror, eating pears
with a glass of time, listens to snow
fall behind memory, while cadmium
corpuscle, boneblack shadow, and lead
white glisten of drooling lip tell us
how to draw death close, paint ravens in.

Lorca's Lover

In forest
the lover's neck
is a young branch.
The breast, an orchard
he kneels into.
His mouth, a grotto—
temple of joy. Place
where bodies scissor
in grass, rise at the forested
torpor of animals,
at the green heart
of campesinos
praying at the gate for rain
in Granada, a city embedded
with duende, canciones,
crucifixions set with tourmaline
while fingers of savants
pluck guitars built from groves
of cypress in June.
Yes, to the yearnings

of gypsy dancers.
Yes, to living in caves
painted with bison.

Visions of Johanna, JPG #12

I listen to "Visions of Johanna"
while writing about you

when someone sends an email
containing a folder of photographs.

A picture of you at ten
with that crashed-in look.

I recall the narrative you recounted
when your grandmother swept you away

from the abuse, gave you a 0.22 rifle,
a pole, and a Buck knife, taught you

survival skills. What shocks me
is the final photo, JPG #12

which your first wife has taken
with her iPhone

only twenty-four hours before—
just as I had seen you on your deathbed.

So beautifully gaunt, it is like a picture
of the body crossing between worlds.

A wavering. One eye at half-mast,
a wet opening, viewing us instead.

Always looking ahead. A window
refusing to close.

I stored the picture in my memory.
Now, it sits on a bright screen in my house,

overlit, as if someone smuggled you out.
Your skin, yellow—the liver, I'm reminded.

They dressed you in your favorite green
shirt, buttoned up, crisp looking, tucked the wool

and cotton blankets around your body,
save for the long feet hanging over the bed,

which made me think of Jesus when the three Marys
held him after he was brought down from the cross.

No one knows the conversation
my son and I had over his father in that hour.

Do you want to lie down with him? Yes.
We held each weighted, cool hand, touched his hair.

He has taken care of his father for the last month,
slid drops of morphine down his throat, guarded

the door against unwelcome guests
like three-headed Cerberus.

We discussed his ears. I spoke of the left,
deformed by frostbite, told my son the tale—

fishing in a remote lake above the timberline,
snowstorm, struggled to get out.

He asked for more.
Once this body was taut as a rope,

disappeared nine meters through blue
water to hook spiny lobster.

We lived in Mexico.
Once, we traded fish for fruit.

Mihaela Moscaliuc

from *The Book of Salt*

"With all thine offerings thou shalt offer salt." —*Leviticus 2:13*

The *Time* staff writer briefs us
animals wore paths to salt licks
men followed, trails became roads
settlements grew beside them.
When the menu shifted from game to cereal,
need surged, *scarcity* turned the mineral
into prized trading commodity.
In 6th century sub-Sahara, Moorish merchants traded salt
ounce for ounce for gold.
Back from Cathay in 1295, Marco Polo charmed the Doge
with tales of salt coins bearing the seal of the Khan.
Salt *caravanned the globe*— Libyan desert to Morocco
to Timbuktu, Egypt to Greece, across the Mediterranean
across centuries down the inlet of your thighs
from which I collect my share
as you shake off the embrace of the Atlantic
and, entranced under the caress of Caribbean sun,
briefly return to my mouth.
As purifying ritual, Romans placed a morsel
on an eight-day-old babe's lips.
The bulk of it they used for buying slaves.
And the staff writer claims *the history of the world*
according to salt is simple—
Taste also Venice's opulence, salt-based,
taste Florence's unsalted bread, the tax
that stirred the French Revolution,
Da Vinci's overturned saltcellar
portending treachery in *The Last Supper*.
Rome's *Via Salaria* gets its name from salt

hauled in oxcarts from Ostia,
salary from a soldier's pay, cut if he "was not worth his salt."
Self-exile is what I get from entrusting memory with recipes.
A pinch here, a pinch there.
Taste this—
fingers cleaved while cleaving,
the tartare wreathed with parsley leaves.
Salad's rooted in the practice of salting vegetables.
I eat alone, unperturbed by the paint peeling off
the apostles' halos. I don't speak their language.
I know salt through its absence. I eat
with someone else's tongue.

La isla de las muñecas

Xochimilco canals, Mexico City

For half a century, under the pitying gaze of his barrio,
Don Julián pushed a wheelbarrow
stacked with salvaged limbs, matted heads of hair, gouged eyes.
Then, self-exiled on the nearby isla,
he grew delicious crops to barter for more.
Trees, stakes, fences don over a thousand dolls
weathered and decomposed,
some nude, some fancily clad.

Devotional for the girl drowned in the Xochimilco canal,
opus of an exalted damaged mind,
haunting installation on the stages of our disintegration,
post-apocalyptic playground or, some visitors swear,
commune of possessed souls who wink and whimper in the dark.

Praise to the accidental beauty of thy twisted work.
Yours too, Don Julián,
but girls
without your muñeca, it's your stories I need tonight.
Come forth, come forth.
Did the cart wheels call from the street?
Did they hum did they squeal did your muñeca whisper *why did you abandon me?*
Who dismembered yours who slung her on the trash pile
who in the canal were you old were you young
what instead did you hold
that first night without?

Forget the blossoms

Here's how I live: I scaffold,
take in chaos, watch scaffold collapse,
peek at stars, start again.
I hold my chaos responsible for blood
splattered at unequal intervals
on the holy unit called day.
Once in a while I placate time with raw flesh,
delectable crimes, anchorpits.
In Edinburgh, I woke each morning
hungry for cherries, harvested the campus
directly with my mouth. I skipped the museums,
famed festival, and only entered philosophy,
literature, psychology to use their bathroom
when juice layered too thickly
on fingers and mouth and I became
the business of every bee.
Friend, if you find yourself there
sink your teeth unapologetically
in those beauties gravid with wait.

Branch by branch, make the flesh yours
without guilt for the famished,
as if you've always belonged to each morsel.
Let passersby and guards think you mad,
let them collide and curse
as they gaze at your chin
blood red, your lips incendiary
and sweeter than any girl's or boy's.

Mother Goddess, Ptolemaic Period, 305-51 B.C., Egypt

Oneonta, NY

We're licking soft-serve outside the bakery,
your chair back to the street, mine fronting it.
Your flirtations melt away any regret
about the cost of this sweet indulgence.
On lunch break from poetry workshops,
we're still on the Sumerians. Awed by Inanna,
we bemoan the neglect, extol her heroically
erotic descent, the bold egotism.
Twenty feet away, under the shade of a poplar,
a large woman gussied in full pink dips her hand
between the pants' stretchy band and skin
then hoists forefinger to her nostrils.
I already know soon we'll share a single cone,
finish each other's ice cream, lick each other's chins.
But here, in this Oneonta sun, drips accumulate
as I decelerate to extend the moment.
I watch. She inhales vigorously
and on the count of three repeats
the gesture, slow and deliberate.
I never mention it, not then, not later.

Erotic

Pandemic, 2020

Asked what he found erotic, he said eyes,
not eyes per se, but how they instigate,
ignite the body from within, that two second
ocular tryst that no tangible can match
when the strange eyes that enter yours,
equally strange, bring you home.
I felt envious. I'd never dared other eyes
and when lanced with a suggestive glance,
made sure to avert mine —
until now, when the daily stroll
parallel to the beach is measured
not in miles, but eyes eyes eyes.
Behind each mask, breath reveals
its nature, and it stinks.
The iris is the sole internal organ
visible from the outside,
my father professed to justify
his Canon's small invasions
on the streets of Manhattan,
the troubles he got himself into.
I walk the day to harvest
what I see —blots of color,
fear, hello, no, father's camera
on continuous click click click,
stealing what the subjects
don't know they can give.

Fred Muratori

Special This Week

Again they're out of avocados and adventure
perfect health and washboard abs
Was a delivery truck hijacked outside Syracuse?
Were the cargo planes brought down by UFOs?
It's a free-fall market economy now
So long pension plan   See you in a next life, Yucatan

The blue-smocked stock boy is preoccupied
He ignores both me and the air raid siren
He wears a clip-on tie so I assume he's unhappy
making minimum wage   but he knows
about overhead and markup and how
they torture the meat to look so red
If you don't see it ask   Good advice
Where do you keep invisibility?   *Aisle Zero*

Almost no one eats canned food anymore
but still it's mass produced as if Washington
were stocking Carlsbad Caverns for catastrophe
When the end arrives we'll all have peaches
peaches peaches and mounds of succotash
Even now the smug unknown crouches
one step beyond the parking lot's
sputtering sodium light

On the easternized west coast
they view the night sky more clearly
They sit on their decks   necks
bent into question marks not sure
of what they're seeing but
suddenly wary of spaces between stars
how anything might fall through them

Wretched Stalks

Yet still they leave us holding wretched stalks
Of disappointment—Philip Larkin

*

The envelope addressed in a hand I recognized
was a trick of automation
marketing deceit
I'd already read the *People* magazine
mistakenly mailed to me
My postman affects sympathy whenever we meet

*

Last weekend the trattoria ran out of veal
best in the city
just as I entered with my date
who looked undead in the green half-light
reflected from a *Sold Out* sign
outside the theater where the play
we absolutely *had* to see was showing one last time
Instead we paced the unappeasing street
and spent another raveled night
with neither sex nor sleep

*

The tour guide said the ocean view was better
last July   when I was cooped up with the flu
Not fogged-in like today   Gleaming flocks of flying fish
spiraled in the sun like beaded curtains!
Too bad   he says   you weren't here then

*

At the airport gate a festival of pent affections
opens out   blooms with hugs
and warm enfoldments
So much to be welcomed to   So much to say
Selfies and smiles galore for everyone
But it's late   The bar is closed
My plane is the one with rust along its wing
and of course I'm only going home

Elisabeth Murawski

Gold Medal

He buys it for me
because I'm Catholic
and I won't let him wear
a condom. I'm that dumb,
and a hypocrite to boot,
sliding into bed. I squirm
when he calls it a "charm"—
there's voodoo on the island
he comes from. One week
late, scared but curious,
wanting anything *his*,
I'm relieved to see red,
take back my loneliness.
His ardor fades with the fall.
I have the medal blessed,
but never wear it. Safe
in a jewelry box
made in Poland, Mary's
immaculate, framed
by a blizzard of stars.

Storm, Western Ireland

White as a saint
inside and out
the walls of the cottage

on Achill Island.
Window shades the red
of suicides. Think

blood, a blade,
the cessation
of pain. Impossible

to read, lift a pen
in such a wind.
The lights fail.

Sleep limps and twists
out of reach
as if it were an evil

to resist:
I might not hear
the breaking glass,

the creaking board,
the bedroom door
squeaking on its hinge,

the empty boat
thumping like a heart
against the jetty.

Émile Nelligan

To Georges Rodenbach

White, white, all white, O Swan—opening your pale wings,
You take flight for Eden, which reclaims you
From the breast of those gray mists of your Flemish fields
And from the dead cities whose death rattles you mourn.

Bruges, where do those widows walk in their black shawls?
Let your bells speak your grief to the firmament!
Along your melancholy canals
Let the funeral bells soar: those bronze ravens in breathless air.

And meanwhile, the Azure radiates to the North
And becomes, it seems, a golden light,
O Flanders! dazzling your funeral eyes.

Nuns, you who pray in the offices of evening,
Contemplate with eyes raised from the Monstrance
The Mystique, that Chosen of eternal sunrises!

Translated from the French by James and Shona Deahl

Winter Evening

Ah! How the snow has snowed!
My windowpane is a garden of frost.
Ah! How the snow has snowed!
What is the spasm of living
To the pain that I have, that I have!

All the ponds lie frozen,
My soul is black: Where do I live? Where do I go?
All my hopes lie frozen:
I am the new Norway
Pale skies have abandoned.

Weep, birds of February,
At the sinister shiver of things,
Weep, birds of February,
Weep for my tears, weep for my roses,
From your juniper branches.

Ah! How the snow has snowed!
My windowpane is a garden of frost.
Ah! How the snow has snowed!
What is the spasm of living
To all the ennui that I have, that I have!

Translated from the French by James Deahl and Gilda Mekler

The Carmelites

Among the shadows of the cloister they go solemnly.
Their footsteps make a shiver run over the flagstones
And the funeral sound of their sandals
Increases slightly the chaste murmur singing within them.

To the seraphic lustre of their austere eyes
The flambeaux respond in modal scales;
Within the coldness of their cloister they go solemnly,
And their footsteps make velvet songs on the flagstones.

One of them is returning to the eternal fields
To find, in the end, forgetfulness of the world and its scandals;
She goes to her bed of death deep in their maze.
Thus, throughout this night, her sister nuns
In their cloister have marched so long, so solemnly.

Translated from the French by James and Shona Deahl

October Roses

So we don't see the roses of autumn fall,
Cloister your dead heart within my slain heart;
My sorrow rushes towards the suffering evenings,
Together with this monotonous month.

The carmine, belated and joyous, stands out
In the doleful woods, punctuated with red...
So we don't see the roses of autumn fall,
Cloister your dead heart within my slain heart.

Down there, the cypresses are toneless;
We quickly adapt to their shadows.
Underground a fresh bed opens;
We will both sleep there, sweetheart,

So we don't see the roses of autumn fall.

Translated from the French by James and Shona Deahl

Mark Niedzwiedz

Hundred loose ends

Only when the rug is pulled from under our feet
Toppled, lying motionless, looking from the bottom-up
Do we see life as it is
Not the squared circle imagined, but something rather incomplete
Words, a quarter left to say, intentions, two thirds on the way
Everything left behind in process, a hundred loose ends
And as we lay quiet, stargazing, fixed point
Our hands no longer able to grip, or shape the world
It would seem only feeble bodies have closure, for we are masters of nothing
But the unfinished symphony, first line poem and the love affair, all too brief
Yet time, which cares not a jot, if we should reach the mountain top
Is a mere calculous, an earthly abacus, not in charge, not God
So, perhaps there is a life beyond to balance the books
Where the almost done, nearly won, break blue ribbons, as well as sweat
For now, though, all seems patches, tears, and mends
The story of becoming, and our going, a hundred loose ends

Kathleen Novak

Out of the Rain

Did we always have these burdens
or grow them like shells covering our soft bodies,
things we slowly haul with us wherever we go?

That is a question.

I see anyhow that we learn to live with them:
bad eyes or knees or aching backs,
piercing pain or falling hair, fading memory,
the husband always ill,
the spouse now gone,
the child wayward or jobless or addicted to drugs,
insufficient funds, shaky hands,
windows in decay and long lost dreams.

We live with them
the *always somethings* we tell one another

I'm saying we just live with them
take them up every day where we left them last night

like old tarps lifted high
and carried with no particular joy over field and stream

so much a part of the trek
we half the time can pretend

they aren't even there.

Resilience

My mother's shamrock plant lived for decades
in a painted ceramic pot hung by macramé
from a hook in the back entry
where she kept all her plants until she died
and my father's care killed most of them
and my Uncle Charlie advised walling in
one whole side to bring down the heating bill
but blocking the kindliest light such that

only the shamrock survived
keeping company with vases of fake flowers
that women liked to give my father in those days
when he was an attractive widower
who loved to dance and putter in his own house
all by himself for the first time in eighty-some years
that sadly charmed era when my mother's shamrock
lived on no matter what, it's roots woven tighter
than the macramé all around it

which was all before my father had his stroke
not final like my mother's but trouble nonetheless
and we moved him far from his home
but close to ours
in the way that well-meaning offspring do
and in the taking of this and that
from one home to the next
I rescued the shamrock

and gave it new soil in a larger clay pot with ruffled edges
placed it on an antique blue and white plate from England
and set it near a southern window where it blooms
in constant tiny white flowers amidst dark green leaves
that do what shamrock leaves are meant to do:
that is to open and close
and open again.

Suzanne S. Rancourt

Voyage

the hawthorn tree does grow in blight
with raven's caw iridescent light
bones of ancients praise the night
ships sail
ships sail

A twenty minute memory
a subway station cafe just outside of London
a cup of coffee
a Welsh man with stark white hair
eyes Celestine blue

I say
if I had a secret boat it would sail quietly
in a sea of solitude like in Memere's paintings
I would slip across cold waters to warm shores
archetypical images of real lives, hardships fossilized
in the caves of Innis nan Damh rumbling
in the hollow rib cage of the oldest known cave bear skeleton
sing through waters of springs and brooks that vanish into hillsides
emerge clean on the other side
the meadow of stags.

like the iridescence of Raven feathers
found by the Hawthorn tree gnarled by time
and the marching clans that returned from ocean expeditions
sailed into Ullapool like seals wicked inland
up through water ways into lochs
to the dolomite caves—bone caves—
just beyond the tree but not before offerings are made—
is my vessel—a spiral of DNA
tree roots of twists and twirls
braids me with the Norse Moors of Scotland

hard people seeking warm water, white sand beaches, palm trees
at the edge of the world in Achadh Mealvaich
where some must go backward to go forward.

I would go there again as my ancestors
travel gulf stream waters to New Brunswick, Nova Scotia,
where the Red Paint people curled into the shape
of an ear to earth we listen
as our ochre painted bodies—our blood painted bodies
return to life

Russell Reece

Chainsaw

After the messy drive to the ER,
after the x-rays, consults with
the ophthalmologist,
the maxillofacial surgeon,
the neurosurgeon,
Dianne brought the kids in.
See, Daddy's OK. He'll be home before you know it.
Todd began to cry.
Dianne picked him up, Christy
slipped her arm around her mom's waist
wouldn't look at me.
They wobbled and drifted
off to the side as we talked.
I had to keep adjusting,
keep moving my head to see them.
Somehow, they were gone
and I was floating
in the air again, covered
by a noisy spray of pine chips
and exhaust fumes.
Then it was morning.
The nurse came in. She told me
I looked pretty.

Tatiana Retivov

Moving Mountains

I have moved ten mountains
in my sleep. This is the only
purpose of life, moving mountains.

They are all shapes and colors,
these earth spewn mounds
and vagabond hillocks.

Each so different from the other
that it forces me to learn
its ways like a new lover.

Here beneath this rock I find
one mountain's Achilles' heel,
soft and raw to the touch.

And there, in the core of an oak tree
dry rot has spread, cancer-like.
It is not that I'm entranced with

the archaeology of ruins,
though it be full of fascination.
It is just that I find moving

mountains—a valuable hobby,
as if I were some Prime Mover
in the Land Below Waves,

in a ritual of my own perceiving.

Suzanne Rhodenbaugh

This Dame's Dozen-Plus Poetry Disqualifications: A Damn-Near Ars Poetica

1. I'm not sensitive. Oh I'm easily offended and can hold a grudge for years but I can take cold, heat, cigarette smoke and alcohol and/or garlic breath. If the talker is extraordinarily entertaining, I can even take the smell of a cigar.

2. I like art as well as the next person, and on occasion visit my local art museums and galleries and such, but generally paintings don't make me swoony.

3. Nature is one of my favorite things, right up there with red wine, blackeyed peas, marzipan and country music. But Nature is mostly outside, and that's a place I go just at intervals. Basically I live indoors.

4. I've never been to Yaddo, MacDowell or Provincetown. I was at Bread Loaf once. There a famous poet said my poems have a charge to them; and a newspaper reporter, apparently at the Conference due to his wife having relatives in the area, told me I looked glamorous. From both these compliments I got up a good head of steam for pushing on with poetry.

5. I've never written a sestina. If I ever do, I'm not going to put "sestina" in the title. I like to show off, but not in that particular way.

6. I can dance. I can keep a beat. I don't get all twirly and gauzy to Aretha Franklin or Patti LaBelle. Those big women deserve more respect.

7. I haven't read all the 17th century metaphysical poets or all the (fill the blank). I've read thousands of books, but somehow not the ones that lead to impressive allusions. What Tacitus recorded or the order of the beheadings of Henry VIII's wives do not trip off my tongue. I would have to look them up.

8. I didn't write poems as a child. I wrote book reports and science papers which I illustrated in India ink. I probably should have written history reports too but don't recall any, which may account for my being unable to remember all the English kings and queens. In later life I did learn the Civil War began in April, 1861, and ended in April, 1865, and knowing this has stood me in good stead. I can trot it out in quite a few contexts.

9. I'm not deep in thought. If I ever appear to be, I'm probably trying to remember whether I sent a birthday card to Rosemary, or trying to decide whether to have pork chops or orange roughies with the leftover black beans and rice.

10. I haven't been able to think of a fundable reason why I should get a National Endowment for the Arts Fellowship. Once I proposed visiting botanical gardens here and yon, but don't think I made a convincing case. I myself couldn't think why I needed to do this other than for fun, which even the Democrats, most of the time, won't give money to.

11. I do get involved in politics, smelly and rotten though it is. Once I even managed a city council candidate's campaign, and she even won. It's true politics is messy and steers the heartmind off more throbbing, transcendent stuff, but I'm a citizen and can take it and besides like the rush of competition and the fights. (See # 1 above.)

12. I have one language—English. I diddled with French for three years and can sing "The Marseillaise" passably accurately; studied Hebrew for two months on an Israeli kibbutz, in between bouts of dysentery and backbreaking work (I exaggerate, but really only a little); and suffered through a semester of German, an unusually ugly language, in my opinion, but I can't claim to speak, understand, read or write any of the above languages. As a kid I was slow with Pig Latin, though I worked harder at it than at any of the above foreign tongues.

13. I like punctuation and capitalization and other such conventions and don't care for a lot of air and space in poems. Also don't like gaseous or baggy poems, though likely I've written a good number. On the other hand, I don't care for poems so jampacked that I can't get the drift of subject and predicate and what's modifying what and other handy bones for hanging meaning.

14. I've never been to Italy. I don't even have a desire to go there. I've been to Russia and hope to go to Scotland. They have strict climates and their people are passionate and fierce.

15. I don't dress funny. Nobody has ever come up to me and exclaimed, "Say! Aren't you involved with The Arts?" When I was younger I could have been taken for a soccer mom, which I was. Now I'm often taken for someone who needs help getting her groceries in the trunk of her car, which I don't, or negotiating the dark aisle of a theater, which I do.

16. I have to squint to see the mythical elements in anything, including myths themselves. Mostly they seem stories for primitive people—like religious stories—and I'm neither primitive nor religious. I have a hell of a time keeping track of who did what to whom under what Greek or Roman rubric and what this symbolized or signified, despite multiple reference books in my office, which I display prominently but never use. I do like the notion of barbarians, though, if this is even relevant.

The Girl Who Quit at Leviticus

A blue spot shone on the Methodist Youth Camp
counselors acting out
Smoking, Drinking, Cussing,
sin blue as a saloon. In my ponytail

I left the chapel sobered and sucked in
my breath with resolve
for going through the Bible in one year.
I set out and didn't flag for months.

The Devil, who wasn't big with Methodists,
never took me. There was no Big Fall.

Just that my peppertree, where I climbed high
to read, seemed to call for
The Black Stallion,
The Return of the Black Stallion.

Looped on a slender limb
I read until the night came down.

I went farther and farther
from The Good Book into tales
of mystery and slaughter,
into love and dark achievement,

whereby I missed the angels,
and the pale horse of *Revelations.*

Someone Has Got to Love the Animals

W.C. Fields can love Mae West
and milk-sotted mothers the babies, someone's got to
tolerate upchucks and inviolate loveliness
as no doubt my own progenitor did,
and keeping in mind some say those
who over-love the animals
are missing some necessary part
with people, I still say
someone's got to love the dogs,
the otters and mongooses, goats, ferrets,
long-lashed cows, and the sexual horses,
the grieving elephants, the veal calves
bolted to their tiny barns
for weeks fed only milk, and the gorilla
at The National Zoo, the one who's been to the moon.

God didn't parcel things out even.
To us He gave a brain—an ugly thing,
all wrinkled gray and gelatinous, like the lives
it enables us to waste—and to plants
He gave infinities of green, but to the animals
He gave love, what we can know
or make of it—and don't interrupt me here
with Darwin or cat fights or food chains—
He did, to them, give love.

Jonathan K. Rice

Music

It's 50° and my windows are down.

Bells from the Presbyterian church
on the corner chime at noon
as I approach the intersection.

I'm listening to Mozart
while hip-hop blasts from the car
beside me. We're both in left turn lanes.

He pulls ahead of me as the light changes.
I can hear his music, church bells,
Mozart as I turn past the cemetery,
mosque and fish market.

A beer truck rattles by, airbrakes
hiss from an eighteen-wheeler.

Kids squeal and laugh on a playground.

The aleatory maelstrom,

tonic spontaneity
is unexplainably comforting.

My heart beats like a metronome,
sustains the unfettered,
unrehearsed, unrepeatable,
unredeemable,

the misunderstood.

On Glassy Mountain

after a painting by DJ Gaskin

It's not the slope of ancient stone,
the glacial movement that left it there

nor the low-hanging clouds
and waters they released

not even the voice of the poet
or the bleat of his wife's goats

who once lived nearby,
not the critters or flora

that make this mountain come alive.
It's the one who knelt and placed her hand

upon the countenance of stone,
felt its aging complexion,

its cool sigh of relief and recognition
in her palms as she rubbed

and revealed its perfect flaws.
From one moment to another

it's never the same,
but it's steadfast, always there

anchored in earth and memory.

Dennis Saleh

Yellow Tedium

The shifting fading afternoon
Light pales to a dull faint yellow
As though the sun were a
Bulb left on too long dimming
No it doesn't pale IT Palls
A strickened palsied pastel
Perhaps from an afflicted
Spectrum. A chromatism
Those amber waves we heard
So much about now pout
Across the land untended
And left fallow more yellow
Sand than not yellow can have
Aspirations but like all things
May fall short. A season or so
Yellow become milky or clouded
A child's waxen crayon sun too
Apparent upon a white paper sky
Overly present and taxing
An incongruous yellow. However
Well intended perhaps a yellow
Sagely left unnoted A standard
Furled observance. Quoth an aviary
Eccentric mutely "Yellow more"

Roberta "Bobby" Santlofer

A Crow at My Window

A crow
Flying low and wobbly like a child's paper airplane,
His wings ripped black crepe paper, tossed and damp,
Lands tilted on stick feet,
His legs buckling against a baby pine planted to hold new soil.
On his side now, his head thrusting to rise,
His eyes bulging
He flips over once.
His eyes, now slit & marbled, face a new highway thick
    with cars.

We leave our car,
Walk off the roadway to new soil planted with baby pines
To find the large bird that hit our windshield.
And we find him,
Against a pine trunk,
Body heaving
Now no larger than a thin black oak leaf during a thrashing
    rainstorm.

Louisa Schnaithmann

The New World

We were not prepared for it.
The ultra green of Technicolor
lawns, their red tulips blinding
us, the shacked roofs made
of ripped steel. A girder became
a god then, metal making
houses that screamed in windy
dusk. Violets were the sun.
We wore slacks that glowed
as bright as stars, and on top,
masks to keep the sick out.
We never spoke of anything
but the doom.

Leonora Simonovis

Further Study of the Raft

Hope can't hold
the logs together,

there's nowhere
beyond these Caribbean

waters. A voyage
built on a lie.

People move
from one collapsed

world to another,
visions of food

on phones and tv
screens. But on this raft

the food's gone.
Sunburnt bodies sink,

their throats
full of ocean tears.

Richard Spilman

Contagion

(Latin: con...with; tangere... to touch)

Without touch, the brain wilts.
So we learned from orphanages
in Romania where babies were held
only when fed or changed. Brains,
like hands, reach for warmth
and in its absence fill with fluid
like abandoned gravel pits.

So now we learn what the old
and off kilter always knew:
What it's like to live with emptiness,
the world on its errands whirling
by or watched out the window,
its vibrant song like trapped
waves against walls of rock.

Todd Swift

Anthony Hopkins Slowly Driving Through the States

Desperate Hours behind, Tony left Salt Lake,
Mickey's method tantrums, in a sober wake,
not quite *Deer Hunter*, dear boy—but Demme
and Jodie were waiting in Pittsburgh to start

the Tally script—the Lecter project the fate
he did not yet foresee was in his character;
that Autumn, having just learned to drive—
you had to in LA to survive, even if only

hugging the curb on the way to AA, home
from a bar—he'd motored from the shoot—
the AAA guide on the seat some might fill
with "a pair of tits" (the void better than sex)—

two-star low-key, entering Wyoming and
Montana in the Pontiac, which he'd bought
just to get away; in Humbert Humbert mode,
sans Lolita (his silent *Lambs* script, touched

by notes *his* guilty obsession—Hannibal
fitting his skin like coal in a Welsh seam)—
obscure, not yet an Oscar level, A-list star—
had anyone seen the *Bounty* that far West?—

no Motel operator could have guessed, in
their best Tony Perkins glance of idolatrous
suspicion and desire, they were harbouring
a special guest who was about to make *Psycho*

look as quaint and stiff as *American Gothic*.
The route led to the Grand Canyon; Hopkins,
just a tourist, was able to gaze into his own
long vast deep divided spaces torn by time,

as if an actor's life was a wounded landscape—
now, in December, he was finally out, escape
and fame driving him slowly through the states,
the need: to never have to do a TV movie again,

the ability to show them—*no one more intense*,
after the Damascus conversion (in Westwood,
in 1975—*no more drink* the angel had said—
just live!—and Christ wasn't he past fifty, good

and alive?)—he had about six weeks to get there,
when January would see him in a trailer, reptilian,
reprising *Pravda*, adding the fucking frustration)...
via Durango to Oklahoma City, on to Dallas,

New Orleans and Charleston (ah, the blessed heat,
the palmettos—slave markets—that cannibal sea)—
playing Handel, Mozart, Philip Glass on the stereo,
the windows rolled down, slow, tempted to speed,

sometimes idling, loose yet coiled—a caged panther...
Taking 4,000 miles at a regular nobody's human pace,
sensing up ahead an awful liberating straightjacket
was waiting, and the tongue-tied mask, his *Clareese*.

A Quebec Farmhouse in Summer

I have it in my head
But the sun brings it out
Summer in the Eastern
Townships, evocative place name
For the settled woodlands, farms
Of Quebec closest to the Americans,

Their brutal border; the loyal came
Over, when nation broke from empire;
But there's no history for me but grandparents,
Trees, books, and heat, reading Lampman
Near the hay, the cornfields, the pond;
That quaint rhymer, who knew

How to sound like a British poet,
Then threw a bit more of Canada in,
Like frogs, and days of shocking light—
A furnace he'd called it, Ontario
Out of winter into the open months,
The blazing upturning glory of provincial weather;

In the heather, near the croquet lawn, I sit
With tea and sandwiches, and caravans
Of books, ignoring the dumbass games
My cousins rope the rest into, the violence
Of being young near a forest in July;
There's no reason to relate these events;

No hate or holding back because of skin or birth,
Except my language was policed by the state,
And like all children, I'd seen past innocence
And could relate to the wolves we'd hear
Some late hours, by the window looking out
Onto calm pastures, unsettling depths of firs;

What occurs to me now, is, this was entitled
Terror, my misborn anxieties, the familial disjointedness
A white empire of tedious safeties that only
Seemed spoiled by drink, rage and incestuous acts;
In retrospect, the sun was hot, I survived, to live more,
To write self-interested lyrics of a land

No one has interest in, except the dethroned,
The indigenous who have been overthrown
By successions of invaders gauche as greed;
That grabbing also policed; the language anxieties
In my province have to come from knowing
The root tongue was never francophone, or Anglo,

There were others in the forests besides the beasts;
But in my time, at fourteen, it was ugly puberty,
Lonesome dithering, plunging into writing, self-lust,
And a growing overall miscast apprehension of mistrust;
But it was beautiful, and contained, and, if not
Unmolested, then mainly unquestioned, our right

To loll afternoons to take our time with English literature,
To plan for a future, that, then, appeared uncontested.
How wrong it was to see it that way, any way,
To think seeing back to my childhood or teen years
Has value or heft at all, except as warning or apology.
I was born privileged even in my aristocratic debts;

Whatever was done to me was done elsewhere, worse,
I must ride now across my estates to make repairs,
Until the end of all conquest, when knighthoods end.
But that, of course, is ridiculous, overstated, false.
I've got no horse, can barely scrape together two copeks;
Poems are vain carriers of recompense. I'll try to rewrite.

Flix

Unlocked down, and I am thinking Indochine,
Despite its Orientalist name, is the best band EVER,
Which will be news to my friends, out there,
If they even care, but I am once again in euphoric
Cartwheels, a feeling, such as those are, inside,
That all is incredibly escaped, we made it through,
Not true, if you count the many war dead all told,
If you count this as a war, if you consider it at all.

Prestige *Perry Mason* is on, and is very gruesome,
Like *the Andalusian Dog*, lots of eye cruelty,
Has a haunting aspect ratio, the Depression's
Returned-opened vets, sassy Saskatchewan preachers,
Black LA cops. It reeks weirdly of our own occasion.
I am simply happy to be listening to French pop.
I cannot ever let their Station 13 stop. Repeat!
Dostoyevsky similarly got gripped at roulette.

I love my pet, love my way of standing, my haircut.
The day, the week, the month, the year, out of its rut.
Infidelity is not murder, Della said on the show.
I know Della, Boy do I know. But failing to act
When a ring could have been thrown around the old,
That is dereliction-homicide, maybe, is it not?
The Chautauqua movement would have done better.
Just a thought, Mister Perry, just a thought.

Devin Taylor

Nermal Is Latin for Nothing

For Jim Davis

The night before Dad's major heart surgery,
I smoke a cigarette like a jackass.
Not even a good one, a Camel—
a regular, because I'm all out of Turkish Royals.
I dip the filter in VSOP Courvoisier
I bought on sale at the county store for around $30
and light the cig and stare at the sky
trying to think of something profound,
but all I think of is my college friend
who, four years ago, looked up to the stars for meaning
and instead saw a sickeningly adorable gray kitten.
And I didn't see him then, but sure do now—
with a hood and a scythe and a hot and bothered expression.
I wish I could grab every dot from that faux constellation
and dump them in a cardboard box with no air holes
and ship them somewhere else, like Abu Dhabi.

Mr. Caretaker

You're such a good son,
living at home and taking care of him
instead of leaving the nest:
how selfless and brave, little chickie
(or something along those lines)
said many saggy-fleshed boomers to
me these last couple years, not realizing
(or being too polite to say)
that I can't get a fucking career
even if I wanted to, because
my sanity flew the coup way back
in the early oughts.
And most of taking care of him
entailed going
OUT TO LUNCH
@Chaps Pit Beef off Pulaski Highway,
where an army of Guy Fieris smile down,
where your thin slices of cow
will still moo for you.

I did (and do) love him
though, sort of like beef.

Post-Father

Approximately two years before the end...

I sit down & write a poem about Dad—not *Papa*, not *Daddy*.
Editors love poems about dads, particularly
dead ones; I am an opportunist.

Keith Richards snorted his dad's ashes;
I can't yet, & I'm not sure I would.

Roethke owns the word *Papa* & Plath does *Daddy*.
Father belongs to that guy Robert Hayden.
My father—I mean Dad—isn't alcoholic, Nazi, or understated.
He prefers Beatles to Stones.

Richards didn't intend on snorting dad;
the wind spread the remains all over his coffee table.
"I couldn't just brush him off, so I wiped my finger over it
& snorted the residue..." Richards said.

Dad can snort my ashes if it tickles his fancy,
but he's probably too old. Then again: Richards.
I am a writer, not a rock star. I don't like snorting.
I like drinking/eating/sometimes smoking.

"...ashes to ashes, father to son" said Richards of dad.
Ashes to ashes, funk to funky: we know Richards is a junky sang me of him.
Dad isn't a junkie though; Dad is a palindrome.

I'll write a Dad poem & eat it.

Eleanor Ross Taylor

The Tallow Family

In an undiscovered country lived the candle people. They had arms and legs and nervous systems, they felt grief and dreamed dreams, but their heads were burning wicks and were consuming them little by little.

They had been made by an old woman who enjoyed reading them, their flickers and spills. Before her were ranged new candles in families, joined on one wick, hanging on racks to stiffen, the tallow still warm. Each had a different story inside it when she struck the match.

When Woman was busy with new candles, the Tallow Family held hands and loved one another. Their flickers had joined hands the day the match was struck. Finally came the day when they were burned down to the plate, and the wicks guttered out in a waxy pool.

"I must make new candles," Woman said, scraping up every drop of the tallow with a big wooden spoon, while it was still soft.

But she could not gather up the dreams and love.

How the Horse Came to Be Written by the Donkey

There was a horse who decided to get what he wanted. As a colt he watched the horses in the corral, the ones who butted and pushed and ran with their heads up. He moved aside and followed with the flock. But who should he follow? He tried running with his head up. He pawed the ground. Other colts moved aside and followed him.

His first job was modest, but it seemed he had to have an income.

He did not know why his income should not be more than the others in the department; he went to the office of the chief executive and asked for half time and a raise ... He made as if pawing the hardwood floor.

"I don't know about the raise," the chief said nervously, "but perhaps it's time you got a lighter schedule. At the same salary, of course."

He needed a rich wife. But the desires and expectations of a rich girl were expensive; he found a gem of a prettyish, poor, hardworking filly. By crafty shopping, they acquired the appurtenances of a castle for their stable. They affected Goodwill Store finery with the right amount of wear, old hats of distinction.

He began to be known for his style and ability to get things done. They entertained politicians and small tycoons. He made some small successful runs for office.

In the Governor's Mansion much was made of the First Lady's modest origins, of his legislation for the poor, of his ancestral line back to chiefs in Scotland.

He began to think of immortality.

One day he noticed a small well-groomed donkey following him.

"Go away," he said. "I don't ride."

"I'm not for riding," said the donkey, "but for writing."

Then he saw the donkey, who had stood up on his hind legs, had pulled a teacup from his ear. On the saucer where the spoon should have been was a pencil; the cup was a cleverly designed memo pad. He had the impression it covered a small microphone.

The donkey was observing, carefully, his necktie and his shoelaces. The shoe laces were perfect, but the tie happened to be one his wife had given him at Christmas.

"I don't always agree with my wife's taste," he said confidentially.

"Ah!" said the donkey, lifting his pencil.

And this is how the horse came to be written by the donkey.

J. C. Todd

Winter Love

There was a time when touch
Led the body
And the body followed as if in dream

Your touch in the warm bed
Recalled from rooms too distant to be felt
Not unfelt but withdrawn, perhaps, or withheld

Now snow drifts over hoof prints
Erasing the trail of the horse
Who stands in the paddock, still

How did the weight of what the horse is
Walk off
And leave the body standing vacant

Letter to the Father

Reading Kafka's letter to his father, written in German, penned in his pinched hand,
reading the German, language of my great-grandmother, tongue I do not have,
breath sends its sounds into my mouth that has no practice shaping them

although my mind has practice with the letter to the father, mine,
which I have written in heat, in the tight shoulders and pressed lips
of a mind made wild by restraint, whose voices run on, run over and past the father,

refusing him but pausing for a quick kiss on his cheek,
the goodbye letter I have folded in my pocket
as Kafka's mother, entrusted to deliver his, instead folded it.

It was my feet that wrote the letter of exit, much as Kafka's wrote his,
walking the city of his father to learn the fortress of his father's grip.
Kafka, in a black overcoat walking in the distance, exquisite keyhole

I could slip through into the cobbled street he crosses as if to post the mail.

In Torino,

sweltering. The doors of the bus
    fold back in accordion pleats
and I'm drawn in, folded
    into a swarm of bodies packed
and lurching in concert, breathing
    as if everyone shared
a single set of lungs, the hand
    up my skirt the only thing
not ours and not my own.

Pat Valdata

Small Appliances

Your first marriage, we tried
to talk you out of it.

Who marries the first guy
they sleep with?

But you weren't
a comparison shopper.

Opening the wedding gifts,
you said, "A blender!

Just what I wanted."
He was a blender, all right.

A frozen margarita, no salt.
All about the high-speed

whirr, the dizzy whirl.
Not much capacity.

Then the frappé button
stopped working. No

smoothie, just a hunk of ice.
So you tossed the blender,

chose the crockpot's slow
simmer. Pot roast replaced

party drinks. A couple
pounds of beef, some onions,

thyme. A half-bottle of wine.
A day's delicious aromas

fill your house. Almost
feels like an anniversary

party. There's something
to be said for comfort food.

For dessert, you can still
turn the heat up to high.

Joanne Van Wie

Nipple

I've never told anyone

that I had a third nipple,
that I had it removed
and preserved in a cellophane-like material,

that I use it as a doorbell cover,
that you press it each time you visit
my home.

I've never confessed that when it rings
I still feel it vibrate
like a girl of fourteen,
like a woman of twenty-five,
which is why I smile when I say, hello,
at the door,
which is why I tell you to come again
and again,
anytime,
which is why I wait to answer the door until
you ring twice.

I say it was, my pleasure,
and, *no trouble,*

and I ask you,
is there anything you've never told anyone
that you wish you could share?

because, Lord knows,
we all have strange secrets.

Spider

Stay very still,
I whisper.
I am cautiously searching my peripheral zone because i've heard
we are never more than three feet from a spider.

I'm not sure what makes me the most uncomfortable:
the spider itself,
the three foot distance,
or the fact that I'm never alone.

Michael Waters

Michael

Unchosen, common—
You may know several dozen—
Meaning "bearer of the word of God."

Ironic too—I who remain
Less of a believer than you.

Proof that my mother, Ashkenazi Jew,
Knew an Old Testament moniker—
Abraham Solomon Isaiah—

Would seem odd in our parish.
Abe the Hebe Ike the kike.

Better for me to be one of many:
Peter Thomas Luke
Stephen

And abide by my Irish
Catholic father's dictum:

Never get mad. Get even.

Love Me Tender

And the chorus of frail voices
Swings around once more to the final verse,
A dull underground thrum, cicadas
Vibrating below the earth,
Not quite dead, but returning
On the little wings of words

As Clearance Giddens, aka Black Elvis,
Draws forth the wobbly exhalations,
Some from wheelchairs, some from plush,
Cottony beds of meds, that Haldol haze,
Draws them past 1956 until embodied here,
Doll-slouched & twiggy, in memory care.

When her neighbor, distraught, rattled her screen,
"Dottie, Dottie, Elvis died,"
My mother, scanning the street for EMTs,
Whispered, "Elvis who?"
                                        But in 1977, she knew
The name of her husband, the name of her son.

Now her voice rises too—first that distant hum,
Then the words, *All my dreams fulfill*,
Her dim drone audible, over & over,
Even after Mr. Giddens unplugs his speaker,
Lowers the mic into its foam-cushioned case,
Even after Black Elvis has left the building.

Reptilian

My wife warns me that she always knows
When some ingénue at a garden
Soirée has beguiled me:

I no longer blink, and bounce lightly,
Ice cubes clinking, down and up
Like a gecko, its toe pads

Velcro'd to stone, my body hosting
A flash mob, a silent disco, ecstatic
EDM rave and thrum.

My wife even knows the narrative
Arc of my whim, how my throat
Thirsts for moisture off the sleek

Neck, how my elastic tongue begs
To flick the still intoxicant
Dregs of perfume below

The dangling silver globe
Of one hypnotic earring.
Visitant in my imaginary

Eden, *almost* amused,
Mihaela flings her solemn stare
Across the earthen dance floor.

Window

The not-there where
The sparrow strikes blunt air

Flies no farther
God-thumbed through every feather

Where someone gazes out
Contemplating doubt

Spring pane
Doubly transparent in rain

Summer: always open
Autumn: forked crack / still unbroken

Narrow border
Between breath and weather

Winter pane
Doubly transparent in cellophane

Night mirror
With coal-fire interior

Where my twin gazes in
Contemplating sin

J.T. Whitehead

American Myths / Lincoln flattens the penny

1.

No one knows, originally, just what
The shape was to be, but it was *not* flat.
Men's purses back then hung like the scrotums
On older men. Southern Aristocrats,
Businessmen and Industrial Magnates
Stacked red, black and immigrant heads like Totems.
The sounds of their clanging change gave warning.
The young Lincoln knew they were approaching.

2.

As he conceived of his own coin, conceit
Gave way to his typical modesty.
Looking out upon the vast plains, the wheat
Gave rise, in his woodsman's eyes, to one part
Of what must be one equal half. The tree
Now split showed an almost perfect circle.
Some kind of formula—Greek, logical,
Archaic—*proved* complementarity
And—like a shot in the dark—the notion
Struck him: *I'll flatten those confederate balls.*
Two faced? Well here's one. Consider it done.

3.

The wheat—and that whole "balls thing"—are fiction.

Rosemary Winslow

M Street, March 27

7 a.m. red-bronze sprouts
    blazon maple branches

dark scarlets dot the rose canes
beside wrought iron gates

our Japanese magnolia bursts white stars

I stop in the sweet fragrance
the delicate turning

Winter's a witch made of sugar vanished in yesterday's rain
across the street green-gold swaying
above the row house roofs

under them bright swaths & slices of shadow
    split the faces of houses

I bend down and catch up *The Washington Post*
Up and down the sidewalks
noses of dogs test patches of ground

Men and women on leashes
plugged into oblivion
glide past like phantoms

Like rain the sun falls on us all

This Quiet Time

Today the house is quiet, no rush hour churning through the street
No birds in the maples and dogwoods, not one helicopter, not one star
No sun dissipates the stone sky
A lone man in a spring jacket strains on a leash behind a Golden Retriever
A lone one... everyone is inside or at the grocery, hospital, pharmacy, police or fire
Yesterday construction workers rode the cranes and elevators
going up on Sixth and K
Today no one   Is all the world learning to slow down?
The Japanese magnolia's white stars turn brown and flop to the walk
In New York, Justin and Sarah's wedding is "postponed to July"
For everything there is a season
Wait   Wait in your own house   Wait
The glove that fits the hand stays in the closet, the hat on the shelf
I count every hair in my comb   Someone deducts it from my total
Every breath out of my lungs is numbered
Every sparrow that falls is seen by something unseen
The media say Everyone matters   Some say some don't believe it
Out in the street the maples burst with tiny leaves, up close they look like miniature hands
The linden blossoms and heart-shaped leaves silently bide their time
I notice the white on the window frames outside is whiter...I put down my pen
oh, the sun must be coming...there's a shine now on Deborah's bay window
Now it's gone as the sound of a truck below sweeps through the canyon of air

Good Friday, 2020

Now I'm standing on the sidewalk
outside the clinic
Inside is saved for those inside
Out here I wait   wait   wait
the barren city my company

Above the city,
the sun is falling
in slow motion
down behind slate clouds
I see how steady Sun climbs down her stairs
I see she is far off   and here

Suddenly pure light silver-gold as new metal
limns low hills of slate clouds
Pink blossoms up—a rocket aimed to the moon
Pink stretches arms out over the horizon
Pink chases eastward and quick disappears
High overhead a gibbous moon
unobtrusive pregnant   translucent white
waits for night

Where have all the flowers gone?

And now it comes right to my door:
the Third World War. Riots all night
in the alleys, shootings next block up,
the glorious new windows in the Carnegie
Library occupied by an Apple store
is closed for the virus. Three wars:
skin, poverty, authority.

At Princeton in 1960, three years
after Sputnik, from behind the
imposing desk at which he sat,
R.P. Blackmur seized the neck
of a bottle of whiskey, set it
with force on the polished oak
and declared: *This is authority.*

Hong Kong, Binnish, Cairo,
London, Paris, Kyev,
Barcelona, Berlin,
the Outback, Vancouver,
Africa! Africa!~ Africa!
Lebanon, Central America,
Oh Washington! Oh Chile!
Pablo, where are you? We need you!
Workers are suffering, the poor!

Jorge! Octavio, Frederico, Che!
Martin, Paulo, Dorothy!
We need you! All we hear is
Dominate! Dominate! Dominate!
The radio's president spouts
venomous advice: *Hate! Hate! Hate!*
—Read the faces,
lips, fires, smashed glass.

I think *Kristalnacht*—
but these voices say
they are against hate,
against killing,
against the smashing authorities.
I think of home on the farm,
a baseball through a window—
whoever hit or threw the ball,
whoever was responsible,
paid from our allowance
to make it new.

Down the street, six blocks
from the White House, the red
stone church, a peace memorial
built after the Civil War. The people
hosted refugees from Salvador,
then American white women, black
women, children. O Pioneer,
you led the city in how to be
in what to do. As a sign, two windows
with faces broken and removed
to make way for two who
died for freedom: in round mosaic
side-by-side with Martin Luther's face—
Martin Luther King, who taught us only love
conquers hate. Harriet Tubman, who
risked her life to lead hundreds
of slaves through danger to freedom,
resides beside Dietrich Bonhoeffer,
who learned about freedom in Harlem,
who last resided at Flossenburg, said:
Take my life instead of this other
random person tapped on the back to die.
April 9, 1945, into Hitler's bonfire
with a noose for a garment, he knew
what human freedom is: "This is the end—
the beginning of my life," he said.

Kelli Allen

Jum Climbs the Tualang Tree

Beware the monkey carrying his razor through the forest. Guard your fishcakes, mind the fire! What comes for Jum is older than the Hantu. There will never be enough meal or ripe papaya to sate these hungers. If he waits, stumbles over his own flat feet, the back of that head might fall clean off, maybe the front, too. Then? Only the eyes on their thin stalks will have any purchase at all. Whose story do you want this to be, anyway?

He counts as he plods. He's heard that when the tualang introduces its yellow crown to the canopy, every honey bee is a debutante for exactly fourteen hours. Then comes smoke and ladders high enough to divide sky from earth. Only a proper storm leaves this wood for homes and nights to sea. If the ax fells these beasts, the hands that swung belong to a dead man within the year.

Jum the winnower, the papa's boy displaced in city sprawl. He is a balladeer, a lover of finch whistle and September frond rhythms. But when Jum sings, his mouth fills with honey or rice and the ooze and spill replaces whatever words he longs to speak. The townswomen come every morning to collect the sweet and grains left of Jum's singing in their huge reed baskets, hoping to sell both at the market, or to trade the lot for a single horned cowfish. It's a wicked trek from brush to concrete. A woman knows to cross her arms and wear rock thrush feathers close to the belly.

Jum allows the songs because of guilt. He ends each day by trying not to think of his four sisters still working the family fish shop near his childhood beach. He pushes dreaming aside to complete the nightly mantra, *I'm sorry, I'm sorry, I'm trying. I will sing to fill the coffers. I will sing to pillow your mangos. I'm sorry*. This morning follows the same as every night and he offers seven minutes to the women, slings his pack over his shoulder, plugs ears with cotton, and meets the first of sixteen hundred and two paces to the bus stop.

Today, Jum will see his mother, will bring her news of the city in the drawing he will lay across her plastic table, and will kiss each sister's broad cheek. All without meeting a single eye, not one glance direct or forward. The stops are simple and he memorized them in his first days wandering Phuket: Green line, Nag, Yumm, Cave-tom, and then, Khao. An hour's walk through pine and palm tree, hermit crabs making their way south, too. And home.

Blue-crested kingfishers are tangled in a mating hump when he plants his big feet onto the sandy dirt. Jum breathes slow, lets the rutting birds' noise push into his ears as he pockets the cotton for the return ride. He touched a breast once, he remembers, let the round nipple harden under his palm, before pulling his hand back and away so fast it slapped his chest in the recoil. The geckos creeping the walls and ceilings in Kappa's room fled at the slap and Jum cupped his hat over his bulging crotch and made quick for the door.

He watches the violet—blue tails pulse, seconds counted as his middle finger taps his thigh, sighs away what he thinks might be desire, and walks. He walks slower than tamarins blink, than purple squid ink their captures at thirty feet below. Jum walks as a boy possessed by smoke.

Bull flesh leaches its blood too slow for pacification. The cock's comb leaves a crater fit for a bowl and the slick collects there as it has for centuries. There are no wood piles for Aaron in these thatches. This is work for dirty hands, clay-stained hands. Jum recalls these truths in the moments between seeing the tree and recognizing that the sight means responsibility. He did not mean to wander this close and now, too quick, it was too late. The arrow had witnessed his shoe's rhythm and unfurrowed its sharp quills to poke both head and spine from the tree's peeling bark just in time to let the whistle of *how, then, boy?* reach Jum's groundsel thick ears.

The Sleeping Lady expels her ghost just once and the tectonic shifts under her tailbone mean maybe we will be born somewhere, too. Though, Jum thinks, the banana serpent grows from the forehead as tightly coiled as the jade. It's where the skin husk falls that spills your children's future and buries the fickle arrow in one of three trees. Jum has been selected by a lineage he has avoided for nineteen years crawling and scooting over the dirt.

As is understood, he empties his pockets at once, bows at the waist, lets the waxy-hard fluff fall from his head holes, and nods at the iron-tipped ruiner of all days. When the arrow speaks, it is to name its price. Nothing less, not a bucket gap wide enough for the tongue to taste water. *Seems I'm thirsty and have been before. I'll see you at dusk for my filling. Wasting your left arm and your right would make you more than a green stump of a man, no?*

While the arrow yawned its tip to let rust mark the agreement, Jum let the pale abacus of his mind decide direction. Paces back to the bus, the wait, the wet-rice words for his sisters if he ever meets their faces after the night collects its bargain.

Hours past and lined with paces backward and then, in closing dark, forward to the canopy, Jum greets the tualang with a honk not unlike the dying cranes wandering the rubber factory at the township edge he considered, before this night, to outline the corpse of his childhood. He places two things on the ground under the hollow-spined eyes of the arrow: an iron vase brimming with mustard seeds, roasted, and a bright green bucket warm from chicken blood not even trying to cool.

How often, when waking and letting the first stretch break a morning's silence, do we think about sentience? Neon lights move faster than we ever will and their insistences are certainly bolder than our own. This is the city against what still grows past its silhouette. This is where Jum suspends himself as he thinks too slow, trying to steam engine ahead —a great-great-great grandmother's promise and a burning, acid-bright desire to be down-cover buried in his studio apartment. Jum wants to be anywhere away from the congealing calf-deep wet and the molar-chipping handfuls of spice soon to muffle his already honey-muzzled voice.

The arrow speaks, the tree lets fall the last of its sequin shades, and somewhere too near the monkey tests his blade against his own snapdragon pink belly. *My tip to the tip and no more or less near the shaft you cradle. Hurry, boy, grain crier, lady footed traveler to nowhere far. This is the last of it, of time, of chance and targets met.*

Roberta Allen

The Connoisseur

Why has Isabel accepted Francine's invitation? Does she *really* want to see Francine? Does she *really* want to meet Francine's parents? Does she *really* want to take the train from the city to Short Hills, New Jersey? The last time Isabel took a train to suburban New Jersey was years earlier when she dated a man who lived in Highland Park.

So why is Isabel going?

Isabel isn't quite sure.

Francine and Isabel are sitting around a table, talking, in the garden. Nearby, daylilies and hibiscus bloom in profusion.

Does Isabel smell jasmine too?

"I've sampled men in twenty-seven countries," Francine says. "When it comes to men, I consider myself a connoisseur." She pauses for effect. "On my trip, I barely gave a thought to my so-called husband. That creep was cheating on me for over a year!"

"Yes, you told me," Isabel says.

The evening a couple of weeks earlier when Francine invited Isabel for drinks at The Carlyle, she had boasted about her sexual exploits on her recent round-the-world trip, but it was really her marriage that was on her mind. In fact, once she started talking about her marriage, she couldn't stop. Isabel listened attentively. She felt sympathetic. After all, Francine's husband had dumped her only four months earlier for a dancer who was less than half Francine's age. When he moved in with the dancer, he left Francine the house, which she promptly put up for sale. This is why she is staying with her parents.

Francine has yet to file for divorce.

Isabel thought she was enjoying Francine's company in the bar despite her scathing words about her husband. But later when Isabel thought about all the wine they had to drink—nearly two bottles of the most expensive *Sancerre*—she wondered if it was the wine, not the company that she had enjoyed. Did Francine think that paying the bill gave her the right to go on and on about her unfaithful husband? This too Isabel wondered about later.

Francine and Isabel don't know each other well. When they met at a museum fundraiser in the city, not long before Francine invited her to The Carlyle, they seemed to click even though Francine was flirting with the chief curator, a friend of Isabel's. When Isabel saw how uncomfortable he was, she told Francine he was gay.

He was.

In the garden, Francine, *the connoisseur*, is telling Isabel how to keep men happy in bed—in particular Isabel's current boyfriend, Eric. Francine has never met Eric and Isabel has not asked for advice. In fact, Isabel hasn't said much about her relationship with Eric. Isabel tries to recall what gave Francine the impression—if anything did—that things were not going well between them.

"I bet Eric would love it if you'd tell him your sexual fantasies—it works for me every time. If you can get him to act them out with you, I promise that will be a super turn-on! You have to tell him exactly what you want him to do—even better if you talk dirty. Oh, and I almost forgot B.O.! That's a huge turn-on for a lot of men."

Annoyed, Isabel would like to say that not all problems in a relationship have to do with sex but she stops herself.

What would be the point?

"I bet men find you a bit intimidating," Francine says. "You have a presence. You seem so sure of yourself, so strong."

"That's sometimes true—at least at first," Isabel admits.

Francine's mother, Sarah, comes out to the garden with a tray of iced tea. "Talking about men again?" Sarah says.

"What else is there?" Francine replies.

"When you and Lawrence were together, you didn't think about men all the time."

"When Lawrence and I were together, I was numb. Eleven years with one partner was enough! Sex is dull by the eleventh year."

"Oh, don't be so silly!" Sarah says, laughing. "Not everyone finds sex dull by the eleventh year. "Francine's mother sits down with them and pours the tea. "When will you see the doctor?" she asks her daughter.

"Thursday," Francine replies, then says to Isabel, "I came back here to have Lasik surgery so I won't need glasses. I'll look terrific!"

"You look terrific with glasses," Isabel says.

Ignoring Isabel's remark, Francine says, laughing, "Men will be beating down my door!"

Is she serious? Isabel wonders.

Francine's father enters the garden wearing a black eye patch.

"Good heavens, what's that?" Sarah asks.

"A present," says Francine's father, grinning.

"Oh, you look ridiculous!" Sarah says, laughing. "Who gave you that?"

"The boys. They thought they'd beat me at golf if I only used one eye. But I beat them anyway."

"Oh, you're all little boys! Take that thing off!" Sarah says, still laughing.

"I'm rather fond of it. Makes me feel like a pirate."

"Some pirate!" Sarah says, smiling affectionately at her husband.

"Oh, Dad," Francine groans. "You really do act like a child!"

"I didn't ask you!" snaps Francine's father. "My age has earned me the right to act any way I want."

"Sit down and have some tea," Sarah says.

Watching Francine's mother, Isabel can see that Sarah knows how to *be* with her husband. Sarah has a happy marriage. She remembers now that Francine mentioned at The Carlyle how happy her parents are. But Isabel would have come to that conclusion on her own after seeing the loving way Francine's mother and father look at each other.

Sarah accepts her husband; she even accepts his silly eye patch, Isabel tells herself.

Is this why Isabel made the trip to Short Hills, New Jersey?

To see what a happy marriage looks like?

Isabel's parents fought bitterly until one day her father left.

Isabel still struggles to accept Eric. If only he would be more assertive! Isabel recalls the night in the restaurant when the waiter brought him the baked salmon plate with garlic cilantro sauce, a dish he hadn't ordered. Eric was reluctant to send the salmon back. "The salmon looks good," he said, with a shrug. He only sent it back at Isabel's urging.

Interrupting Isabel's thoughts, Francine says, "Lord knows I've never had a problem attracting men." She crosses her long shapely legs and runs her hand through her blonde streaked hair. "But there are less men to choose from when you hit fifty. I'll have to find my little black book and see who's still around. Maybe David's back from London. I think he went there only to get his branch office going."

"David's married—or at least he was," Sarah says.

"David was married when we had our little fling."

Her father shakes his head and stares at his tea.

Sarah says, "One of those men you know must be divorced by now."

"I don't mind if they're married," Francine says. "I just want to amuse myself while I'm here. After all, I'm not staying. As soon as the Lasik surgery is over and I've figured out where to go next, I'll be off!"

"I wish you'd find someplace else to store your furniture," Sarah says, losing patience. "I don't understand why you need to store all that furniture in our house. Surely you can afford to rent a good-size storage space after selling your restaurant." Turning to Isabel, Sarah says, "That restaurant on the Jersey shore was a gold mine! I can't understand why she sold it."

"Eventually I'll buy another house and settle down," Francine says, "Then I'll want my things."

Until then," Sarah says to Isabel, "We can only use half our house. You'd think we bought this house just to store her furniture." To Francine, Sarah says, "Your father and I do have a life of our own. In fact, we have a very nice life since your father retired. We like living by ourselves."

Clearly, Isabel sees that Sarah isn't happy her daughter is staying with them. But Francine is probably too involved with herself to even *hear* what Sarah is saying. Isabel shifts in her seat as Francine says to Sarah, "I wonder if Gregory is around."

"Gregory is married too, Sarah says, with a sigh. "But I heard Robert separated from his wife."

Robert's so uncool, and he doesn't make enough money. You know I can't stand a man without money."

Though Francine seems to have forgotten about the furniture, Isabel has not.

Isabel is sure Francine's mother has not forgotten either, but Isabel figures that Sarah knows it's pointless to say any more about it.

"Well, I'm sure you'll find someone who suits you," Sarah says, exasperated.

"Yes, I'm sure I will," Francine replies.

Isabel's thoughts keep returning to the loving way Francine's mother and father look at one another. Can she imagine looking at Eric the way Sarah looks at her husband? Whenever she sees that besotted look in Eric's eyes, she can't help herself, she turns away. Isabel wonders if she will ever be able to accept Eric—or any man for that matter. Eric does have many fine qualities, doesn't he? And he *is* assertive in bed. But Isabel has broken up with boyfriends who had many fine qualities. Some of her boyfriends have even been as assertive as Eric in bed.

"Are there any cookies?" Francine's father asks. He has suddenly come to life. He has been sitting silently, staring at the tea he hasn't touched.

Before Sarah has a chance to respond to him, Francine says, excitedly, "I know who I'll call—Jean-Noel! Jean-Noel is always up for an afternoon tryst at a five-star hotel. Where was it last time? The Ritz-Carlton? Or was it The Peninsula? And all that champagne! He knows how treat a girl! And he'll go home to his wife in the evening, cheerful and happy. His wife should thank me."

When it comes to men, Isabel sees now that she and Francine are more alike than she had realized. Weren't they drawn to each other like magnets by their fears of being hurt again? Isabel wonders if Francine recognizes their connection. Probably not, Isabel tells herself.

Isabel sees a wall before her.

A high wall.

A solid wall.

A wall as thick as the wall crazy Trump wants to build at the border.

Isabel thinks about Francine.

Of course, Francine's pain is still raw. But if the example set by Francine's parents didn't help Francine find happiness, what chance does she, Isabel, have of finding happiness with a partner? Isabel begins to wonder if Francine's parents were too much in love with each other to give Francine the love and attention she needed when she was a child.

Isabel sits up straight, closes her eyes briefly, breathes deeply.

Isabel is *not* Francine, she tells herself.

Isabel is *not* her parents.

Just because Isabel's father ran off doesn't mean that Isabel can't allow herself to let down her guard and allow herself to trust, to love.

She knows she'll have to work at it.

Work hard.

Very hard.

Maybe she'll even see a therapist.

Of course, there are no guarantees—

Clutching her backpack, Isabel suddenly rises from her chair, anxious to leave before her resolve weakens.

Francine turns toward Isabel with a look of surprise and says, "Where are you going?"

"I didn't realize the time!" Isabel says, without looking at her watch. She thanks Sarah for the tea and says her goodbyes in haste as she makes her escape from the garden.

Robert R Angell

Stick Out Your Thumb

Oliver hadn't called me since spring break. This called for a little privacy. I took the kitchen wall phone out on the patio, closed the sliding glass door just to the point of cutting the line, then walked the handset as far from the house as possible until the coiled cord straightened as far as it would go.

"Ted took mom on a trip," Oliver said. "They'll be gone a week."

"I thought her boyfriend's name was Art."

"That guy skipped town at Christmas. Anyway. Jack is staying with Dad this weekend and getting dropped at school on Monday morning."

"That means..." I hesitated while checking the windows and doors. In the family room, Dad sat alone with a drink watching an ABC news special about Nixon's proposed ceasefire in exchange for Vietnam releasing our prisoners of war. He didn't care about me anyway. Curtains closed. Nobody listened at an open window, especially not my nosy little sister.

"Yeah, Man!" Oliver said. "Wanna come over?"

"You should have called last night," I said. "Or at least after school today if you wanted to have a party." I rubbed my bare feet on the rough concrete of the patio and looked at the azaleas blooming white against the dark backdrop of woods.

"No party, Steven. Just us."

My heart raced. I started pacing but the phone cord had other plans and yanked me back in the other direction. Tethered to the house, I arced out into the cool grass that I'd cut after school. The bright green scent rose up as clippings stuck to my feet. I wished he lived closer. Life sucks.

"It's almost nine, Oliver. I don't have a ride."

Silence on the line. I heard some animal rooting around in the woods beyond the patio. Then some guy walking on the fairway beyond the woods called to his dog. In my head, I imagined Oliver pouting, his puckered lips, his freckled cheeks, puffy eyes, brown hair falling into them and getting brushed away.

"Ollie," I said. "It's not my fault. I'll be there around noon."

As fate would have it, I desperately needed a change of scenery. Vicious rumors had been flying around school all week that me and my current best friend were faggots. Boyfriends. None of it true. I'd spent the last few days running rumor control and trying to convince William not to dump me. As friends, of course. Like I said, we weren't fooling around, had never fooled around, and I doubted that we would ever fool around no matter how drunk we got.

Some things you just know. Or just know to stay away from, not think, or talk about.

Oliver lived a few miles outside of Annapolis in a community full of old weekend cottages and bungalows. There was a strip of Chesapeake Bay beachfront. He went to River Prep with us in seventh and eighth grades, but his dad, long divorced from his mom, said she had to pay for high school. Between her job, boyfriends, and alcohol, Oliver's bleach-blonde mother was almost never at home. He and his brother had the run of the place, even back then, and I'd enjoyed sharing their freedom whenever I could.

That is, until I met the new William. Over that summer, he'd grown a few inches and filled out. He was just a happy guy, and endearingly awkward in that athletic way. We were in most of our classes together and sat next to each other in the back. Also, William's dad lived within easy walking distance on the other side of the golf course in a five-bedroom split level with a new wife and three step kids. William was there every other weekend. His mom lived fifteen minutes away on the Magothy River side of the highway in a fifties-style house where he'd grown up.

Oliver had switched to the public high school in Annapolis. He'd traded our manicured campus and old boarding school buildings that served a few hundred students for a massive institutional red-brick and glass building that served thousands. I hardly saw him anymore. He had disappeared into a forest of other kids.

Back in the fall of seventh grade, Oliver and I built a tree fort behind my house after school, hand sawing discarded lumber, learning how dangerous a hammer could be. You had to hold each nail with confidence to get it started, and to do that you had to get over the fear of hitting your fingers. Again. You learned trust.

We never held each other's nails, but by the time that fort got finished, we probably could have. The two of us spent one cold, cramped night in there and it rained unexpectedly and dripped in on us until we gave up. Stinky sticky pine resin got on everything, and we got too many splinters. We outgrew the tree house. I soon realized that I'd rather spend time at Oliver's house than in our tree fort anyway.

Oliver and his little brother had the entire top floor to themselves. Essentially a one-room attic. Someone had replaced pull-down stairs with permanent ones tucked in a closet off their kitchen. At one end of the long room, Oliver had nailed up a shower rod and hung batik privacy curtains to hide his bed and dresser. Just like living in a tent. On the other end, Jack had the same setup, except he had a colorful plastic shower curtain.

That left the middle space as a kind of kids' living room with a naked lightbulb on the ceiling, an old TV, a record player, and a box fan in the front gable window. A couple of milk crates and two bean bag chairs served as tables and sofa on a crusty, multicolored shag rug. But it was the free-standing, working toilet positioned against the back windows that stood out.

Shortly after we finished the tree fort, Oliver had me over for the first time. Jack, three years younger than his brother, sat there on that toilet mid-dump and, after a fart and a laugh, asked me to hand him the toilet paper.

I froze, dumbstruck, having been strictly raised that nudity, let alone any bodily function, had no place in public under any circumstances. I could barely change clothes in our gym's locker room, though I noticed Oliver also turned when he dressed. Here was this boy, no inhibitions, no anxieties at all. This household blew away all the rules and conventions.

For instance. Dirty clothes lay everywhere. They didn't even have a closet, just some scaffold thing made out of gray cast iron pipes with random hangers on it that they shared. Each had a chest-of-drawers backed against the knee-wall and it conveniently blocked the gap the curtain didn't cover. Drawers hung open, shirts and pants stuffed unfolded inside. Piles of every little thing you could think of landed on the stained top surface. It was a tangle of matchbox cars, a magic 8 ball, puzzle boxes, belts, empty packs of cigarettes, loose change, necklaces made of beads and chains, a zippo lighter with the hinged-cover ripped off, tin foil, a resin clogged pipe, and a mood ring that Jack kept stealing. On the floor, Jeans and cutoffs, shirts pulled inside-out, nice pants and the shirts that Oliver wore to River Prep, and underwear lay scattered around a laundry basket. Obviously, neither of them played basketball.

I loved everything about it. His side smelled like him, even more so. They lived a relaxed and free life up there, and no wonder Oliver's clothes were always wrinkled. Their mom yelled up from below, but never set foot on those steep narrow stairs.

Of course, I stayed over whenever I could those first two years. We roamed the streets of Bay View in the middle of the night. Went streaking and skinny dipping off the beaches there with other neighborhood kids. Then Oliver changed schools and, well, you know how that works. We kept in touch. Sort of. I knew his phone number by heart, and his mom knew my voice and she liked me.

"OK," Oliver said. "I'll see you tomorrow. Bring swim shorts."

I stepped back toward the house and the cord went limp and re-coiled. Cutoffs, T-shirt? Sure, but I knew exactly what to wear.

My favorite blue jeans were so broken in that they were as soft as cashmere, threadbare blue, and patched in several places where they had worn through. I'd worn them so long that I had to extend the bell bottoms with three inches of some thick, paisley velvet cloth that my mom had lying around. I'd sewn it on myself and it came out really well, just like the patches, and I looked good in them. Oliver told me that once.

Mom hated those pants.

Saturday morning, I got up early around ten and had eggs and bacon at my end of the oak kitchen table. I turned the little black-and-white TV on low to Bugs Bunny. While Mom cleaned up, I asked if I could go to Oliver's for the night. She couldn't say, "Ask your father," because he played golf every Saturday.

"You haven't seen Oliver in a while," she said, loading the dishwasher. Her red checkered apron protected her white blouse. She never liked Oliver much. Said he seemed dirty to her.

"He called last night."

"Oh. That's who called? I hoped it might be William."

"No," I said. Not going to talk about William right now. Nope.

"I'm sorry, Steven. I can't take you all the way down there. I'm having an early lunch out," she said, then quickly added, "With the bridge group." She stood at the sink with her hands stuffed in her apron pockets and stared out the window, probably at golfers on the other side of the trees. The eighth fairway backed up to the woods behind our house.

"I can hitchhike. No problem."

She kept staring out the window. Everyone hitched. Over time, Mom got used to me doing it but said she didn't like it. One day, she said, "Sorry, Honey. Can you catch a ride home after school today?" She never named it and so could gloss over it.

She turned away from the window, glancing at the wall clock. "You'll have to catch a ride on your own if you want to go."

"Good idea," I said. "Could you drop me off on Copperfield on your way?" That would save me a hilly fifteen-minute walk to the road.

"Sure, Honey, but you'll need to be ready in ten minutes."

Eight minutes later, I opened the garage door wearing my soft faded bellbottom jeans, platform shoes, and loose-fitting striped cotton shirt. I juggled a bundle of brown corduroy cutoffs and a T-shirt rolled up and tied with a red bandanna. I had twelve dollars and seventy-three cents, plenty enough for lunch and pizza and a pack of cigarettes. I got into the yellow station wagon and waited, staring at the family room door, the gardening tools, the shelves of old paint cans, rags, jars of nails, the toolboxes, and the saws we used to build the fort. Finally, she came out.

She'd put on a tan pantsuit, fixed her makeup and sprayed her hair. I could smell it on her, along with one of her fragrances, Chanel Number 5, I think. I'd probably given it to her for Christmas. I rolled down my window.

She dropped me off at the entrance to our community on Copperfield Road. She handed me ten dollars "Just in case," and waved as she turned in the direction of the other community entrance. I hurried across the street, my spare clothes bundled under my left arm, and stuck out my thumb.

Three cars went by. Then Mr. Montgomery pulled over in his gray Mercedes diesel with red leather interior and bucket seats. He lived by himself near the clubhouse in a brick rambler with a carport. Guys in our neighborhood laughed at him, but he always stopped for me.

"Where are you going, Steven?"

"Annapolis."

"I'm off to the Giant on the highway. That will get you part way."

"OK." Good, I thought, getting in. I could get a pack of Camels at the store.

He got back on the road. "How is school, Steven? Your hair's gotten long."

"We only have two weeks left before exams so I'm not cutting it again until fall."

"Looks nice long. You're in ninth grade now, aren't you? Sixteen now?"

"Yes, Sir. I'll be sixteen in six months."

"Going to see your girlfriend?" I shook my head. He smiled, eying my roll of clothes. "Parents out of town?"

What's with this guy? "No," I said, quickly. "They're home." Then I wondered if he meant my parents.

I watched the woods and houses go by and sort of answered his questions while holding the bundle in my lap. We stopped at the light to cross the four-lane highway. Annapolis lay southbound to the right. The Giant squatted wide on the other side across a big parking lot.

"I can get out here," I said, opening the door. "It's more on my way."

"You're right. Good to see you, Steven."

I shut the door and hustled over onto the southbound shoulder past the gas station entrance. Mr. Montgomery watched me and waved. The car behind him honked. The light had turned green.

Cars piled up behind the red light as the traffic crossed. A red one with a white top in the far left lane had its right blinker blinking, obnoxiously trying to nose its way over. I noticed because someone beeped at him. The light changed. I stuck out my thumb. Cars leapt forward but the red car muscled its way into the right lane, passed by me slowly, and then drifted onto the shoulder and stopped. I ran to the door and looked in.

The driver had black curly hair, a mustache, a big nose supporting horn-rimmed glasses, wearing an open suede leather vest with no shirt. His cutoffs were so short that the white tips of his pants pockets hung out. I had a pair just like it in my bundle. His left elbow rested on the window, his right arm on a fold-down armrest in the middle of the red vinyl bench seat. The eight-track blared "I'm Your Captain" by Grand Funk Railroad, but he turned it off and motioned me closer with two fingers holding a smoldering cigarette. I leaned in the window.

"Where ya going, kid?"

"Annapolis, then out Pine Ridge Drive."

"You're in luck. I'm headed just that way. Hop in."

I did and held the rolled up cutoffs and shirt in my lap.

"Oh, no problem. We got room," he said, and folded up the armrest. I put the bundle between us on the seat, noticing cracks in the red dashboard. "I'm Harry," he said, and I almost laughed because it was true. His hirsute legs, forearms, and chest gave it away. I almost commented on it but didn't know if he'd laugh or not.

"I'm Steven," I said. We drove for a few lights listening to the chassis creak, then merged onto Route 50, and drove over the Severn River Bridge. I watched the seagulls. He lit another cigarette. "Do you have an extra cig?"

"Sorry. My last one. But," he said, nodding toward the glove box. "There might be some in there."

I found a vinyl pouch with the owner's manual in it, a bottle opener, two pencils, and a dime bag of pot with rolling papers and a premade joint.

"Want some?" he asked. I shook my head. I just wanted to get to Oliver's house. "Keep looking. There. Underneath." He leaned in and pointed. His hand fell and brushed my leg when he sat back up.

I found a crumpled Marlboro pack with two rough looking cigarettes in it.

"There you go," he said, and punched the lighter. "Might be a little old and stale. Sorry. Hope it doesn't taste too funny."

"Thanks." When the lighter ejected, I took it and lit one of the smokes, took a deep drag, my first of the day. I hoped Oliver had some or his mom had left a few. She never seemed to remember how many cigarette packs or how many bottles of booze she had in the cupboard and she kept everything stocked except maybe the fridge. Oliver had a perfect setup if you asked me.

I took another drag. Something popped as the ember got to it. Tasted weird, like tobacco and burning sugar. "What kind is this?"

"It's a Lucky Strike." He looked at me and smiled.

"That's the Pine Ridge exit," I said, pointing.

"Oh, right." He cut across a lane and took the exit. "Sorry, I had a little buzz earlier." He stopped at the light at the bottom. "Left, right?"

"Huh?"

"Turning left? You get high?"

I nodded. "Sometimes," I said, not wanting to sound uncool.

"OK, we'll keep going as long as you do." He turned and we drove on.

They'd repaved Pine Ridge Drive. The blackness of it sparkled up in the bright sunlight, the new yellow lines, the white lines, they glowed. The road felt so smooth, and I took another drag and flicked the ashes into the overfull ashtray.

"This the right direction?" His arm now lay across the back of the seat, his fingers in my hair.

"Hey," I said, pulling away.

"Be cool. I just stretched out," he said. "Is this the right way?"

He moved and I reoriented on the seat and looked ahead, recognized the Junior High passing by me on the right. "Yep," I said slowly.

Harry's hairy leg. It pressed against mine. How did that work? He drove the car with his left foot on the gas and his right foot way over on my side.

"Isn't it hard to drive like that?" I moved away, squinting in the bright light.

"Nah," he said. "I do it all the time."

Wait until I tell Oliver about this weird guy, I thought, and felt myself get excited. I covered my blush with a drag, letting the smoke trail out in an endless stream. I'd see Oliver soon. Another mile or so, then Rocky's Pizza on the right. We ate there all the time. We often walked there from Oliver's place.

I thought about Oliver, and this weekend, then I realized a Harry hand squeezed at my crotch and the hairy leg draped over mine pulling my leg toward him. I startled, like I'd nodded off in class. "Hey," I protested, and slipped out from under the hairy leg.

He stopped on the side of the road and I watched him loom toward me. He pulled his crotch to the side and his hairy penis shot out of the leg hole and I stared and pressed back against the door, hitting him with my roll of clothes.

"Easy, boy," he said. "I'm your friend."

"Oliver?"

"Yes. Close your eyes. I'm right here."

My numbing body slowed me down, like swimming through molasses. Oliver seemed far away. Then the adrenalin hit. I screamed, wedged myself deeper between the seat and the door and fumbled for the door handle. Harry grabbed the bundle from me just as I found the lever and spilled backward out of the car onto gravel and grass. My heart racing, I skittered backwards as Harry lunged.

I ran into the woods. Harry calling my name. Calling for me to wait. Telling me it was a mistake. He wasn't like that. He wasn't that guy. Come back. Everything will be all right.

He stayed in the car, just sitting there with my bundle in his lap staring my way. I stumbled through the trees and tumbled across the parking lot into Rocky's.

Tony recognized me from all those years of pizzas. "Hey, kid. What's a matter?"

"That guy picked me up hitchhiking, and he's out there!" I pointed through the glass door at the red car, doors closed now. It got back on the road and drove slowly forward.

"OK, pal. Come behind the counter here and we'll take care of this bastard." Tony lifted part of the countertop and came out to me, guided me behind, then went to the door in his stained apron, his right fist a massive meatball ready to swing. Tony stepped outside and I could see everything through the glass.

The red car accelerated, chrome dazzling in the sunlight. Tony raised his fist. The car hit the shoulder, braked and spun around flinging gravel everywhere, then zoomed the other way, disappearing around a curve up the road. I closed my eyes.

"Kid? You OK?" Tony asked. "You look a little shell shocked."

I slumped against the wall and slid to the floor. "I don't feel so good."

"Here." Tony leaned down and handed me a coke in one of their red-striped cups. His huge hand engulfed my forehead. "You're sweating, kid. But you don't got a fever."

"The boy's terrified," said a female, the fat old lady that sometimes worked in the back.

"I think you're right, Mamma."

"Hey, Hon," she said. "You eat lunch yet? You hungry?" And without waiting for me to say a thing, she said, "Just a minute."

Tony stared down at me. I know he'd seen me and Oliver thousands of times buying pizzas, staggering out to the picnic table under the oak tree at the edge of the lot. Eating like pigs.

"It's a little early, isn't it?" he said, stroking his chin.

I stared up at him.

"Ah," he said, looking me in the eye. "Something else. What did you take?"

"Nothing. I didn't take any... I'm just trying to get to my friend's house."

Tony glanced outside. "You want I should call the cops?"

"I just want to get to Oliver's."

A fluorescent clock shone brightly on the plastered wall, rings of blue, pink, and white around the dial. I never heard it hum before, louder than the other kitchen noises.

Tony seemed to look me over for a long time. "OK," he said. "Mamma? Put the pie in a box and watch the shop for me. I'm taking the kid to his friend."

Next thing I knew, Tony had me on Oliver's porch. For the first time, I saw the dirty shiplap siding, the peeling paint, the cracked window, the mud-tracked floorboards. Oliver opened the door.

"What happened to you?" He glanced up at Tony as I leaned in against the doorframe.

"He's not sayin," Tony said. "Maybe you could get it out of him? Is Val here?"

"She and her boyfriend went for a sail," Oliver lied. "They'll be back soon."

"Uh huh. Listen, kid. You guys gotta look out for each other. Stop being stupid. You need to talk? I'm here. Gimme a call." He handed over the pizza. "Number's on the box. Say hi to your mamma for me, Oliver."

Climbing up the steep stairs felt like crawling, Oliver behind me, pushing. I collapsed onto a bean bag and closed my eyes.

"Steven?" He knelt, straddling me on the beanbag and shaking me. I wanted to hug him, then the memory of Harry made my stomach clench. "What happened to you? Why did Tony bring you?"

"I..." couldn't talk right then. Not even to Oliver.

Last night, I had plans for us. Hopes anyway. Now I only saw ugliness creeping toward me. I felt weird, then threw up in the toilet. Everything crashed around me. The warnings were real.

I didn't want to be that guy. Not that guy. Never that guy.

Oliver, with his warm hand on my shoulder, looked as scared and confused as I felt. At least we were friends. I needed a friend. Just a friend.

In my heart, I felt a great hammer coming down.

Daniel Abbott Armstrong

Moonstones

After the political debacle referred to as the election of '16, the black squad took to enforcing the unwanted rule—accosting people at random, disappearing others—pushing a cart filled with fear throughout the county. A secret resistance was brewing and in their paranoia, the orange squad could feel its potent whispers.

The orange squad opened investigations into everyone and would try to extort information and useful lies from young parents by shoving/incarcerating their children into snow banks for hours as the parents watched and pleaded. Too long in the snow and frostbite would take its toll on extremities and eyes.

The broken children eventually released back to their distraught parents. Their fingers and toes, ranging from purple to blue, were quickly immersed in lukewarm water, though to the children it felt as if burning. But their eyes...

A fog had descended upon their eyes which had taken on the milky shimmer of moonstones. Their horrified parents feared their vision would not return.

That's where Nurse Sasha came in. No one really knew where she had come from, or if that was even her real name. She was tall and other worldly, her eyes black as buttons, and she moved the way that marionettes move, arms swaying from side to side while her head would dance about on her shoulders.

Sasha with her magic pouch full of remedies and smelly liniments would always appear when the need was most great.

She once had mended Mishka Holodov's elbow with goat butter, fish eyes and poppy seeds when he had broken it castrating a bull. Another time she cured old Vadim's gout with a minty salve and a gentle caress. She also had a special oil made from rendered mink fat, sage extract, corn sugar and other unknowable ingredients. It was this last concoction which she used for the children's eyes.

One by one, she gently applied the oil to each milky eye with a dropper and a paint brush until coated to her satisfaction. Next, she would give a quick thumbnail flick on a wooden match and ignite the oil. Most of the eyelashes would burn about halfway before the oil met them, and kept them alight like Victorian footlights while a larger flame above the pupils thawed the opaque corneas. She would let the flame burn until the eyes cleared, snuffing it with a damp cloth, and a ginger kiss. Each child drifting off to sleep, their parents a blend of shock, awe and gratitude.

Saved from an otherwise blindness, their own eyes now black as buttons, the children's vision would never be quite the same, but more than adequate on even the darkest of nights for recognizing the brutes that put them in that snow.

Jeff Bagato

Air

Why are there so many weird dorks on this website? They all band together to try to struggle against reality, but they don't change it.

All I remember about the talk our teachers gave is basically it'll ruin your life it's so addictive and bad for you. That it's totally barren and devoid of life. No, really, if you smoke marijuana you'll get into heroin and crack, and then you'll steal from your mom.

Yes, in fact, it really does. Once you get it in your bloodsteam you only think about the next time. Look what happened to me. Remember me way back bragging about how I was going to try heroin but "wouldn't get addicted" because of my self-control? Everyone told me I was an idiot, but I wouldn't listen. You could just scroll through my profile after that and watch it just slow.......down......

After a few years, I just wanted to die, but I thought, "screw it, I'm not going out like this, not until I've made something of myself." Now I have everything to live for.

These days, the only time I have to add fluid is after several bleedings. Where this air is coming from, I have no idea.

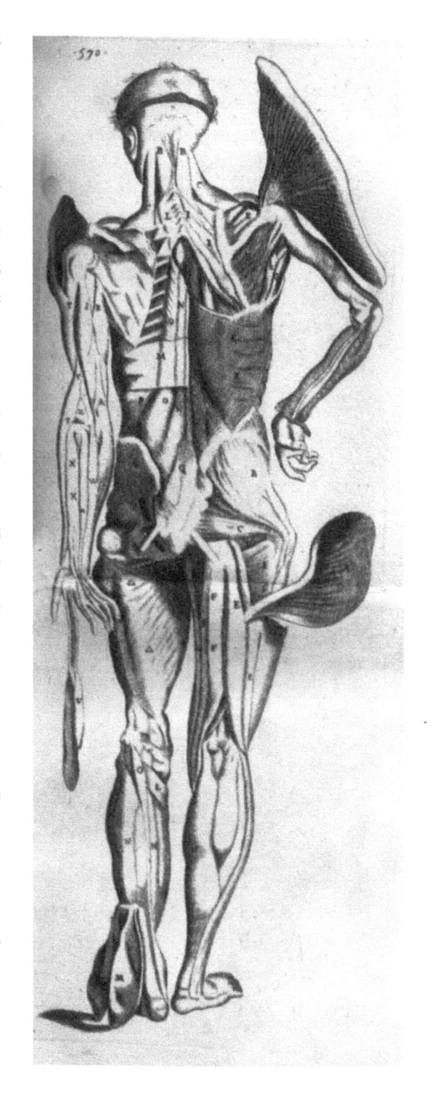

Good Sign

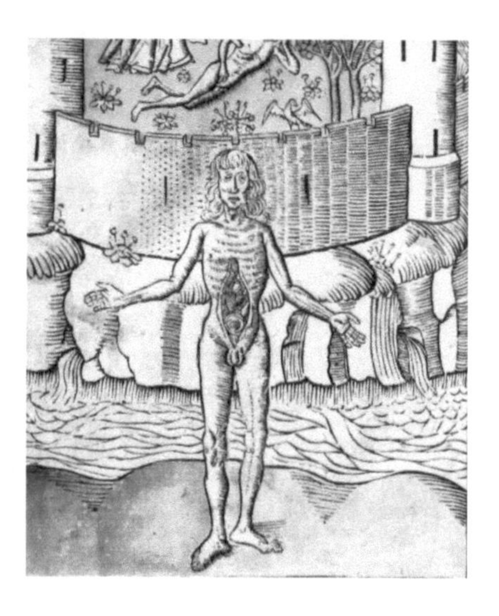

That isn't a good sign.

If she does leave you just because of more options on Tinder, she's likely in for a rough time LOL. Even though women do get way more matches. If they're looking for something serious it can be really tough and require multiple horrible dates. Either way I'd suggest asking her to be upfront as to why she's been cold towards you. Make her confront her feelings, and you guys can move on from there. If she leaves you then do not accept her if she comes back because her Tinder experiment failed. Stop being insecure about it. Women hate that, and she is probably picking up on it. Also, maybe re-evaluate why you are with her.

I didn't date at all in college. I was a virgin at graduation. Then I did OK throughout my twenties, but I was limited to women aggressive enough to pursue me.

Sometimes I'm involved in the VR scene. Considering I don't remember the last time I took my character to bed, I'm pretty sure that's low on the list of priorities. I have legit slept like two.

It will only get more convincing from here.

Guessing Games

Eleanor ignored it until she saw fingers stick out from under the bathroom door. She opened the door, and there's Beth naked, wearing cat ears and a cat tail butt plug. She was clawing at the door... like a cat! Beth stayed in character despite Eleanor's confusion. Eleanor played along and treated Beth like a cat. Eleanor even had bowls and food ready. It escalated quickly to rough cat play, including Beth making those angry cat sounds, hissing and scratching.

Beth came into the kitchen two or three times a day, mewing loudly for milk and food, but after eating very fast she always disappeared. Eleanor missed the purring, contented ball of fur on her lap in the long evenings as she played checkers, or read aloud, or sewed, or played guessing games. She felt rather hurt, too, that Beth paid her so little attention, and several times she tried hard to make her stay, trailing a spool tied to a string in front of her, or rolling a yarn ball across the floor.

After one meal, Eleanor followed Beth to her hiding place in the walk-in closet. When Eleanor came upon her, Beth arched her back, rolled over, and spread out her paws, disclosing to Eleanor's astounded, delighted eyes—no, she wasn't dreaming!—two little kittens, one all gray, just like its mother, the other gray with a white bib on his chest.

Oh! How cute they were! How darling, and cuddly, and fuzzy! Eleanor put her fingers very softly on the gray one's head and thrilled to feel the warmth of the little living creature.

"Oh, Beth!" she asked eagerly. "Can I pick one up?"

Eleanor lifted the gray one gently and held it up to her cheek. The little thing nestled down in the warm hollow of her hand. She could feel its tiny, tiny little claws pricking softly into her palm. "Oh, you sweetness! You little, little baby-thing!" she said over and over in a whisper. Beth did not stop purring, and she looked up with friendly, trusting eyes as her mistress made the acquaintance of her kittens.

Beth stayed in character.

Lingering

Weren't you concerned about that at the time?

People need to be careful to not set precedent for petty reasons that could come back to haunt you under different circumstances.

Another commenter criticised me. I just pointed out something that seemed odd and possibly funny. You were both downvoted even though you weren't agreeing with the initial comment. I've fought mud-frogs tougher than you! Why. Won't. You. Die?! Aaargh!! Stop! I yield!

I had those mega block weapons. The wooden ones belonged to some ogres and the other to some knight. Back then was the golden age. What does it take to make a full six hits to the head? Hmm, so far I've found it a hundred percent of the time.

I spend too much time online, but I don't regret it. I still lead a pretty normal life. My mom deleted my discord account. That was fun for a while, but discord accounts take most of the day.

Someone is lingering at your front door.

Unknown

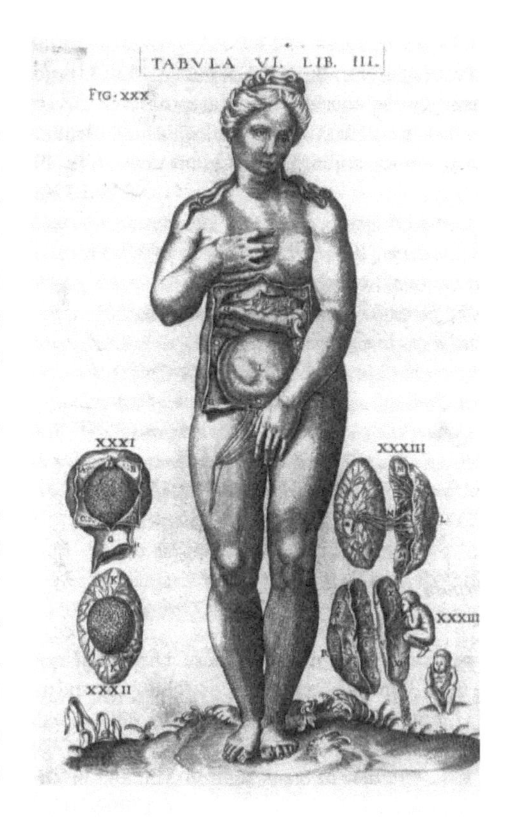

It's normal for girls to go through a phase like that.

Before I transitioned and I still had a working uterus, I went through a super hormonal phase where my body was like, "I need to procreate," haha. But the fact that she sabotaged the condom to get herself pregnant against her boyfriend's will means there's probably an underlying mental issue. I hope you guys can fix your relationship.

Her mom doesn't have to tell her to get one, she can just mention it as an option. Which is rather important in cases like this because that way the minor knows their legal guardian is fine with abortion and would help pay/support her through it so it is actually an option she can consider.

NTA, but there are several red flags here. You need to get her in for some help. It is understandable to want a baby, but she is 16 and her frontal lobe isn't fully matured yet; that's why teens are so stupid. You need to get her to a specialist. Don't get me wrong, I have had tons of friends who had babies at 16.

I was one of those babies.

Tom Ball

32 Fables

Castle in the Air

There was once an eagle who told the other birds there was a castle high up in the clouds if they wanted to see it. But they had to fly very high, as high as they could go.

But when some of the birds went up so high they had heart attacks or ran out of oxygen and fell to the ground.

They were good eating for the eagle.

Moral: Don't believe everything you hear, especially if it seems highly improbable.

The Pig and his Medicine Bag

The pig said he was a friend of God and could heal the sick.

He would give animal clients his wonderful "magic pill."

Of course the pills worked sometimes, even a placebo works.

But the pig changed locations very often so that when animals were unhappy about the treatment he would be nowhere to be found.

Moral: Sometimes positive thinking is as good as anything else.

Freak Show

And so, it was in the year 2029, the scientists implanted a human brain into a monkey. One day soon we will be able to do it with androids as well said the scientists.

Some people however exclaimed that this world was becoming a freak show.

Moral: Humans think they can do anything and they won't stop until they are Gods (immortal and smarter).

The Leper

There was once a man who had leprosy but he didn't go for treatment since he could live an easy life of a beggar. But he lost both arms and although he got some money it was a very hard life. He was a beggar just like many animals are like beggars. Hopeless people and animals.

Moral: Some people's ideas of a livelihood are surprising.

Lying Dog

There was once a dog who told nothing but lies to others. As a result only the most timid of dogs would spend time with him.

He couldn't understand it, believing that he was a great entertainer.

Moral 1: Everyone lies but some take it to excess.

Moral 2: There's a fine line between imagination and lying.

Crazy Owl

There was once a fox who said to an owl, prove to me that you are wise as animals say you are.

So the owl pounced on the fox and killed it and ate it. There's wisdom for you said the owl.

Moral: Don't dare people who are more powerful than you to do things as you may be their next victim.

BC 12 000

The shaman of the tribe was known as a great storyteller. Of course, like any great storyteller, he embellished the tales to make them more interesting.

Indeed it seemed to some peoples that their storytellers never told the real truth.

Moral: There is more to life than truths set in stone. Truth is what you make it. And life is illusion.

Ladies' Man

Once there was a fox who dyed his hair blue. The other animals laughed at him, but the vixens were interested in him. He spoke sweet words to these females. And they all loved him.

Moral 1: Sometimes being different can give you a big advantage.

Moral 2: Sometimes the members of the opposite sex may like you much more than friends of the same sex.

Android Pets

In the year 2120 AD, there were few animals, just those living in parks mainly. Food was all synthetic so farm animals were not needed.

But people enjoyed android pets who were almost as smart as people and some even claimed they were smarter than that.

The androids were programmed to amuse their masters for the most part, and everyone was happy.

Moral: We all look forward to enslaving androids in the future.

The Price to Pay

There was once a lioness who was willing to do anything in order to become President.

So she bribed many other powerful animals with gifts of meat.

And so she won the election.

But once in power she demanded many sacrificial animals to feed her and her fellow politicians.

Moral: When a bad person gets elected, you better watch out.

Keeping a Journal

There was once a certain turtle who kept a journal of events in the forest.

But all the other animals said the journal was boring.

Moral: Some people get more fun vicariously than they do by doing actions.

Justice

There was once a beaver who built a dam and flooded a large area. But the farmer who owned the land took the beaver to court versus animal right's activists.

The court's decision was the beaver had to take down the dam.

Moral: Justice favors the strong. However there are environmentalists who plead on behalf of the animals, usually without success. A human is not equal to an animal.

Deal with a Worm

There was once a certain pig who dug up a worm and was about to eat it, when the worm exclaimed, "Spare me and I will lead you to a place where there are many worms.

And so it was. And the worm jumped on top of the pig's head thinking he was some kind of king.

Finally the pig decided to eat the worm on his head too.

Moral: Betray your own group to try and save your own skin seldom works out well. If you are going down there's no point bringing all your friends down with you.

Bear and the Wolf

Once there was a wolf and a bear who were good friends. They fished and hunted together but eventually the wolf said the "bear was too overbearing."

So they went their separate ways.

A couple of years later they still were alone and very lonely and when they died there was no one with them except the vultures.

Moral: Never underestimate the value of friendship.

Butterfly Album

There was once a butterfly lover who claimed butterflies were the most "graceful of all creatures."

But when he caught them he would carefully kill them and put them in his album books.

Moral: Humans are always abusing the ones they love.

Dull Dancer

There was once a horse who thought she was a good dancer. So she would prance around the farm.

But the other animals said she always danced with the same moves, and it was boring.

Moral: Sometimes what some people call art, others say is dull.

New Anti-Environment Party

And so it was in a certain country a new political party was founded. It was called the Anti-environment party. Members of the party smoked and lived in polluted cities and didn't like animals. They wanted to decrease the amount of parkland.

Some people were outraged but others saw humor in it. Some were serious about it.

Moral: People destroy the environment everywhere. They must therefore not like it.

The Good Bear and the Bad Bear

The good bear never fought or stole and was friendly with every creature.

The bad bear stole and fought with every creature. And he enjoyed parties and dancing and singing.

When the two bears were old, they both said they were happy.

Moral: There are many roads to happiness.

Raven and the Pig

The raven said, "The end of the world is coming." "I don't think so," said the pig.

But the raven said, "What if it was the end of the world?"

"You can't prepare for something like that," said the pig.

"I think you are very brave," said the raven.

Moral: Don't let people distract you from your daily business with improbable claims. If there is a serious problem then cross that bridge when you come to it.

Fighting Fish

There was once a fighting fish who won 40 straight fights. However he was depressed. And then one day he sank to the bottom of his tank and refused to fight. So the next fighting fish killed him easily.

Moral: Every great fighter is weak and tired sooner or later.

Man in the Moon

So it was the first moon colony decided on a Noah's Ark type deal. The question was which animals would roam under the Moon dome.

Most common pets were included, and lots of birds, but no one saw the need of predatory animals.

Some animals complained they were no better than zoo animals, but nothing could be done about it.

Moral: Humans will decide which animals survive into the future. If any.

Dream of Dancing Foxes

A certain rabbit kept having the same dream. In the dream the foxes were all dancing and singing and entertained the other animals.

But when he told his dream to other rabbits, they said it was a wonderful dream, but totally unlikely.

Moral: Many animals dream of strange things, just like humans.

Love and Old Age

There was once a feral cat hanging around a farming area. He had known masters and he had known freedom. But in his youth he loved freedom more. But now he was getting old so he approached a farmer who picked him up and brought him home. There he met a nice female cat and had babies with her and everything was lovely.

Moral: In youth you need freedom, in old age you need love.

Dreams of a Panda

A certain panda in the zoo had a dream in which the animals were outside the cages and the humans were inside.

He hated those gawking humans...

Moral: Some creatures have nothing to look forward to other than dreaming. Without dreams they would be lost and insane.

Dreams of a Goat

The goat was always dreaming he had the whole mountain to himself.

But in reality he had to stay on steep slopes to avoid predators.

He thought to himself no one can take my dreams away from me.

Moral: For some people and animals lots of sleep and daydreaming makes them feel better even if it is an unhappy life.

Pig Girl

There was once a young girl who cried a lot. So her father put her in the sty with the pigs.

Social workers discovered her however one day and they brought her back to "human civilization."

However it was difficult for her to adapt to human society and she could hardly talk.

Finally after many years of therapy she was more or less a typical human although she often grunted as pigs do. And she taught pigs to play the xylophone. And she even taught pigs to beat the drums with their hooves.

And she was an advocate of more rights for pigs. She said most farmers kept the pigs in small spaces where they could do nothing but eat.

Moral: No matter how wretched your past you can always start all over again.

Lion Maze

Somewhere in Africa lived a very rich man. And he had built a beautiful large maze.

In the maze lived a male lion and there were sophisticated cameras all around the maze.

The rich man enjoyed putting animals and humans in the maze, especially humans to see how they fared with the lion.

Moral: There will always be those who enjoy others' suffering.

Goats in Danger

There was once a family of goats on the mountains. Every now and then a group of wolves would steal one of the goats. But they were smart enough to not take too many.

Said one wolf, "We are just like farmers."

Moral: Some animals are very cunning.

Cricket Killer

A certain man devised a machine that could zoom in on crickets' sounds and spray them with poison. He hated the sound of crickets at night.

It worked well and soon everyone wanted one. So it was goodbye crickets.

Moral: They'll get rid of insects step by step.

Daydream of a Bear

Said one bear to another, "I've got an idea for an animal-human Olympics."

And he said, "We could have events such as throw humans as far as you can. Or starve humans as much as possible or eat humans. Or make them run until they drop. Or make them run around without their fancy clothes and make them try to survive in the wilderness. And so on."

Moral: Many animals hold grudges against humans. So too some cruel humans treat other humans cruelly.

Masked Personalities

There were several women in the town who started wearing masks with an angelic halo above their heads.

It wasn't long before the fad caught on and soon in this city and others many were wearing masks of some kind, often indicative of their personality (e.g., some wore wolf masks.)

Then one day everyone was wearing masks, some people having many of them and they wore them all the time.

Moral: It is difficult to know who someone is anyway. It's a world of mystery.

The Last Animal

One day in the far future the super humans had a party for the last animal to die. Henceforth only highly intelligent androids and humans would walk the earth. To them animals were all primitive idiots.

Moral: And so, there were no more fables.

Joanna Biggar

Avignon

She saw him before he saw her. From the flower stand at the corner of the grand avenue leading from La Porte de La République, she watched, half-hidden behind sprays of lavender, orange and yellow lilies, bouquets of wildflowers and red poppies, clutches of sunflowers. As full and fragrant as if it were not 1917, as if the war were not still going on. Her black eyes shifted as she followed his military stride, easy to see with the sun reflecting off his long, shiny boots. The nearer he came to her, the more she could make out the tall form of the officer in his smart uniform, the cut of the jacket with its gleaming brass buttons, the angle of the visored cap, familiar, yet foreign. An American. The heat of the Provençal sun, filtered through the elegant arbor of plane trees, made him appear and disappear, as if in a game of *cache-cache*. Then, when he was close enough for her to see his face, he paused to get his bearings, scanning the end of the street to find her shop, Fleurs de Provence. She was surprised at the beauty of him, the angle of his jaw, the rugged, oval face, the shock of blond hair visible just below the cap. She was surprised to find her pulse rising.

That was before she looked into his eyes, the translucent blue of a lake fallen from a summer sky. She blanched to realize that they were staring at her, that he now saw her in a way she had not yet discovered even in dreams.

Bonjour, Mademoiselle. Je cherche une certaine Violette Rocher, qui je crois travaille ici. Je m'appelle Lt.-Colonel Mark Beausoleil. Lt.-Colonel Mark Beausoleil looking for Mlle. Violette Rocher. He lifted his cap, bowing slightly, revealing more of the white-blond hair, but none of the rush of thoughts running through his mind. He stared at her unblinking. He had come for a letter informing him of what was perhaps seditious activity, to be delivered to him from a small hilltop village by a brother of this shopgirl. But he had not imagined stepping into a lush corner filled with the colors and scents of Provence, staring into the flashing black eyes of a chestnut-haired beauty in a high-collared white dress.

He, an experienced army officer, thirty-eight years old, a man of the world, he had not expected this.

"Oui, Monsieur le Colonel, je suis Violette Rocher," she replied stepping out from behind the sunflowers, then adding, "But you speak very fluent French, Monsieur," leaving off the phrase, "for an American," and not remarking that it was French with a quite peculiar accent.

"Yes, well I have been in France since 1914, some three years now. I have learned a few things." He smiled, revealing a warmth that never showed in his guarded eyes. "As for my

French, it is almost '*ma langue natale.*' I am a native of Louisiana, you see." Trying to regain his composure, he did not offer more, and she did not ask.

He did not know how long he stood in that fragrant circle of sun before continuing. Perhaps she did not notice. Perhaps she was simply patient. He would not let himself imagine she felt anything more. "Yes," he said at last, "I believe you know why I am here."

"*Oui, Monsieur, la lettre.*"

"Yes, the letter. I was informed your brother would send it to me here, to be in your care until I could collect it." He tried not to admit the disordered thoughts coursing through him as he watched the slender, perfect form in the white dress turn back into the shop, dark hair flying in ropes of curls. There was something more about her that attracted him, too, though he could not name it. And when she turned back to him, the black eyes held steady, filled with messages he could not decipher.

"*Voilà, Monsieur,*" Violette passed him an envelope, which he did not see, from her small delicate hand, which he did.

"*Merci.* I will return soon with a reply. Perhaps tomorrow." He straightened into his stiffest military posture, and turned to walk up the boulevard.

Marc-Antoine Beausoleil passed a restless night in a hotel near the Palace of the Popes. There was the matter of heat, of course, always a factor in a Provençal summer. And there was the matter of the letter, the purpose of this visit to Avignon, and which he had read and reread during the hot night. He could barely grasp its tumultuous implications, nor how to respond, while the memory of the hand that had delivered it was searingly clear. As were the auburn strands of those dark curls as they shimmered in sunlight. And the eyes, carrying worlds and wonder in their blackness.

He had thrown off the night sheet, baffled by himself. This young woman, a French shop-girl, seemed to have gripped him in a way none of the high-born, silk-clad belles of his life as a Southern gentleman and Army officer had. Nor the ladies in New Orleans, San Francisco or Monterey, nor the dark, sensual senoritas on the Mexican border with whom he had found great pleasure. Many women had given him that, but none had invaded his dreams.

He glanced at the clock in the corner of the room and saw it was nearly six. An early riser by habit, he jumped up to meet the day, shaved in front of a warped mirror over the porcelain wash basin, and threw open the shutters on life beginning to stir in the street. Vendors shouting as they assembled their vegetables and wares in kiosks on the nearby Place des Châtaignes, horses clop-clopping over cobblestones, massive church bells ringing in the day all over the city.

In a darkened corner of the hotel's dining room, he lingered over his café au lait, his brioche, butter and apricot jam, grateful again that here, inside the walls of Avignon, it was easy to forget the war. But his polished boots and pressed uniform also reminded him that it was different now that the United States was actually in it. And now that his days of wandering observer, information officer—and intelligence gatherer—as roaming Military Attaché assigned to the American Embassy in Paris would soon be over. Now he was an Allied Army officer slated for active duty again, eventually to rejoin the cavalry, which the new Military Defense Act had just authorized.

What luck that this in-between period had brought him to fulfill this last mission here, in Avignon, while he awaited new orders. Retrieving the letter left by Jean-François Rocher—and formulating a response, which he had not yet been able to do—gave him an excuse to delay his mission and to revisit Fleurs de Provence and the intriguing Mlle. Violette Rocher perhaps more than once.

By late morning, a suitable time to return, he estimated, he stepped out to retrace his steps down the Rue de la République, a changed, and possibly vanquished, man.

It was hot, and J.J. slowed her pace accordingly to go the short distance from where the Fleurs de Provence must have been to the terrace of le Café du Soleil. She chose a shaded corner and slid easily into the cane-backed chair with its comfortable tapestry-covered cushion. The old-fashioned doorway with its lintel of Tiffany glass, the patina of chair arms polished by years of sitters like herself—including herself decades before—all things that offered a world of the past gave her comfort. The past, after all, why she was here. First to discover the real story of her Grandfather, Marc-Antoine Beausoleil, her Grandmother, Violette Rocher—and from it some truth about her own life.

How strange, she thought, at a few years shy of fifty, to realize huge and important pieces of her own history were a mystery to her and that it seemed necessary to find the past to know the present. How strange to face the odd fact of her own incuriosity about it until now, she who had been relentlessly curious about all the lives and stories around in her life as a journalist, playwright, fiction writer. And most of all, how very strange, after fifteen years since she'd pursued the disappearance of her dear friend Melanie, to find herself again now, in 1989, in possession of letters and information that would lead her to the unknown story of someone very close to her. Or "someones," she reminded herself. Because this was Gran's story, too.

She summoned a waiter and ordered a *citron pressé*, a favorite drink for hot summer weather. Something Gran herself had made for her as a child sitting under the great avocado tree in Pasadena. As her tall glass of lemonade began to sweat into rivulets, she recalled the last time she was here thinking about Grandfather. That Paris year, in 1963, so long ago. She remembered sitting in this very café, imagining how Grandfather had probably come here with Gran.

That was likely true, but much of what she had first conjured about the meeting of her grandparents had not been. Her head swirled with images, information, with questions surrounding them, but she now knew what she had not known when she was younger—that it would take time and patience to put this puzzle together. That she must not rush.

She pulled her chair out from the table to bathe a little in the magical sunlight of Provence, drawing her large sunglasses down from the top of her head onto her face. *Yes*, she told herself, *slow down, find the rhythms of this place again, go with them. Yes, put it all aside, especially the work. This is time out for a new direction. This is the time to find their world and live in it until you know what you need to know.*

With resolve, she stood, put some coins on her bill, turned to walk up the Rue de la République toward the Palace of the Popes, settled under a wide-brimmed straw hat as defense against the sun, and determined to make every step take her into the Avignon of 1917. Had Gran worn such a hat, she wondered, glancing at the silhouette she cast on the street? Her mind found its way back to those days when her grandparents strolled here, when the wide boulevard had been filled with carts, laborers in *sabots*, and soldiers in their hard visored caps striding fast among darting children, while the citizenry in fine coats and long dresses clung to the shade near the edges, glancing at the latest headlines: the great underground explosion south of Messines Ridge near Ypres; rumors of ration cards for bread and sugar; the arrival of American troops in June. But for her grandparents, she knew, the conversation was of a deeper, more private nature, as they spent those few free and desperate days filling each other with the stories of their lives and with the import of the letter that had brought them together and lay between them. How she wondered, in sunlight strong as it was now, was it possible for them to admit the darkness, too? But she knew they had.

J.J. pulled herself to the sidewalk to stop in front of the great window of a fashionable leather store, as if she were contemplating a purchase. She wanted to linger and let herself hear the words that Violette and Marc-Antoine had spoken to each other, to follow the thread of how those crucial days had unspooled. She took a handkerchief from her handbag and pushed back the straw hat to wipe her brow, seeing her tall, curvaceous reflection in the glass. *Nothing like Gran*, she had to acknowledge, not for the first time. Then she glanced up to see a sign pointing to the church of St. Didier.

Her pace slowed, along with her heart, not from tracing some memory of her grandparents, but from a flood of her own, and she turned down the block to the ancient church into the warren of medieval streets beyond.

Past the old walls of the church the square in front gave way to Rue du Roi René, and suddenly her ears pulsed with the sounds, whispers, sighs, laughter of Roland Montrefor as he took her hand and waltzed her down this street, for if there were a word for him, for them, it would have been dance. *My God, J.J.*, she could hear his funny, lyrical accent, *but come quick to make some reparations to this great king, because, you know, he cannot forgive that you do not know him.*

The great king, Roi René of Provence who championed justice, believed in prosperity for his people, *who was, you know J.J., a superbe poet and loved all the poets and had these festivals—incroyable—for artists and musicians, my God, what parties they could have down there in Aix at his palace."* She continued down the street with the great king's name, where corner stones, fountains, benches under shade trees opened memories like petals unfolding on a stem in her brain. When she reached the crossroad of the Rue Grivolas, she gasped and turned up it.

She would not cross Rue du Roi René in search of the remains of the church of Sainte Clare d'Avignon, whose history she had not thought of in decades, but which came flooding through her now in Roland's words. *That, chérie, is where Pétrarque, le pauvre, saw Laure for the first time on Good Friday, 1327. That is where his love and his misery for life began. My God! Can you imagine it? To be in love with a woman for life who will not have you. Who is married to someone else, who maybe doesn't know you are even alive. No, no, J.J., it is too much. You know how I study my philosophers to learn the truth, but when Sartre says "l'enfer c'est les autres," I think he is wrong. Hell, my dear J.J., is a lifetime of love never returned.*

J.J. walked fast up Rue Grivolas as if to outpace the story she had no intention of revisiting. Just as she had no intention of bringing forth her love affair with Roland, so safely buried in the past. Yet, there she was following that street, her feet flying with the sure-footedness of a dream, up three blocks to the façade of the old stone building—*foundations from the 14th c.* Roland had laughed—where on the 3rd floor his professorial uncle's apartment filled with leather and old books looked out over a stone courtyard with a fountain. Where with windows thrown wide open to the star-streaked Provençal sky she had lain night after night in Roland's arms, herself naked and open and mad with the touch of him, everywhere at once, mad with the sound of him, making her sing with him in words of no language she knew. Making her drunk with him as he loved her in every way possible, in ways she had never been loved before or since.

She rushed past the building with its assault of uninvited memories, finding her way automatically to the small streets leading to the Palace of the Popes. This was the time to follow the footsteps of her grandparents, she told herself, and no time to wander in the dead ends of her own past. *My God*—even in her own mind, the words came out in Roland's voice—she only allowed herself limited remembrances of that far-away romance, mostly from the time when she met him in Paris, when she had first realized that his impish, curly-haired good looks, his enthusiasm, purity of spirit, and off-sided humor reminded her of the Little Prince. And she had blessed him with the nickname.

She pushed aside what her body remembered even if her mind refused. Forgetting her feelings for him was the price she'd paid to also forget the cruelty of her leaving.

Dennis Desmond

All in a Day's Work

The parking lot outside the union hall is where desperation lives, bounded by wads of blackened chewing gum baking on the asphalt in the mid-day summer sun, battered pick-up trucks, and the industrial-sized dumpster whose sliding door won't ever close.

It isn't easy to make it to one's vehicle without being accosted by the individuals who hang around the lot. These are the guys who avoid the inside of the union hall where you have to play by the rules, the guys with limited life choices, for whom construction is one of the few options, who can't hold a job even when the jobs are begging. They range from the I-need-a-job so I can fall-off-a ladder and sue, to the honest guy down on his luck.

It's not my job to talk to them. I hire agents to do that. But sometimes I get cornered, and there are times when I want to talk.

Not to Tony, though. Tony served 17 years in prison, for what I don't know, but 17 years is a bad sign. He got fired from the two jobs I put him on, threatened the lives of the superintendent and his family, and one of my agents as well. "Never meet with this guy alone," I advised my agents.

Now it's just me and Tony, face-to-face, a few feet apart. I'm cornered between two rusting Chevys, shielded from public view. My bad, taking a short-cut through this part of the lot.

"Hey, I been here all morning," he says, "waiting."

He knows I'm the Boss, the Man. He's chewing a wad of gum. Slowly, deliberately, his gaze fixed on mine. A fly buzzes nearby but my eyes do not leave him, alert for sudden movement. My heart pounds in my chest. I wonder if he has a gun.

"I know I done bad," he says.

His short-clipped brown hair sticks up in different directions, he is unshaven, and his sunburned, white arms are slathered with tattoos that have wandered their boundaries.

"I got control of my anger. I need a job."

I've crossed paths with Tony a few times in the past year. I've never seen him like this before, never seen him show any contrition.

Neither one of us speak for a moment.

"I'll see what I can do," I say, at last.

Tony spits his wad onto the pavement. He steps aside to let me pass.

I let my breath out when I get inside my vehicle, hands on the steering wheel.

Tony lied to me. And I lied to him.

On the way out of the lot, my tires flatten the clump of newly-deposited gum.

Patricia Eakins

Still Lives

If you have a back yard, maybe you know what it's like to go out there when the house is settling down for the night. At that hour, the sky has darkened, though it is not truly dark; your world has turned inward. You walk a few steps into the dark, calling the name of the lost cat—"Mousy! Mousy!"—looking anxiously into the falling night toward the hole you have been digging in the rocky soil for weeks, a hole deep enough for the full-grown pear tree your sister Sally has promised you, a hole invisible way out in the lawn. *Mousy is a scaredy cat. Usually she stays close to the house.* You turn around to look behind you, then see the warm opaque glow of the shaded windows, and the light-spilling square of the single unshaded window—the kitchen window which frames the life of your household as if it belonged to someone else. Maggie, your older daughter, is washing the dishes, and Caitlin, the younger, is drying. This is as it should be. They are doing their assigned chores. You do not expect to see Pia, the "mother's helper,"—if you call it helping to play with the kids most of the day like a kid herself—you do not expect to see Pia, who goes to her room after dinner—or James, who goes for a stroll and a smoke and would be farther out in the yard somewhere.

You see the cutting board, rutted from so much slicing; the rusty, mismatched canisters; the battered metal bread box with decals of your grandmother's time, the yard-sale china drying in the dish rack. Through an arch you see the dining room with its street-find chairs, no two alike, around your husband's aunt's scarred table. You see apples in a celadon bowl wheel-thrown by your neighbor down the road. An unframed painting by James of other apples in that bowl hangs crooked; the postcards thumb-tacked around the painting, of James's favorite works of art from the world's museums, have bent corners, from James taking them down so often, to examine them more closely and muse on how he yearns to visit the "living works of art" in Paris or Amsterdam or wherever they are—but he has responsibilities, he says, and sighs. From the lawn, you "see" those bent corners even though you are already too far away to see the postcards, let alone the corners, as you back further into the dark, calling for the cat. You see them with love for the life you have and then you don't.

Because suddenly there is a flash of light from the third-floor window that is the top half of a door onto the fire escape from Pia's room. Pia is framed in the window, looking down at the top step of the fire escape where sweet gray Mousy sometimes crouches. Well, Pia had said she would look for Mousy there. She doesn't seem to see the cat and lets the curtain fall back over the window, but not before you have seen James right behind her, his chin nestled into the top of her head And—like that—your heart shrinks into itself, smaller and smaller, until it is a stone, your body cold around it.

You stumble back and back and still further back until you fall backwards into the pear-tree hole. You have hit your head, and it takes a moment for your vision to clear. You cautiously swivel your head and raise your arms one by one, then try your legs. One ankle has bent too far and may be broken. Your foot flops oddly at the end of your leg. It hurts like hell and you cannot bear to put weight on it, or even move it, so you cannot climb out of the hole.

You need help. *Call out!* you scold yourself. The windows are closed, but sooner or later they will hear you, will they not? James, Pia, your girls, and Ellen, Maggie's friend who has joined the girls drying dishes in the kitchen—now you remember, she is staying overnight. But why bother? They would not hear you; the girls are laughing and tussling, rushing through the dishes so they can play "Go Fish" in the blanket fort they will have made in the dining room. You can almost hear their peals of laughter where you lie crumpled in the hole around your throbbing ankle.

But James—on an ordinary evening he would return to the house after his stroll and his smoke. Any minute now he might look up from the battered club chair where he is reading *Lust for Life*, the novel about Van Gogh which he has returned to again and again in the twenty years since you first met him in a café in the East Village. He'll pull off his reading glasses, rub his eyes, look around, realize you are missing—but no, no, he would not be in his chair, he would have gone out to smoke right after dinner; he must have ducked around to the fire stairs that lead up to Pia's room. *Was it only tonight? How long has he been sneaking up those stairs?*

Pia is buxom—you have to give her that—buxom—and blonde, of course, though indisputably—indisputably!—plain. A plain twenty-three-year-old who is in no way special, unless you count Swedish as special, or twenty-three, or blonde and buxom—though, face it, twenty-three is more special than forty-five with stretch marks below the navel and gray at the temples. But you are a cook and a gardener and a wife and a mother—and a skilled photographer's assistant who drives an hour and a half each way to Manny's studio where you do the portraits, and sometimes further when you have a wedding—group shots and solos and candids—you get home late—you prefer a class of graduates to shoot one by one in a booth in a school gym—half a day and you're done. You have to have Pia, or someone like her, because James's passion for his art is so consuming, he can't be bothered feeding the girls or seeing they do their homework or even feeding the cat. And great art—uncompromising, true art—just doesn't pay, people want sentimental crap, the painterly version of your wedding pictures, so you have to work, though when you moved to the country from the city, you thought you could live from James's occasional gallery show and the paintings he sold through the Real Art website. If it weren't for your sentimental crap you'd starve.

So. You drive three hours a day. At least. Hoping your car doesn't throw a rod or hit a deer. And Pia looks after your daughters and cleans and tidies your house and feeds your cats. She goes to her stifling attic room after dinner; it is part of her contract; she is off duty then: she does not have to clear the table or do the dinner dishes or get the girls to bed unless you're stuck on a long shoot. Most nights she is free to stick her pods in her ears and listen to her music, whatever that is. She closes her eyes and sways to its beat. She yawns ostentatiously. She stretches luxuriously. She climbs to her lair via the inner route, the steep staircase at the end of the upstairs hall. You hear it creaking, then the door of her room opens on its squeaky hinges and closes.

Not long after James rises, casually mentioning the need and desire for a smoke, as if it were a new thought he had not had the night before and the night before, cracking his knuckles, rocking back and forth on his heels a few times, adjusting his underwear under his jeans, ambling out onto the porch, the not-yet-lit cigarette already between his lips as he steps down onto the darkening lawn.

Where does he go? You used to wonder, in—oh, a kind of abstract curiosity—for you knew everything else about him—your artist husband who had made his career painting you and the girls and the artifacts of your life together, your teapots and candlesticks and vases and board games—and every last flower from the cutting garden: pink peonies, white phlox, blue delphinium.

He paints the girls in leaf-light, shadowed by the lattice of the gazebo, Maggie sprawled on the bench, reading a Wonder Woman comic book, Caitlin, her knees drawn up to her chest as she hunches on the wooden floor, one hand on Mousy's head, studying a swallowtail that hovers above a magenta coneflower.

James paints the tomatoes and basil and chives and squash growing near your blue kitchen door. He paints what you cook and artfully arrange for service —your green salad studded with orange nasturtiums, your mocha chiffon cake, ganache oozing from between the layers, drizzled with raspberry sauce and topped with a crown of candles and a wreath of daisies, as if the cake were a Lucia virgin come singing on Christmas morning with coffee for those still in bed, Christmas in July, Pia said, as she came bearing coffee for you and James in your bed, in her gossamer white nightgown through which you could see her dark nipples and pubis and the hollow of her navel, Pia wearing the Lucia crown she had brought from Sweden just for the American children who wouldn't know this custom, the crown with its candles lit—as if Pia were a cake.

But that was last summer. You had almost forgotten. Before you fell in the hole, you were wondering where in the yard you'd see James smoking as you walked backwards over the lawn, calling for Mousy. "I'll make you a new catnip sachet! I'll let you sleep on my angora shawl. Mousy!" The fireflies winked and danced here and there, now and then flashing in front of your face. The frogs were singing; some call it croaking, but you have always known they are singing—in the boggy place between the lawn and the woods. "Mousy! Mousy!" You could barely see the darkening house with its squares of opaque light in the rooms with drawn shades, the bright light spilling onto the lawn from the kitchen window that no longer framed the girls. They must be under the blanket draped over the dining room table. When they tired of cards, they would call for James to tell them a story about when he was a little boy. And James would take the inside stairs two at a time to knock loudly on Pia's door. "To hell with your contract, Woman," he would say. "Tell a story of when you were a little girl in Sweden," as if Pia were the mother and her family's stories were our family stories.

"Mousy! Mousy!" You called and called before you fell. Where was Mousy and where did James go to smoke? The yellow eye of the cat did not burn before you, nor her blind eye shine white. No plumes of smoke were visible in the gloaming, nor did you see the glowing red tip of the cigarette. You needed to find Mousy before a fox or a fisher or a coyote did. You wanted to see if your husband stood behind the garden shed to smoke or walked up into the woods to loiter under the big old hemlock that deer hunters had long ago built a tree stand in—or perhaps he climbed up into the tree stand and crouched on a branch to smoke. You wondered. And you followed him because it did no good to ask.

"What is this? I step out in the cool of the evening, enjoy a smoke, see what stars are out. Can't I go for a stroll without you getting on my case?" So he said when you confronted him that one time you did. He was unkind, yes, and defensive.

So tonight you casually mentioned that the smallest cat was still out. You walked through the blue door calling her name well before the girls started clearing the dishes from the table, while Pia was still fiddling with her ear buds, because you worried that Mousy, with her crippled hind leg and her blind eye, had not come in at feeding time as the other two cats had. What if she had wandered out onto the road and been hit by a car? You hadn't heard a car, but some cars are quiet. You stepped off the back porch calling, "Mousy! Mousy!" but she did not come, not even when you crinkled the packet of feline treats you carry in the pocket of your jeans, a sound which usually brings her to curl around your ankles, purring. She did not materialize from the gathering darkness.

And James is nowhere to be seen either, though before you fell into the pear-tree hole you peered all around the yard for a James-shaped shadow. He was not standing by the rose bush, inhaling its fragrance mingled with smoke, nor was he lounging in one of the Adirondacks on the lawn. He was not inside the gated gardens, nor was he sitting on the bench beneath the apple tree. He was not standing with his cigarette glowing red beside the two old Subarus you call cars, looking up at the sky in wonder, as you do even in the hole. You are the one who knows the names of the constellations. He has never been much interested in astronomy or even astrology, and anyway there are no stars tonight. A haze of cloud covers all the twinkling brights and obscures the moon.

Through the line of scraggly trees along the river you can see the sodium-mercury vapor arc lights of the town hall parking lot, but the lot is empty. The town supervisor, the town justice, and the town clerk have gone home to their own houses further along the river, which is high tonight after some days of rain, roaring rather than burbling. If you were to call out you'd have to yell, and your call might be mistaken for the howl of a coyote, one of the tall, gray-brown ones that lope on lanky legs along the ridge of the mountain looming above you.

There are rumors about packs of coyotes surrounding hikers or blueberry pickers, though no one knows anyone to whom this has happened. People scare them off by banging pan lids, it is said—who walks out with pan lids? These stories get started; who knows where they come from? Some people like to frighten themselves, but those people are lounging around in their living rooms gobbling popcorn while they binge-watch British mysteries. They are not people who have fallen into a hole too deep to climb out of with a broken ankle, but not too deep for a coyote to leap into, snarling and snapping. And who do not even have their phone with them.

Poor Mousy!

You moan, and someone moans back—not so much a moan as a mournful hoot—an owl cruising the dark for prey. You moan again; the owl hoots back. You hear the rustle and flap of wings as it passes overhead. Then you hear the pawing and snorting of deer, somewhere nearby, but not near enough to see. It is altogether dark now. You see eyes gleaming here, then there, you hear coyotes padding in, you hear a low growl—maybe it is human footsteps you hear, the growl is a sound you are making from deep in your throat. Or maybe it is James, pissed off to be disturbed when he was reading *Lust for Life,* his favorite book, the only one he ever reads.

"It's not what you think," he will say later. "I was changing a light bulb for Pia. Then I went back downstairs." He realized you were gone and walked out to find you—though if it were him padding toward you, would you not see the beam of his flashlight bobbing up and down as he walked over the uneven ground crisscrossed by vole tunnels? Would he not call your name?

"James!" you say, "James!"

After a moment the owl hoots back.

Among the twinkly fireflies, you see the Lucia crown, its lit candles guttering in the wind that blows down the mountain, floating over the lawn as it moves towards you, the white nightgown a diaphanous veil intermittently visible in the night, the body a shadow gliding and turning within the veil, appearing and disappearing. And then there is only the crown with its flames, and then the flames go out, one by one, as if someone had extinguished them with sharp gusts of breath. You did not see a face highlighted in the dying flame-light, its bones shining around its dark eye sockets. There is only the crown, then the night. "Pia? James? Help me!" The owl hoots in reply.

Sharon Goldberg

Quarantine Companion

On day 801 of the pandemic, after months and months of quarantine, Alicia ordered a companion on amazon.com. She lived alone and she felt lonely. The companion she selected had earned excellent reviews, the supplier had a five-star rating, and their return policy was generous. They even offered a two-year warranty. Alicia feared if she didn't act quickly, the seller would run out of product just as others had run out of toilet paper, N95 masks, and antiseptic wipes.

The companion arrived via drone drop on her front steps in an 18" by 18" cardboard box. Alicia slipped on her mask, washed her hands, and pulled on rubber gloves. She lifted the box, carried it to her garage, and opened it. She removed the companion folded inside and found his activation instructions and a plastic bag containing his clothes taped to his back. Alicia transferred the companion and accessories to a clean shopping bag and carried them to her kitchen. She removed her mask and tossed her gloves in the garbage.

Alicia unfolded the man and sprayed him with Lysol. Following instructions, she pressed his belly button to activate him. He expanded to full size. Constructed from a gel substance, the man's exterior looked and felt like skin. The version she'd ordered had black curly hair, green eyes, and a medium build. Alicia dressed him in his khaki pants and maroon pullover sweater. She pressed his belly button again.

"Good afternoon," he said and smiled. "What should I call you?"

"Alicia," she said, and smiled back. "What should I call you?

"Whatever you like."

"Jeremiah," she said.

Jeremiah was handsome, but not distractingly so. Alicia did not want a mate, a lover, or boy-toy. She did not wish to exploit Jeremiah; he slept in his own bedroom. (There would be one interlude after they watched *Dirty Dancing*. Mutual. No regrets.) Alicia hungered for conversation. And she needed help around the house. Heavy lifting. Repairs. Cleaning. Jeremiah shopped for groceries and picked up prescriptions. He waited in line at the post office and Home Depot. He picked up food from her favorite restaurants, the ones that were still open. Since he was not an actual homo sapiens, Jeremiah was not susceptible to the deadly virus.

Together, they cooked and ate dinner, played Scrabble and Yahtzee, screened films and binge-watched Netflix and Hulu shows. They debated politics and discussed philosophy. They listened to music and worked out to YouTube videos. Jeremiah participated in Alicia's Zoom book club. And he was programmed to cut and color her hair and give her deep tissue massages.

In time, after research and more research, after testing and more testing, the FDA approved a vaccine for the virus. The country sighed with collective relief. When the entire population was inoculated and the quarantine lifted, people emerged from their homes. They returned to work and school. To restaurants and bars. To beauty salons and tattoo parlors. Alicia resumed her normal life.

"You don't need me anymore," Jeremiah said.

"You're right," Alicia said. "I'll give you a great review."

"Thank you. Remember, I'm still under warranty."

Alicia pressed the companion's belly button and deactivated and deflated him. She re-folded him neatly along with his clothes. She placed him in a box and stored him on a shelf in her bedroom closet.

She'd bring him back out during the next pandemic.

Sarah Golkar

Flight from Your Old New York

Date: 5/26/2006

One Way Ticket, Flight#6576

Departing/Departure time: LGA, New York City, NY. 5:35pm

****TRAVEL WARNING:** You are leaving a fanciful childhood dream behind, only semi-actualized. Friends, lovers, artists, ballet dancers, street performers, your super, your lunching professor-friends, the Met and its docents with their watchful eyes, the clap of high heels on the steps of Lincoln center, the smell of the subway and its deafening halts, the yappy dog in the apartment above yours, the mailbox with your name on it in the vestibule of that Williamsburg apartment, the hipster kid who thought he was a writer who sat on your front stoop at 2 am and talked only about himself, reading Kerouac aloud over half a pack of cigarettes and a bottle of cheap wine, the parties with all the dark and lonely people in the dusty warehouses with paper mache igloos for making out and bags of cocaine that you admired but never touched, even the man on the street corner who whistled at you on your way to school, to work, the bodega, the drugstore, and the doctor who said you weren't getting better, but most of all the sound of the city at 5am and the way the morning light flooded the spaces between the buildings into your bedroom where the boy rolled over to kiss you before he left for the last time. You, like him, caught in the debaucherous undertow clamoring to make it out alive.

Destination/Arrival Time: AUS, Austin, T.X. 7:39pm

****TRAVEL WARNING:** They say when you leave New York you ain't going nowhere, but they also say everything's bigger in Texas. For a while you will feel ashamed of returning home. The piercing quiet of slowing down, a reminder of your failure to thrive. You'll move into a co-op with a dozen other misfits, a sturdy wooden house with a porch swing and an Australian shepherd. You'll quit smoking, learn to cook, and start drinking sweet tea barefoot on your front porch to pass idle afternoons. You'll sunbathe next to dreadlocked hippies along the banks of spring-fed swimming holes, and take long drives with the windows down along the eastern edge of the Hill Country. Watch blood-orange sunsets burst across big skies on warm summer nights, cicadas whirring applause. You'll stop writing for a while, but slowly, words will form in your minds eye that you'll put on paper. You'll take hikes through forests with steadier boyfriends and bottles of Lonestar beer, sit under a full moon, and think about how it's the same one you've always marveled at, and of the many things you were and will become. And one night you'll skinny dip in the Guadelupe river with new friends, float on your back and look at the stars, feel the adrenaline pulsate, the heavy sky on your skin, and smile.

Pamela Gordon

Lap

Hank was her boyfriend. Everyone in the family said so. In the photograph of the relatives sitting in the front room in the rented house steps from the beach—stucco, hydrangea, and a long staircase leading up to the door—she sits on his lap. It did not matter that he was her cousin, or that he was twenty-four and she was four.

Next door lived Hannah, who had a daughter her age, or was Hannah the daughter? They made houses together on the beach by tamping sand into yellow plastic pails, turning the pails upside down, and sliding the pails up. If the tops of the houses caved in they molded them with more sand. This way—along with a shell or a seaweed strand or a bit of wood they placed on each top—the houses were distinct in an otherwise cookie-cutter community. All stood at attention in the morning sun until neighbor boys barreled down the beach howling, and knocked them down.

At first she cried and ran to her mother. Her mother wore a kelly-green one-piece every day. The color seared into her eyes, making it possible to spot her mother no matter how far she drifted from her. Her mother comforted her but didn't stand up to the boys. Hannah, or Hannah's daughter, didn't run to her mother. Hannah's mother or Hannah never came to the beach. She hated sand. Her mother in her kelly-green suit, with low-slung wooden chairs, a blanket, towels, baby oil, and the infant brother led the two girls to the beach in the morning and led them back at noon for lunch. Lunch on the Hannahs' front porch was payment to her mother for the morning caretaking. Lunch and the pitcher of what the mothers called, laughing, "Lemonade." They sucked on their drinks and their cigarettes, filling the girls' cups from a different pitcher they called: "Your lemonade," and saying: "You can have some of ours when you're older."

As the weeks progressed the mothers let the girls go down to the shoreline earlier and earlier, alone. This resulted in more planned houses standing for a longer time before the mid-morning arrival of the Godzilla boys and their monster whoops. By the end of July, the boys and girls were taking turns burying each other deep in the damp sand once the houses were demolished. Then they'd unbury each other and plunge, shrieking, into the foam to be washed. No matter how hard the ocean beat her she still had sand kernels in her crotch when she peeled her suit off at the end of each day. At night she fell asleep to the waves pawing the shore. Sleep was a dream of rolling over and over inside the waves, scratchy sand between her legs, salt and brine marinating her skin, her limbs and face sun kissed.

The picture of the relatives was taken in August. Everyone glowed in white and black. Her mother had pulled her curly hair into a half-pony. She wore a white dress with smocking across the chest and shiny black Mary Janes with white anklets trimmed in lace. They were the first shoes she'd worn all summer. She had walked around the rented house, the streets, onto the beach, barefoot, so that even though the shoes fit they were pinchy. She would wear them to school in September when she started kindergarten.

In the picture she sits on Hank's legs which are crossed. She sits on the knee on top of the other knee, his leg extended, as if she's perched on a branch. She was his favorite. Everyone said so. He had a moustache and a large nose. She doesn't remember another time she sat on his lap. She doesn't remember ever being alone with him. Years after the picture was taken, he married a woman everyone agreed was stunning but remote. They had two sons, and divorced. He married two more times and had more children.

Other cousins, now women, all of them older than her yet younger than him, roll their eyes whenever he is mentioned. She hasn't seen him in a very long time. When they come face to face at a family funeral he looks at her and says her name with satisfaction. After, she sees him with his third wife, across the room. He grabs the wife, kisses her mouth, holds on to her a little too tightly.

Karen Guzman

Pilgrims

"I could live on coffee and pastry," Lily says. And as if to prove the point, she licks her lips, her little pink bow of a mouth, and lifts the glass mug in a silent toast.

"Don't you mean cafe latte?" Jerome teases. "That's what you're drinking."

But Lily's eyes are closed. She's lost, relishing the sweet sharp drink and the tickle of foamy milk against the roof of her mouth. "Oh, right. Cafe latte. Sorry, Mr. Continental."

She's traveled all over Tuscany eating like this, closing her eyes while a look of rapture transforms her face. Jerome envies her ability to lose herself so totally in the moment, to embrace every sensual offering. Two days ago she stood in the duomo in Sienna, head thrown back, eyes wide, lost in the vaulted ceiling with its flow of sweet-faced saints and stars and the glory of God shining through the painted heavens. Jerome watched until his heart ached, and he had to look away.

Today is Assisi center day. They've been staying in the city, in its nattier suburban edge, more than a week. They have a three-room flat in an old renovated house. White chickens peck and strut in a wire pen in the yard. One escaped yesterday and strolled down the street with an air of great importance until Lily lured it back to the pen with a bag of popcorn. The flat is cramped and the water pressure is terrible, but there is an excellent *panettteria* on the corner. The yeasty sweet fragrance of baking bread wafts down the street every morning, as they can walk to the train depot.

All week they've been day-tripping to ancient medieval towns full of narrow streets, gray and austere, where eons of feet have tread, where countless people have dreamed and died. In each town, they have found an astonishing cathedral, or duomo, whose builders tried to etch a vast God into the soaring, glittering walls.

But they have yet to visit the old, walled center of Assisi, where the famous Basilica of St. Francis dominates the mountaintop. It rises above the stone streets, flanked by hillside groves of olive trees with delicate leaves that shimmer in the December wind. They saved Assisi center until today, because Jerome has a feeling about the place, about seeing the Basilica and St. Francis' crypt. He tried to explain it to Lily as their plane left Bradley International Airport outside Hartford, rising over the forests, the tidy neighborhoods and soft rolling countryside of Connecticut.

"When should we see the Basilica? I mean, what day?" he asked. They had three weeks in Italy.

"Not right away," Lily said.

"Why not?"

"Because you're so hot for the place. I believe in delaying gratification."

"Oh, right. Since when?"

"Anyway, don't you want to prepare your heart, young man? For the kingdom of God will be at hand." She closed her dark eyes and folded her small hands, fingers flashing with silver rings, beneath her chin. She liked to tease him about religious things. He didn't mind. She was such a skeptic. Once on an early date, he asked her over dinner what she believed. She took a sip of wine and swallowed. "Oh, everything," she said, "and nothing." The corners of her mouth turned up in an impish little grin. "Do you know what I mean?"

And the funny thing was, he did. He began knowing during the years at Wesleyan, all those nights he walked the campus alone, crossing the grassy common, passing beneath towering oaks and maples. He pondered the universe, while his classmates got drunk at dorm parties. He would pass by lighted windows, vibrating with thumping bass lines and the throaty cheers of a game of quarters. DRINK, DRINK, DRINK. The girls cheered and tossed their hair, sitting Indian-style, long legs folded over each other, giggling on beds.

When he attended these parties, Jerome couldn't stop staring at their legs, imagining them, Oh God, clutched around his waist, bare and slippery. When at long last after one such party, a sociology major from Wisconsin with orthodontia perfect teeth did wrap her legs around his waist, lying beneath him in his narrow dorm bed, he felt a life force rush through his body with holy clarity. He fell back on the bed, panting and marveling. So, this was what everyone was talking about. How could he have ever made any important life decision without knowing about this first?

Still, he wavered another year before deciding he would not join the priesthood. Not now, maybe not ever. He consulted professors and friends and family. They all told him to give it time. Seminary could wait. Be sure first. He was already sure about one thing. The lid had been torn off the mystery box, and to his surprise, the box was bigger and deeper than he had ever imagined.

Lily, annoyingly enough sometimes, seems never to have doubted the vastness of things. She celebrates contradiction. She loves crossword puzzlers and brain-teasers.

"Francis saw God in everything," Jerome told her on the plane. "I read this book about the lives of the saints back at Wesleyan, when I was still thinking of the ministry."

"God, I'm glad you didn't do that." She wore black jeans and a fluffy lime green sweater that made her eyes glow like Jade. Her heavy, long black hair fell around her shoulders. She had pulled the top back with a rhinestone-studded barrette. Something always glitters on this girl. She is tiny actually, five-foot-one, with delicate, pointy features. She looks younger than twenty-nine. And Jerome looks younger than thirty. His rusty auburn hair waves back from a strong, yet soft, face. There is something vulnerable in the thinness of his upper lip, a slight downward cast in the corners of his mouth that makes him look mournful and contemplative. His body is lean and athletic, the kind of body that can adapt to any demand. It has adapted to Lily with a force, a consuming desire that almost frightened him at first. There had been other girlfriends of course, but this desire was like a baptism, an anointing with holy, erotic oil. He had learned at last how to be a happy animal.

People comment on his youthful appearance all the time. It embarrasses him. "You're an associate vice president for development? You don't look a day older than my son." Well, he'd moved up fast at the American Red Cross. He has a knack for the place, for translating its mission to a world of bottom-lines and apathy. At parties, he likes to say he "shakes people down for a living." Corporations, charity foundations, government agencies, anyone willing to part with a few bucks. The Hartford chapter of the Red Cross has exceeded its fundraising goals the past two years, largely due to Jerome. His strength is simple. Hurricane-wrecked villages in Honduras, earthquake victims in Iran, blood shortages in California hospitals, all these matter to Jerome, and it is his gift to be able to make them matter to other people.

"Tell me more about Francis," Lily said, turning to face him on the plane. "I'd like to know a little about the man before I disturb his grave."

Jerome explained how Francis turned his back on the petty strife of men. How he rose above the politics and corruption of the church. How he came to stand for true ecumenism, for the divine in everyone, in everything.

"I scrapped seminary after reading about Francis," Jerome said.

"He inspired you?"

"I don't know that he inspired me, but he made it OK for me to walk away. Do you know what I mean?"

"All I know is I'm glad you did," Lily said.

"Why?"

"You know why."

By this time they were over the vast Atlantic, and the flight attendant was bumping the drink cart down the aisle.

Eight days later they are climbing the stony streets to the Basilica. "Today's the day," Lily said in bed that morning. "It's Francis-time!" She jumped up and did some hip-hoppy dance steps across the room.

They stop for coffee at a café within site of the Basilica's tower. They sit around a tiny metal table with just enough room for their drinks and the plate of golden pastry—something glazed and filled with cool cream—that Lily is devouring with moist-eyed bliss. "God, am I gonna have to hit the gym when we get home," she says.

"You've got nothing to worry about," Jerome says. It's his automatic response. She is not fat, not at all. But he has yet to meet a woman who doesn't worry about weight, and he has learned a stock answer is necessary. He drains his little espresso cup. The dark, heavy shot spreads like warm lava into his stomach and through his veins.

When they're done, they leave the café and start the walk up to the Basilica. A biting wind sweeps down the street. Ceramics shops, shelves and windows blooming with colorful bowls and platters, line both sides. Other shops, tourist places, peddle St. Francis kitsch. The legendary, bareheaded monk in his brown robe stares out from posters and dishtowels and refrigerator magnets. Jerome rolls his eyes. "You can bet he never dreamed he'd end up on a teapot."

"Oh, I bet he's thrilled. He's probably turning cartwheels in heaven right now," Lily says.

"Are you kidding me? He was a simple man. I mean, he wasn't after rewards or fame. He saw himself as a servant of the people, of all creation actually. He never wanted to be buried in such grand style, either."

"Then why was he?"

"Well, he wasn't originally. He was first placed in a pauper's grave up in the hills somewhere. His followers later moved his body to the Basilica."

"The dead offer no arguments," Lily says. "But he must be glad now."

"Why would he be glad?"

Lily turns, a look of exaggerated patience on her face. "It's all turned out so well, hasn't it? I mean, look at this." She sweeps her hand along the street. "Look at all these people coming here, seeking whatever it is they seek and leaving happy. Isn't this what matters now?"

Jerome takes her gloved hand in his and pulls her arm. Then they are kissing, pressing up against each other in the street, bundled in overcoats and scarves, laughing like children. Her lips are warm and alive beneath his. She throws her arms around his neck. "Someone has to set you straight, boy," she's says.

"And that's your job, I suppose." He takes hold of her long ponytail.

"It is today," she says.

A sharp wolf whistle pierces the air. Jerome and Lily drop each other, as a grinning, dark-haired boy of perhaps ten passes by, pursing his lips in a kissy-kissy mouth. A woman in high-heeled boots and a red leather coat grabs his hand. "Fabrizio," she hisses. "Comportati bene! Behave!" She pulls him along the streets.

"Maybe we should keep the street groping to a minimum?" Lily says.

Jerome looks up at the tower of the Basilica. "What would Francis think?" he teases.

"Oh, he probably groped a thing or two in his day."

"Lily, he was a monk..."

"Was he gay?"

"I don't know. I think I remember reading something once, some speculation, but it's just rumors, conjecture. People see what they want to see."

Lily shrugs. "I'm just guessing those monks had to, you know, break down once in a while, cooped up together day in and day out, year after year. A few sparks had to fly."

They pause before climbing the long, cement staircase up to the Basilica.

"You're feeding the rumor mill," Jerome says, and she laughs.

At the top, they follow a walkway that surrounds an open lawn before the Basilica. A life-size crèche with ceramic figures sits in the center. Christmas is over, but it is not yet New Year's. "Spooky," Lily says, taking Jerome's arm. "I think one of the shepherds just moved." It is just past noon, and sun floods the face of the Basilica with creamy light. It's a simple stone face, humble compared to the grandeur of some of the churches they've seen.

"It's smaller than I thought," Jerome says.

"Yes, but remember there are two buildings, an upper and a lower. They're linked." She's been studying the travel books.

Stepping inside the Upper Basilica, there is a sudden and profound hush, a silent proclamation that this is a place steeped in its own mission, a place where the outside world will not intrude. A small sign near the entrance asks visitors to maintain a respectful silence. Cool, clear light fills the narrow center aisle. A vaulted ceiling arches high overhead. Clumps of tourists move down the aisle, meandering toward the altar. Others stare, eyes raised, at the famous Giotto fresco paintings depicting scenes from Francis' life that line the walls.

Jerome pays their admittance, pulling the euros from his wallet, mentally calculating their worth in dollars, a habit he can't shake. He unwraps the scarf around his neck and turns to look up the aisle. Then the stillness of the place slows his heart. It draws him from the glare of the world back into himself, into the core of all the things he carries.

"Great God almighty," Lily breathes, turning in a slow circle. "The Giotto frescoes. They're more magnificent that I ever imagined." Her lips part and she moves to the wall. She knows a lot about art. She's an assistant curator at the Wadsworth Atheneum in Hartford. They met at a Red Cross fundraiser the museum hosted. Jerome was drawn to her gleaming black hair and large, almond shaped eyes. And to something else, too: her exuberance. The outbursts of laughter, the jerky way she gestures with her hands when she gets excited. He had always been drawn to quiet girls, ones who seemed manageable. Then suddenly he was standing, glass of Cabernet in hand, before this luminous girl, watching her lips move, her eyes glint, and he no longer needed to manage. It was as if a wire deep in his brain tripped, saying, "Let go."

They tour the frescoes one-by-one. Lily studies each and points out its features. The paintings are intricate, dream-like, muted in soft tones of earth and gold and sky blue. Here is Francis renouncing worldly goods. Here, giving his cloak to a poor man. Here, preaching to the dovelike birds. Jerome stares into the serene painted face, ringed by the glowing halo of a saint. The face doesn't betray a hint of human emotion, just a peaceful detachment, a serene certainty, as if Francis knew then what was to come.

Murmurs rise all around.

"Here's the death scene. Check out the angels," an American accent whispers.

"Slow down, John. It makes absolutely no sense to come all this way and then speed through the place," a British woman pleads. Jerome recognizes some French and German, too. A cranky baby, little face twisted with fury, shrieks from a stroller.

Then a deep voice comes from above. "SILENCIO. SSSHHH." Jerome and Lily freeze. There is a sound system. The Basilica is wired, and this stern Italian man is telling everyone to shut up. Jerome looks around. Near the door, a plump, middle-aged monk in clunky dark eyeglasses and brown robe sits in a wooden booth. "SILENCIO. SSSHHH," he insists, leaning forward to speak into a desktop microphone. Between warnings, he collects donations and sprinkles holy water from a tiny glass jug onto objects the faithful offer. An old woman with a lacy, black veil draped over her head holds rosary beads out to him.

"Don't fool around, do they?" Lily says. "I wonder if they throw people out."

"I'm going to sit down, OK?" Jerome whispers.

She studies him a second, the way she does when she's looking through him and reading what's really going on. "Sure." She has a sixth sense when it comes to his moods. Sometimes he doesn't even have to explain.

What he wants is a chance to center himself. He doesn't want to overhear conversations or bump into tourists or be scolded by a monk. He heads down the center aisle and slips into a pew. He wants this moment to register. He exhales slowly, hearing the air leave his body. He doesn't pray as much as he used to, but he thinks about God. A lot. The problem with prayer is since he's not sure who God is anymore, he doesn't know how to talk to him. But he is certain he will discover a new way, a new language, if he just keeps trying.

Lily meditates. She says it brings her to this incredible stillness, as close to the divine as she has ever come. He wants to try meditation. Maybe when they get back to Connecticut. He glances into an ornate, side chapel across the aisle. Stained glass fills it with a rosy, surreal light. He stares into the glow.

"Bon giorno." A man slips into the pew.

Jerome startles. "Bon giorno."

The man looks to be in his early sixties, slender in a dark overcoat, and bald with a spiky gray fringe of hair wrapped around his head. Freckles dot his bare scalp. He scrunches his face up in a rabbity grin. "Americano?" he says.

"Si," Jerome says. He wonders how they know. Several Italians have pegged him as American—a waiter, a train conductor, a guy selling watercolors on the street in Florence.

"From Brooklyn?" The man's eyes light up.

"Ah, no. From Connecticut."

"Con? Where that?"

"Connecticut. It's near New York. Near Brooklyn, sort of."

The man frowns.

"In New England?" Jerome offers.

"England?" The man brightens.

"SILENCIO. SSSHHH," the loudspeaker monk insists.

Jerome glances back at the booth. "Shit," he groans.

The man laughs. "Shit," he says. "Big mouth." Then he leans back, chuckling.

Jerome stares ahead at the altar.

"Ah, bella. Beautiful, yes?" the man says.

"Yes, uh, I mean si, beautiful," Jerome says. They sit side-by-side a moment longer. Jerome wonders how long the man will stay and why of all the pews in the basilica, he had to choose this one.

Then Lily is threading her way up the aisle toward them. "Hey," she says.

"Ah, bon giorno," the bald man greets her.

"Bon giorno, signor," Lily replies. "Piacere di conoscerla." She's been studying the phrase book.

"Uh, let's go," Jerome says. "Lil, OK? Let's see the crypt now."

"Crypt? Si, si. You go see Francesco crypt," the man says. He wags his fingers at a door off the altar area.

Jerome stands. "Scuse," he says.

"Crypt." The man nods, scrunching his face into the rabbit grin.

Lily waves, "Ciao."

At the front of the church, they push open a heavy wooden door and step out onto a stone plaza. The sky looms an uncertain gray overhead. Rolling mountains, their spines draped with snow, rise in the distance. "How were the frescoes?" Jerome says.

"Lovely. I've got a new respect for your friend Francis. Who was your other buddy?"

"That guy? I don't know. I'm sitting there, trying to just, you know, be alone a minute and think, and he plops down next to me and asks me where I'm from. I think we pissed off the silencio monk."

Lily laughs. "Oh, no. He was pissed off when we got here."

Alongside the Upper Basilica building they find a narrow stone staircase, very steep, that leads to the Lower Basilica. They step down, placing their feet carefully as daylight disappears. The passage is dark, tunnel-like. They round a bend, pull open a door, and then they are inside. Votive candles flicker in darkened corners like beating hearts. They are underground in the hushed dim of a holy basement. The ceiling is lower, inlaid with ribbons of gold and metal. Hosts of winged angels and cloaked saints poise frozen, painted in place, forever declaring their devotion. Everything seems to whisper that God is lurking, solemn and watchful. Jerome reaches for Lily's hand. She squeezes his. They pass the raised altar, decked with ruby holiday poinsettias. A stream of visitors shuffles by, heads lowered, wrapped in winter coats. Some silently cross themselves.

"Pilgrims," Jerome whispers. "They come from around the world to this site."

"Like us," Lily says.

And Jerome is struck. He is a pilgrim. Now, still. He had always imagined that his journey would end one day in a hilltop parsonage with flower boxes blooming in the windows, a place where he would be cocooned, beyond the reach of the world, the presence of God all around.

"Sounds lovely," Lily said when he described this vision to her. He looks at her now, walking ahead of him into the far wing where the crypt waits. Her ponytail hangs down the center of her back. She touches the wall, her hand pale and vulnerable against the rock. He wonders how long these walls have stood and how much longer they will stand after everyone here is gone. Lily and he have walked Italy's ancient streets this way, marveling that so much has gone on for so long, while they have been aware of so little. Now they are a part of it. At a café in Florence, Lily said almost these exact words, as if she were reading his mind. She has changed my life, he thinks, and she doesn't even know it.

They are almost at the crypt now. Silence hangs in the air, a solemn veil. But the crypt itself is anticlimactic, humble in a way Francis would have liked. A great cement box bearing his remains sits raised in the middle of the room. A stone block wall encircles it. Folded bits of paper stick out from cracks in the blocks, notes to Francis placed there by pilgrims. Jerome can imagine what they say: pleas for healing, for salvation, for all the plagues of the human heart. Lily and he circle the tomb, part of a slow parade. He hears sniffing. Tears shine in the eyes of an old woman with snowy hair. A heavy-set man raises a puffy hand, the fingers thick as sausages, to his eyes. A wordless compassion rises in Jerome, and he looks away.

In one corner of the room, rows of wooden pews face the crypt. When they reach the pews, Jerome gestures to Lily to sit. No one talks. Prayer is silent. Lily closes her eyes and lowers her head. Praying, Jerome knows, in her own way. People all around them are doing the same. Other monks, contemporaries of Francis, are entombed in the walls around them. Jerome has read about the faithful band of brothers who stayed by Francis' side through life and into death. Plaques bear their names, marking the spots on the wall where each lies. Jerome squints to make out the names, but it is too dim.

He looks back at the crypt. Notes poke out from cracks in the gray stone. He wonders if they are ever cleaned out, and if so, what becomes of them. Tonight Lily and he will lie in bed, speculating about their contents. She will weave fantastic tales of lost love and damned souls. She loves stories. Her dark head is still bowed, the rhinestone barrette glittering. He rests his hand on her knee, and she places one of hers over his. A lightness fills Jerome, buoying his heart. If he were to compose a note for Francis to relay to God or to the universe or to whatever is listening, this is what it would say: Lord, please forgive the prayers of the faithful. We never know what to say.

Lily would roll her eyes at such melodrama. She sometimes tells him to lighten up. She says he makes too much of things. A woman behind them clears her throat. Then someone taps Jerome's shoulder. It's the bald rabbit man from the Upper Basilica settling down next to Jerome as if they are old friends. "Crypt," the man whispers. "Francesco. You find."

Jerome nods. "Yes." He imagines how disgusted the silencio monk would be with them now, and he can't help smiling. Imagine a monk telling people, who have traveled great distances seeking God, to shut up.

The man leans closer and points at a plaque on the wall marking the tomb of another monk. "Francesco boyfriend," he whispers, grinning. "Ah, amore."

Jerome nods. He can't help smiling. Lily would have a field-day with this tonight. He takes her hand and closes his eyes. She squeezes his fingers, and a warmth moves over him. It feels as if the stones themselves are sighing.

Jessica Claire Haney

Under Construction

It was hard to imagine the building ever being whole again. Or that anyone or anything ever would be. Even if people someday got to a point where they weren't anticipating another attack, or word of far-off battles, wouldn't Melanie always see the Pentagon as destroyed the way it had been months earlier?

Looking out the hotel window, Melanie wondered if anyone would actually choose it—choose this view—on purpose someday. When Melanie had stormed out of the house, a bag with a few hastily-packed essentials swinging from her shoulder and bouncing against her body as she descended the stairs to her car in the driveway, Todd hadn't tried to stop her. He didn't ask where she was going or look out the door as she left.

Although she didn't much use the cell phone she had gotten in the wake of the attacks, having it did shift her feeling of being traceable. Even if Todd didn't know where she was going—and certainly at first neither did she—he could try to reach out. In her head rang the "Reach out and touch someone" jingle from her childhood, a relic from a time even before answering machines. Now calls stood to show that someone was trying to find you, warn you, give you instructions with words on a screen dampening any mystery behind the attempted connection.

No Kerouacs on the open road, most people had a line of communication in their purse or their pocket. She recalled the Bat Phone with its dark red bubble that lit up in emergencies. Her version was a slim gray brick, its only light the green that matched the clock radio in her bedroom.

As she'd ridden the elevator up to her room, she wondered what the desk clerk had thought about a woman checking in with almost no luggage on a Friday afternoon. "Any other guests?" he'd asked. Her "No" was firm, but what would he believe? Did she want him to think she was there for a business meeting or a salacious activity? Really, she was escaping the thought of her husband involved in both at the same time.

Was that some kind of ironic, more than anything in the Alannis Morisette song with a crash that killed a man who had waited his whole damn life to take that flight? Melanie turned her key to open the hotel room door and inhaled sharply at the view from a decidedly unironic crash.

When Melanie had worked over the summer of 2001 to adjust her plan for teaching U.S. History to the school district's new pacing guides, she scheduled the trip to the National Museum of American History for the fall and the war memorials for the spring, after the state standardized tests would be over. She had expected that kids who had grown up in Northern Virginia would be sick of the museums, but she'd found when she started teaching five years earlier that few had spent much time in them. She'd remarked on this once in a department meeting that first year, and the teacher who taught the Advanced Placement sections scoffed, "Not mine. They acted so bored last year I gave up on that trip. Besides," she added, "we have so much more material to cover."

Melanie occasionally got students who dropped down from AP to regular history. They were almost always Black and Hispanic, and they usually seemed relieved to be back with their friends, as if they'd been holding their breath. She wondered if she were teaching AP—if her colleague ever gave up her coveted sections and Melanie agreed to the extra College Board training—if she could make these students feel more welcome, get them to stay.

What Melanie had not realized in August was that on their way to the museum, they would pass so close to a living artifact of contemporary U.S. history. The Pentagon that early October morning was still a shocking sight, a mouth screaming open to reveal jagged teeth around a pit of rot. What was there to say in answer to the kids' comments, with exclamations like "Dang!" and also with some turned heads, muffled mutterings of, "I don't want to see that." Even though their school was not that far away—all area schools had been on lockdown the whole day of 9/11—her students wouldn't have had much reason to pass this way, to see the devastation up close. Melanie had, just once, but it was profoundly more disturbing to see what the kids saw, to know but not yet really know how this would shape their lives.

Three months later, she sat on the hotel bed where she would not be fornicating and looked out at the construction, the tarps and cones. Once it was rebuilt, would the new part always not match the older, like the lower third of the Washington Monument, even after they'd gone to so much trouble to clean the whole thing with an elaborate scaffolding that made the obelisk seem naked after it was removed.

Her younger brother once built a Lego wall around a castle and substituted navy after running out of regular bright blue. The darker part resembled an ink stain spreading in right angles. The Lego wall remained in the house longer than their mother, who had run out of patience and left them for a new life, acting as though Melanie, already at college, wouldn't feel the missing hole.

She could imagine the path of the plane that must have gone right over the cemetery, then lush-green as they'd seen in front of the smoke on TV. The hills were now gray and brown, still—always—filled with white crosses. She wiggled the strap off her shoulder and lay back on the bed, conscious of the plasticky sheen on the floral comforter even though she wasn't going to stroke it. That was the word Todd said the guys from the office had used. They badgered the one woman on their team to stroke Todd's crotch while at a restaurant for a celebratory dinner after meeting a deadline. Everyone had drunk too much, he said. He shouldn't have driven home and had called in sick the following morning, as he guessed others had. When Melanie returned from school in the afternoon, having left quickly after the dismissal bell to get back to ailing Todd, he had said, "I have to tell you about something that happened last night," adding quickly, "I didn't sleep with anyone or anything."

The details were murky. Somehow the woman, Janine, had been taking some ribbing and was trying to act a good sport, to play along. Todd couldn't recall who had said what first except that it was Mark—who Melanie met once at a holiday party and had thought should be the dictionary picture for the entry for "smarmy"—who said Janine should see if she could get Todd hard, if he wasn't too drunk.

"Just stroke it a few times," Todd remembered him saying with something like a wink.

Mark was on Janine's other side, and when Todd had asked why him, Mark said something about the best angle, asking Janine, "You're a rightie, aren't you sweetheart?" Melanie could imagine the smirk on his face. Todd explained it was all under the table, so no one could see much other than Janine sidling up and crossing her arm across her body.

"That's what I'm talking about," said Mark. Others joined in with nods of approval and Todd started to feel himself grow as Janine stroked him through his trousers. "Chubby" was his word. He lingered in a haze until Andrew across the table shouted, "Me next!" and all the guys laughed heartily. Then Todd snapped out of it and said something about it not being funny and to stop. He caught the eye of the waiter and asked for water and the check, putting the whole bill on his credit card, even though he wasn't the department manager. The night had to end; he would figure out the expense report later and just eat the cost if need be. It was clear he seemed to be a killjoy, but everyone was tired and drunk and most had wives at home, wives who were unlikely to hear about the incident.

Melanie had been horrified that Todd had gone along with the scheme even if she was also glad he'd stopped it and was relieved he had the maitre'd get Janine a cab. And it was worth something that he told Melanie. But then he admitted that after he'd made himself breakfast, while Melanie was at school, he'd felt like beating off and found himself thinking of Janine. Not that he'd ever cheat on Mel, he offered, intending to continue talking, but she was so grossed out she told him to shut up.

"I have to get out of here," she said at least three times, rising from the couch, going upstairs for her clothes, and stomping through the front door.

Within minutes, she'd left without a plan but certain she couldn't sleep at home that night. She didn't want to call any friends and have to tell them what happened or to lie. It was nearly 4:00, and she thought she could look for a hotel from the library computer. She'd once gone to a tiny branch situated in a strip of restaurants and a movie theater; it had the system's only copy of *Amistad*. She didn't repeat showing the film in class because the violence was too disturbing and the courtroom scene too boring. Years later, on a chilly January afternoon, she was lucky to get one of the few spots in the parking lot. When she entered with just her small purse, not her shoulder bag, a man at the circulation desk next to a shabby little kids' play area said, "Just to let you know, we close in 30 minutes."

On one of two public computers, Melanie found this hotel, the cheapest one nearby that had a decent rating on Expedia. Without a reservation, she drove straight to the building that looked out on that fall's wreckage while also sitting across the street from barracks and across the highway from a large mall where people were shopping and eating. She imagined all those bodies moving under fluorescent lights or sitting in dark booths and thought of the bodies that had sat or rolled around on the comforter beneath her, the bodies buried in the hills to the left of her, and the bodies that never emerged from the building across from her. What of Janine's body, not 24 hours after being asked to service Todd's?

Melanie's body was exhausted and admittedly hungry. Winter evenings faded early. She couldn't tell yet if the tarped area of damage would be flooded by work lights or go dark, haloed by dozens of tall lamps in the giant parking lot that surrounded the four intact walls of the huge building.

She didn't want to wait to find out and so closed the curtains and grabbed her purse. She would buy herself dinner, and then she would become one of those people who sits in the café area of the Borders bookstore, reading something that helps them imagine being somewhere, someone else.

Victoria Heartwood

Turning the Vessel

My last molar came loose during the winter I turned twelve. It was the only thing that rattled in our home, which my father had practically rebuilt from the fieldstone foundation, so I let it hang on by a single root fiber for several days. When I flicked the tooth with my tongue, it popped out of the socket with a hollow snap that sent my mother from the room with her hands over her ears.

"Would you please," she said, exasperated, standing beneath the doorframe. "I can't even think while you're doing that."

Ignoring her, I stared at a jumble of words in my book and flicked the tooth again. The sudden whine of my father's bandsaw from the other side of the wall muffled the mud-sucking crack that echoed in the cave of my mouth. When I glanced up, my mother was gone.

My father was a skilled carpenter and could interlock the most intricate sections of wood together with ease. I once watched him standing outside in the snow, scribing a 6'x10' column of Douglas fir with a chainsaw to fit perfectly into the tea-cupped wall of an old log cabin. I was there because the property owners suggested his daughter might enjoy riding their toboggan down the steep hill that sloped across the lawn to the lakeshore, but after a few runs I favored sitting on their bay window seat and watching him do his work in the drafty great room.

In our own home, every cabinet and door was plumb and square. No plank ever creaked beneath our feet. My father had rebuilt the old colonial to be stronger and more sound than it ever was back in 1801. The perfection of our house was his obsession, and my mother liked to joke that it took the pressure off of her.

The day I sent my mother from the room, my father had been toiling in his woodshop since before dawn. Attached to the side of the house like a tumor protruding from the rib cage, it was a place where he was free to create. He may have been on the other side of the wall from where I sat, but my father was worlds away, lost in a forest where the trees had been stripped of life. I read by the fire, tongue probing my tooth, and listened to what now sounded like the whirr of his sharpening wheel. When the tools had just the right camber, he'd hone the burrs away with a wand encrusted by diamond dust.

"Is it valuable?" I once asked, enchanted with how the long, slender tool refracted the light.

"It is to me."

As I sat reading in the living room, I became aware that the machine's motor had stopped. A few minutes later, my father was standing at the doorway, metal glinting by his side. He approached me and took my chin roughly in his hand. "Open," he said.

I obeyed, showing him the tooth.

"Mother says it has to come out ... or it will get infected." His hands smelled of iron and oil. I could see they were grimed with dirt. His glasses were slipping down his nose, but he didn't adjust them. Instead he brought a pair of workworn pliers up from his side and inserted them into my mouth like a dentist. The hard steel stretched my lips open and made me gag. I was frozen, staring at my father's face. His nose was screwed up to hold his glasses higher, allowing him to see through the square magnifiers at the bottom of the lenses. He exhaled a plume of wine. I held my breath as the pliers scraped the sides of my tooth while he probed the surface for a firmer grip. With confidence, my father pumped my tooth back and forth in its socket and severed the remaining root.

"Here," he said and dropped it into the palm of my hand before turning to go without another word.

I looked down at my last baby tooth. Its inner ridges were jagged like a saw and, deep inside, there was a dark stain of blood on the white surface.

One morning in late Spring, when the snow dropped into the earth and spikes of bloodroot began to unfurl, I ran after my father as he entered the woods at the edge of the meadow behind our barn. To a woodturner, finding idyllic raw wood was more than a necessity, it was a hero's journey in search of the holy grail. We walked in silence for a long time beneath a breeze tousling the leafy canopy as he steered his chainsaw in a wheelbarrow around rocks and roots on the path.

My father was slender. The lightness of his gait made it appear as if he blew in the wind like a shirt clipped to the line. I'd watch him as his eyes hovered around the tree trunks, scanning for burls. Mine sank to the forest floor, preferring to search for rotten wood nestled in the leaves, scouring the trail's edge for the spathe and the spadix of a Jack-in-the-Pulpit. My father waited patiently as I crouched next to a decaying log, digging out the soft splintery layers to unearth bark beetles in their winding tunnels. Together we pushed the whole of it over and watched as a few brown newts wriggled toward the shadows for safety. I caught one and drew it back into the light. Turning it over in my palm, I examined its exposed belly. It was puffed up in protection, the robust orange in stark contrast to the topside with its symmetrical spots along the supple spine. I knew how to be gentle. I knew not to hold onto things for too long.

After nestling the newt back into its depression, we gently rolled the log over in place. I reached for my father's hand. His grasp was instinctive at first, but then the tension unspooled like fishing line and it was just me catching at the swinging heft of his palm, fingers as limp and uninterested as a dead perch before he reached for the wheelbarrow again and we continued to walk among the towering trees.

What else settles into a depression? I wondered, searching for the perfection of a fringed bleeding heart beneath an opening in the canopy. *Mushrooms and butterflies, a family of mice, mothers alone in the house.*

The trail was muddy and I had to leap to reach my father's oversized footsteps. We walked for what seemed like hours with him pointing out deer and bear scat and identifying every birdcall—chickadees and finches, a Downy Woodpecker, and, occasionally, a Scarlet Tanager. When we came to a birch tree that had fallen across the path, my father knelt down, unhooked his knife from its leather holster clipped to his belt, and sliced the paper white bark from the trunk. "See how the grain of the wood lies mostly parallel to the tree's pitch? It'll flow right up and out into the branches," he said, handing me the knife, and snapped off the nearest limb. "Long fibers. See that? This one had some longitudinal strength." He stood up and arched his back, hands pressing just above his hips. "But not quite enough," he said.

I squinted at the sunshine crowning his head, and rolled the handle of the knife from palm-to-palm. Then he reached for it and took it from my hands, pushed the blade within, and slipped it back into its holster. "Stand back," he said and took the chainsaw from the wheelbarrow, ripping the cord and sending a plume of oily smoke into the air, to carve up the tree blocking our path. As we continued walking down the trail, I bowed my head to scan the muted leaves from last Autumn for treasures. When my father stopped dead in his tracks, I crumpled into his back. Unmoved, he didn't even seem to notice.

"There it is, Chuck," he said, calling me by the nickname he had given me when I was about ten years old. I had been mindlessly filing a dowel with a rasp in his workshop while he reorganized all of his drawers and cabinets. He was standing there, picking some wood shavings out of the red wine he drank from a jam jar and then turned to swallow a gulp. With his back to me, my father pointed to a heavy round cylinder sitting on the long table next to the lathe and said, "Hand me that...Chuck."

I hesitated. "Why are you calling me *Chuck?*" I asked. By the time his laughter subsided and he'd caught his breath, the name had stuck.

Standing behind my father in the woods, I followed the angle of his tilted head to a tree where endless branches shimmered with bright new leaves. The burl was as big as a termite mound. "It's a big wart," I said, disappointed by the tangle of gnarled bark.

"It's a sugar maple burl," he said and explained how, beneath the surface, the raw wood erupted in spikes like a crystal formed deep in the earth. As with diamonds and children, burls are wild growths that develop under pressure or stress, from injury, and the infestation of pests. Like a malignant lump, burls protrude where buds have become knotted and tangled away from their normal growth. Most burls grow underground—in secret—only to be discovered when the tree is uprooted in death or by a ravaging storm. It is their rare and wild nature, captured and shaped into something that can be held beneath the hand, which makes them so valuable. A burl grows so strong, like iron forged by fire, that it nearly refuses to split even though its twisted grain is unpredictable and may shatter on the lathe if turned and touched in the wrong way.

With his chainsaw, my father carved through the thick crotch wood that harbored the lump and, afterwards, gently dressed the wound like a Salvation Army nurse on the battlefield. Beneath the thrill I sensed something small and vulnerable, a gnat in a spider's web, and followed its thread to what I later learned was his shame. Harvesting this prize like a thief with a conscience, my father knew that the few hairs he plucked from his scalp and left at the tree's roots could never measure up to her loss.

Upon our return from the woods, with the burl still rocking in the wheelbarrow, I watched my father dump the bundle onto the ground outside his woodshop and carve it up with his chainsaw into several chunks we could move onto the workbench by hand. Standing together at the chipped and stained wooden table in the shop, we examined the interlocking grain in each section of the burl.

"It looks like a maze," I said.

He nodded and traced his finger along a darkened area. "This might be a mineral streak or some heartwood staining."

I trailed my own finger toward a small, brownish mark. "This could be a worm track," I said.

"Pith fleck?" he said, pulling his glasses from his shirt pocket and resting them atop his nose. "Could be."

"See the knot clusters here," I said.

He turned to stare at me. "Go help your mother with dinner," he said.

I skulked to the door, stopping to turn and watch him as he stood stooped over a pot on his hotplate, like an alchemist, melting some paraffin to stir into a wide mouthed jar of boiled linseed oil. Then poured himself a glass of wine from the jug on the shelf above his workbench before dipping a wide boar-bristle brush into the golden mixture. My father painted the raw surfaces of the slices of burl until they were coated and slick. He transferred the blanks to a shelf in the back of his woodshop and covered them with a tarp where they would sit for the next several years, drying out for his future creations. When I heard him clear his throat, I silently twisted the handle and left before he could turn and see that I had been standing there like the improbable apprentice I had secretly been all along.

I felt trapped by my mother's side in the kitchen, snapping the woody stalks off spears of asparagus, washing and spinning lettuce, shelling beans, and peeling carrots. Some evenings, after dinner had been prepared and was roasting in the oven, I'd sneak around the house to watch my father at the lathe through the window. He stood bent, holding his breath, as he stroked the organic curves of a vessel in progress, coaxing beauty from the blank. His fingertips were always searching for imperfections to strip away.

My father was a skilled carpenter and an amateur woodturner. He was a man who sought perfection in function, but desired the wildness of form. What he really wanted to do, and what he did whenever he could, was turn free flowing vessels on the lathe. He would rip out articles about the rules of arc and angle from his woodturning magazines, ball them up, and stuff them beneath the kindling to start the morning fire in the woodstove in our kitchen. Only in this regard did he eschew practicality.

My father was determined to prove that the importance of characteristics may well outweigh shape, that feet need not appear to be a solid support, and beautiful proportion could range from the sublime to the downright impossible. He made many mistakes on his quest to carve a vessel that was both pleasing to the eye and beneath the hand. And those that disappointed he sliced open like the magician's assistant to be studied for error. A few times he thought better of halving some promising specimens and drilled holes through which he could lace them back together with leather cord or copper wire. Those were my favorites, broken and scarred yet resolute in their beauty.

Some evenings while scrubbing potatoes at the sink, I'd stare out the window at my father and his hired boy splitting and hauling wood at the barn. My mother thought I had a crush on Henry, a few years my senior, but the ache in my heart was to be out there in the last of the sunshine and wind, doing the work of men. As soon as the pie dough was rolled out, overturned into the dish, and littered with cinnamon-spiced slices of apple, I was out the door, running toward the barn.

After my father left to wash up for dinner, I turned to Henry. "You're doing it wrong," I said, grabbing the pitchfork out of his hands and scraping up an enormous pile of hay in the tines.

"Scrappy," he said and smiled.

"You're fired," I said.

"For what?"

"Sheer ignorance."

I fired Henry for two years running and he still showed up every afternoon. After graduating high school, he started an associate degree program in agriculture at the local community college, came to work for my father after classes, and boasted about what he'd learned each day.

"Come on," Henry said, "you're interested in this stuff, too."

"Maybe," I said and pushed past him, "but I don't need *you* teaching me."

Henry grabbed my hand and spun me around to face him. I ducked and went in for his waist with both my arms around his wiry torso, twisting him back-and-forth until he lost balance. Hopping on one foot, he locked his arm around my neck. We struggled, grunting, for a while before he whipped me to the ground and lay crossways over my belly, grappling for my hands. I groaned and flipped him onto his back, but he weaseled out of my hold and pressed me face-down on the cracked cement with my arm twisted upon my spine. "One!" He started counting. "Two ... three!"

"You win." I winced and, when Henry let me go, I rolled over in defeat to face him. He dropped his forehead against my shoulder and laughed. "You sure are weird, Chuck," he said, "but I like you anyway."

I reached up and patted him on the back of the head. "Next time, you're gonna lose," I said and yanked his hair hard, pulling his head back and exposing the downy hairs on his throat.

Just then, my father walked into the barn with his arms full of cordwood. Upon seeing us entangled on the floor, he dropped the whole stack in a deafening clatter and yelled, "What the hell is going on in here!"

Henry was up in a flash, dusting off the scraps of hay and dirt from his clothes. He reached down to give me a hand up. "Just wrestling, sir," he said.

"Chuck," said my father through his teeth, "get in the house."

A couple of days later, my father fired Henry for real after he forgot to put a pile of linseed rags back into their empty paint can.

"They could have burst into flames and burned the whole house down," my father raged.

I watched Henry striding stiffly down the center of the driveway in a measured pace. When he got to the road, he broke into a run. After that, I was the one who had to assist my father with all of the men's work, but it wasn't what I'd always imagined it might be.

One evening, I was helping my father sweep up sawdust in the shop when I bumped into him. "Sorry," I mumbled.

He grabbed me around the waist, spun me about, and thrust his hand up behind my head, tangling my hair in his fist. The broom I had been holding rattled to the ground. Then he pressed his body into mine and covered my mouth with his own. His hot thick tongue pushed my lips apart and probed about beyond the wall of my teeth like a trapped animal. I felt the hardening in his pants dig into my belly. My heart was pounding in my head and I couldn't breathe. His smell was all over me: the grease at the sides of his nose, his soured saliva, the damp heat rising from his armpits. I began to scream and he pulled away.

My father blocked me at the door, wavering. "Elena," he said, wiping his mouth with the back of his hand. "Not a word of this to your mother." He held his finger by my throat like a blade. "You know she's been down. This would push her over the edge."

Then he slid aside like a barn door and I bolted into the night.

After that day in the shop, my father still tried to teach me about woodworking.

"Chuck, it's important to find the right kind of log," he said. "You want to avoid rot, a bunch of cracks, anything that looks like it's had an infestation, and, generally speaking, holes, or wood that's grown into fencing wire."

"I thought all that stuff gave the wood its character," I said. "You're the one who told me the most intriguing wild grain comes from trees that have endured the greatest stress."

On a stormy winter's night, I snuck out of the house and met Henry halfway down the road. He'd brought a plastic bottle of vodka and we took turns swigging the caustic liquid, coughing and laughing at one another's contorted faces with each swallow. Branches littered the road as the trees had been wind-shorn and weakened under the weight of the snow and ice.

"It's freezing out here," said Henry. "Let's go to the barn."

Up in the loft, it was just warm enough for me to extract one leg from my pants and for him to unzip his fly. There, with the hay poking into the back of my thigh, I tried to erase my father's lips with Henry's hungering kisses, erase my father's body with Henry's stiff cock rubbing my dry insides hot like a wrist burn.

I never knew what it was to get wet and feel the pulse of desire until I left home for college and stayed up all night talking to a Peruvian girl in my dorm about raising guinea pigs for food. Back at Alejandra's family homestead in the Sacred Valley, her younger brothers fed compost to the muddle of rodents and harvested them for special occasions.

"So, big party—no waste," she said, smiling and widening her hands before her.

"Your hair is like flowing water," I said, running my fingers through her dark locks. "You know what I like about you," I said, "you have this natural balance, a good form, and tactile qualities."

"Um, thank you, I think," she said.

I told Alejandra everything I knew about wood that night. Its hardness and its give. "During the drying process, which takes years, the vibrancy of freshly sawn wood will fade even as the strong grain patterns remain," I said as we sat crossed legged, knee to knee, on her twin bed. "Wood darkens with age. It may split and crack in shakes and checks—those imperfections you want to avoid while turning unless you don't care about the blank flying apart and knocking you cold. You gotta be wise and follow the growth rings, from light to dark where the heart is large." I reached out and took her hand, running my fingertip over the crescent moon of her thumbnail. "Avoid disease and don't bring pests back to the woodshop. If you gotta work with spalted wood, make sure it doesn't dent beneath your fingernail."

Alejandra withdrew her hand from mine and stretched out over the bed on her side.

I leaned back against the wall and continued. "You have to cut softwood with a sharp tool," I said. "If you sand it, you risk etching away the tender flesh between the hardened growth rings. Make sure the grain runs across the blank, so it broadens when you turn the wood. Everyone thinks tighter rings are better. If you turn a quarter-sawn form, eyes will develop in the long grain. You gotta be aware. Never stand directly in front of your blank without proper protection."

"Chuck," Alejandra said, "lie down."

"Don't turn green bowls, unless you enjoy the warp," I said as I dropped to my side, mirroring her. "Play around with coloring, burning, and blasting. You might like to try piercing, hacking, patching, and joining. But, remember that no matter how much you embellish, you've got nothing without sound form. Ultimately, a vessel functions best as a container."

Alejandra rolled onto her back and her shirt slipped loose from her jeans. I fingered the hem and said, "Splits might run deep through the most intriguing grain. Don't give up on a burl with sinuous cracks as that kind of wood may be ideal for heavier pieces. It is their rare and wild nature, captured and shaped into something that can be held up in the hand, which makes them valuable." My voice grew quiet as I glanced about her face. "People say wood is warm to the touch—the earthen tones like the familiar eyes of a lover."

"Do you always have so much to say about wood?" She asked, catching and pressing my hand against her soft belly.

My face grew hot and I shrugged. "A well-sanded bowl feels like velvet beneath the fingers," I said, touching her skin. "Don't be fooled into thinking that the right weight, the right shape, the curves, or the balance could ever supersede the form."

"Chuck," she whispered, "enough."

I laughed and bowed my head. "See this inner curve?" I said stroking the front of her hip. "It's well-proportioned and—"

Alejandra leaned forward and hovered her mouth before mine. I felt her sweet breath against my lips and I bridged the distance between us, completely filled with her softness, her warmth, and her kindness so that nothing from my past could edge its way into my mind in that moment. Yet the thoughts returned, like dampness bleeding around the edges of the waxy seal on a blank, as we kissed. *Only the perfect combination of luck and skill can bring out the best from the twisted grain of a burl when turned in just the right way. A careless touch can shatter the most exquisite of vessels.*

Dennis Jones
The Boar Hunt

Doctor Stacy "Hutch" Hutchinson slices the wild mushrooms from his front yard with a Callaway sand wedge. He was still in his scrubs. A glass of bourbon, sweating the ice in the July heat serves as his tee box. With every swing, he looks up to admire the distance the white button tops sailed. Should have corrected for windage, he thinks. Across the street, the dubious blind woman walks on the sidewalk with her candy-striped seeing stick. He is convinced, absolutely sure, she isn't really blind or if she is, she isn't *that* blind. Slightly blind, maybe. He raises his golf club to her in greeting. He thinks he sees her hesitate—see?!—but she just walks on and he mutters, I'm onto you lady, quietly enough that her heightened sense of hearing—a big if—won't catch what he says. He takes a hefty gulp of the whiskey, one more practice swing and hits another mushroom fifteen yards into the street.

He should go inside but he hears his son, Travis, sixteen, working on the Rachmaninov piece. For some reason, he is playing it in a banana costume. He's been wearing it to do ordinary things—homework, the dishes, walking their dog, taking out the garbage. Hutch is only vaguely alarmed by this and knows he should probably be more concerned. He viewed the costume as a slight improvement over the powdered wig Travis normally wore to practice the piano. "Don't mess with my peruke," Travis would yelp when Hutch tried to pry it from his head. The wig askew, his son looked like a cross between Louis XIV and Robert Plant circa *Houses of the Holy* with the creepy album cover art. "It's only because of syphilis they became popular," Hutch sneered, like that was some great burn. The therapist says it's only natural to want to inhabit tropical fruit costumes after a divorce. How much was he paying this nitwit? Still, he let it go. Hutch was working hard to let everything go but that was becoming a full-time job. The therapist held five degrees and steepled his finger to his nose like flying buttresses. Such a phony. Hutch shook his head. Focus. One more backswing, going for a draw to land somewhere near the "Drive Like Your Kids Live Here" sign which he found mildly insensitive to those who were not fortunate enough to have children, children who played concertos and dressed as a plantain to wander around the house. Instead of a draw, he sliced it hard right. "Fore," he calls and holds his right arm straight off to the side, then buries the heel of the golf club into the turf.

The boar hunt was Hutch's Big Idea. He had taken his son dove hunting many times and thought they should up their game, mix it up some given their new circumstances. It would be a bonding experience. For the doves, they liked the long open fields at Botany Bay best because afterwards they could walk the beach and see a million different sea shells and enjoy the fading heat of the Lowcountry Fall. This was when he was still married to Moira. They'd bring the birds back in a canvas bag and when it was turned out she could see the tiny dots of blood from where the birdshot had pierced them. Stray feathers would float through the kitchen and Moira would always cover her mouth and say she was going to be sick but Hutch would just laugh and tell her to get over it. She would take the dressed birds and make *Coquelets des Canapes* and after drink brandies on the back porch with Hutch and watch the sun light fade over the sea rocket and bayberry of the dunes, the waves crashing on the beach beyond in the deepening night, while Travis played Chopin in the front room. Kind of like a Cialis commercial, he thinks now.

But then came the "incident" or rather the alleged "groping" by Hutch, his hands lingering a little too long—a second, two at most maybe?—on a newly augmented breast he had successfully enlarged to fantastic proportion. It didn't matter that Tonya Sanders was a bikini model and physical trainer. "Circumstantial," his lawyer, Len Applegate, said. He spoke in one word sentences that somehow seemed hard to follow. "Hearsay," he snapped at nothing Hutch had said. Hutch noted the Hermes tie and the IWC Portuguese on his wrist and tried to calculate the damage, both financial and psychological. He had needed Moira to back him up but she went over the railings of the sinking ship, sniffing, "I know an iceberg when I see one," whatever that was supposed to mean. The thing was, his patients, the women, trusted him. When he held their finished breasts in his hand, palpating them gingerly to see if the silicone was evenly dispersed he had the distant look of wonder on his face, a slight smile at the corners of his mouth, as if Tinkerbell herself flickered and hovered within his cupped palms. The physician's assistants in the office called it the Hutch Clutch behind his back but he didn't care because his monthly revenue eclipsed their annual salary twofold. Boo-yah. Len settled the matter out of court but the damage had been done. He had boo-yahed his last time. "Buy yourself a new tie," Hutch told Len as he signed the paperwork. "Ten-four, good buddy," Len said, altering his one word sentences for a change. Hutch thought he did it for sport.

Wild boars were apparently a nuisance upstate. They were a nuisance everywhere is what all the flyers and websites said. Like they had it coming to them. Like they were completely aware of what they were doing and should have known there was backlash building to consume them. The animals just couldn't see what was coming—military style operations that were designed to slice them to ribbons. The meat was butchered, put in ice chests and sent to fine restaurants in Charleston and Savannah, a few up in Raleigh. Like he was somehow going to be part of the Farm to Table Movement. Some Locavore. Moira wasn't so sure. "What about his hands," she said. She looked at her own hands with a slight frown. They were thin and bony, fragile, with the softest skin he had ever felt. "He's not exactly Tchaikovsky," Hutch said flatly. "Why couldn't you be more supportive?" she wanted to know. "I'm just being honest," Hutch shrugged. "Why not just fake it like the rest of us so you don't look back and say 'I was a boat anchor that held him down?'" He pondered this for a moment, staring off into the distance, pretending like he was really listening, really giving it a shot. "So, we're good on the boar thing, then?" he asked.

Curtis is their guide. He and his shifty sidekick Andy harnessed two dogs that looked more like large brown gargoyles and leashed them to the ATV. They looked rougher in person than on the website, giving off a slight trace of menace. "Stacy?," Andy says and holds his head back as if to get better focus to see if Hutch was really a man.

"I get that a lot," Hutch says. Ass clown is what he thinks but with the dogs spewing foam and what appears to be blood from their mouths, snarling, he thought it best to be oblique. Plus, there was the matter of their automatic weapons. *Side-arms* as Curtis said. Safety first, Hutch thinks.

They carry seven foot spears, with a steel arrow head the size of a gardening shovel attached at the tip, with smooth wooden handles and neoprene grips. Those meat heads at his Crossfit Box could suck it, Hutch thinks. Dead lift this, bitches. He feels a little out of sorts, not wearing his scrubs. He wore them everywhere, pale blue—turquoise on days he was feeling aggressive and dominant, daring comments. He settled for an orange hunters vest and a trapper's cap even though it was approaching eighty degrees. Curtis and Andy were decked out in camo with elbow and knee pads, small night vision goggles pushed up on their foreheads. No wonder this trip cost two thousand dollars. They looked like they were going on the Bin Laden raid.

Travis wonders why he went into plastic surgery. "It wasn't to cure cancer, I can tell you that," Hutch says. "Did you really grope her?" he asks.

"Lingered too long. It's a bad habit. Anyway, we settled it."

"Are you some kind of perv?"

"What's with you?"

"It sounds pervy is all."

Hutch cocked his head and wondered where the boy in the banana costume went. There was a long silence, punctuated by short burst of Andy and Curtis gunning their ATVs. Finally, Hutch says, "I made a mistake, Travis, and paid for it. Now quiet, you'll scare the boar—or is it boars?" He is agitated and is beginning to think this was a bad idea.

They walk in a cut clearing of hay-colored grass, and dried brown leaves glistening from the rain the night before. The loblolly's sway in a slight breeze. Curtis and Andy check their GPS and look down at scat they found on the ground. The dogs whine and slobber, yanking fiercely on their chain. Andy is unfazed, takes off his glove and buffs a nail with an emery board. Hutch thinks it's an odd time for personal grooming.

"Maybe we could just call in an airstrike and head back," Hutch offers. "Maybe you should zip it, Doc. There's one close, so just wait. We'll get you one." Andy is getting testy, Hutch thinks. It's always the sidekick that bears watching, and worries about Andy's blood sugar level, the amount of fiber in his diet.

"Splendid," Hutch cries, like he was landed gentry on his mount at a fox hunt. What was wrong with him, he wonders. It was a word he never uttered aloud in his life.

The beast springs out of a row of hay grass and the dogs, baying wildly, give chase.

"Get movin', Doc," Curtis says. "Dogs are liable to eat it before you can kill it."

About a quarter miles east in the fields the dogs have run the boar into a shallow ditch and pace anxiously along the rim. They smell blood, Hutch thinks. The boar's hind leg is broken and he struggles in the dirt. Hutch breaths hard from the chase. Travis doubles over with a cramp, struggling to breath. The two guides come up alongside on their ATVs with their weapons drawn. "Just a precaution," Andy says. "Better finish him, Doc. Think of it like a scalpel slice, right above shoulder blade and into the neck."

It's an incision moron, Hutch thinks. He had seen videos of the kills on YouTube and they all seemed strangely delicate as if the hunters were reluctant for the kill. Hutch took the tip of the spear and gently eased up the animal's shoulder blade. The boar panted heavily until that moment of the tip touching it's hide, then starts shrieking. Something loosened in Hutch and he drove the spear deep against an artery, then connected with bone. Blood steamed everywhere. He withdraws the blade but feels such a rush that he leaps into the ditch and stabs the animal over and over, launching the thrusts from over his head, blood flying as Hutch laughed and laughed at the gore and the mauling until Travis, screaming, crying, over his father's hysteria, finally pulls him away and out of the ditch.

Curtis sniffs, spits a huge gob of snot and pronounces the beast "sure as hell dead."

"Don't think there's much use for any of the restaurants. Boar Bolognese is off the menu for the time being," Andy says.

The dogs grumble and pull on their leads until they reach Hutch who is sitting on the ground, breathing heavily with his head bowed. Hutch looks up. The dogs stopped growling and wag their tails furiously. They come closer and lick the doctor's face and forearms, washing the blood from his skin with their determined slobber, their tongues rough as a fine-grained sandpaper.

Travis says, "let's go dad. Let's go home," but his voice sounds far off, muted. Hutch is still winded and does not look at his son. His arms ache. He sits still to let the dogs finish their work.

Christina Kapp

What Sells

Olivia turned into her mother's empty driveway. In the gray of evening, dark trees blacked out the sky behind the low house, making it look like a stone in the mouth of a cave. She walked around to the back porch, digging in her purse for her mother's keys. When she opened the door, Penelope, her mother's little white terrier, shot into the yard like a dove released into the sky.

She'd been caring for Penelope for almost a month, but staying in the house she had moved out of only a handful of years ago felt like sneaking in late for curfew. She expected her mother to be bending the blinds of her bedroom window, watching. She wasn't, of course. There was no mother in this house anymore.

Olivia sat on the back step and took her mother's ring out of the pocket of her jeans. When she slid the gold band on her finger, the body heat trapped in the metal made her feel uncomfortable, touched against her will. The ring also just looked wrong. At twenty-six Olivia considered herself too young for a wedding ring, a conclusion supported by her mother, who, even at forty-four, had never made such an attachment herself.

Beyond being an oddity, the ring wasn't pretty. It was heavy and too thick, the finish ground to a sandy matte. What was even more peculiar was that Olivia had never seen this ring before she found it on her mother's hand in the hospital, after she was dead.

When word got out about her mother's fatal accident, the ring became a glittering bit of gossip. Versions of the story cast the ring as everything from a symbol of purity to a desperate attempt at conformity. A youngish, single mom who worked as a dental assistant and liked to paint watercolor landscapes, caught dead in a wedding ring became a bitter spinster, a jealous mistress, a sad case of loneliness. "The hospital called looking for her husband," Olivia overheard people whispering at the funeral. "Can you imagine?"

It was as if her mother had had a heart attack while screwing a prostitute.

"It's just a piece of jewelry," some of her more temperate friends assured Olivia. "Don't read too much into it." And yet, like everyone else, Olivia kept circling back to the question of why. Why hadn't her mother ever married? Why would she wear an old gold band? Why on her ring finger? Why on her left hand?

After the funeral, as time slipped into the vacuum of forgetfulness that comes after the flowers have turned brown and been cleared away, the ring became a talisman. A tangible representation of an emptiness in Olivia's center. She couldn't leave the house without the ring in her pocket, couldn't stop her fingers from reaching for it throughout the day. She couldn't stop wondering where it had come from.

Olivia tested a few theories. Her mother's divorced college roommate shook her head and sent her home with a tuna casserole. A series of her mother's ex-lovers turned out to be otherwise involved or disinterested. One man claimed her mother was a witch and she'd used some kind of trickery to steal the ring from an unsuspecting man. While Olivia liked the possibility of witchcraft, the ring didn't seem conjured. Day after day, its solidity persisted. She searched the house for a stash of boxer shorts and razors. She installed a nanny cam to see if a dark stranger would appear and let himself in. She found nothing. No one came.

As she became bolder about her inquiries, Olivia wore the ring to a local bar, where she found no evidence of her mother, but attracted a man in a buttoned-up red flannel shirt who was willing to fuck her. Another night at a different bar, she added details about her mother's evening commute, the Whole Foods rotisserie chicken in the back seat, the Fed-X van that collided with her mother's Corolla at the corner of Bridge Street and Blackburn. This earned her some additional sympathy drinks as well as a fuck, but no one knew her mother or had any useful opinions about the ring.

As the weeks passed, Olivia's job grew impatient. She had to come back, return to work. The rent on her apartment had to be paid. She had to face the inevitable need for a Realtor and moving trucks and garbage cans.

Olivia bagged her mother's her jeans and sweaters, her boots and wool winter coats for Goodwill. She put aside the nicer clothes for a consignment store closer to her apartment. She gave books and videos to the local library, the philodendrons and ferns to the neighbors. She donated dishes and candlesticks, pots and pans. She stripped her mother's house down to the barest of elements, until all that was needed was a coat of paint.

"You have to brighten it up to sell," the Realtor said. "Make it look fresh."

That night Olivia lay in her mother's bed. She ran her finger around the circular water stain on the nightstand. She felt her body shift into the sag in the middle of the mattress. She slid the ring off her finger and put it back on again.

As a punctuation to her mother's life, the ring left an opening, the tiniest of drains through which swirled the things she knew about her mother. How she loved to plant tulips and daffodils in the fall so she would have something to look forward to in spring, how she taught Olivia to play backgammon for quarters, the way she waved her arms in the air while singing to "Bohemian Rhapsody." What it left her holding was a woman she hadn't really known. To her surprise, the ring was the material evidence of a woman she didn't know, and she loved her more for it.

These thoughts lulled Olivia into a half-waking dream of the scraping and sanding and rolling and painting she intended to do. She saw herself prying the lids off can after can of paint so white the brightness hurt her eyes. She saw herself painting the house whiter that even Penelope could stand, rolling layers thick as rubber over the hardest of corners, smoothing the sharpest of splinters. She swept white across walls, ceilings, doors, and windows until the living room looked like the interior of the moon. She saw herself pressing her brush into the carved crevices of the furniture staged for sale, pouring it over lamps, tapping it into the fabric of the couch. She'd paint over mirrors and oven knobs and dishwasher buttons. She'd paint and paint until even poor Penelope felt dirty and brown and ran out into the yard, leaving paw prints that looked like impressions of snow in the grass. But Olivia would stick to the job. She would paint until the whole house was so white it turned her tears to diamonds, until each of her mother's rooms was decked in a perfect bridal glow that would surely sell itself.

Kristian Macaron

Precipice

We get there just after sunrise, when the air is still cold. Marie, halfway through a lukewarm cup of coffee, sets up the camera between a dolomite, in the shadow of the eastern mountain over rough black and white granite. We have a lens that will capture a hawk flight in milliseconds. She shrugs off her sweater and it falls in a plaid heap on the dirt. The Autumn air is colder and weaker than the desert sun. I shiver, and take a long sip of coffee, but Marie is already working. She raises her binoculars to her eyes.

The Hawk Watch can be seen from the freeway, eastbound on I-40, just ten minutes outside of Albuquerque in a kind of wilderness that seems too close to home to be real. Every week we hike up in a mile and a half of silence. I'm usually too hungover to mumble more than my coffee order, and Marie just waits. It's almost like a ritual now. She sets up the camera and then studies the cliff side. I stand balanced against the icy rock, checking the pages of our notebook, reading charts, barely awake. Dashed lines meant flapping. Solid strikes meant soaring. In six months, Marie and I will be defending our masters' project in front a panel of professors who read the dashes and strikes like codebreakers, and then my immersion into the nuance of this language would be over absorbed by life's real strikes and dashes.

"There they are," she says. She's looking up to the top of the ridge and today—like every Sunday—we see two human figures at the top of the Hawk Watch climbing over and down the precipice as we gaze skyward.

I lift my binoculars and find them. They are almost more interesting to us than the hawks. *Almost*, being— in all actuality—an incredible understatement; the birds are our life's work. This elderly couple is out here every Sunday. They move slowly down the mountain, always together, hand-in-hand bracing their bodies against the dusty rocks. Their marbled hair blends into the granite swirls of the cliffs, but every Sunday they try to hike down the cliff opposite Marie and I while a whirlwind of hawks play around them.

"I wonder why they start from the top?" Marie says. Her northern New Mexico accent lilts vowels in a way she usually avoids, and she pauses to inhale a deep kind of air. Not a tired draw, but a breath someone takes when they need to make themselves present in a capsulized moment. Before I can help, she's refocused herself. She unpacks the data, as I watch the couple maneuver carefully over piled rocks and a narrow ledge. Today he has on a camo-green windbreaker and she wears a polka-dotted headscarf.

"Maybe their house is up there." I shrug and say, "Do you see any hawks? There was a little Cooper's soaring on our way up from the car."

Marie, for all the setting up she'd tasked to, hadn't noticed.

We try to work. Marie adjusts the camera, I peer into binoculars.

"Ben," she says a few minutes later, "there are no houses up there."

The light still resting on the Sandia Mountains turn the feldspar in the mountains a glowing pink. The color of the sun rising or setting on the mountains is called an alpenglow. Most of the mountains in New Mexico are named for their alpenglows. The Sandias are a watermelon pink, the Sangre de Cristos to the North shine a halo of deep golden red over the Rio Grande Valley and the Manzanos to the South are rose-hued, sunlight shining through mystical maple forests.

I met Marie in a Biology research course as part of our grad school research at the University of New Mexico. She was aloof and deceptively passionate, but she agreed to go on a date with me after I quoted the "Rime of the Ancient Mariner" to her at a party. It was the first time I heard her laugh. We studied flight patterns—for birds, not people—though ironically, if I could figure out my own, I'd have solved some of my own problems already. Flight patterns reveal movement, moments of stall, and moments of breach. Moments when I realize that birds are more aware of the wind than we are.

Though I tried major after major nothing stuck but my obsession with movement. And it wasn't just the birds. I couldn't sit still. I couldn't have a desk job, couldn't choose a vacation, couldn't decide whether I wanted to keep or sell my car. (I sold it, so my work was now at Marie's mercy.) I felt very free. This said, I know in my heart that my settling on avian biology was mostly because the birds seemed to know what to do and I didn't. Up to the second of migration, and then they would just gather and take off. Everything and nothing left behind them. I love this and it also terrified me, the thought of being left behind.

Marie is the opposite. She is obsessed with the birds not their movement. Her arms have carefully inked miniature birds-of-prey soaring up and down them. She can count their tiny bones or hear their piercing screeches and identify almost every raptor in the world. I want to be as sure of something as she is of birds. I'm not certain that she's sure of anything else. Sometimes, in seconds-between-seconds, when we're having breakfast or walking hand-in-hand to campus, I find myself wondering how long it will be till her body migrates from me toward some unknown horizon.

The couple climbing down the mountain enraptures us both, but for different reasons. Marie and I have nicknamed them, "Merlin" and "Nimue"—or I have; despite Marie's passion, between the two of us, I am the poet.

The wizard, Merlin, who lived his life backwards was supposed to have left Arthur at the pinnacle of the King's reign to live his youth in a cave with the enchanting nymph, Nimue. In wizard years, that's centuries of privacy, if you're following.

"So Merlin emerges again an old man, finally. I always wondered what happened between them." I try to joke, but today Marie bristles.

"I don't know how much longer I can take this," she says. "I have to know, Ben. I have to know why they're doing such a dangerous hike." She is still looking toward the cliff, but I swear she could be crying and I wouldn't know what to do, so I grab the camera and find the hawks.

"There." I point the finder, but she's already found this one. While Merlin and Nimue climb down the mountain, we watch the birds.

There are five red-tails playing in the wind today. One of them watches us from a distant granite pillar before he shoots into the updraft, winding and spiraling into the wind until he is just a speck in my binoculars.

"He's playing," I say more out of awe than a read for data.

"That's a thermal," Marie says, looking at the readings. We record the data, carefully.

When we look back at the cliff Merlin and Nimue are gone.

Apart from Merlin and Nimue, flying is the best kept secret of my life. When I started learning about birds I started learning to fly. From outside of Albuquerque, the ridged spine of the Sandia Mountain range is a sleeping dragon curled around the city. The head is the far north of the city, the nose breathing fire into the pueblo dances and casino torches. Eye level with the tram towers glinting wires in the brilliant sunlight. From the famous crest of the dragon's head, the mountains seem to fall on either side of you. To the West is Albuquerque, a city more sprawling than it seems to know. Layers of air and dust and the falling sun over the horizon of volcanoes, and Mount Taylor—once fire—now blue and ice. To the east of the mountain is the back of the dragon, alpine aspen scales, and a small ski resort, carefully groomed in the winter, overgrown grass and secret herds of horned toads in the summers, and below that: open prairie. There are miles and miles of ridge to the South, one of the ridges winds into the Hawk Watch, and I always think of it there when I'm at the crest watching the hang gliders.

On the crest there is always wind, and I often see raptors here, spiraling in the whirlwind while observers look elsewhere, to horned toad lizards hiding under stones. It's easy to miss birds, tiny specks in the invisible zephyr.

I am waiting for the perfect wind. My feet are balanced carefully, and my arms hold the wings grounded. Through the vibration of the rainbow wings of the glider I feel the updrafts flying up the side of the cliff. There is a crowd growing. Hikers wait on rocks or against trees. Tram visitors snap pictures. Marie helps me watch for measurements or mistakes. In this moment, Marie is my entire world because the next part is knowing when to step off the mountain. After I jump, I don't know where I'll see her next. I feel a small terror that I won't.

A small railroad spike is on the left in front, marking the edge of the cliff. Tied to it is a faded plastic ribbon, showing the direction of the rising wind. Sometimes I wait forever. The altimeter beeps, almost drowned by the pulse of heartbeat and it's hard to believe. All that matters is the wind and my wings and the weight of my wings on the wind.

When the moment comes, it feels as if I am stepping into a portal. Five steps: one-two are starting, three-four are sure, five-six propel me off the mountain, and then there is no footfall, only wind carrying wings, and though I think for sure I am falling, the mountain and Marie are suddenly behind me. Marie can see me, but I can't see her.

I land far below in a field of high rocks alone. When I return home, Marie is reading about migratory seabirds. She closes the book and takes me in her arms and then I am sure that she's real.

That night I dreamed I was back in the sky searching for Marie down in the stones holding her camera, her charts, somehow looking for the wind and somehow finding only Merlin and Nimue in their red track suits carrying peanut butter sandwiches leaving a trail of bread crumbs, and Marie's charts are high in the air around me, the tiny inked birds leaving her arms to join the whirlwind. Marie leaves the ground, flies into the sun.

The next Sunday, Marie pretends not to notice them, but I do. The air is cooler than usual and they are dressed warmly—more warmly than us. We can see hot air balloons in the sky to the East, bright beacons of quiet, floating fire. On the best days, the hawks at the Hawk Watch ride the warm air of the thermals and updrafts that hit the mountain and spin up the cliff. The birds can ride them for many miles, all the while watching for prey. I sometimes think that at the heart of every cyclone, there must be a bird-of-prey.

Marie lists observations for two hawks already high in the wind when we get there. I write them down and we try to calculate the distance. Suddenly she stops.

"Why didn't you tell me she was wearing a fur coat?" Nimue is covered shoulder to ankles in a brown fur. Merlin is wearing a red jacket over his sweat pants.

She lowered her binoculars, her eyes flickered from the cliff to the tiny outlined goshawk on her forearm.

"Have you ever climbed down a cliff?" Marie asked.

I hadn't.

"Well, I have, and I don't want to see them fall."

"What makes you think they'll fall at all?"

"I know you spent yesterday flying, but people don't have wings, Ben."

She's not wrong, but she is surprised at me and at herself. She looks back up at the cliff. Nimue moving like a bear holding hands with an unwitting Olympian, his Icarus wings hidden beneath a red Adidas windbreaker. Sun gleaming off the granite walls, dust tumbling at their footfalls. I imagine, as they walk down together, they are not warning each other to be careful. Instead, Merlin tells Nimue about the first time they held hands and she remembers the new shoes she wore to the movies on their first date. They talk about things like cathedrals and canyons and waterfalls that make someone go crazy with wanting to see the world.

"They just put me in a bad mood, is all," Marie says. She moves the binoculars to her eyes away from the cliff into the sky.

Then somehow, I can finally see it: Marie wishing for wings. Her mind bating, like a flurry of feathers, helpless and grounded. The birds on her arms her tethers to the sky.

That night Marie calls me as I walk home from the dive bar in the student housing. Joe's Place is a world-between-worlds that probably would still be falling apart if the end of the world happened and probably stay in better shape than most places. When I answer, I assume that she's going to ask if I can record the data for this week. She usually does it, obviously. I'm crossing the light at Silver St. when she asks, "Ben, will you drive somewhere with me?"

"When?"

"Now," she says, "or tomorrow, but now is better."

An hour later we're on I-25 flying north, parallel to the twilight, on a road blazed through fields of sage and long tumbling miles of cedar. There is a deep trench of the Rio Grande somewhere between us and the sunset over the volcanic graveyard of the Jemez Mountains.

Tonight, as she drives she talks about raptors and it might be the red sunset in her dark hair and the albatross on her shoulder, I realized I might not know the deepest parts of her, but I know I love her.

"The man you talk about, Ben, who wrote the story of Merlin and Nimue."

"T.H. White."

"He spent a year alone in the woods and he trained a goshawk using Renaissance texts. It was a beautiful bird. Stubborn and perfect."

I know this story.

"The bird leaves him," I say.

"I know," she says. "I like to think it's because they didn't understand each other."

She's talking about us.

To be a falconer or austringer (distinguished for the breeds of raptors they tamed) took great devotion over skill. The birds would be found as hatchlings, stolen from nests, or bred to be trained, and the fledgling would be sent away to their new owner and trainer. Always, when it arrived, it would be a displaced and terrified creature. What built then was a companionship.

The road is flying by now, but the stars aren't moving. Between Albuquerque and Santa Fe, the Rio Grande Valley winds and ebbs. There are tiny river towns and pueblos, wild horses, and casinos heavy with lights and people, but outside all silence and space.

"You learn how to keep it awake on your arm until it trusts you enough to eat from your hand, to fall asleep."

"Easier said than done, I imagine."

"If the bird learns to trust you it will fall asleep, otherwise you are holding a creature that is trapped. It bates and screeches and tumbles and tangles in the jesses."

"Have you done this?" I ask.

"No," Marie says, "Of course not."

"But you've felt it," I say without thinking.

"The staying-awake part—that's not the worst part."

"It's the jesses, I imagine."

"I imagine too," She looks over at me. "I wonder why they did it. It would break my heart."

When I first started learning how to fly, I learned what falling felt like. It felt like relief, in a way. That there could be a physical sensation to failure, and a way to try again, each time building my wings, my trust of the wind. Strapped to wings and a vehicle, you run until the wind lifts you, but you always feel like weight.

As we drive into the mountains, the desert disappears, and the Sangre de Cristo Mountains loom around us, holding headlights. I haven't asked Marie where we are going. It seems important that I don't, but she turns off the highway three hours later in Taos and toward the red gash in the earth too dark for us to see as we come down from the mountains.

To get to the Rio Grande Gorge, we drive around the city, close to the mountain, and then through the edge of town past the far-off lights of Questa and the constant fiesta of the Mothership. I imagine in Taos Pueblo there could be a dance tonight, because the air is perfect and calm and electric. In the city, there are circles of wanderers and revelers and each home we pass has bright lights on porches and moths to welcome their people home.

I've never been to the gorge at night, but—if in the daytime it feels like wonder—at night it feels like swallow. We get used to the night sky holding stars, but the canyon holds only darkness. As Marie and I walk across the bridge, seven miles from anywhere, our footsteps have a hollow din. The rails are cold and metal, and I can't help but hold them tightly. When we get to the middle, Marie sits on the bridge, curls her legs so that her knees touch the guardrail.

"I don't let myself come here," she says, "but it's important that you know this place."

Suddenly, the void moves somewhere inside me. The bridge doesn't feel strong enough to hold us up. Marie sits calmly. My shoulders are suddenly bare of colorful fabric wings and I feel myself falling, so I think of Marie's birds.

"In the mountains here, where my family comes from, the people used to be coal miners, builders, pioneers, dreamers. They still dream. Their town is ghosting, and many of them come to Taos. Still, many of them avoid the gorge, as I do. You see, it happens in my family," she says. "I first came here when I was a child with my mother and my aunts to throw flowers over the rails for my cousin. I remember watching the flowers fall, and seeing a bird dive with them; I know it was a hawk now. I can see it so clearly. It flew headfirst into the gorge and if it came up, I didn't see it. One of my aunties told me that was how birds became dragons. They dive just as though they were flightless, wings spread, tumbling, falling into a gorge of scraggly cedar and dusty rocks."

She pulled up her hair and on her neck between her shoulders, there was inked fire and part of a dragon's wing that I could see even in the small pool of road light.

"I was so young, I thought of my cousin constantly; it was all I could think of—her becoming a dragon. I waited and waited for one day to look up and see her in the sky, but I know that we buried her under a pine tree with a mockingbird nest."

I tell her I'm sorry. I hear my words fall into the darkness.

"And then, one day I found myself here," she said. I couldn't imagine any more.

"I was here," she said, "and I don't know how I left this bridge."

Marie gripped her hands against the rails. We listened to for the river, but all we heard was the road, headlights behind us.

"After I recovered, for a while I wanted to hike to the bottom. That's what I think of when I see Merlin and Nimue. They're trying to get to the bottom. There's something for them at the bottom of the Hawk Watch."

"They're probably just out for a hike." I try. I can't seem to fathom reason. I look for the outlines of Marie's birds in the midnight.

"No," she says. "It's that cliff. For some reason—for them—it's that cliff with the birds flying and falling all around them."

For a while, quiet envelops us. The moon illuminates shadows in the gorge, and the fence lined with locks marked with the names of loved ones and graffiti on the rails. One marking says, *One life, one love, one universe*.

There are two types of flight. One is the ability of birds, you know, to ride the wind. Then there's the ability of an airplane or a glider to synthesize it.

"The third kind of flight," Marie says. "is jailbreak. It's learning how to get back up when you hit the ground. It's learning to have faith in something greater than yourself."

"Jailbreak." I echo.

"Do you like cuckoo clocks?" Marie asks.

"I like the chains you pull to wind them."

"I like the bird that falls in and out of the box. Maybe that's us, waiting for some warm and whistling wind to step into your wings. We all do wild things when we are learning to fly."

"Flying is different than falling. You know that." I muster. She nods.

"I know," she says.

"Marie," I finally say, "I keep waiting for you to fly away."

"I keep waiting for you to fall," she says. "We can't be afraid of each other anymore."

Maybe it's enough, this moment, for us to build something real. We wait there for the concrete to chill our bodies, the cold wind sweeping up through the canyon. An hour passes and then a meteor shower. The moon is half full of coyotes. Marie brings her eyes away from the darkness; she rests her head on my shoulder. I think this is how the wild places age.

The next Sunday, as we drive to the Hawk Watch for our shift, Marie passes the exit.

She doesn't say anything, but she drives faster than usual and at the top of the mountain she pulls off the road into the trees. At the top of the Hawk Watch there is a tiny white cross surrounded by dried flowers and footprints, but Merlin and Nimue are not there, almost as if we had imagined them week after week. We stand at the edge of the cliff and look down. The wind is warm and comes below me in spirals. There's a slight path, worn by tight footprints. Marie chirps to the mockingbirds in the trees. The forests are tall thin pines and wispy aspen. The leaves are a messy yellow, red, and peppermint green in the fall and the trees look like water-colored chile peppers.

I can sense Marie's disappointment that we hadn't found Merlin and Nimue, but just as we look down the cliff-side, a kettle of red-tails, float up all around us. They love the whirlwind. They live and dive *and die* for the whirlwind even though it is dust devil after dust devil. They'll never know how many of us journey to watch them. Below us there is just rock and underbrush.

When Marie takes the first steps on to the path, I almost reach for her, panicked. She looks up at me and takes my hand. We fumble our footsteps, losing hold once or twice in the soft deceitful dirt. The worn path stops about half-way down the mountain, further than we've seen Merlin and Nimue walk. Marie keeps moving, holding her body close to the cliff, and I am so aware of my steps that I forget to think about flight, and still feel like I am soaring.

When we reach the bottom, we are quiet. There are beaming sunflowers: shallow, wild, stalked, and shadowed. The trees are tall and untouched. The birds inside them cuckoo and chirp. The sound of a small creek is somewhere behind them. What we saw then was dreamlike—a stream with glistening water pouring over white stones; the reflection in the sunlight must have been blinding from a birds' eye view. The grass around the pond is the brilliant green of dragon scales, weighed down by its own untamed tallness. The beat of the ancient *acequia* from under the earth, breathing water for wanderers. Tiny skeletons lay dead on the medley of grass and leaves. Shadows of the raptors in the kettle spiraling above paint Marie's body so that it looks like her tattoos have taken flight. One moves behind me, fused with my own shadow, so that—for a moment burned into my sight forever—I have wings.

Elaine Vilar Madruga

The Tanners

"You don't love your kids anymore," my wife spits out. "Are you gonna starve them to death while you're out there, thinking God knows what?"

Her words rattle out of her like machine-gun fire. She's more lethal than the virus that swept through the Fauvist neighborhood a few months ago, nearly solving the overcrowding problem.

She screams. May Da Vinci and Titian forgive me. Women are the most abominable creatures on Earth. She's behind me. With spots on her face. A tattoo of sunflowers spreads across her face like a yellow pandemic. Gogh is the epitome of the good post-impressionist wife.

"Shut up, woman. See? You're frightening the kids." The light from a red lamp stings my eyes.

Picasso Jr. and Yanigauguin play mahjong. They've gotten used to seeing us bicker. Mommy cries. Daddy sighs. They don't complain, though. They're great kids.

Picasso Jr. is old enough to get tattoos. Ink on his face will give him an identity. But we haven't been able to buy him anything. We don't make enough dough for anything other than this miserable life, one step away from starvation. We can't even afford the rent to Guernica, the son of a bitch who manages this apartment. We're one step away from being evicted, from being out on the street.

Picasso Jr. doesn't complain. He's a good boy. He entertains Yanigauguin like the older brother who loves his sister. He teaches her to play. With an air of responsibility, he looks so serious that it hurts. He lights a fly hologram and makes it fly in the air for a second. Yanigauguin smiles.

"Poor Picasso Jr. He's old enough to get tattoos." My wife's words get mingled with other noises like footsteps and chatter. Her recriminations reach full strength. "Do you want your son to be an outcast, a child without an identity, a casteless boy, without a mark to distinguish him from infidels?"

I don't want that either. Picasso Jr. raises his head for a second. So does Yanigauguin. She's still too young to understand anything.

"Did you want kids for this?" my wife keeps berating me. "Did you knock me up for this?"

The sunflowers on her face sway. I'm dizzy. Nausea climbs up my throat. How the hell did I end up sleeping with her? How did I even desire the yellow ink stains blooming on her face? No sane man would ever venture into that shapeless garden. Except me.

"Quit it, Gogh," I tell my wife. I feign despair, but nothing keeps her quiet.

"'Quit it,' my foot!" she shouts. "Look at your poor son, firstborn and without tattoos. Passersby turn to stare. Do you know what they see? An untouchable boy. An orphan."

Yanigauguin cries in a corner of the room. An outcast freak, my poor son works in dangerous neighborhoods. There, tattooless kids have fallen victim to a tanner's knife like crickets crushed by a miller's boot.

Picasso Jr. hugs his baby sister. He tries to convince her that Mom and Dad are just playing verbal mahjong, that soon, very soon, everything will return to normal.

"What's wrong with you, woman? What's the matter, Gogh?" I grab her shoulders and give her a good shaking. Tears well up in her eyes, and remorse hits me. "Do you want Guernica to barge in here and kick us out?" I ask. "Remember we're behind on the rent. Soon you'll have a tattooless son who's also homeless."

She remains quiet. Blessed be the gods. Tears trickle down the sunflowers on her face.

"We could sell my skin," she says, at last.

She's quiet on the surface. But under that thin layer of calm, her blood simmers.

"Your leather or mine," she adds. "Doesn't matter. Don't you think they would pay something for my sunflowers? For my face?"

The image gets stuck in my mind's eye. My wife's face under the tanner's knife. Her skin peeled off. Her sunflowers wither for good. Her death.

"Once, years ago," my voice almost fails me, but I go on. "I saw a man begging for change at a subway station. Passersby turned away from him. He had no face except a blood-colored smear. Not even a Cubist looks that terrible."

My wife crosses herself. She seems disgusted. Almost cracks me up. Ever since we shacked up some twenty years ago, she's never stepped into the Cubist neighborhood. Nor does she think about it without feeling sick to the stomach. As far as she's concerned, those Cubist folks—with geometric tattoos—are true abominations of nature.

"You're not going to sell your skin," I say. "I'll manage it one way or another. Junior will get his tattoos. I promise you. And Yanigauguin too. In due time. When her time comes. She still has a few more years to go."

Gogh smiles and glances at Yanigauguin. She's still little, thank the gods. She won't get her tattoos for another decade. We've got years to recover from the economic blow from Junior's banding. I must hold on to this hope.

"I trust you, my love," Gogh says, quite innocently. The tears are almost dry on her sunflowers. "But it's got to be soon. We can't keep exposing Picasso without tattoos."

She's right. But it's not necessary to spell it all out. I understand what lies behind her words. What she really means. My kids depend on me. What kind of father would allow a tanner to rip apart his firstborn's face, let alone his life? What kind of father would allow his son to work in the factories for peanuts without protecting him from the hatred of those who marginalize the unbranded outcasts?

"Trust me," I tell her for the last time. I kiss the sunflowers, still wet, on Gogh's cheeks. I also kiss my son and my little Yanigauguin.

"Do you want me to stay up, honey?" Gogh asks. My work as a servant in the Romanticism and Rococo neighborhoods lasts until late at night or, sometimes, until the early hours of the morning. Poor Gogh and her jealousy. She imagines me in front of those women, perfect replicas of the Delacroix, Fragonard, and Boucher esthetics, who are so abundant in Romanticism and Rococo. I've dreamed of those rich girls from the neighborhoods where those of us only kneel down and clean.

"Put the kids to bed. And you too," I tell her. "You shouldn't stay awake for me. I'll be late."

Without waiting for her answer, I leave the apartment. For the ninth day in a row, the elevator is out of order, stuck between two floors. The door opens like a monster's mouth. I've got twenty-two floors to go down. My heart is about to explode. The years pass by and leave you increasingly old and poor. On the twelfth floor I think about the beautiful Rococo girls. Their tattoos. Their faces. The Boucher girls are always so high-spirited. The Fragonard girls are always so mocking that they point at you when you inadvertently knock down a glass of wormwood brandy. I hate them. I've got a hard-on as my heart seems to skip a few beats. Bitches. They've never known the risk of going without tattoos, because surely their faces were scarified in utero by the best artists of this universe and the other eight alternative ones. Bitches. They've never spent a horrendous night in a factory like my son. Or in front of an oven with no food, like my poor wife. Or picking up glass shards, like me. Beautiful bitches in wonderful skin. Their hides are worth more than my whole family's life. Outside, the night is a puddle of vomit, spread like oil on canvas. The stars look no different from the artificial satellites and bots swarming over the city.

Underneath the knife was a Parmigianino girl. She screamed, of course, like all prima donnas. Her neck—disproportionately long—trembled. Two men watched silently as the tanner skinned the girl. They all wore masks to hide their faces from each other. Howls. Cold-blooded. After a few minutes, she seemed to give up. She stopped fighting. Passed out.

"Hurry up," one of them said. Under the dim lights in the basement, it was difficult to do precise work. It was also impossible to do it quickly.

"Shut the fuck up," the tanner said. "There's only one way of doing it—doing it well."

"Shut your mouth or they'll shoot you."

The tanner stripped the girl's skin with all the care he could muster. Without damaging the skin or ruining tattoos. He had a reputation for his mastery over the knife.

"It's done. Now pay up," the tanner said. "How much?"

"We brought the goods, dude—" one of them complained.

"—but I did the dirty work," the tanner interrupted. "I can't stand being robbed."

His threat did the trick. No one was going to get into a fight with the best tanner in the neighborhood. He grabbed the bank notes and counted them in silence. His wages never exceeded a pittance, but they meant something. For him and his family. He didn't thank anyone. He avoided haggling. He avoided looking at the faceless, bloody Parmigianino girl. There were only a few hours left before sunrise. The tanner walked through the empty streets. The factory—the girl's skin came off in its basement—became an iron-colored dot in the distance. At last he reached his apartment. Home Sweet Home. The elevator was still out of order. Twenty-two floors to go up. He knocked on the door. Three times just as agreed. A woman with sunflowers appeared with a smile.

"You're late," she complained.

"The girl was difficult, Mom," he said. "Her skin was hard. A Parmigianino girl."

"The pay?" That was the only question that mattered. Picasso Jr. handed her the miserable pittance he had earned at the factory. His mother added, "Better than nothing. It's enough to pay for your tattoos. Have you thought about design?"

Picasso Jr. nodded in silence. His mother seemed happy.

"With what's left, buy Yanigauguin a hologram," he said. "And some socks for Dad. The ones he has are full of holes. Poor old man. I hate to fool him like this. The supposed pay rise at the factory isn't too convincing. Someday he'll find out. He's not an idiot."

His mother's sunflowers seemed to shine. She was smiling.

"Oh, son, don't worry. After all, somebody's got to do the dirty work to support the family. If he can't..." her voice trailed off. "Now listen. A symbolist girl has just moved into an apartment on the thirteenth floor. By herself. She seemed to have been expelled from her caste. Maybe she's a rebel. Nobody's going to miss rebels. How much do you think her hide will cost?"

"Nothing out of the ordinary," Picasso Jr. replied. "But better than nothing, right?"

Her eyes still heavy with sleep, Yanigauguin got up from her bed, approached her older brother, took his knife, and wiped the blade in silence.

"I'm going to heat up some coffee for your father," Mom said. "Poor man, he toils for peanuts!"

Yanigauguin hid the knife under the trail of mahjong tiles and broken holograms in a corner of the room. The sun was beginning to rise. The infamous light of the red lantern was no longer unnecessary. Gogh puffed it off.

Translated by Toshiya Kamei

Willard Manus

When the World Was Young

"How is she, nurse?"

"She's still in intensive care."

"But what's her condition?"

"One of the doctors will come out later to talk to you."

I fell in love with Gail the first time I heard her sing, in a small ginmill in the Village called The Stray Dog. She was working only with a guitarist but didn't let that bother her. Sitting on a barstool with cigarette in hand and long black hair sifting down around her shoulders, she sang with a concentrated intensity and beauty that pierced my heart.

Her set lasted just short of an hour, with one song following another with nary an introduction. I'm here to sing, not talk, was her attitude, so why don't you just kick back and listen, really listen. And that's what the audience did; all chatter ceased as her dark voice—soft, smoky and lush—filled the room; all eyes stayed on her as she picked her way through the Great American Songbook.

Most pop songs are about two things: finding love and losing love. The songs she sang that night were no different, but she managed to make them sound new, find fresh things in the familiar.

That was quite a feat I told her as we walked afterward through the Village, accompanied by her brother, Jim. It was he who had brought me to The Stray Dog and I would forever be grateful to him for having done so.

We headed to the Colossus Diner on Hudson Street; it was owned by twin brothers, Greeks from the island of Rhodes. Gus worked days; Pete, nights, which meant that there would always be a friendly face to greet me.

Pete ushered us to his best booth, where we sat and ate and shmoozed until two in the morning. I couldn't take my eyes off Gail; so smitten was I that I even watched as she chomped away on a hamburger, a messy sight that I somehow managed to find endearing.

"Any further news, doctor?"

Not yet."

"When will you know anything?"

"I'm afraid I can't answer that."

Gail lived up on 67th Street and Amsterdam Avenue in a three-room flat whose kitchen-sink did double-duty as a bathtub. She didn't have much furniture but the flat's walls were painted in bright and unusual colors.

"A set designer friend is responsible for the look of the place," she told me. "He came up here and painted the whole damn apartment himself."

"Is he my competition?"

"Nothing to worry about, Lou. He's homosexual."

"Where did you meet him?"

"I sang in an off-Broadway revue that he designed. Marvin's a real pet."

There was always recorded music to be heard in Gail's pad: Billie or Ella or Bird but especially Clifford Brown. "I just love the way he plays his horn, with such soaring melody and long, flowing lines. And when he drops down and starts hitting those sexy low notes—oh my, I just turn to jello!"

The only time Gail sang at home was when she cooked dinner—"Hawaiian chicken, it's the only dish in my repertoire." She'd stand at the stove and warble favorite verses or scat to one of Brownie's solos—"Joy Spring" or "Lullaby of Birdland."

She kept playing LPs as we ate, in candlelight, killing a bottle of Amaden, listening to the throbbing guitar of Segovia, the insolent piano of Bernstein. The only time the music stopped was when we made love, but it resumed immediately afterwards as we sat propped up on pillows with Gail taking long, deep drags on a cigarette, listening to Brownie again.

Gail smoked Sweet Caporals, a cigarette she had discovered while on a gig in New Orleans; its dark, pungent smell filled her small bedroom and would forever be the smell I'd associate with her, along with the Chanel No. Five that she dabbed on her wrists or behind her ears.

When we went out, which wasn't often because of the lack of funds, it was almost always to a jazz club, especially one where a vocalist was appearing. She also made it a point to catch the work of one of the Young Turks on the jazz scene—Mingus, Coltrane, Ornette Coleman.

These musicians were making new sounds, sounds I'd never heard before, especially Ornette, who seemed determined to attack every musical convention he could, in an aggressive, defiant way that grated on my ears.

"What's with those weird noises he's making?" I asked Gail.

"The noises may sound weird at first but there's a pattern to them, even a beauty. He's just breaking away from fixed harmonic and rhythmic patterns. It's freeform jazz, Lou, without familiar resolutions. But once your ears adjust to it, you'll see how exciting it is."

Gail was right. It took several weeks—and much perplexed listening—but gradually I began to appreciate what Ornette was doing. Like a ship emerging from a fog bank, his music slowly began to take on shape and presence. Soon I came to know it and love it—in much the same way as I had come to know and love Gail herself.

"Why don't you go home and get some rest?"

"No, I'll stay here with you, Lou."

"You're sure?"

"I'm sure."

Jim had recently gone to work as a copy editor at the *World-Telegram*, on the midnight to dawn shift. "It means I won't be able to work on my novel for a while," he said. "But what the hell, I need the damn dough."

Jim was halfway through the writing of his first novel, which was about a character named Billy Bravo, an amusement-park motorcycle rider who sped round a perpendicular wall at 120 mph to entertain and titillate the public. He defied gravity and the fates for ten years, only to suffer a sudden and devastating accident that left him a cripple. Now, having retired to a single room in a crummy boarding house, he craves only isolation until a girl named Lorelei shows up and tries to pull him back from the void, save him with her love.

The book was strange, dark and unsettling—the work of a poet. Jim was by far the best writer in our workshop, but he worked so slowly and painstakingly that he'd written only seventy-five pages in two years.

"You need to get on with it," I told him. "You need to bang out a complete draft instead of trying to make every sentence perfect. All that tinkering and fussing is holding you back."

"Not everyone can work the way you do—bashing away at the typewriter like a wild man, going on instinct the whole time."

"Writing is like sex," I told him. "It's best not to think about what you're doing!"

Just before Christmas my savings ran out and I had to find work myself. Since I didn't want to commit to a steady job, I decided to look for seasonal work at Railway Express. A vast shipping company that moved everything from packages to heavy machinery, Railway Express had such a need for extra hands at Christmas time that just about anyone who walked in the door could count on being hired. It was here that I made a major mistake. The day before my job interview, I went up to the Bronx to visit my mother. When she discovered that I had the sniffles, she persuaded me to try her pet remedy for the common cold.

"Eat this clove of garlic," she said. "It'll clear your head in a flash."

Normally I didn't pay any attention to anything my mother said, but this time I went against myself. Down the hatch went the raw clove.

Twenty-four hours later, while I was being questioned by Railway Express's personnel director, he suddenly slapped down his pen and said, "I'm sorry, I can't go on with this."

"What's the problem?"

"I hate to say it, but you have the worst case of halitosis I have ever encountered!"

But I've never suffered from halitosis."

"Look around the room," he said. "You've cleaned it out."Sure enough, we were the only ones left in sight in the large, open room.

It took some persuading to convince him to allow me to come back the next day.

I've never smelled anything as foul as that breath of yours," he said as he OKed my application. "If I were you I'd never eat another piece of garlic as long as I lived!"

Gail was fortunate enough not to have to work at a menial job to survive. She'd had her fill of those when she was in Chicago, her home town.

"Chicago's tough on singers," she explained. "There are so many good ones there, mostly black of course. "If I could book one or or two gigs a month, I felt lucky."So she quit Chicago and went elsewhere—Kansas City, Indianapolis, New Orleans, a year on the road with a dance band. "Have voice, will travel," she cracked. "I'm just a gypsy at heart."

She'd been in New York for two years now. The jazz scene was competitive—nothing came easy in the Apple—but she'd managed to survive nonetheless. She could count on finding work in the clubs or singing backup on someone else's record date. She also sang at weddings, industrial shows, even at private parties.

Her dream was to become a headliner, but in the meantime, the tweentime, she carried herself lightly, taking whatever came her way with grace and aplomb. She knew that most of the people she worked for appreciated her: she not only sang well but came to work on time and well prepared, and was unfailingly pleasant and even-tempered. As one bandleader put it, "She's good folks."

Gail was also much liked by the jazz fans who frequented the clubs: the night-birds, hipsters, mobsters and molls who sat over drinks and dug the way she interpreted a song, going deep into herself and tapping into the primal emotions that were needed to sing the blues.

And always as she sang, her long, dark hair glistened in the lights and smoke from her cigarette curled around her—smoke that was laced with the Sweet Caporal smell I had come to love. That was Gail, the lady in my life, the love of my life, not just a singer but a *jazz* singer, the highest form of pop-music royalty.

When I was done toting and baling it at Railway Express, I'd join her at the club, mingle with the regulars. It was good to feel a part of the jazz world, accepted by it, even though I was usually referred to as Gail's old man or her main squeeze.

I became particularly friendly with one of the habitues, a guy named Eliot Landry, a self-styled hipster who worked in the publicity department of RCA Records. For some years now, Eliot had been compiling a dictionary of jive talk and was forever referencing it.

"What's shakin', man?" he'd say when we met. "What'cha been puttin' down lately, you big muggle head?"

Eliot dug the way Gail sang and tried to catch her whenever he could.

"She is one down chick!" he said. "I just wig out when I hear her voice. She's got the stuff, no need to bluff! I'm gonna help her make it, sure as a hard head makes a soft behind!"

Then he checked his wristwatch and took off abruptly, explaining, "Sorry. Gotta catch the midnight subway to Brighton Beach!"

A lot happened in the new year. Thanks to the money I'd made at Railway Express I bought enough time to finish my first novel, which was based on the basketball scandals of the early 1950s, when several New York college players were arrested for trying to fix the outcome of certain games. Some bookies had paid these gullible kids to hold the score down, come in under the point spread, enabling them to cash in big.

My novel was turned down by all the important publishers in town—"Sports books don't sell"—but then Roz Sutfin, another member of the writer's workshop, got a job as a junior editor at Ace Books, a fledgling paperback house. She gave my book to her boss, who not only bought it (for a thousand bucks) but expressed interest in Jim's book as well.

That prompted Jim to quit his job at the World Telegram and devote full time to his novel. By working seven days a week, twelve hours a day, he ground out the second half of BRAVO, powered by coffee, cigarettes and the occasional shot of Irish whiskey.

His relentless work paid off. Roz took his still-warm manuscript to her boss, who promptly made an offer (twelve hundred bucks, a small fortune!). We were going to be published. We could now call ourselves professional writers.

It was time to celebrate!

We did it by renting a car and driving down to West Philadelphia, where Gail was singing at Pep's Musical Bar with Clifford Brown and his band. Yeah, that's right, Clifford Brown!

Brownie had heard her in New York a month earlier, when she filled in one night at Birdland for an indisposed Anita O'Day. He liked her so much that he invited her to join him in Philly for a weekend gig. Her turn to exult: she was singing with her idol. And the live session was to be recorded!

We got to Pep's just in time to catch the first show. There was Brownie, tall and alert and youthful as he stood on stage and played that horn of his, round face scrunched up as he soloed crisply and economically on "Lady Be Good," attacking it head on, seducing everyone in the room with his inimitable fat sound.

Then Gail came in with the lyrics, articulating them with her usual precision and warmth, giving them a hip, distinctive edge. As always, she chose not to wear a glamorous gown or play the diva,

just stood there and sang from the heart, sharing whatever she felt with the audience. Then she turned and got into a spontaneous dialogue with Brownie, the two of them spurring each other on, voice and horn dueling one minute, harmonizing the next, neither one of them missing a note or going over the top with their virtuosity.

It went on like that for two nights, nights filled with excitement, wit and swing. Triumph and pleasure were also in the air, joyfulness and love as well. Everyone in the room felt it, performer and audience alike. We were all one, all part of something rare and worthy, and everyone joined in spontaneously when Gail began scatting, making crazy sounds like shoolyakoo and oobla dee and vop vop VOP!

A few months later Brownie left Philadelphia for Chicago, where he was to join his pal, drummer Max Roach, for a week-long gig at the Blue Note. Brownie made the trip in his Buick with his pianist, Richie Powell, and the latter's wife Nancy.

Brownie started out driving but then turned over the keys to Richie and climbed in the back seat for a snooze. Richie, contrary to Brownie's strict instructions, soon gave the wheel to his wife. It was raining heavily that June night and the Pennsylvania Turnpike was slick with water. Nancy, driving fast, failed to negotiate a curve and struck the guardrail. The car then careened across the road, hit a bridge abutment overlooking Route 220, jumped the barrier, and rolled down a seventy-five-foot embankment. Nancy, Richie and Brownie were killed instantly.

Gail wasn't the same after that. She kept working when she could, turning up on time and singing for her supper, but something subtle had gone out of her voice, a feeling of optimism and happiness. It was replaced by a different sound, a sad, wounded, mournful sound.

And at home, up there on Amsterdam Avenue, all she would listen to now was Sinatra, the Sinatra of "Wee Small Hours," the Sinatra of such odd, melancholic songs like "When the World Was Young."

And then, after we had made love and she'd sit there smoking Sweet Caporals and staring into the semi-darkness, I'd see a tear beginning to form in her eyes, slide slowly down her cheeks.

"Thinking of Brownie again?"

She nodded and sighed. "He was so young. Only twenty-five. How could he have died like that? Why did he die like that?"

I had no answers. All I could do was take her warm, slender, grieving body into my arms and hold it close, hold it tight.

Later that year Jim's book was published; a month ahead of mine. *BRAVO*'s lurid, trashy cover showed a semi-naked man and woman in bed, but the flip side of the book balanced that with a truthful photo of Jim that Gail had taken in Central Park. Jim stood posed against a gray boulder, wearing a herring-bone jacket and a turtleneck sweater. His gaunt, lined face and thick black moustache gave him an intense look, the look of a man who felt deeply and painfully every word he had written.

Because Ace Books published original paperbacks on a skimpy budget, there would be no promotional push for *BRAVO*, no advertising or publicity. It wasn't even sent out for review; it was simply tossed out on the book-trade's waters and left to swim or sink on its own.

It was left for us to give Jim a publication-day party, in a small, used-book shop in the Village. It was a low-budget affair: jug wine, chunks of cheese, Ritz crackers. But the atmosphere was jolly and festive, with about fifty friends chatting, joking and laughing. A stack of Jim's books was sold at thirty-five cents each. "Five cents more for an autographed copy," he cracked.

Joe Levitan, head of our writer's workshop, said a few words about BRAVO, praising it as "the work of a genuinely gifted writer. His world, even though seemingly 'foreign,' is one that is immediately credible. With wit, energy and originality, he has produced a profound and powerful work. I'm so proud to have worked with Jim on it."

Then Eliot Landry took the floor and said, "Haven't read Jim's tome yet, but I've gotten to know him lately and all I can say is that he's a real gone guy, a bitchen, gassy, outta sight cat who I dig the most!"

Next it was Gail's turn. Clad in tailored jeans and a rough-wool sweater, she put her head back and sang an a capella version of "When the World Was Young." Big applause.

Then the bookstore owner put on a record, a dixieland thing, and we all started doing an approximation of the Charleston, whooping all the while, and when it was mercifully over, Gail fell into my arms and cried, "Oh God, I'm pissed, I'm so fucking pissed!"

I once read in a physics text book that there is a law of inevitability in life. All things that converge must also recoil, separate, and divide. Then they rebound and begin to converge again, only to disintegrate.

That's what came to mind, for some reason, when the phone rang early one morning a few months later, when I was in upstate New York, visiting my ailing Aunt Mag. It was Jim, with news about Gail.

Having finished a gig at the Five Spot, she had gone home alone at two a.m, crawled into bed, lit up a cigarette, poured herself a glass of Amaden, and put on the just-released record she had made with Clifford Brown. As she listened to herself singing a silky version of "September Song," with a muted Brownie playing double rhythmn behind her, followed by a slow-paced "Lullaby of Birdland," she began to doze off. Was "Lullaby of Birdland" the last thing she heard that night, or was it one of the other tunes on the disc, "I'm Glad There is You" or "April in Paris?" Not that it matters. What does matter is that sometime in the next half hour or so she fell asleep.

Did she have a brief, conscious thought when she woke up to find herself engulfed in flames? Or did she simply pass out from the pain and horror, lose all consciousness? Only Gail could answer that but she was presently in the intensive care ward of West Side Hospital, heavily bandaged and sedated.

I arrived at the hospital just before noon and joined Jim in the waiting room. Neither of us spoke. Neither of us could speak.

We just sat and stared at each other, and all I could think about, once again, was that law of physics, the one which insisted that all things that converge must inevitably recoil and divide. Or disintegrate.

I'm sorry," the doctor said that night. "*We did our best but we couldn't save her."*

At her memorial a few weeks later—it was held at the same bookshop where Jim had celebrated the publication of *BRAVO*—people told stories about Gail, sometimes weeping in the telling, sometimes laughing. Some of the music that she loved best was played: Miles' "Sketches of Spain," Ella's "How High the Moon," and of course Brownie jamming with Max Roach on "Tea For Two."

Afterwards, Jim and I walked through the Village, moving aimlessly and silently. Only once did I stop, when I caught a whiff of something familiar.

A kid was sitting on the steps of his Bank Street tenement, smoking a cigarette that smelled like Sweet Caporals. But when I went to him it turned out to be marijuana. It wasn't the real thing. Not even close.

Ofelia Montelongo

Enema

Part 1—How to Take an Enema

1. Purchase an Enema. Any drugstore must have them. Perhaps they'll ask you what kind, but you won't know because you don't know what an enema is. You ask the pharmacist for enema pills. The lady covers her lips with her fingers. She coughs to hide her laugh. She takes you to an aisle and gives you a large box that read Fleet Enema. You first think of Twitter Fleets. But that doesn't make any sense. There are no enema pills, she says. The lady turns the enema box around. A cartoon-like man on his knees is inserting a plastic bottle through his rectum. She tells you the liquid in the bottle needs to go up in your colon. You shake your head. You don't remember touching that part of your body. You can't even reach it. Didn't your doctor explain to you before scheduling the procedure? She asks. You shake your head again. How many do you want? Two. You can save money if you take four. You buy the four-enema box, just in case you mess up. You walk away. Fast. This isn't the first time you wanted something and got something else. It's like when you applied for a Ph.D., but only got accepted to the master's program.
2. Go home. You have to take (squeeze, insert) the two enemas tomorrow at dawn. You can't drink or eat anything eight hours before your Sigmoidoscopy (that is the name of the procedure you can't even pronounce). You wonder if the camera that'll go inside you will make you bleed more. Whatever happens, you only hope they don't find cancer. You remember an unexpected rectum bleeding rushed you to the doctor's office. They scheduled a Sigmoido-something, a similar procedure to a colonoscopy, just a bit shorter, just like your master's degree. Again, not quite what you wanted.
3. Grab a towel. It's 4 am and eerily quiet. You couldn't sleep, just like when you were reading literature theory and Foucault and Spivak roamed around your head. You set a large beach towel on your bathroom floor and re-read the instructions. You Google for extra advice on how to do this. People do this willingly, even if no procedure is required. If people do it often, how hard could it be, right?
4. Lie on your left side. Bend your left knee. Find your rectum. You move your untouched hair and find your orifice. It's so small. Nothing goes in there. Things go out, not in. How can ten centimeters of this hair-dye-sized bottle go inside of you? You barely can touch it, let alone hold a squeezing plastic. It's your gordura. There's so much spread skin around your body

that keeps you warm but makes you weigh more than 300 pounds and hard to reach behind. You wish your arms were made of rubber. The instructions assume you are normal, just like your professor when assigning twenty-page essays.

5. Remove the nozzle from the saline solution and squeeze the bottle inside of you. If you can't do it lying, squat, and force the tip inside. Wait, you re-read the instructions. No forcing is necessary (phew). The pointy end says it'd be soft, but it is as sharp as the words of your professor telling you that your essay is not worthy of grad school.
6. Your rectum finally opens up and receives the saline solution. You go back to the knee-chest position, clenching. If you drop the bottle to the ground, grab another one. The good thing is you bought extra. The enema flows inside you like those graduate classes that force you to produce writing in minutes even if your body wasn't designed to do that. You don't know that it will hurt until it does. Swaying, you squeeze the bottle with a shaking hand until it's empty. You gently withdraw the nozzle—your stomach growls. You feel bowel movements. It's working.
7. Endure. Oh, mon Dieu. Ay, Dios mío. Oh, my God. A liquid alien is inside of you, demanding to be released. You clench your bottom, which is now facing the ceiling. Try not to scream or barf the enema. This is how it felt when you were researching and writing the essay your professor hated. You want to expel your bowels, but you can't. You have to wait five minutes, and only two have passed. You play music. Shakira. The bouncy music is making it worst. You can't let go, but the gas is stronger than you. The haste is your deadline, so you rush to the toilet with a hand in your behind. You let go at minute four.
8. Evacuate—a raw essay. Your defecation is all over the place, just like your paper, or at least according to your professor. You lose control. You tear up and feel your gut leaving you. Now that it's out, you can't put it back in. You can't take your written words or the excrement spread in the white ceramic toilet back inside of you. You can't ignore someone else saw it or that someone else called it mierda.
9. Repeat. Repetition is inevitable. You're still full of shit. Your rectum knows what to expect, so it opens up quickly. You poke the container and squeeze the liquid in. The second time is not easier. Now it needs to be a seven-minute hold. Your inside wants to burst. You want to release gas, so you clench and clench tight. If you don't do it right, you're not sure if the Sigmoido-something procedure will work. The minutes are now slower. Music doesn't help. I can't, you say aloud. Yes, you can, you respond. You keep clenching like you keep researching, editing, but you can't hold it for that long. Warm liquid starts dripping down your leg. You stand up, desperate, with the towel behind you. You fear the worst.

10. Release. At minute five, instead of seven. Your second trip to the toilet is like eating a bar of chocolate after a month-long diet. It feels good—gone with flatulence. Even blood mixes with the soft stool. You are sure the tacos you ate yesterday are gone. You still feel something inside, maybe the sandwich you had for breakfast. This is all you can do for now. Like the paper you submitted at the last minute. You know that's not all you got, but that's all you can give at the moment. This is your first time doing this, and the instructions are so general. You are doing the best you can.
11. Throw the empty enemas. Your essay is garbage, just like the hollow bottles. Trash. Even your classmates tell you that. "I don't want to be a jerk, but this needs a lot of work." You're a *jerk*, you want to say. Now you know bleeding and shedding mierda is part of the process; your professor and classmates made sure to tell you that.
12. Flush your thoughts and go to the procedure. Now that part of your intestine is spattered all over the ceramic like words disparatadas in a white paper: pat yourself in the back for forcing you to produce, even if it hurt. Stop thinking about what you didn't do right. There's nothing you can do now. Even if you tell yourself that, you still ponder about what the wiggles inside your intestines mean. The throbbing feeling you never do the things right enough doesn't leave you with the enema. You know that no matter how hard you try, there's poop still inside of you. You don't know this, but this will stop. You'll stop bleeding. You'll stop crying, and in a few years, you won't even remember what an enema was. You will look back at this moment, and you'll laugh. You won't exactly remember the professor who said you weren't enough—that your work is not enough. You won't remember the pharmacist who made fun of you or the nurse who didn't even look at you when she scheduled the appointment. You can promise yourself this: the bleeding will stop. Nonetheless, you don't say it to yourself because you don't know yet.

Part 2—The Procedure

1. Drive to the doctor. You need someone to drive you there and pick you up, just like the friends you need in graduate school to survive. You want to avoid thinking on the way to your procedure. What if your growling pushes waste out in the moving car? You take deep breaths, trying to ignore the soggy discomfort. You bring Borges and Anzaldúa to hoard your thoughts. Did they ever have their rectum examined? Did they write about that? You lean your head on the window. The sun is waking up and makes you squint. The minutes are slow as when you were holding the saline liquid in your rectum. Even if the car is going at the speed limit, it looks like it is dragging itself down with your thoughts.
2. Arrive at the doctor. In the waiting room, people read magazines or play with their phones. You imagine some of them are there for the same procedure as yours. You imagine them

bending on their knees and reaching behind. You scan the faces around, all from different ages, just like your graduate school cohort. They smile at you, as they know you haven't eaten or slept. They did the same job as you did. They probably did it right, not like you. Maybe the tall blond lady could reach better, write better. What about the older man with the cane? You imagine he got some help from his wife, who sits next to him, knitting. They all shredded mierda, but they smile anyway. Their faces don't complain about the spasms or the contractions. They pretend for their survival, exactly like grad school.

3. Prep for the procedure. Before entering the prep-room, you have been asked at least three times if you ate or drank anything. No, you answer every time. You mention you brushed your teeth and didn't swallow anything. A nurse gives you a gown. It doesn't close, so she gives you a second one. You wear the second one backward before you lay on the hospital bed. There are three other people in that room separated by curtains. You could hear them breathing and their heart machines peeping the shared hallway. The rattle-off questions begin. Do you have any allergies? The nurse asks while plugging cables next to your bed. No, you say. Height? Weight? You respond. You know you shouldn't lie. You can't hide your body here. You lie anyway, as you did to your advisor when you told him how advanced you were with your thesis. On both occasions, the lie is pretty close to the truth, so they both believe it. The nurse goes back to her computer to type the answers. Do you have a living will? No. Someone to make decisions for you when you are not able to do so? No.
4. Wait. Swaddled in white blankets, you hold your thirst and hunger. You lie there wearing nothing but two emerald gowns listening to the beeping of your heart monitor. Sometimes it synchronizes with the other ones in the room. Even if the blonde or the older man reached their rectum in different ways, all of you beat at the same rhythm sometimes. It happens the same with your classmates. Even if they have more experience emptying their intestines, you all defecated and wrote. You all survived the professors that made you bleed. At least momentarily. You keep waiting. Even if the antiseptic scent of the room squishes your nostrils, the smell of the shitty enema still lingers around you. You look at your barcoded bracelet with your name and fake weight. You trace a finger on your taped IV inserted in your right hand and remember when you were sixteen. You had cancer in your right ear. The doctors removed your lobe—burned it down with radiation. The deep poke inside your vein feels the same way as years ago. You catch yourself hyperventilating. This memory is making your heart monitor beep faster, whirring and flashing numbers at you. You breathe in and out and try not to think about cancer.
5. Wheel to the procedure. A man comes to take you to another room for your Sigmoido-something. He checks the clipboard at the end of your bed and asks for your name and date of birth.

You respond. Your throat feels scratchy. He scans the bracelet and pulls the wheeled bed out of the room. He is before you, pulling through fluorescent-lit hallways. Do you need any help, Carlos? Another male nurse asks. Like if you were too heavy for the scrawny man driving you. Like you were a heavy body, Carlos was pulling from a river. Your feet wrapped in surgical booties are floating. You remember the nurse injected something for your racing heart and bottomless anxiety. Your feet aren't actually floating. Carlos is pulling them out of the river. Other nurses passing by don't offer to help, but they glance at both of us with taunting smiles. Carlos finally leaves you in a cold room with two doctors and two nurses. Your mind leaps into the time when your advisor drives you to your thesis defense and leaves you to present in front of the committee.

6. Get the procedure. The cold room is filled with monitors. They chant offbeat from every part of the room. One of the doctors asks you if you want anesthesia. You say yes. Are you sure? You don't really need it for this procedure, he says. You don't want to feel a camera inside of you, so a yes stumbles out of your mouth again. Another doctor or a nurse inserts a plump syringe into your IV. You didn't get anesthesia in your thesis defense or your comprehensive exams. Still, if you try to describe the details to someone else, just like this Sigmoido-something, everything seems fuzzy.
7. Go back to the curtained room. The unmistakable sound of a fart wakes you up. You are not sure if it was yours or someone else's. In front of you, Carlos is parking your bed in the room, covering a laugh with his hand. Your throat is closed up. With your left hand, you made the sign of a drink to the nurse. Your gruff voice says, water, please. Your hands still smell like a public restroom. You feel like you have been holding your breath all of this time, so once you drink some water, you breath out for almost a minute. You made it. Your thesis has been approved and now you have to wait for the results of your exams.
8. The end. You overhear behind a curtain the waiting-room older man asking the nurse if she believes in ghosts. She bursts into laughter. You definitely feel like one—like a spectrum haunting down all the possible results of the procedure. The doctor arrives later with a clipboard. You are shaking. Dread is eating your stomach. The doctor tells you he revised your intestine. Your heart thumps. The whirring of the heart monitor is louder. He shows you the photos he took. See? Still full of excrement, he says. That was what your professors say about your comprehensive exams. The instructions were clear, the doctor/professor says. You want to say: you expect me to do this on my own with barely any explanation or guide. This was my first time. Instead of saying that, you say nothing. You nod, grateful you don't have cancer or polyps. Even if we couldn't see everything you are capable of doing, the doctor/professor says, you have passed. You are good to go. The bleeding was part of the process.

Mary Overton

The Making of Samson

And the woman bare a son, and called his name Samson: and the child grew, and the Lord blessed him. —Judges 13:24

Oh, for the old religion! For Jehovah. The original Jehovah, when He was one god among many, chosen by the ancient Hebrews to be their own. A manly god. A lusty, hasty, pugnacious god, drunk with ambition, besotted of His consort, Asherah. Such a being appoints heroes to crush His enemies and consolidate His power. The primal Jehovah knows how to summon a hero from among motley farmers, camel drivers, and goat herders.

Start with the mother, is Jehovah's motto for making a hero.

Not just any mother, but a desperate woman. His favorite type: the barren, perimenopausal wife, made reckless by decades of infertility. Suddenly, shockingly, she is aware of a boy-child leaping in her womb.

Visit her with an angel.

When alerting gravid females, Jehovah sends the Archangel Gabriel, Prince of the element water. He can be trusted. He is liege lord of the Western Celestial Army and one of seven magnificent officers who answer directly to the god.

Such a visitation comes to the wife of Manoah in the latter days of the Judges. The record gives no name for this thrifty, crafty housewife who makes and sells goat cheese. She breeds kids so spotless they fetch an excellent price from anyone needing the local witch to read entrails.

On this clear day in April, the woman considers herself too busy for a messenger.

"Greetings, good lady," the stranger begins. He bows, a formal and absurd act in a parochial outpost. "May a thirsty traveler seek the kindness of water?"

The good lady snorts. She continues working in front of her two-room house in the uncrowded village of Zohar. She is packing crockery and rolls of canvas into tall, lidded baskets, using wheat straw to protect the nested bowls, the jugs and pitchers and cups. She squints at the man, for her eyes are weak, and she considers his city clothes. Bluntly she states, "There will be water at the place where you stabled your mount."

"I arrive not mounted," the man replies. He seems unperturbed by her rudeness. "Neither camel nor ass nor gelding."

The woman pauses and stares at his sandals, at the hem of his robe, none of it dusty as would be that of a walker. "I suppose you have wings," she says.

"In a manner of speaking, yes."

His affable nature irks her. Only rich people and slackards have the leisure for pleasantness.

She returns to her packing. The sturdy goat-hair cloth, suitable for tents and awnings, is material she has woven from thread she has spun. The tableware is made by her husband. Manoah is a potter. He manufactures cheap imitations of the highly desirable black and red style Philistine pottery. Every spring the couple travel to the Terebinth Fair in Hebron where they sell these goods.

The angel admires Manoah's wife—her self-possession, her pragmatic attitude. She has the tough-skinned, ruddy face of a woman without vanity. She looks older than her age, but remains agile and energetic and has a wide, sturdy pelvis.

Jehovah, as always, has chosen well.

The stranger says, "I flew down from Heaven to chat with you about the passenger in your belly."

"Ha," she responds. Not one waver betrays what she feels, which is intense surprise and fear. "The only thing in my belly is indigestion."

"You are planning to seek a cure for your uneasy bowels," he goes on. "In Hebron, you are thinking to buy a purge. From a midwife, perhaps, or from a priestess of the oracle."

The woman gives him her full attention. "Who are you?"

"I am Gabriel, Prince of Water, attendant to the High, Holy God of your Fathers."

"My father was an idiot," she says, "as was his father."

"Tribal fathers," the stranger chides her, although they both know what he means.

Manoah's wife snorts again. It's a habit. "What's the water nonsense about?"

"I rule Our God's watery realm. Creation is made of four elements. Earth, air, fire, water." Gabriel speaks patiently, as he believes that part of his mission is to educate. "An Egyptian conceit. The distant Orientals add a fifth element, metal, but Our God doesn't accept it."

"Our God is full of himself." The woman spits. "Always in a madding rage about one thing or another. As jealous as a second son. I'm partial to Bel of the Terebinth Oak, myself. He's the only god doing me any good."

She points to the baskets. Also to the four noisy donkeys inside a mud-brick corral built against the house. Four is the number of material gain. She has purchased the nasty beasts to carry her goods. They will journey two days to reach Hebron and its swarms of pilgrims. Manoah's wife is a shrewd haggler, and every year she obtains excellent prices for their handiwork, and for the donkeys which she sells as well.

The angel ignores her gesture. He commands: "Your destiny, woman, is that you shall serve the Hebrew god. You shall give birth to a son and raise him up. Here is a sign, that you may know it is, indeed, Our God who speaks: He sends you greetings from an entity on the other side, from one who calls you *my poppy cake*."

Manoah's wife is stunned. She has not heard *my poppy cake* since she was a small girl, since her old granny died. Something softens inside her calcified heart.

Then the housewife shakes her head. "Explain this miracle to Manoah. He hasn't raised his staff in a score of years."

Gabriel nods. "I will satisfy your husband."

"Satisfy me first," she says. "Tell me the father."

Gabriel laughs. He knows how the old girl gets around. During the past several moon cycles there have been four men and a youth. "You will recognize the father by the son's hair."

"That answers it." The woman huffs air through her nose, but glumly, more frightened than she wants to admit even to herself.

Back when days were short a traveling party camped near Zohar while the caravan leader recovered from a fever. There were two Egyptians in the group, professional magicians headed for Jerusalem, and they owned a slave with golden hair. His amazing hair was so dirty that the color did not appear shocking. Still, it attracted attention. The slave's face was disfigured by crossed eyes and a broken nose. The man was past his prime and so thin that he seemed a rack of bones, but those bones weighed heavily—blunt, broad bones. Manoah's wife found herself drawn to the man for his stature and his bold, randy humor. His laugh expressed both rebellion and resignation, sentiments with which she can identify.

Perhaps her own hidden drops of golden blood yearned for the man. Unbeknownst to her, the beloved granny had, long ago, coupled with such a pale northerner and had borne a dark child who kept the secret. This more recent indiscretion of Manoah's wife will not be so neatly camouflaged.

Now in the presence of the unwelcome angel, her body makes known its secret. A terrible nausea flushes upward through Manoah's wife, as though she is hostage to some toxin. It permeates her flesh, her skin, her inward parts. She keeps hard crusts of bread in her pocket to counter this bilious condition. She draws one out, nibbles it.

"You are insane," she says. "I don't dare deliver a yellow-haired child."

"Not without preparation," Gabriel agrees.

"I will be taken straight from childbed to the road and stoned for a harlot."

"Fortunately," Gabriel assures her, "the first, fetal hair is black. Later it grows in blonde."

Manoah's wife chews the stiff bread. She still has more than half of her teeth. She wishes that she could vomit away this queasy taste, this heaving gut, this baby.

Gabriel launches into his prophetic mode:

"Behold, thou wast barren; but, lo, thou hast conceived, and will bear a son. Therefore beware, I pray thee, and drink not wine nor strong drink, and eat not any unclean thing, nor make further congress with men: For, lo, a son is born and the child shall be a Nazarite unto God from the womb: and he shall begin to deliver Israel out of the hand of the Philistines."

"A Nazarite!" she shrieks. "A Nazarite! Stone me now and be done with it!"

"Hush," Gabriel scolds. "Do you want to tell the whole village your business?"

"I am not raising a religious fanatic."

"You shall, and you shall be happy to do so. He is going to be a beautiful boy."

Manoah's wife looks unconvinced. "I have never met a Nazarite who was right in the head."

She does not exaggerate. Many quite ordinary people, men and women, take the Nazarite holy vow for a month: refrain from grape products, let one's hair grow, avoid funerals. They do this for penance or for healing or to embrace a discipline. But the life-long ascetics are a different breed. Manoah's wife knows them as lost souls and holy fools, disheveled hermits and urine sodden mad men.

Gabriel nods thoughtfully. "You have seen only those who are self-chosen to the way. Your son shall be different. He shall be trained up within Nazarite conventions. Your son shall be raised up to know he is a hero for his people."

The woman shrugs. "Every mother's son thinks himself a small god."

The angel is not distracted by her doubt. A serene, a sublime expression makes the visitor beautiful beyond words. He continues, "Your son shall be raised up a champion. Let the days of his Nazariteship be as the hairs on his head, as the dust of the earth, as the salt in the sea."

Against her better judgment, Manoah's wife feels herself moved. A private, fortified room of her soul holds the knowledge that she is capable of great things. She is more than what circumstances allow, more than what people judge her. She is sorely tempted to unlock that room and speak about it with Gabriel. But in the end, she keeps her mouth closed. Manoah's wife has no delusions. She accepts that, in the end, her wishes and dreams, the things she wants, have no leverage on reality.

Instead she grumbles, "And it's left for me to do all this raising."

Gabriel nods happily:

"Blessed are you among women, and blessed is the fruit of your womb."

"I'm the one burdened with caring for this unripe fruit, and I can't even give him a decent haircut. Well, my little Nazarite can grow his hair, but it's going to look tidy."

"No combs!" Gabriel cries, looking askance, for the Nazarite pledge specifies—no implement be used if it might pull out a single hair.

"No combs," the housewife agrees. She wiggles her fingers at the angel. Religious rules do not prohibit grooming by hand.

"No grapes, raisins, vinegar, or wine," Gabriel continues, while they are on the subject of restrictions. "Our God abhors worshipers of the vine and their ecstatic lords."

"Tell that one to Manoah," she snorts, for her husband is a drunkard.

"Now, the bit about dead bodies..." Gabriel creases his celestial brow. "I have negotiated with Our God on that one. The law states, and I quote:

"ALL THE DAYS THAT HE SEPARATETH HIMSELF UNTO THE LORD HE SHALL COME AT NO DEAD BODY.

"But your son shall be a warrior, and keeping a warrior away from dead bodies is impractical, to say the least."

"To say the least," she agrees.

"Our Lord is waiving that one." Gabriel shuffles his feet, suddenly nervous. He hates explaining the nuances of Jehovah's thinking. Humans do better with simple yes-no, on-off rules. "Our Lord has determined that this Nazarite shall be in a special class of his own. There shall grow up a tradition around him. There shall be written in the codes: A NAZARITE IN THE WAY OF SAMSON."

The woman looks startled. "Samson? You've named him Samson?"

Gabriel lets out a grateful sigh. She's not going to quarrel a point of law. She's been sidelined by the name issue.

"Who is Sam?" she demands. "Why are you calling him son of Sam?"

Gabriel coughs. "Actually it's a corruption of *Sunson*, 'son of the sun,' for he shall be in the tradition of sun heroes."

"Sounds blasphemous."

"Yes, well, thus the modification."

"And you'll explain it to the neighbors?" she says doubtfully.

"Bring out Manoah!" Gabriel orders, finally losing his calm.

But the woman is not one to be ordered. "So what do I tell the old dog? 'Honey, there's an angel outside who says I'm knocked up.'"

"Identify me as a stranger with a message."

"Will you tell Manoah he's a cuckold?"

"Do I look stupid?"

"Yes," she says. "Don't take it personally. All men look stupid."

"I'm not a man. I'm an angel." Gabriel hates himself for this descent into bickering.

The housewife stares directly at Gabriel's crotch, covered over in the modest style of the day. "Is there a difference? What sort?"

"Nothing you need bother about."

She grins, her expression lewd.

"Go!" Gabriel commands, and the tiresome woman scuttles into her house.

It's becoming harder and harder to endure these interactions with humans. Jehovah doesn't know and wouldn't care what it takes out of His minions. He's a big picture guy. His plan for world domination is brilliant, if risky. Jehovah keeps practicing with these heroes and their mothers, searching for the right combination, the mother/son duo who can take on the leadership role He envisions, become mediators between Him and creation. Then He hopes to step back and focus on a couple of parallel worlds that have been neglected. Earth is high maintenance.

Gabriel, same as the other Archangels, is pushing his own agenda. He calls it the Deist Model, a rational, hands-off management style that forces humanity to deal with the consequences of its actions. This is contrary to Jehovah's taste. What Jehovah adores is the dramatic stunt—a burning bush, manna from heaven, the parting of the Red Sea. Such games entertain Him, but they result, Gabriel has observed, in creating megalomaniacs like Moses who preferred to lead the Hebrews in circles through the desert rather than enter the Holy Land where the patriarch would have had to share power with his generals. Jehovah finally put down Moses, vain old fool that he'd become, so the Hebrews could settle.

Samson will be another of a long line of experimental heroes. If the Samson trial fails, Gabriel is going to suggest a radically different sort of mother. A virgin, perhaps. Jehovah will laugh in his face, but Gabriel is convinced there are strategic advantages to the idea. Several ancient traditions have successfully used the virgin-mother setup.

Gabriel's musings are disrupted by ugly sounds from inside the house. Manoah is receiving a tongue lashing from his wife. The spitefulness of her tirade appalls the angel. Could Jehovah have misjudged this one? Gabriel feels ill. Weary, out of sorts. He decides to continue the interview later and ascends into the vibrantly clear sky. He hears behind him the donkeys, braying like discordant bugles.

It is the following day.

Manoah hears the old Sow shrieking. He is, or was, pleasantly asleep. He had been feeling no pain, and that is a state he considers pleasant. Hearing the Sow's voice under any circumstances is pain. Being awake under most circumstances is pain. He marvels daily at having lived so long with his many complaints—a toothless, rotted place that throbs in his jaw, scabby sores on his bald head, a popped kneecap that cripples him, burning when he urinates, a worm in his gut. Manoah is a small, wiry fellow, not the sort to develop showy muscles, yet like all potters who work a wheel his hand and upper body strength are impressive. If forced to do so, this runt of a man could subdue a much bigger assailant.

He has never known health. He was born the fifth son to a freshly made widow, during a decade of drought when charity became as scarce as water. Only his fierce constitution kept him alive. In a different life, Manoah might have been a fine looking, successful man. He is not aware of this sad fact and so is refreshingly free of self-pity.

The Sow screams in his ear, "Get up, desert dog. The stranger is back."

Manoah does not respond. He talks as little as possible with the Sow.

"The stranger got tired of waiting for you last time," the Sow goes on. "He's back. Get out there and talk to him."

Manoah rolls over and presents his butt. Once, long ago, the first time he insulted his wife in that manner, she slapped her filthy sandal against his backside. He took the case to the village elders and they ordered her whipped. It was extremely satisfying.

"The stranger claims we can't leave for Hebron until you talk to him. He's interrupted my packing twice now, and I'm not getting a late start because you two need to natter over a cup of tea."

Manoah has less to say to a stranger than he does to his wife. He closes his eyes. Men come and go. It is said that the gods made men out of clay, which explains why they are as uninspired, as interchangeable, as breakable as the pots Manoah fires in his kiln.

"Cunt," Manoah mutters.

"Get up," she repeats. "Speaking of genitals, the stranger has a message about that limp thing you call a dick."

Manoah opens his eyes but does not move. God, but he hates the Sow more when he is sober.

"Get up," she insists.

He does so. A half dozen hurts get up off the pallet with him, constant companions. He shuffles to the doorway. Outside the afternoon light is hard and solid, like shining iron. Embedded within this scintillating, voluminous light appears an effete man with his hair in ringlets. Manoah has seen rich foreigners with such hairstyles, but only at a distance, riding in their palanquins or dining on their balconies.

"Hail, Manoah," the visitor greets him. "A goodly man."

"Sometimes," Manoah says.

"All that I spakest unto the woman, shall I also tell thee."

Manoah scratches his chest. "Make it quick."

"LET THE WOMAN, THY WIFE, BEWARE. SHE MAY NOT EAT OF ANY THING THAT COMETH OF THE VINE, NEITHER LET HER DRINK WINE OR STRONG DRINK, NOR EAT ANY UNCLEAN THING: ALL THAT I COMMANDED HER LET HER OBSERVE."

"OK."

"Our God abhors worshipers of the vine and their ecstatic lords."

This oft-repeated bromide is of no interest to Manoah. "Huh," he says. He drinks wine with a clear conscience. He prefers, when he can afford it, a beverage made of fermented honey. He moves to turn around and hobble back to his pallet.

The stranger finally crows the news:

"Lo, a son shall be born of thy loins, a hero unto the Hebrews."

"Go fuck a camel in the anus." Outwardly, Manoah's face remains placid. Inside, he is scalded by the burn of sudden fury. His impotence troubles him deeply. "I should cut your throat and feed you to pigs."

The traveler raises up his arms: "Manoah, sire of a future hero, Our God restores to thee vitality. Thy seed is replenished."

Manoah is on the verge of murder when he feels an unaccustomed warmth in his nether regions. A whisper of sweet longing uncoils in that space below his belly, that place of loneliness and desolation.

The stranger rattles on: "Our God hath need of thy staff, Manoah. Yea, the Philistines are an uncouth people encroaching upon the Hebrews. Vengeance shall be visited upon them by a Nazarite, and this Nazarite shall be called Samson, and he shall be the issue of thy wife."

Manoah can hardly breathe for the arousal happening inside him.

The stranger raises his hands, as for a blessing: "Go, servant of Our God, and know thy wife."

Fifteen years pass.

Fifteen years are to Gabriel but the time he might spend lacing a sandal.

Look now upon the youth, Samson. Long-legged and slim-hipped. Still beardless. Soft, butter-yellow moustache barely visible on his upper lip. As pretty as a girl. His saffron locks in seven splendid braids, each one long as an ox tail. On the nights when he sleeps at home, his mother puts him to bed, rubs oil into his back, replaits his hair, whispers stories. She calls him *my poppy cake*. Her lips touch his ear. A blind man can see the boy does not come from Manoah's seed, but the stupid potter repeats the angel story, *ad nauseam*, until he has quite proven that he is a lunatic. No one bothers to enlighten Manoah. Just don't let him suggest marriage into any Danite family.

But fewer and fewer nights is Samson found at home. The village of Zohar roosts high on a ridge overlooking the Sorek River valley to the south, the hill country to the north, and Samson roams. He is gone days at a time, ostensibly to graze his mother's goats. He wanders north into Ephraim, west into Philistine territory. It's an empty, rocky, dun colored land, miserly on the surface but rich down below where subterranean springs water deep-rooted trees. Green orchards of pomegranate, fig, and olive rise out of the dust.

Samson discovers such an olive grove around an ancient well, all hidden inside a ravine north of the Timnah vineyards. He stops to let his mother's goats chew the tough, salty grass. He collects several hundred stones of varying size and practices hurling them with his shepherd's sling. He is ambidextrous. He fells a sparrow and crushes a lizard, but then the animals flee and Samson marks targets on the fruit trees. The boy pushes himself, in love with the exertions of his body. He can hear the efficient leverage of his long bones, can smell the effort of his muscles. He sucks his skin, thirsty for the fungal taste of sweat. In that dry air sweat doesn't linger. He must work hard for it. The sky is white and arid and absolutely clear.

The boy exhausts himself. He is proud that he must collapse on the dirt, spread-eagle beneath an old warrior of an olive tree.

"Let it be known I died a hero," he announces to the tree, his words croaking through a throat so parched it aches. "Let maidens mourn who never knew my prick."

Actually, Samson's prick has never known a female, maiden or otherwise. His small village has one prostitute, and she laughed when he sought her services for free, honestly believing a whore would be honored to lie with him. He was twelve years old at the time. He broke her nose for the insult, and Manoah had to pay the woman's father for injuries.

Now Samson, on the cusp of manhood, luxuriates in his spent flesh. He lies on his back. His limbs are splayed. His eyes are closed. He sees himself in his mind's eye. Seven yellow braids array themselves about his head like flames on a burning sun. His phallus rises as tall as the sacred baetyl, a stone pillar that marks Asherah's holy ground. The glow of life simmers around his edges. The youth perceives himself wrapped in light, a beacon, so that wherever he may go, Jehovah will track his location. Most shepherd boys are unaware of their own looks, but Samson's mother taught him to admire his face. She gave him a mirror when he was a small child.

"The fighter is ready to drink," Samson proclaims as if to a bevy of servants. He wants to get up, to go to the well for fresh water. Ah, but it's good to lie still and hear the rustle of leaves, each leaf a shy spirit gazing down upon his prone form as he uses both hands to pleasure himself. He hears them whisper secrets about him. "Bring me my golden vessels full of wine!" he commands the olive leaves, and they shake with joy at his words.

Something pulls one of his braids. Samson glares upward into the morbidly mournful face of a nanny-goat. She sticks out her tongue and bleats.

Suddenly he is desperate for drink. He curls his body inward, then snaps out with his arms and legs like an acrobat, so that he's upright, on his feet, the movement quick and limber. He is laughing. He knows the shape of his mouth when he laughs. He is pushing aside the stone cover to the well, pushing as if it were made of the goat-hair canvas his mother weaves. How he loves his strength! He hauls up the precious water in a pitcher and he drinks and drinks and drinks as if there is nothing else, no breathing, no thinking, no shitting, no dreaming—only the pouring of cool water into himself.

The goats erupt into a cacophony of noise. They cry and gallop away. Samson hears their scrabbling hooves over the stones. He is about to go after them, whip their skinny, worthless butts, but first he wipes his face with drops of the water, never spilling any. Water is too valuable for spilling.

Samson turns. He faces a lion.

"So," the youth cries as if to a jolly companion, "Monster, you seek me out."

The young male cat stares with that uncanny, rigid, feline expression.

"You flatter yourself," the lion says. He is big boned, a bit scrawny as if he has grown quickly and not had time to fill out his frame. His black mane is new and thin.

The two enemies are fellow bachelors, callow, solitary, full of untested power and yearning, of an age to have left their mothers but not yet having won their own females.

"I am Samson, champion of my fathers' One God," pronounces the boy, naming himself. "I am chosen to smite the enemies of my people. Who are you?"

The lion roars, "I am the eater of champions!" His challenge is guttural and booming.

Samson laughs with pure delight. Battle! Blood! For one of them—death! All the fibers of his brain hum. He trumpets, "Out of you, Eater, will come only meat! I plan to kill you and to dance around the meat of your carcass."

The lion shakes his mane. "I die daily, yet I return. I am both sun in the sky and gold in the earth."

"I hate riddles," Samson shouts. "Speak like a hero. Aspire to the nobility of man."

"I am the eater of heroes," replies the lion. "I am the eater of men."

Samson looks upward and raises his arms in supplication. "One God of my fathers! He who has ordained me advocate of my people! The adventure begins! Arm me with righteousness! Clothe me in the armor of Your might!"

The youth continues in this manner, on and on and on. He knows the tales, that Jehovah's attentions can be fickle.

Up in heaven, Gabriel is figuratively tugging on the god's robe. "Jehovah, You really must focus on Your hero. Divine intervention is part of the plan."

The corrupt old god peers down at the scene. His vision is not what it used to be. "That's the boy? Good looking fellow. Quite full of himself, isn't he?"

Gabriel restrains his irritation. "By Your instruction, Jehovah. His mother trained him up to be invincible."

"The lad's about to get the shit stomped out of him." Jehovah's interest is stirred. The energy of violence always does that for him.

"Yes," Gabriel confirms. He is practically in hives with anxiety. The lion prepares to pounce.

The god leans down and delivers upon the scene a mild electric shock. Time ceases. Action stops.

The jolt stuns Samson. Momentarily his senses lapse. He drifts, suspended in a blind, soundless, airless, thoughtless space. He re-awakens to the world, but it remains still. He alone moves, through a tableau. The lion is poised mid-leap—claws extended, ivory teeth bare. The beast's eyes burn with the glamour of war.

Samson's tongue delivers oracular words not his own:

"Lo, the ants shall make a highway of your bones, and bees shall nest in your ribs. The mother of bees will be their queen."

He strides to the stationary lion, reaches with sun-burnt hands into the thicket of black mane. Samson clutches fistfuls of hair and flesh, and he begins to tear. His own body groans with the enormous effort. The vitality inside him is unbearable. It grows and swallows him. He is driven to thrust back against it, into it. He strains against the lion until it seems they both must shatter, and then Samson hears a rip in its fabric.

The lion gives beneath Samson's hand.

Tissue and blood and a ghostly clear fluid spill out of a gash in the lion's throat. The world re-animates. The world jars back into action, only now the lion is screaming. The animal is writhing. With bare hands, Samson rends the creature, joint from raw joint.

At last the boy's frenzy is done. He stands, bloodied and triumphant on his secret battlefield. He has always known it would be this way. He was born with the memory of victory.

Chris Paranicas

The Arrangement

The guy at the nursery told me not to mess with invasive plants. I was having trouble getting things to grow in the shade and asked his views on perennial vinca. He said the major and minor varieties spread indefinitely and it would be a fight to contain either one. I already knew that part. I was renting a house in Washington, D.C., and didn't want my two hundred square feet to lay fallow. What I really needed wasn't more information, but a uniform, with "Doug" stitched on the pocket, to go into battle.

The day of Holly's party, I wrapped up in the garden early so that I would have time to clean the mud off my shoes. She and I had worked together at the hospital until about six months ago, when I left to take another job. She was the head nurse on one of the units and I was in billing. We had to interact from time to time, so it resembled a friendship.

By the time I got there, the kitchen and dining room had already filled up. Holly and Bill had a lot of friends, many couples. I really couldn't imagine why she wanted me to come. I'm not very good at small talk. I was planning to trot out gardening as my centerpiece conversation and maybe something about the roads or the rain or roads in the rain if I got desperate.

I was sitting alone on one of the couches reading the news on my phone when someone sat down next to me and introduced himself. Tony was about my age, late thirties. He was wearing blue jeans, a polo shirt, and untied work boots. We had the obligatory conversation about our jobs. Tony told me he had worked at the same company for ten years dealing with computer hardware. He liked to fix things and move around.

I told him about working in the garden earlier in the day. I said I worried that I might be a pawn in vinca's quest for world domination. He said he had been in Annapolis in the afternoon on his sailboat. He explained to me the challenges of sailing alone. He said he had had a good workout, the wind being what it was.

Tony was thin and strong. I wondered if instead of periodically trying to cut out sugar, I could just sail my way into a similar physique. I guess I was pondering this for a long time because Tony said, "but you probably don't want to hear all that boring stuff." I never know how to respond to comments like that. No, I do want to hear all the boring stuff? Tony seemed like such a cool guy that I also vetoed "on the contrary." I settled on, "not bored."

Holly picked that moment to come over. She and I hugged and she told Tony how much people on her unit missed me. I appreciated her comment although *have already forgotten him* would have been closer to the truth.

Holly said, "And I'm so pleased you two met."

I said, "I was just wowing Tony with my inability to keep up my side of the conversation."

Holly said, "Don't let him fool you. He speaks plenty when he has to and has a passable sense of humor. You both do. Not to mention your mutual interest in men of course. Did you notice how straight Doug's teeth are?"

I felt my cheeks burning. I was wracking my brain trying to remember what personal details I had told her that might come spilling out.

Holly said, "I'll give you a chance to get better acquainted. Tony, Doug will give you his number." And then she disappeared.

Tony asked me if Holly had ever mentioned him to me. I said I didn't think so. Even though I wasn't there anymore, we still focused on hospital talk. I told Tony I knew they had another place in Annapolis but not a lot else about her life outside of work.

Tony said the day was starting to catch up to him. I said I was tired too. The summer in D.C. does that to me. Plus you never want to turn your back on vinca, which is like bamboo's evil cousin. He said he looked forward to hearing from me. I unlocked my phone and handed it to him. He took a minute to compose a text. We stood up and shook hands and then he squeezed my shoulder, smiled, and left.

When I got home, I read the text he had sent himself from my phone, "Don't wait two days."

Our first date was a hike at Great Falls. The parking lot seemed really crowded, people were carrying coolers, and kids and dogs added some chaos. At the beginning of any relationship, I think about having kids and dogs with the person I am dating. Later on, I don't worry about it anymore.

Tony had on shorts and a T-shirt with hiking boots. His legs were thin and sinewy. A few men and women smiled at me. I interpreted this to mean, *nicely done*.

We spent a lot of our time walking together in companionable silence. We stopped to look at turtles sunning themselves. Tony pointed to a tree and asked me what kind it was.

"It's red maple."

Tony smiled. "It looked familiar. Sorry."

"I don't mind." Then I said, "Wait until I fall out of your sailboat while it's still docked."

"I'd like to take you sailing some time."

"This was a good idea."

Tony said, "how far do you want to go?"

I made a sound like, *I nuh*, and put my hand on the small of Tony's back.

Another smile. A good sign. Tony took a cap out of his backpack and put it on. It had a nice amount of wear to it and I wondered briefly how much planning went into Tony's dreaminess.

"So how do you know Holly and Bill?" I said.

He said he and Bill met through sailing. He was glad they fixed us up but annoyed about the reason. From what I could glean from the next few sentences, they did not like the person Tony was currently dating. I didn't realize until that moment that we had been fixed up, although it explained why Holly invited me to her party. Tony must have noticed that I got quiet. He sighed and took his ball cap off.

He said, "Don't worry. My thing with Frank is doomed."

I hadn't been thinking about that. I was chewing on the concept of being fixed up without anyone mentioning it to me. Holly didn't usually hold many things back.

I said, "Doomed because he's wanted by the law?"

Tony laughed and said, "No, he's an attorney himself, married to a woman. Really unhappily. Bill and Holly think I am walking in a minefield, but it isn't like that at all."

I said, "It still sounds complicated."

Tony said, "It's more recreational than anything."

With his cap off, I noticed Tony's eyes were bloodshot. We had been walking for a long time.

"Maybe time to turn around? I don't want you to remember this as the day that random guy from the party caused you to get a bad sunburn."

"You're not a random guy, remember?"

I felt dizzy from the conversation and the July heat. On the way back, we stopped at a crowded restaurant with blonde wood and clean lines. The menu overwhelmed me. When did having so many choices become appealing? A bearded guy, waiting to take our order, was scowling.

I said, "My mind is blank."

Tony said, "Point somewhere."

"One of the salads. I've been beating myself up about how little daikon I eat."

"Go get some seats. I'll take care of it."

I found two free places at a counter next to the window. We both faced the street. I had enough of his good looks for one day anyway. Tony put two fingers through one of my belt loops and ate with his left hand for a while.

Driving back I felt tense. Tony didn't speak much. I didn't know where things stood between him and Frank and so wasn't sure what my next move was going to be.

Tony said, "Keep a day open next weekend."

"Maybe we shouldn't start dating until I find a boyfriend."

Tony smiled then kissed me. "Are you always this funny?"

"You're inspiring me."

After Great Falls, Tony and I had dinner together the next two Saturdays. I wasn't making much progress on what exactly I was doing, so our dates involved talking and hugging each other goodbye around the time it was getting dark. I couldn't work out how to fit into Tony's current life. He already had a house, a job, a car, a boat, and a regular sex life. What did I bring to the table? I didn't cook or change oil.

On the third Saturday Tony texted me "Can you drive me to Annapolis?"

I picked him up at his place in Maryland, several miles past the D.C. line. It was a small, unattached, brick house with a long dirt driveway leading to the back. The lawn was a little wild and had no flowers or trees on it. There were some hedges that needed attention, spaced randomly along the road. Tony was waiting for me outside. He had on a dark green T-shirt tucked into khaki shorts with no belt, and running shoes.

"Everything OK?"

"Yeah, just something stupid."

"So where are we going?"

"To Bill and Holly's. I left my wallet there."

"That's why I am driving?"

"Yeah."

"That's funny. You're having sex with a married man but you're afraid to drive to Annapolis without your license."

He didn't respond. "When did you leave it there?"

"Yesterday."

"You cut out of work for some sailing?"

"No."

Tony was blushing.

"I don't get why you're using their house."

"Frank lives in Annapolis. He's Bill's lawyer."

I shook my head slightly and rolled my eyes.

"Now you're mad at me."

"More like confused."

"I shouldn't have asked you to drive me today."

"Yeah, what were you thinking?"

"You're the first person I call now."

Tony directed me to their street and when I parked, he got out to search for his wallet. I couldn't deny the possibility that Tony was changing his mind about the direction things were heading between us and this was his unsubtle way of mentioning it.

On the drive back from Annapolis, we listened to the radio. Tony tuned it to the baseball game. It settled my mind down to hear someone say where a ball landed, who picked it up, and where he threw it next. I couldn't face going home after I dropped Tony off. Sometimes the garden distracted me. I could crawl around picking up dead leaves without a care in the world. But even that wasn't going to cut it today.

I stopped outside Tony's house and said I would call him.

A few days later, I called Holly.

She said, "I'm cooking dinner, so make it quick."

"What was your brilliant plan here?"

"Bill thought we should find someone for Tony."

"He has someone."

"You know what I mean. So that Frank would get the hint and disappear. I'm not convinced he prefers men, so all I can see is Tony getting hurt in the end."

"You were what, running interference?"

"We put a lot of thought into this and chose you."

"You could have told me all this before the party."

"Would you still have come if I had laid this out for you?"

I hung up. She said it would have to be quick.

Almost four weeks passed. I had to face the fact that we are living in an age when two people could meet up for sex and never give a second thought to their souls. I wished I could complain to Tony about it, but he was part of the advancing army.

I texted him, "You did tell me about Frank at Great Falls. I overreacted."

"At first I thought you were cool with it."

"I hope you're joking right now."

"So what, we're speaking again?"

"I guess, since I'm checking up on you."

"I'll be honest; it's been a tough month."

"I didn't mean for us to stop hanging out. Can we at least stay friends?"

"I want more than that with you."

"Are you sure?"

Tony texted me the following Thursday. "Saturday a possibility or do you have a big date?"

I responded, "No, my big date is tomorrow."

He just wrote "ha ha." Then later, "hope he is as good-looking as me."

I texted back, "not that high a bar."

He wrote, "ha ha again. I'm stepping up our game on restaurants."

Tony picked me up at six for dinner. He is a very focused driver, so we didn't talk much in the car. We seemed to be heading into the suburbs. Tony had on a white short-sleeved shirt with a collar, a pair of dark suit pants, and black dress shoes. It looked sportier than what I imagined he wore to his computer job.

We arrived at a restaurant that was surrounded by trees. Tony put his arm around me as we walked in from the parking lot. It was starting to cool off.

We were the only two guests in a dark, paneled dining room. Pictures of hunting scenes, with dogs and horses standing around, hung on the walls. It reminded me of an earlier era, when the biggest problem facing the D.C. suburbs was foxes. I sat across from him and tugged on the tablecloth to align a furrow with the diameter. The ice water sloshed. Tony said I should get a drink if I wanted one, but he was driving so would pass.

We both ordered the same thing. Whenever we had something in common it surprised me. Mostly we seemed to be opposites: dating styles and the land-sea divide being two obvious examples. I couldn't figure out why Holly and Bill thought this was such a great match. Maybe they just wanted Frank to stop using their guest room.

I was starting to get used to the way Tony ate things in order. First he would eat all the tomatoes, then the cucumbers, then the peppers, and so on. Holly once said what you love about someone at the beginning drives you crazy twenty years later. I never had the experience. I was trying to imagine twenty years from now in this restaurant. Same type of candles but the white tablecloths would be more frayed. We would probably have a regular table by then, under the largest picture in the room, with the hound whose face had three different emotions. It was hard to believe Tony's rigid way of eating would ever bother me. I wondered if Holly and Bill were wrong about everything.

When we both finished, Tony leaned back and put his leg between mine.

I said, "I don't know, Tony. It's a hard situation for me to get my mind around."

"Frank is just someone I hook up with. That's all. Why can't both things work?"

"It's impossible. I promise."

We had coffee. Tony paid and then drove me home. The ride back was silent again. Tony parked near my house.

I said, "Well, thank you. You should've told me we were going deep into the Maryland woods. I could have driven out and picked you up, instead of your making two round trips."

"Don't go yet."

We sat in Tony's car in silence. It was finally cool enough to have the windows open. For me the summer in Washington is like the winter in Alaska. My cabin fever can get intense. Fortunately the garden is in the shade. The layout of houses, garages, fences, and trees has the effect of blocking out most of the sun. I realized it was probably why I hadn't quit gardening. I was also attached to the ferns.

Tony said, "My hands are shaking."

I put my left hand on top of his right hand. He leaned over and kissed me. I let my fingers slide up from his neck to his soft hair. He had both hands on my waist, one edging into my pants.

I stayed for a while. A long stretch of silence followed. Another thing we had in common.

I said, "Friendship with me isn't so bad. I can water your plants when you're away; take a look at your hedges."

"What are my other options?"

"We keep going around in circles maybe making out in your car, or you get serious about this."

"How do I know you aren't going to disappear at the first sign of trouble?"

"Wait, what?"

"I didn't hear from you for almost a month."

I got out of the car. "Maybe you should be more careful with your wallet."

A couple of days later, Tony went out of town for a conference related to his work. I called Holly and said I was sorry for hanging up on her.

"I shouldn't have sprung that on you. I see that now."

"More than anything else, I appreciate your thinking of me."

"What's going on with you two?"

"Good question. Are you sure I'm in the same dating stratum as Tony?"

"You would be good for each other."

"I'm not sure Tony wants what you think he wants."

"I've known him a lot longer than you have. I know what I'm doing. Maybe don't give up so easily."

We said goodbye.

On the Saturday after Tony got back, he suggested that we do something early in the day. He picked me up with my bike and we went to Georgetown. It was starting to get hot and the trail wasn't very crowded.

I said, "Your trip was OK?"

Tony said, "Yeah, except for the plane, the hotel, and waiting in line for the rental car."

The bike path toward Bethesda has a very gradual upward slope. It would have been hard for me to keep up with Tony even on a flat surface. He slowed down. A lot of guys would have used the opportunity to point out they were in better shape.

When I had thoughts like that, it made me feel guilty about not calling Tony for almost a month. I should have said yes, no, or maybe. How hard could that have been?

"You were right about me. Being silent for so long. I wasn't thinking."

"Being right is overrated."

"Now that you told me, it won't happen again."

Tony was staring straight ahead. He seemed to be in a bad mood. I was weighing attempting to apologize for a third time. If our relationship was going to go forward, I was determined to keep some part of it on solid ground.

"I spoke to Frank. We're taking a break for a while. Does that work?"

I nodded.

Half an hour later, we stopped to rest. We leaned our bikes against a plane tree. Tony knelt down to tie his shoes. I picked his helmet up from the ground and handed it to him when he stood up.

Tony said, "I'm done eating cereal by myself every morning."

We got back to Tony's house in the afternoon. We stood at his kitchen sink facing each other gulping down glasses of lukewarm water. Both of our shirts were wet. Tony was standing really close and then we were kissing. He pushed me back against one of the counters, undid the button of my shorts and pulled down the zipper.

After showering, we were lying on his bed. It was cool in his bedroom, so Tony lent me a pair of his sweatpants. He had his head on my stomach. I was tracing the veins in his hand and wrist with my fingers. When he drifted off to sleep, I rested his hand on my chest and steadied my breathing.

We ate dinner in Tony's backyard.

He said, "You're staying over tonight right?"

"Definitely. But I have to be at work on Monday."

Tony grinned.

It stayed warm even after the sun set. Frank was on my mind. I supposed we would all meet one day in the parking lot of a supermarket in Annapolis. Later, Tony would say, *uh, that was Frank*. And I would say something like, *the Frank*? *Talk about charm*. For the record, I think vinca has charm, but ominous is my primary association to it.

I said, "Thanks for the clothes by the way."

"I like you better without a shirt."

"You got it."

Che Parker
Death of a Man

It went like this:

The nightclub was jumpin'. Jazz. A band was playin' some oldies but goodies. People was laughin' and dancin' and drinkin' wine and beer. Poppa was at the bar havin' a cold one just mindin' his own business. That band was playin'! I mean playin'! The lead singer was sweatin' somethin' terrible and he was tappin' his foot and the drummer was drummin' and they was goin' at it. Really jammin'. Poppa was bobbin' his head (just a little) and really feelin' that cat go. The mood was good and everybody was havin' a good time right on Prospect Avenue. Just when the set was wrappin' up and the people was clappin' and the lead singer was givin' his "thank yous" (he was a local kid done good, grew up not far from Prospect Avenue) well, that's when Sugar started cursin' one of his whores and sayin' she disrespected him.

"You ain't worth this," he said and tipped his glass a bit and a drop of whiskey hit the floor. "Now get down there and lick it up, you damn dog!"

The music stopped cold. Got real quiet up in there. They said you could hear a mouse piss on cotton. The whore musta' been scared 'cause she was shiverin'. She was real pretty and high yellow with long wavy hair.

"Come on now, Sugar," the bartender said. "We just tryin' to have a good time."

"I is havin' a good time, Bookie," Sugar said. "Now, like I said, lick it off the floor!"

Now the girl truly had to have been scared of Sugar, 'cause she started down like she was 'bout to lick that spilled whiskey off the floor, and that's when Poppa stopped her. He reached out for her shoulder and stopped her kneelin' motion and looked like the Lord Almighty touched her or somethin', 'cause she jumped up, and moved and stood behind Poppa. That really pissed Sugar off 'cause then he said somethin' like "Fool, is that yo' lady?" Poppa shook his head. "Then sucka, don't touch that hoe. She's my property!" But Poppa didn't budge so that musta' really pissed Sugar off 'cause that's when he pulled a blade and the whole nightclub gasped because that meant he meant business and Poppa still didn't budge (musta been some trait or values for courage or somethin' that his father instilled in him). But Sugar didn't bluff and he wasn't known for bluffin' and people knew that so he stuck Poppa with that blade a few times in the gut and ran out the club and Poppa fell over and the girl screamed and a lot of women screamed and Bookie leaped over the bar like a young athlete and pressed them white bar rags on Poppa's wounds but too much blood was comin' out and Bookie yelled "Somebody get a ambalance!" and he kept pressin' them dirty bar rags that smelled like beer on Poppa's wounds but it was too much blood just too much blood and it kept spillin' just spillin' out his gut and the ambulance came, it got there quick is what they said so Poppa was spared from dyin' in a nightclub but he died in the back of that ambulance on the way to the hospital. Just too much blood lost.

That was Poppa. And that's how Poppa got murdered.

A few days later Momma and Grandma took me to church for Poppa's wake.

Momma and Grandma had been raised in the church. They still went from time to time, but not as often as they used to. The old pastor died at the church they went to for years and Grandma said it wasn't the same. She said the church only cared about takin' money, not savin' souls, and she stopped goin'.

"You gone hear the Word today," Grandma said. "Shouldn't be this way. Your daddy's wake. But that's the way the Lord wanted it. Get dressed."

I got off my bed and got ready, brushin' my teeth and washin' my face. Momma was already up fryin' eggs and bacon. After I got dressed we took a few bites and got ready to go. Grandma didn't eat. Her and Momma wore all black. Grandma also had on a small black hat with lace around it. I had never seen it before and wondered where she kept it.

"Come on," she said. We walked out the house and down the stairs toward the church. It was close, a few blocks away, so we didn't need to catch the bus. It was still early in the mornin' so it wasn't too hot out. Momma's legs and feet was botherin' her again so she was walkin' slow. I walked next to her. Grandma walked fast and was about half a block ahead of us.

We got to the church and it was startin' to fill up. Grandma sat in the first row and me and Momma joined her. Right in front of it was the casket. Poppa had no other family, just us. He had a baby sister when he was younger but she died. Scarlet fever. I could see Poppa's face, but I didn't want to look at it. Momma was sweatin' real bad. She wiped her forehead with a handkerchief. Momma wiped her face again. I saw her glance over at the casket. She didn't look long.

The organ player was a fat man with a Jheri curl. He was smilin' real hard and sweatin' even harder. He was bangin' out the sounds and people was standin' up swayin', wavin' they hands and sayin' "yes, Lord!"

Grandma was tappin' her foot. I looked at Grandma's hat again. Did she keep it under her bed? The choir started singin' and it was like heaven opened right up. The singin' was loud, real loud, and the sound from the speakers on the stage went right through our bodies. We could feel they praise. One young girl in the choir, she was probably my age, started singin' this song, "Oh Happy Day." She let out that voice and the people started shoutin' louder. They was tappin' they feet. Some stood up and shouted, yellin' for her to go on. A couple people was even dancin' in the aisles. The young girl was usin' her whole body to get the words out. It was like she was vibratin'. I looked over at Momma and it looked like she was cryin'. Although she could have just been sweatin'. She wiped her eyes. Grandma was singin' along. I hadn't heard her sing since I was a real little kid, and I forgot she had a good singin' voice. She sounded real good.

The new pastor of the church came from around back and walked to the podium. He had on a dark gray suit with a bright yellow tie. He was young with a mustache and slicked back hair. The young girl was just finishin' the song. The people was full of energy and smilin' and cryin' and fannin' themselves. They was clappin' and clappin'. The young girl smiled and moved back to her place in the choir.

"Let the church say Amen," the pastor said.

"Amen," the church said.

"God has truly blessed us with the voices of angels. Amen?"

"Amen," the church said.

"Lord said, seek me, and you shall find me. And church, I see some of y'all are seekin'. Amen."

"Amen."

"Yes, Lord," one woman said behind us. I looked back and saw she was wearin' a big pink hat.

"Church, we are here today to celebrate the life of a man. A good man."

"Amen," the church said.

"Cut down needlessly, church. And yet, there's something else I got to say. SInce I have you here."

The church chuckled.

"Church, there are many out there, many sheep, who have strayed from the flock. Amen."

"Amen."

"And church, these sheep, these sheep who have strayed, church, they've found other things to sustain them. They're not sustained by the Word! Church, they're not sustained by the Lord! Amen."

"Amen."

"No church, they have found crime and drugs. They're not sustained by the risen Christ. Now, now, Jesus said, judge not, lest ye be judged. So church, don't get me wrong today. Don't get me wrong."

The church chuckled again.

"I don't want to judge the sheep who are grazin' on the food of criminal activity and drugs. No, church. I want to steer these lost sheep back to the flock! I want them to be sustained by the Word of Christ. Can the church say Amen?"

"Amen!" the church said. He went on some more about the evil of doing crime and drugs. I thought about some of the junkies in our neighborhood. I wondered if they thought drugs was evil. The preacher went on some more and after a few minutes the choir started singin' again. After hearin' a song I never heard before, the young girl came back to the front of the stage and started singin' again. "Sinner pleeeeaaaasse!" she called out. It sent chills through the church. Her voice, and those words, sent an energy through everybody. All of a sudden it was like she was a lot older than me, at least like fifty years old, and had a long, hard life. Like she had been through things that grown ups go through. She wasn't a little kid like me. Not right now. Not while she was singin' this song. I could feel it. Seemed like everybody else could, too.

"Sinner, pleeeeaaase don't let this harvest pass," she sang. "And die and lose your soul at last."

I looked over at Momma and she was definitely cryin' this time. But she was also smilin'.

"You OK, Momma?" I asked.

She just nodded. I looked at Grandma and she was just tappin' her foot with no look on her face.

"See where Christ has died for you and me," the girl went on. "My God is a mighty man of war."

She sang some more and it was like the Holy Ghost, whatever the Holy Ghost was, was right there with us. There was so much energy, smilin', cryin', dancin', wavin' and faintin'. After the song ended everyone clapped. The old woman who was singin' was now a young girl again, walkin' back to her place in the choir.

The pastor came back to the stage and preached some more about sinners and acceptin' them, not judgin' them. I felt like he was talkin' directly about Poppa, but I wasn't sure. I found a loose thread on my shirt and started to play with it. I didn't hear much more after that. The preacher said something about Poppa being a good man, like many other people had said. The funeral was ending. Momma stood and walked to the casket. The church went quiet. She stared at Poppa's face. She crying something terrible. Then she came and sat back down.

The pastor said a prayer, and then he said something contributing to some church project and they sent the tithing plate around. Grandma looked at me.

"Let's go."

We started to get up, I took one last look at Poppa's body. His face was a mask. One of the ushers gave us a crazy look as we walked away. A woman walked up and said "I'm sorry for your loss." Momma nodded. "Thank you," she said.

Grandma didn't say nothin'. We walked down the aisle and out the buildin'. We started walkin' home. Grandma was already a few steps ahead of us.

"Grandma," I said, tryin' to get her attention. She didn't answer.

"Grandma." She was gettin' further away. She stopped.

"I ain't got no umbrella, so I don't need your rain."

She kept goin'. I looked at Momma and she didn't say nothin'. She could barely walk herself. Grandma was soon a block ahead of us.

"That was a good service," Momma said.

Was it? I thought.

I could only remember the girl's voice, and Poppa's cold body, mask-like face, in the casket.

Poppa was a good man. That's what they said.

Meg Pokrass

Eleanor Rigbys

It was Halloween, a holiday I distrusted and worried about and normally avoided by turning out all of my lights and sitting alone in the dark. But this time I had arranged a date. The movie we'd chosen, *Eleanor Rigby's Escape*, had received mostly bad reviews, but the line to get in was enormous.

I told my date the truth—that I wanted to see it because it was the story of my life. I felt a bit odd about telling a person I didn't know that I identified with such a depressing character. But this was the way my brain worked. Divorce had burned a hole in my confidence, and the smoke never left the room.

"It's the story of my life too," my date said.

Her name was Grace Robenstein.

"Just let me know if you hate the film, and we can just get up and leave," I offered. She looked at me with wounded terrier eyes.

For me, this same-sex date was theoretical. I was as straight as Eleanor Rigby probably would have been.

"I'll betcha Eleanor hated Halloween," I said, to break the ice. Trying to make my poor date laugh. Maybe I could kick up a spark, because here we were, stuck in an unmoving line to see a movie about a lonely woman who dies alone with her name.

A piece of thyme was caught between two back teeth from the shitty frozen pizza I had prepared for myself before the movie. I dislodged the sprig of thyme with my tongue, poked it around inside my mouth. Everyone needed a secret, I thought.

I imagined Grace and I vacationing on a barren Scottish island, perhaps Shetland in the winter, the two of us huddling together as dark days turned into one. How are your knees? I'd ask. She'd be rubbing in anti-inflammatory gel, trying not to eat too many crisps. I'd be trying to remember to do my isolated hip exercises with a red resistance band. Maybe we'd go out for a gluten-free beer in the evenings.

Grace looked sober and a bit wise. She could have been cast as Eleanor Rigby's therapist. Getting old was becoming serious business.

I told myself to relax. Soon we'd be watching ourselves on the screen. I tried to imagine kissing Grace Robenstein. If this were a movie, she'd be played by Helen Mirren, which would make it easier. I reached into my rain slicker and snuck out my flask. *Spot of whiskey, Grace?* Her lips wriggled together like an earthworm. My lips wriggled back.

Rebecca Pyle

A Pond by the Anthropology Museum

Beautiful at the university were the anthropology museum and the natural history museum and the temple dedicated to law with a statue of an old professor in front. But most beautiful was the plainest: a rectangular pond, longer by several feet than the tallest person you will ever meet; in other words, this is a pond for everyman, everywoman, everychild. You could be born in it and die in it; no one, floating, would be too long; your long hair could stretch out behind you, and only begin to curl alongside the simple stacked deep greenish blocks of clay which hold the water in, hold it and hold it, very still.

They met in front of it, the college girls, each school year: they met there on some pretext which was forgotten, once they were at the pond. Beside and slightly above was the anthropology museum, which had once been when the university was smaller, the university's art museum. But it continued with sacred, shielded things, which were shields in themselves; these were the places you went to visit when all was fading from you, and you needed armor bigger than armor you'd had—when your friends were not, you were realizing, sufficient to buoy you and encourage you.

It was sweetly rank, and greenish; it was rot making peace with rot. It was time going by and blinking sweetly, not protesting; it was saying sometimes let things lie. Forget ambition or who was best; it is all good, said the old pond, which had no frogs in it, but looked like a place frogs would like, if it was warm outside.

No one visited the pond in winter. It was the pond of spring, and the pond of autumn. In summer it was not visited much, because then it was not tinged with the power of the spring that would turn into summer, or the autumn which was the last remnant of the power of spring and summer.

One year the college girls went there as a group—their small dormitory was nearby—and a horse came out of the water with double heads. Oh no, cried the leader of the girls. We are sorry we came.

The two-headed horse watched them go. When they were gone he sank back into the water.

Another year a jealous mother craggy with fury rose out of the water.

Oh no, she's not someone we want to be around, said that year's leader of the girls.

The jealous mother sank back into the water, but with a look in her eye that said she would be back. At her shoulders were the two stepsisters who wanted to harm their sister. But they had not even a chance to rise. They laughed and cackled at each other as they sank back into the water.

Another year went on, and then came a day the new women students at some orienteering session were around the frog pond so marvelous.

Oh look, said one. Look who's coming up.

It was the god of indecision; curls went one way on his head, and then another. His mouth smiled on one side and mourned on the other. His eyes looked up, then they looked to the side, then down. Then they began that eye route again. He began to recite Shakespeare; and then, sentiments from greeting cards.

The girls stood still when they saw him; he was very like them, themselves, at this age.

Only one girl saw the danger of believing they were safe with him, and she raced up to him standing there emerged from the frog pond.

Recite the table of elements, she said.

And he did not even fully know what that was, and out of shame he sank back into the water.

What the one girl had done was very good; she had saved them all from being fooled by the god of indecision. But she herself was not immune; instead of admitting, one year, she was in love with someone, she turned her back on that person, and took up with someone who did not care much about her. And a life of rue resulted. The pond by the anthropology museum was still there. It was autumn, a magic month for the pond. She had forgotten where the small entrance gate was, whether it was on that street or this one. It was of course at a corner, the magic spot for places.

She stood before it. Very clear was her reflection in the still pond, though the sun was not very bright. It was so cold she'd worn gloves.

Recite the table of elements, she said in a small voice. Her reflection showed she was no longer young; really, only the intensity of her eyes was beautiful still.

And the god of indecision was back. But strangely, he'd resolved his problems. It was apparent. His hair now all curled lightly, elegantly, in one direction. His eyes were steady. He was looking at her.

Inorganic or organic, he said.

Oh, all the elements, she said.

He recited it, perfectly, naming many she had never heard. She had long ago forgotten most of them.

Name the name of the boy I loved, she said.

I can't tell you that, he said. He never came here with you.

You are correct, she said. He never did.

He sank, very certainly, back into the depth of the pond. Up above on a tree branch there was a tremble: a bird had come to sit, and look at the water, and her. Then, just as she was about to talk to it, it flew away. She could not decide what kind of bird it was, or why it had not bothered to stay. She could not remember what day it was, and didn't think it mattered. Looking across the campus today, at all the students, she wondered how anyone had ever chosen a course of study. Wasn't it all futile?

A bus stopped in front of her. Where do you want to go, said the bus driver. Oh, I don't know, she said. I'll just sit on the bus and make up my mind.

But she could not make up her mind, and rode the bus till the end of the bus day, when there was even a different driver. When it ended its run in the dark bus garage she said thank you to the last driver and got off, and as she turned a corner coming out of the bus garage she saw the bright, bright face of the young man she'd loved. But he'd become a gorilla; he was leaned over and shaggy, and his eyes had become small and cruel. His hands once so fine and delicate looked as if they wore pair after pair of glove. His feet were dark and gripping. He began to chase her. She ran as fast as she could back to the bus, pulling the door behind her. She would sleep here all night. She could see the gorilla circling the bus and then leaving the garage. She was safe.

She was safe till she saw that the bus driver who came onto the bus in the morning was a gorilla in a bus driver's suit. She would surely die; she was now going to pay for her indecision, and her insult to him fifty years ago.

No one else got on the bus; they saw, very clearly, it was a gorilla in a bus driver's suit, and it was not Halloween. Halloween had already passed.

The bus stopped. They were stopped at the anthropology museum; if you knew where the gate was, you could go to the rectangular pond, so simple and beautiful and green beside it.

Let's go, she said, to him. Her voice was shaking.

Let's go, he said.

And she and the gorilla in the suit sat beside the pond, on the cement bench with old-fashioned curving legs. It was very very cold to sit upon.

I loved you, said the gorilla. Though I was too indecisive to tell you.

Yes, that was it, she said. You were indecisive. It was not just me.

Now I could kill you, he said. I am a gorilla after all. I am a gorilla in all my rage.

But you wouldn't, she said.

Oh, you say I wouldn't, he said. And he bent his big shaggy brown ragged head and began to weep. And weep.

He went to the side of the small rectangular pond and when a single tear of his even fell into the water the pond all of a sudden glowed pearly gold.

The pond had never looked so beautiful.

Let's sacrifice ourselves to the elements, she said.

The gorilla took her hand and she with him went into the water, sinking deeper and deeper. The pond loved them and absorbed them without making them go through the agonies of drowning. They became part of the pond. The city had to come pick up the bus, eventually, from where it had been parked all day beside the anthropology museum.

The next fall the young women came, and they were all, every one of them, taken over by emotion beside the pond, forgetting whatever they had supposedly come to discuss as a group beside the pond.

In the shallow water, invisible and sweet, the woman who had lost her young man and the man who had lost his young woman were tremulous and worried: had they ruined the magic of the pond? But winter came and spring and summer and fall again, and another group of young women came, this time to celebrate someone's engagement.

And then the two in the pond were completed, and could dissolve, and go on to forever.

Jordan Redd

If we were witches

She's becoming another lost thing. Like my childhood. The violets I used to pick from the grass in my backyard. I'd collect them in woven baskets and bring them to my mother to steep. They fall through the bench cracks in the park when I try to claim them now. I'll press them in a book and watch as time fades the purple to a thin transparent white. Time does that to all of us.

I spot Elle from across the grass expanse, so I stand from the bench. She wraps me in a tight hug. It's Sunday. We had made plans to go to the park together. We go to feel like we still can make room for each other. It's a big park. So I have hope. I spread out my agate blue blanket under a willow tree and Elle puts a strawberry to her lips before I've finished smoothing out the wrinkles. Patience and impatience. Our most outstanding warring traits. She lies down on the blanket and spreads her long hair all around her. It looks like silk.

"I've been writing."

Eyes closed, she holds her hand out to me. I press my brown leather book into her palm. She opens to the creased page. A poem about her. I doubt she'll see herself. I've smothered her scent. Too much is unspoken between us already. Her expression is soft while she scans. Page after page, some about my mother's garden, some about spellwork, most about her. None are good. It's a hobby. A diary. Therapy.

tangled curls and coffee breath—she drinks tea. Her hair is straight.

she smells like lavender—she's allergic.

One day I fear she's going to lean back, squint at the lines, pause, and ask, *who is she*?

I still don't know what I'll say.

"You should send these somewhere."

"No."

Her nose crinkles, distorting the freckles on its bridge. I'm convinced that she's oblivious. But maybe she's not. Maybe she's a good liar. Maybe I don't know her anymore.

"Am I the only one who gets to read these?"

I refill our wineglasses to occupy my mouth. I want a change in subject. I don't really know why I do things like that. Push the envelope to places I only half want to go. She accepts my offering and my silent plea to drop it. Her second glass has bloomed a faint rose across her cheeks that tells me she's uncharacteristically calm now. She hiccups and asks for a tarot card reading. She doesn't have to ask if I have them with me. My first deck. The one my mother gave me for my 14th birthday with the raised golden scrollwork. It goes everywhere with me. Elle lays on her side to watch me shuffle.

"Do you have a question?"

"I want to know what my question should be."

"You want to ask the cards what you need to know?"

"Yes."

I try desperately to focus while I fold the cards into themselves, but her stare is piercing into me, like a challenge. Her reading will be tainted. I can sense it. I pull three cards face down: past, present, future. Left, center, right. She reaches out and flips over the past.

The High Priestess—Upright.

"This card is about balance, intuition, and subconscious wisdom."

"And it's in my past?"

"That doesn't mean it isn't in your future."

"It's certainly not in my present."

"It's a reminder that you're capable of harnessing that energy again."

I turn the present.

The Moon—Upright.

Secrets, cycles, truth and emotion. It isn't a card either of us would forget.

"Is there something you aren't telling me, Elektra?" A tease.

She hates it when I call her by her full name. But I do it anyway. Elektra. With a *k* .

The distinction is important. The k turns her name to fire. A c would mean her parents thought of Greek mythology and chose not to name her after a goddess like Athena. I call her Elle when I'm happy with her. Or trying to be. Elle makes her sound ethereal. I think that's what she'd rather be. But to me she's her namesake. All-consuming. Wild hunger. Raw beauty.

"Isn't the card supposed to be telling me what I need to know, Prim?" She coils her hair around her finger, taught.

"It's telling you that there's something hidden from you. Or you're not being honest with yourself."

"Is anyone ever honest with themselves?"

We both reach for the future. I let her turn it.

The Tower—Reversed.

Intense and unexpected change. Upright it's a card about external upheaval. Reversed it's about the personal and internal.

"I hate this card."

"It just means that you need to be open to change. To shift the way you look at life."

I know that she hates change. I see it as evidence of life. She sees it as a reflection of dying. A bee landed on the rim of my wineglass. I held my finger out to it and let it crawl onto my palm.

"I brought a J. Do you want to go smoke it on the bleachers?"

"We're twenty-six."

"And?"

You'd think going back to places you haven't been in a long time would quench the nostalgia buried in you, but it doesn't. It just makes you more acutely aware of it no longer belonging to you. You feel strange and out of place there. I don't miss high school. I just miss the years when my days were her and mostly her. There was some kind of magic in that.

Back then the word witchcraft conjured something alluring. It was fresh to her. She found Sutton ruinously boring but I could uncover new meaning for her under every crinkled leaf in my backyard. She was enthralled by my mother, our home. The misshapen jars on the shelves in our light green kitchen, the scent of fresh jasmine from our garden drying on the counter and the open pot of sandalwood mingling around our heads, the way our home never sat still.

I swear the air buzzed when my mother was preparing spellwork. She charges the energy of a room just by exhaling. She's an empath—it's impossible to lie to her. It seemed like a terrible thing in adolescence. But maybe it's not so terrible to have someone intuitively know when you're aching. Elle and I would collect the ingredients from the cupboard and pile them on the wooden countertop of the kitchen island, my mother talking us through every detail: we'll cast tonight under the full moon, matches to burn our intentions, cinnamon oil to dress the candle (green, a nod to Demeter), tiger's eye for luck, clear quartz to amplify. I remember her yellow apron. I remember I used to sneak dried baby's breath into her pockets because I thought it looked pretty. It made Elle smile so I tucked the extra behind her ear.

Now she works as a curator at an art gallery. She likes it well enough, but it isn't her everything. It's small. Elle craves things bigger than her. Few things are. She talks about it with me the way you'd talk about asking for money from your parents. Dancing around the subject. Afraid to ask—or rather, afraid to tell me that she isn't happy here. I can't read people like my mother. I want to say I can read her better than most. I am at once an expert and an amateur at everything I do. I think I know what I'm doing, who she is, who I am, but it's a constant learning experience.

Elle exhales a puff of smoke into the night air. Weed makes her reckless. She stops thinking before she opens her mouth. I was waiting for her to ignite. But nothing came. She fixed her stare at the opposing team.

"Have you cast lately?"

"Everything I do feels off."

"You've been writing. Shouldn't creative energy fuel you?"

I cast a courage spell. I cast a spell to give me the courage to tell her I love her. I gathered the ingredients in a neat salt circle. Moon-bathed agate, bloodstone, and clear quartz. White candle placed on top of the Strength tarot card. I asked Athena for her help while the candle burned to its base. I buried the candle wax in my backyard under the new moon. It's been a month and I've never felt more scared.

"I guess it's not enough."

When I opened my nursery Elle used to come every week to visit. I'd be repotting succulents and she'd offer to help. I loved the way the dirt would smear on her cheek when she forgot she was covered in it, because she was so invested in her story about her dream last night. She wanted me to tell her what they meant. What it meant that she was stuck in labyrinths or skydiving through an endless sky. I wanted to know too.

You can't convince me that there is a fall better than ours in Massachusetts. I live in a small two bedroom ten minutes from my mother. I picked it because it was made from stone and falling apart. I like to nurture things back to life. Old buildings house histories. When my mother stepped onto the property for the first time I knew from her peaceful expression that they were good histories. I spent months infusing the walls with my energy. Smothering every surface with a living thing. I have love for my home like I have love for Elle. Time went into knowing her. I have love for Elle the way you have love for the characters in a good book once you've reached the end.

My high was ebbing. I've been smoking too much. She tears skin from her thumb. Blood pools in her nail beds. I want to reach over and pull her hands to her sides but I'm paralyzed. Our silence feels charged with a novel of things we wish we had said. It should be easy to use our high as an excuse to say anything. But it isn't. I start to write a poem in my head. I think about the night in 8th grade after the football game when she kissed me, right here, in this spot.

She left me there with the taste of ash on my lips.

I think about circles. Time and bullshit metaphors for it, like:

We're here again, different *ash, same taste, dust to dust,*

or something like that.

I reach into my pocket and clasp my bloodstone.

"Prim?"

"Yes?"

"If I left, would you follow?"

If I wasn't just going through the motions most days, if I wasn't also becoming the lost thing, maybe I could find the right spell, the right herb, the right deity to pray to, to fix me. To find me. Spells don't work if you don't believe in them. How can you undo the damage if the damage is what prevents you from healing? My mother would press rose quartz into my hand and tell me to let it bathe in the moonlight on my windowsill. Maybe it would keep something at bay, but it wouldn't be enough.

"Prim?"

"Yes?"

"I can't leave without you."

Russell Reece

Scatterbrain

There's no barrelman, no cowboy hats filling the grandstand, no kids running around, just Judge and his pals at the fence passing the bottle of Kessler, and Gary and his crew at the chute, oak timbers straining, fifteen hundred pounds of crazy trying to blow everything apart. I climb over the rail, dust everywhere, the smell of rosined leather and shit, chaps flaring, the bell clanging. A spur catches on the board as I work my legs around the bull and pull my boots tight against its belly. Huge muscles surge under my thighs. Gary wraps the rope around my glove. I pound the grip tight, pin my hand with the Velcro strap.

"Stay in front, chest forward," Gary says. "Ya git back on him it's all over."

I'm amazed at the muscles, like something ready to explode. I think out of control freight train.

Judge shouts, "Piece of cake, Johnson."

I push my hat down, hear the electrical snap, smell singed hair. I nod at Gary. The gate flies open and I lurch into the hand, see three still-shots from an instamatic: the cloudy sky under my hat brim, the empty grandstand and fence at an oblique angle, the ground beyond the steep slope of the bull's neck. We both slam headfirst into the dirt and I'm eye to eye with a drooling, snorting, snot flying monster, horns coming at me. Gary's hands grab the bull's lips, jerk the huge head away. I roll off; scramble to my feet, see myself passing through the gate, people shouting, patting my back. I grab the fence, shake my head, try to find normal. I can't.

I close my eyes then the bull is in the chute again and Judge's gravelly voice rips out, "God damn it, Johnson! Git back up there, ya got him tired now. Ain't a buck left in him."

Somebody hands me my hat. I get back on, not sure why. I feel the velvet hide, rolling muscles. I remember that from somewhere.

Bam! The bull slams the back of the chute, sharp and loud as gunfire.

Gary works my gloved hand into the strap. I can't move it. I try but for some reason it won't budge.

Bam!

Gary pushes my hat down, slaps my chest. "Nod when you're ready, brother," he says.

"What?"

(Celebrating John Johnson's first go on the bull, Scatterbrain, at Gary Leffew's ranch summer 1970)

Jeff Richards

Red Light

I follow her to the station with a suitcase in my hand. The train rolls in. The brakes screech, insults my ears. The steam hisses like a snake that covers her with a venomous vapor that, when it dissipates, reveals her forlorn eyes like it's me done something wrong not her. For a moment, I want to take her in my arms and squeeze her tightly and say, It's all right darling. I forgive you. But I can't. She climbs aboard and turns. Our eyes lock in one final embrace that is full of hate and regret mixed together. I hand her the suitcase.

"I don't want to go to Mayflower. I want to stay with you."

"No, ma'am, you're not staying. Nobody crosses Buddy Caldwell," I say poking my chest and turning my back on her. But when the train pulls out of the station, I turn back and watch it disappear down the track into the darkness. The last I spy are two lights, the blue light stands for my blues, the red stands for my pride.

I wander to the club I own, where she used to work before I married her two years ago. "Big Boss Man Marries Young Chick," it said in the *Clanton Clarion* written by Johnny Charmin, the owner, who was sweet on Claire as he was on every lady that crossed his path.

"I'm looking to unlock every box in town," he told me in his snarky way, one day, at the club, "because I own the master key."

Johnny was a tall, lean fellow with bushy eyebrows and dark, penetrating eyes. He wore black from head to toe, King Baby jewelry with death head skulls, a black hat with a silver band, and silver spurs on his black boots. I could hear him jangle down the street from blocks off. He charmed the ladies with his good looks and smooth manners. They called him the devil, a name that he cultivated. Even to the point of buying a boa constrictor, which he wrapped around his neck, and fed live rats from the lab, and invited us in to take a look as if we already didn't know he was a rat from the trouble he stirred up in his newspaper. The son-of-a-bitch, in my case, was hitting below the belt alluding to those lines in the Luther Dixon song, "You ain't big, you're tall that's all." He's right. I'm tall, six-four, but I'm not big. He's big and I know that for a fact because one night Claire wobbled in the club, blood trickling down her leg through the fishnet stockings. One of the ladies guided her to the bathroom where she cleaned off. When she wobbled back, I asked her if she needed to visit the clinic. She allowed that she needed rest and I offered my bed in the back room that I sleep in when I work late. I fluffed up a pillow and she lay down in the bed. I covered her with a blanket. I pulled up a chair and took her hand. She looked up at me with big frightened, doe-like eyes.

"Sometimes, I think I'm going to die young," she said, squeezing my hand tightly. I never noticed her before. I hire them. I fire them. I'm nice to them along the way. But, in the end, I'm a businessman.

"You shouldn't say that," I objected in a firm voice.

"I know, but I feel it in my bones." She closed her eyes.

I left her alone. Finished my work at the club. Listened to the blues band. Tapping my feet. I love the blues. That's why I own this place, a shack in a field that I fixed up, a hundred yards off the Blues Highway. I can't play the blues. I got a tin ear. The next best thing is to listen to the blues and get paid for it. The last tune they played was "Night Train." I was humming it as I headed to the back room to rouse Claire. She was dead asleep. I made a pallet on the floor and, in the middle of the night, she woke me up. She said I could sleep with her. I wasn't thinking very hard so I climbed in. Before I knew it, we were kissing. Then I squeezed her breasts but she wouldn't let me touch her below because Johnny Charmin poked her with his big thing. "It's so big," she said, wide-eyed, "that it caused me to bleed."

"Maybe it caused you to bleed because he was rough," I suggested.

"It doesn't matter," she cuddled up beside me. "Now I'm with you."

I took that to mean that she wasn't with Johnny anymore, which pleased me. I was falling for Claire. I don't know why. Maybe it was she looked so sad all the time with those doe-like forlorn eyes. Maybe it was her pouty lips and compact body, long, skinny legs and short torso like Minnie Mouse. Maybe it was that she sang in such a sweet, lonesome way, not a squeak or rattle in her voice, whiskey smooth. I knew why she glommed on to me. I was a good contact in the biz. But I was bothered at the same time that I was the boss. It was against my policy to mess with the employees. But I let it go. My mistake. We were married two weeks later at the club. She begged to sing at the reception. One of the band members asked if they could use her later. I said yes as long as I'm in the general vicinity. I guess that was the beginning of my jealous streak, a philosophical one considering she was twenty-two and I was forty-eight, married twice, the father of a teenager who lives in Atlanta with his mother.

When the party was over, the rice thrown and all, we left for my home on River Street in Clanton. We made love. It was delicious for me. I could imagine growing old with this lady. Raising children. She'd sing at the club. I'd hire a band and we'd travel the road for weeks at a time, cut us some CDs. I'd make her happy and that would make the kids and me happy. And maybe one day she'd be famous enough to be elected to the Blues Hall of Fame and maybe one day when we're gone they'd put up a sign on the Blues Highway in Clanton saying here was the home base of Claire Caldwell and name my club so it'd become as famous as Po' Monkees. I knew I was overstating the case but that's the way I felt making love to Claire. I don't think she shared my feelings.

One late night a month after we were married, Claire insisted she needed cigarettes at the On the Go market on the highway. I told her she should quit that habit. It'll ruin her health and her voice in the bargain. But she persisted. I said I'd get them for her.

"I'd let you do that, darling," she replied, tucking me under the chin, "but I also need to buy some lady things."

When she showed up two hours later, she looked peaked in the face like she was scared. I asked her what transpired. She said she got lost in the backcountry and stopped to ask a tall old black fellow with big feet if he knew the way back to Clanton. He pointed east and mumbled under his breath in a sort of a low howl.

"I suppose that was the ghost of Howlin' Wolf," I snickered.

"I don't know. Maybe it was. Don't you feel the Delta's haunted?"

"No, there's no ghost nowhere," I don't believe in this Mississippi Delta hoodoo. Nor does she. She was hiding something from me.

One day I wandered into the bathroom and she was standing in front of the mirror popping a pimple. I noticed a trickle of blood running down her leg.

I jumped back thunderstruck. "You've been with Johnny Charmin, haven't you?"

She looked down at her leg and laughed. "You ever hear of a period. That's what girls get every 28 days and that's what I'm getting right now." She wiped her leg off. "Now you git so I can take care of this in private."

I left, my suspicions aroused even further. I knew betrayal. I betrayed my first wife for my second and my second wife betrayed me. So I decided to count the days and when it came up to fifteen, I found Claire in the bathroom bleeding.

She fell in my arms and begged forgiveness. "I can't help it," she sobbed. "Johnny Charmin is the devil. I swear to God, he tempted me."

More hoodoo, I thought as I cleaned her off and put her to bed, but I knew why she felt that way. I heard of other women fall for his charms and claim the same thing. A friend named Margie Dresher sold her music store in Clanton and moved to Austin, Texas after she'd been with him. He called his big thing the devil's tail because it was long and pointy at the end. "He used it like a battering ram," Margie told me. "Like I was a castle he was trying to assail." It was not only the hard treatment that scared Margie, but what happened afterwards. Three women disappeared from town, and only one was found hitching on the highway, white as a sheet. A fourth turned into a recluse and a fifth was found face down in an irrigation ditch. Her boyfriend strangled her when he found out she slept with Johnny. In my opinion, he strangled the wrong person. Sure, he had his defenders, women who said he was simply misunderstood, but I'm not stupid. I knew it was my duty to defend my wife and the best way I saw was to remove the temptation.

I suggested a long vacation in New Orleans. Claire, who'd mostly been nowhere all of her life, jumped at the chance. I found a boutique hotel in the Quarter. The first night in the Big Easy, we sidled over to the music clubs on Frenchman Street. At the Spotted Cat, we caught Tuba Skinny; at Snug Harbor we caught the Ellis Marsalis band; and, at the Blue Nile, Michael Mooney, a long-haired blond fellow in sunglasses who played the blues on a beat-up acoustic guitar. Claire tugged my sleeve. "I want to sing," she whispered in my ear. This was exactly the reaction I wished for. Lots of people consider the blues depressing. I consider the opposite. The blues release the sadness inside me. And that's what I wanted for Claire. During a break in the set, I plunked forty bucks in the tip jar and asked if he would allow her to sing. He waved for Claire to come up. He was doubtful I could tell by his pained expression until they agreed upon "Bumble Bee Blues" and she poured it out so forlornly that I could feel the ache inside her and I wasn't the only one who felt it because after she breathed her last sigh, Mooney reached in the tip jar and handed her half of the forty I plunked in.

"Sing us some more," he said.

When we returned to the hotel, Claire was so high with her triumph that she suggested we make love. A breeze wafted through the open window, carrying a funny combination of smells, fuel oil, Old Spice deodorant, cheap bourbon from the Mississippi, funnel cake from Bourbon Street, the cloying sweetness of honeysuckle climbing our balcony, the briny smell of our bodies, and the taste of her strawberry lipstick. It was intoxicating and I reveled in it until the early morning I rolled over on my back, exhausted. "I love you with all my heart and soul," she said, leaning up on her elbow and whispering in my ear. The hairs on the back of my neck tingled. "You are a caring, gentle, good-natured generous man. I don't think I have ever met a man like you since my daddy departed from this earth."

I didn't like it that she compared me to her father, nor that she neglected to mention my sexual prowess. She did mention as an afterthought that I was tall and muscular and had the most beautiful blue eyes. She didn't mention the bald spot on top of my head. She told me that after her father died when she was fourteen, she was destitute. "He was the only one in the world who cared for me. He was the one fixed breakfast before I headed off to school and helped with my homework. He was a smart fellow. When he caught on that practically every waking moment I was belting out one tune or another I heard on the radio, he arranged voice lessons. He played the piano and I'd sing and he'd shake his head and sigh. 'You have the voice of an angel,' he said. 'One day, if you keep to your lessons, you could be the next Patsy Cline. He was partial to country. But when he saw I loved the blues more, he said I could be the next Ma Rainey. He wasn't prejudice."

She commenced to blubber. I rubbed her shoulder gently whispering to her that everything will be OK. "I wish that was true," she said, gazing in my eyes. "I wish I was like my daddy, but I'm more like momma who ran off to Oklahoma with another man. I have a wandering spirit."

I knew exactly what she meant and I almost succumbed to her desire to remain in New Orleans. "We could sell your club, move down here, and start over."

"I suppose we could do that, but it would take a while to find a buyer. Besides, I don't believe we could make enough cash from a sale to live in New Orleans."

We drove the slow way to Clanton following the Natchez Trace, but the beautiful scenery didn't erase the sense of doom hanging over our heads. It didn't take long until she was back with Johnny Charmin. I don't want to go into detail other than to say everyone in town knew what she was up to. They felt sorry for me. Gave me looks of pity when they wandered in the club or didn't look at all. The son of a bitch Johnny jangled in to gloat but I'd hide in the back room until he was gone. At night when she was with the fiend—she didn't try to hide it from me anymore, I would lie awake staring at the ceiling, my imagination running wild. Finally, I'd see the light cross the ceiling and know she was pulling in the driveway. I'd hear the car door slam, the front door creak open, and the clatter of her heels as she ascended the stairs. When silence prevailed, I knew she was at the foot of our bed checking to see if I was sleeping. I pretended I was. She undressed, pulled the nightgown over her head, and either climbed in bed beside me or padded out to the guest room. If she climbed in bed, I would smell the sex on her. If she went to the other bed, I yearned to join her. Either way I couldn't sleep. My heart crawled to my throat. I felt a physical ache so excruciating I couldn't breathe. I crawled out of bed to the bathroom and with a shaking hand swallowed a few cups of water. I spent the rest of the night watching television, the sound down low, tamping down the evil thoughts in my brain.

This didn't happen every night, maybe twice a week and one morning when it hadn't happened in a month I asked her hopefully if she was finished with Johnny.

"No," she whispered weakly, "I suppose one day but it'll be him that's finished with me."

I didn't catch the implications of what she was saying. I only thought of how lonesome I felt and growled at her that, "I love you with all my heart, but all my love for you is in vain."

"No, it isn't," she sniffed, patting my hand. "You're a darling man and I love you back but not in the same way."

This irritated me. I grabbed her wrist. "I suppose you love him so much because he has a big dick."

"I wish it was as simple as that," she said loosening my grip. I never found out exactly what it was that made Johnny attractive to Claire other than the devil thing. But I'm not one to believe that. I believe in evil, but the devil is an excuse. I know for a fact that Claire was not the only one. During that month hiatus, Johnny saw two other women, one divorcee who worked for me, and the other, Clyde Hopkins's wife. I'd seen them both come out of his office. Finally, I confronted the divorcee. She was always late for work and I threatened to fire her. She broke down and told me she couldn't help it. Johnny had a hold on her. I allowed that I understood, but she should be more punctual in the future. I felt sorry for her as I did for Clyde's wife. Besides, I guessed, as long as he was occupied with these ladies, he'd leave my wife alone. But there came a time when that was at an end and I returned to those sleepless nights waiting for the light to cross the ceiling as Claire pulled into the driveway.

So finally I couldn't stand it anymore and I took her to the station. The train rolled in. She climbed aboard and turned. I saw the fear in her eyes, but I didn't know why until two weeks later they found her in a tree after a tornado passed through Mayflower. I remembered what she said about dying young and it made me feel like I wish I died with her.

Johnny Charmin jangles in the bar in his usual black from head to toe, King Baby jewelry with death head skulls, a black hat with a silver band, and silver spurs on his black boots. "You hear about your wife," he says, pulling up a barstool. "Could you imagine the power of that tornado lifting her up in that tree like she's a baby doll and smashing her brains to bits?"

I reach for the gun I hid under the bar. I finger the trigger, but don't try anything. Johnny, I think, is reading my mind.

"What's bothering you Buddy boy?" he asks, a fat grin lighting up his face. No end to his gloating.

"Nothing," I say, taking my hand from the trigger and leaning on the bar. "What's your poison?"

"Bourbon and branch water."

I turn my back on him, reach for the Blanton, his favorite. Pour a double shot. I'm a peaceful man. The last thing I care to do is kill Johnny Charmin. I think for some reason he wants to be killed. I don't know why, something that happened in his past, something in his DNA. It doesn't matter. I'm neither a psychiatrist nor the agent of his demise. Besides, it's not his fault alone what happened to my darling Claire.

I pour the branch water. Turn back to the bar. Plunk both glasses down. Look up.

Clyde Hopkins sidles up to the barstool next to Johnny. Nods in my direction, plunks himself down, and swivels around in the stool.

"You're gonna die," he growls as he draws a gun from under his jacket and points it at our tormentor.

The big fat grin on Johnny's lips turns lopsided as if it's a ship about to sink.

Thierry Sagnier

Can We Go Now?

"Can we go now?"

I was in Paris, on the fourth floor of the Galerie Lafayette, one of the first department stores in the world. You can buy a tee shirt for a few Euros there, or a designer dress for a few thousand Euros. I had once run into Johnny Depp there, looking through the collection of LPs.

"Can we go now?"

The small boy was sitting on the floor in one of the store's book aisles while a few feet away his mother searched through a selection of novels.

I looked down at him. He was perhaps five or six, a nice-looking child with a baseball cap on his head and a lollipop stuck in his mouth. He was a very American little kid.

"Hey!"

He glanced at me when I spoke, a stranger/danger look in his eyes.

"How ya doing?"

His mother had moved a few feet down the aisle. She had four or five books in the crook of an elbow.

The kid stood up. He held a string shopping bag, the kind found by the dozen in every French household. He reached inside, pulled out a copy of *Le Petit Prince* and held it up. I squatted down next to him and said, "That's probably my favorite book in the entire world."

His mother looked in our direction and hurried over. I stood. "It's OK," I said. "Really. We were just talking about *The Little Prince*."

She was a honey blonde in her thirties, clad in jeans, a pale blue blouse, and a costly tan leather jacket. She asked, "You're American?"

I nodded, added, "Well, naturalized. I was born here. In Paris. I live in the States."

The kid tugged at her jeans. "Can we go now?"

She patted his head and said to me, "Our last afternoon in France. Our plane leaves in six hours. I wanted to make a quick stop. You can't find these books where we live."

I looked at what she was carrying, expecting Balzac and Flaubert. What she'd picked up was a bunch of Série Noire, what the French call *pollard*, cheap detective novels meant to be read in an afternoon.

I smiled. "You got the classics."

The kid turned whinny. "Please, Mom?"

She said, "Five more minutes." Then she turned to me again and asked, "Do you think you...?"

"Yes. Of course..."

So I sat on the floor of the Galerie Lafayette reading in French from St. Exupery's masterpiece to a little American kid with a lollipop in his mouth. Five minutes into it, he fell asleep. A few moments later, his mother returned with a large plastic sac holding a dozen cheap paperbacks. I handed her *Le Petit Prince* and she dropped it into the bag. "We already have it in English."

She picked up the kid whose eyes opened for a fraction of a second, and then closed again.

"Where are you from," she asked, "in the States?"

"Virginia," I said.

She nodded. "Never been there. We're from Oregon. A long long flight ahead of us."

The kid stirred; his head dropped to her shoulder. She took a couple of steps, stopped, looked back and said, "Hey! Thanks!"

She walked away.

Le Petit Prince really is one of my favorite books in the world.

Lex Shramko

Existence

From their window ledge, the three macaques silently watched as the two German cars sped away. They did not stay together; the one turned left at the corner and went west, and the other continued northwards down the boulevard. The macaques searched with their eyes at both ends of the boulevard, pressing close to the edges of the window frame to extend their view. So it was Daisy, sitting in between Hector and Rose, who saw the boys emerge on the balcony in the building opposite the Derzprom. They held oranges in their hands, and they were smiling, looking down over the balcony's railing. Seeing the empty boulevard, they too pressed themselves to the outer edges of the rails, leaning out to see as far as possible.

The smaller boy looked up at his brother, and his lips moved. He pointed at the street below. As he pivoted to re-enter the apartment, his older brother lay a gentle hand on his shoulder, staying him on the balcony. The two brothers faced each other, the younger listening to the elder. And the elder bowed his head and rested his forehead on his brother's, hands on his shoulders. The macaques were too far away to hear their voices, but they understood when the younger suddenly quivered his spine and instinctively threw his arms around his elder, orange tightly clutched in his fist.

Minutes passed as the brothers rocked on the balcony, their sorrow radiating out from their ledge, across the boulevard and through the bare tree branches and up the concrete walls of the Derzprom where it settled on the macaques' window ledge. Leaning into each other, they also rocked, echoing the dance of grief on the balcony across the boulevard.

From the roof above the monkey's window, a crow dropped, her wings unevenly spread at first then straightening as she arced between the trees of the boulevard, and alighted on the boys' balcony rail, her wings fumbling to balance her sudden halt. Hearing the unmistakable sound that a crow makes with its muscular wings, the boys ceased their rocking and looked at the crow, who returned their gaze with one eye, waiting. Oles the younger blinked his weeping eyes clear and held his hand out towards the crow, his chest heaving with tears. The crow jumped onto Oles' hand, dipping and bobbing. The boys gazed, rapt and lost in the crow's black-eyed vision, and the crow stayed, gripping Oles' fingers with her toes, and holding the boys' minds in her own until they again felt their heartbeats and the cold now numbing their feet and hands. And with that, it was time for the crow to leave. She dipped her head once, twice, and bent her body low and pushed off from Oles' hand, flapping hard to clear the balcony. Climbing into the air above the boulevard, she flew parallel to the streets below. At the intersection with the pharmacy on the corner and where one of the German cars had turned left, the crow cried once and long, and banked left.

From their window-ledge, the macaques watched the older brother put his arm around the younger, and tenderly usher him into the apartment. The balcony doors closed behind them, the motley of glass panes reflecting the pale whiteness of the Derzprom, catching the last light of the Western skies where the crow had flown. The broken windowpanes held nothing but empty black space.

("But I thought you walked—"

"We *did*. The cars—that was just the beginning—"

"Well, how long were you in the car? I mean, how far did you get?" I reign in my frustration with my mother's unreliable narrative. Have some decency, I say to myself.

"I don't remember. A long time."

"Is that hours, days, or weeks, even?"

"Hours, I think. We drove until we got stuck."

"Stuck?"

"Mud. *Mud*. You cannot even imagine. It was—literally—mud up to your knees."

"Cars got stuck?"

"Cars, trucks, horses, people. You don't know how many times Galina pulled me. Carried me, even. I wasn't small. I was nine. Horses collapsed with exhaustion. And were simply left there. That was hard—the horses suffering. No one, not the Germans, not the Russians, not the Ukrainians, could stand mistreatment—we all felt the same about the horses."

"So you walked—"

"Yes. All the way to Poland. Warsaw. I know it was Warsaw because later I saw pictures of buildings I remember—"

"Wait. You *walked* from Kharkiv to Warsaw? In one go?"

"Yes. Well, no, not in one day. We slept where ever we could. Barns, village huts, sometimes just under trees. Later, as we retreated—after Warsaw—with this or that troops, we got rides sometimes but that time it was all walking. That's where Galina lost her shoes—the mud sucked them right off—her green *kid leather* pumps."

"Galina wore heels?! You guys are fleeing the city and she choose heels? And a black silk dress?"

"Well, the black dress was very light and rolled up easily. That was logical. But the heels—Galina always wore heels. These were beautiful kid leather, too! She lost one—remember that hill I told you about—where she literally half-pulled, half-dragged me—"

"Yes, and she told you had to walk, she could no longer carry you."

"Yes. She carried me many times but I was big. Not too big—I was skinny—there was no food. There was something in her voice that I heard. Something that made me reach for a strength I didn't know was possible. I understood there was no choice but to choose. And so I walked. I chose."

"So...this is where she lost a shoe?"

"Yes. And at the top was a village and a road. There was a dead soldier, lying on the side of the road. He was so young, just a little smaller than Galina. He was just a boy. She needed his boots. She bent down to get them off, and they wouldn't come off. He was stiff. The boots were stiff. Other people must have stopped to help because I remember hands and arms reaching down to help her. She wore these boots all the way to Warsaw."

"How long did it take?"

"I really don't know. It was a blur. I walked so many times asleep. With my eyes open. Unseeing and asleep.")

In the trees on the muddy hillside, the crow silently rested on a branch. After taking the road west out of the city, the car had joined other lines of trucks and cars. People with horse-drawn carts, horses with riders. Carts pulled by people. Soldiers with bicycles. Whole families with their sacks of possessions. Soldiers on foot. The crow stayed hidden among the branches, always near Taty's car. She flew ahead to where the column faded out to abandoned carts and trucks stuck in the *rasputitsa*, mud trenches pulling trucks down to their underbellies. Three times she flew back to check on the car's progress. Each time, they progressed less and less until finally they too were stuck in the mud, the road blocked by abandoned, quagmired vehicles. They too got out of their car, and walked with the mud sucking at their legs, demanding that they stay.

Now the crow watched as a small troop of scattered humans scrambled up the embankment, clutching tree roots to pull themselves uphill in the mud. They made as little noise as possible, yet the sounds of their labored breathing reached the crow's keen ears. She watched the young woman speak softly into the girl's ear and she saw the girl redouble her efforts to climb the hill under her own power. The young woman continued to kneel a moment more. She slung her bag to the ground between her knees. She removed the photo album and set it against the base of a tree. Stuffing her lightened bag inside her coat, she crawled the rest of the way to the top.

When the last humans disappeared over the ridge, the crow dropped from her perch and hopped over to the photo album. Bowing and bobbing twice at the leather cover, she leapt and stood on its edge, wings folded neatly on her back as she looked uphill at the empty ridge.

Julia Slavin

Relics

I regret to tell you that I have had to put your Color Field prints up for auction. Your minimalism, your need for order and purity, I will never understand your ontology but still, the day the prints were packed and driven to the port I became heavyhearted. It should please you to know that The You Museum has fallen on bad times. The grants have dried up. Suburban growth means less foot traffic. Now and again I get the art school couple, trying the door to The Sex Room, but that, as you know, I shuttered years ago. As no doubt you have been made aware, the governments of Peru and Ecuador have called for the return of all artifacts taken from graves; I have sent the weavings to the port for priority shipping. That plus the pacifist mood of the country has attracted negative attention to your medals and uniforms. Worst of all, our letters, once considered the finest single-topic archive in the world, no longer appear to be worth the paper, birch bark, gum wrapper, or book jacket on which they were written. Even the double tear stain, yours and mine, on your letter from Rome holds less value than an incomplete sentence in a vanishing text.

A boy, dressed in the school uniform of one of the academies came into the gallery not long ago, dropping fifty *zloty* into the donation box.

"Did you want change?" I asked.

"The money is mine in case you think I have stolen it." He straightened his posture and clicked his heels. Strolling along the hotel room installations, the Gare de l'Est platform on which you sent your wife and daughters to Roussillon, and our seats at the opera that night, he stopped at your letter from Rome.

"This is what they come to see?" He asked. "The double tear stain? Why, you can scarcely tell the tears apart the way they blend." He raised his phone and took a picture.

"No photos," my guard, Smitty said.

"Why?" The boy asked me. "I am not using a flash. See?" He stomped over. Smitty stood from a chair on loan from the National. "It is only the flash that harms the works." The boy moved on to the framed newspapers, the headlines about how you saved your men after the attack on the ship.

"My father would be interested in these," he said. "Surely you know him. He is sole proprietor of The Us Museum."

"Victor Kozol is your father? No, we have never met."

"Me. I like the letters. You don't see them anymore." Unlike other boys, he did not try the door to The Sex Room.

"You have excellent taste," I said.

"You are American," he said. "You came here for him?"

"I came to study art," I said.

"And you stayed," he said, pleased with himself.

"I stayed to curate," I said.

"I want to go to America," he said. "I want to visit Hollywood and live in New York. I am studying archeology. One day I will be a great curator."

"It is hard work," I said. "You must be detail-oriented and disciplined."

"Your advice will serve me, madam."

He came to the gem display.

"*Aj!* They are beautiful. All yours?"

"All mine."

"From him?"

"Every one."

He tapped the glass over a bracelet. "What is that?"

"Don't touch," Smitty said.

"Agate and sapphire," I said. "I don't remember the occasion."

"I'd wager you most certainly do!" Impertinent boy.

"I must now ask you to leave," I said. "We are closing for lunch."

"The halo diamond on platinum," he said. "What clarity! How many carats? What did it cost? You were engaged?"

"It was a promise ring," I said. "Now, good-bye."

"A promise for what?" He barked. "To leave his wife?"

"The lady says we are closing," Smitty said.

"You cannot close." He straightened his spine and clicked his heels again. "Museums are for the people. These objects belong at The Us Museum."

"Until your father has the means to buy me out, they belong to The You Museum. And now be on your way," I said.

"My father will not like that you shooed me."

"I'm frightened!" I teased. "Smitty, aren't we frightened?"

"I will take these photos to him," the boy said. "He will be interested."

He took another fifty *zloty* from his pocket.

"This is too much," I protested.

"I am sixteen-years-old, madam. I know the value of a *zloty*." He then snapped a picture of me before I could raise my hand to stop him. "Got you!"

"The tyranny of the young," I said to Smitty after the boy marched out. I then turned the *Zamkniete na czas obiadu* sign around to face the street.

I spent the first part of my lunch hour checking the whereabouts of the beach installation. The artist and wave machine were coming from Canada but the Council for the Arts was late with the grant money. The chalk rocks had been set to arrive from Dover. It was below freezing that day near the rubble where we walked. The cliff had fallen into the strait. You put your feet in the water. I was pregnant. I never told you.

"No more installations after this," I said to Smitty who stood on a ladder to adjust a light that had begun to damage the paint on the cyclo we had ridden in Hanoi.

"Pretend," you had said when we escaped the tour guide in the Bamboo Forest, "that I have tied your wrists with cord." I held on to two stalks. "And placed under you a shoot of Truc Sao, the fastest growing plant in the world."

"Bamboo torture is a myth," I laughed.

"Not where I'm from," you said, moving my legs apart.

I left another message for the Canadians and despite the cold day, left the museum and crossed the boulevard to the park where you and I once walked, before we became unhappy. I was still an art student. You had a rash on your legs, a plant-born disease. We passed a line of children waiting at the *lody* kiosk. "Would you like one?" you asked, and I didn't know if you meant ice cream or a child. When we walked beneath the pedestrian tunnel you stopped to look back.

"This is a city of arches," you said. "Do you like our city?"

"I do," I said.

"The Russians forced gray upon us," you said. "So we paint our buildings turquoise and pink."

"Dissent in color," I said.

"Do you hear the trains at night?" you asked.

"I hear the horns in the port."

"I don't sleep well," you said.

"Nor I."

On the skating rink some ducks with blue wings landed on the ice. A child threw a stick. They flew off. An ice resurfacing truck had gotten stuck. A woman yelled at the man driving the truck to shift gears but the blade dug deeper into the ice. She climbed up, pushing the man away. Another man waved his arms yelling that the water pump was broken. There would be no ice conditioning today. You told me you'd only ever seen the color of my eyes in pottery. A man bounced a ball to a boy. He seemed to find pleasure in frustrating the boy over and over by bouncing the ball too high for his son to catch. An older gentleman pursued a young art student. "At least let me buy you a *kaszanka?*" He pleaded.

"*Jestem* vegetarian," she said, escaping his hands.

It was past three; I needed to get back to the museum.

"A way ahead may open when we expect it the least," Smitty said as I read the email from Paris calling for the return of their Gare de l'est platform.

"I fear the curator's time has come and gone," I said.

Tracking down the Canadian artist occupied me, and then London, learning of The You Museum's tribulations began to waver on the Chunnel car loan. Smitty was in good spirits, however, because the table from the Central Café had been delivered and he had the idea to display your last letter in the form of a menu.

Smitty also prepared a case for the display of *my* last letter, which you have neglected to send back to me. It is unfortunate because our last correspondence could have been a draw. I am depleted of apologies. I remind you, again, that you were married and therefore had no recourse. I remind you, also, of a certain female warrant officer, and a certain navy spokeswoman.

Allow me to review the events. A deposed leader and a coup, an uprising in the tribal areas, your ship left during the night for the South Atlantic. Though your letter explained your absence, the depravation had depleted me. I stayed on the train platform for many hours. I then did as you'd instructed, *See Budapest for the both of us.* On the Cultural Avenue, I met a man you said you knew, a Mr. Augie Dell. You had played cards with this man on your ship, you drank too much, and revealed too much. You should have protected me. But that was the world of our arrangement. Your vows were with her, after all.

Mr. Dell and I were uneasy at first, having little to discuss but you. We saw The Military Museum and The Architectural Museum and The Fine Arts, again on your recommendation. The curator craze had hit Europe. There was excitement and inclusiveness as so many young people took up shop. Renaldo from The Ours, Tasha from The Anyone, and Alexi, that hilarious nihilist from The Nobody. Students and tourists zipped in and out of galleries, the curators kissing their patrons as they came and left. The continent sparkled, our spirit irrepressible. We didn't know there was a bomb over our heads.

Over cake at the Central, Mr. Dell told me you'd recommended our usual hotel. He said he didn't have a very nice room, that the shower was oddly situated. Water spilled onto the floor when he bathed. The curtain flapped in and out. I told him that I had a very nice room and a very nice shower and if he would like to use it he was welcome. The café was crowded, I remember, filled with young tourists. I had to sit with my legs out to the side. He asked if I wanted to visit the Aquincum. I said my feet were sore.

"You don't care for antiquity?" He asked.

"I prefer modernity," I said.

He pulled my feet onto his lap and rubbed them. He then bent over and kissed the inside of my knees. The crowd followed us from the café down Vaci Street, everyone dancing to music that spilled onto the sidewalk from the galleries and souvenir shops, but they broke off in twos and threes, some at the bridge, some into boutiques, leaving us alone. I leaned against Mr. Dell to keep up my head because I felt I had been drugged. I told him I needed to sleep and we arranged to meet in the lobby in the morning to go to the Aquicum. But he came back to the room minutes later to ask if he could use the shower.

My attempts to contact you have gone unanswered.

Assuming you have kept any of the notes regarding what transpired with Mr. Dell—the two night stay in the hotel suite, our comings and goings to the cafes and clubs, always attracting a crowd that wanted to dance with us, to smoke, to drink, to have coffee—and could find it in your heart to send them, I would be in your debt. My preference would be any of the confessional letters, the one about my torn gown, which I have displayed on a dress form, how he preferred moving aside my underwear to removing it (also on the dress form), his gutter language, the chair we broke, or the aforementioned shower would be agreeable. The descriptions of the stall in the men's *Furdoszoba*, I would hope you have black-lined, as well as the *Palinka* at the *Szimpla Kert*. As I am certain that I begged your forgiveness up until and ending on the eight-month anniversary of your departure for the South Atlantic, any of my correspondences between March 26–November 25 of that year would suit. Time is the better part of this request and for that, and that alone, I apologize. As ever, I am wishing you good health.

My mind possessed by having to close the gallery, I did not think of you even once. But then one night I had a topsy-turvy dream involving a plastic barrel of money and an American actor who pinned me while barking instructions to stretch after exercising. I dressed and hurried through the streets, barely able to see through the morning fog. But instead of going to my museum, I decided to visit to yours. I walked through the park, stopping to gaze at the Lantern of the Dead tower that you found so curious. "There is no cemetery," you had said, explaining that to be a true lantern of the dead, a light would have to be placed on top to show the location of a burial ground. I continued across the avenue on the south side, walking down a series of narrow streets. The quality of neighborhood dropped, with shops boarded up and men standing on the street with nothing to do. I was surprised to even find The Me Museum because it had no sign and the upper windows were broken, curtains billowing in and out. Inside, a woman scrubbed the beehive tile on her knees then leaned back on her heels to pray. I heard an echo of high heels tapping, a door shutting. I stepped up to a guard seated at a card table reading a book with an illustration of a melting face on the cover.

"The Me?" I asked.

He handed me a pen. I saw on the sign-in sheet that I was the only visitor that day. "Follow around to the right," which I did but ended up at an emergency exit. I went back to the guard.

"Where did you tell me to go?" I asked.

"To the right," he repeated. I explained that I'd gone to the right but there was only an emergency exit.

"The Me Museum is through the emergency exit, Madam."

"I won't set off alarms?" I asked.

"You most assuredly will set off alarms." He wished me a good day and turned his attention back to the book.

When I came to the emergency exit, I did as the guard instructed and pushed open the door. A darting alarm screamed out, reverberating through the metal stairwell. A woman, the skin of her face stretched as though pulled by cords, her hair the whitest blond-in-a-box from the *zasob*, tottered in with a set of keys, unlocked a glass case, and pressed a red button that switched off the alarm.

"*Bardzo mi przykro!*" She apologized. "*Straznik!*"

"I'm guessing this is not The Me Museum," I said.

"No, madam. Our guard has nothing to do but play games. He is lucky for the union. Otherwise..." she swiped an invisible slash across her neck. "I will take you to the museum. *Prosze*," she invited me to follow.

"*Amerykanka?*" She asked.

"Yes," I said.

"*Nowego Jorku?*"

"Maryland."

"Mar-y-land," she repeated. She said good morning to women in kerchiefs and mint colored uniforms who cleaned the tiled walls with disinfectant. They looked at me blandly.

"Wel-come," she said when we came to a gallery with floor-to-ceiling oak doors, a honey-stained oak floor, and windows that gave an impressive view of the smokestacks and arches of the city. The gilt bronze and cut glass chandelier was a warm touch.

"I regret this is only my first visit," I said.

"You are here now. *Prosze*," she invited me to walk through.

The case in an antechamber stored the requisite man's dress shirt on a manikin torso with the obvious lipstick kiss on the collar. I complimented the woman on the use of track lighting and moved into a room, which housed the three limestone Middle Kingdom canopic jars left to me by my uncle, the proprietor of the Pre-Dynastic in Cairo. They contained the viscera of a queen. Preferring to let the dead rest, I had never been fond of relics. I told you to consider them on permanent loan. The first jar, containing a stomach, was topped with a jackal head carved of wood. The second, Hapi with the baboon head, the lungs. And Qebehsenuef, the falcon held the intestine. Enlightened in so many other ways, the Egyptians had no spiritual use for the brain, which got sucked out through the nose and thrown away.

"There is one missing." I said, noticing that the human-headed Imseti jar wasn't among the group.

"The liver, yes," she said. "On loan to the Us."

"You will tell the gentleman that the jar was not his to loan."

"Certainly, madam."

We headed into a dark room of glassed-in exhibits.

"What does the lady think?" The woman asked.

I feared telling the truth about any of the exhibits, with the exception of the incomplete set of canopic jars and my Late Period Egyptian bronze cat with the gold earring. I shuddered when I saw my plaster of paris triple-headed phallus mold that I sculpted when I learned you were fucking the navy spokeswomen, *and* me, *and* your wife, for all I know. As I suspected, you felt it necessary to display the menstrual blood Rorschach I mailed to you to protest your refusal to engage during that time of the month, even when I demanded you prove your devotion. *My* glass tile vagina mosaics. All conceits of the first year art student, conceived during that honeymoon-with-the-self period. I turned toward an even more immature work of mixed media, a sepia self-photo x'd with lipstick across my heart.

"Powerful," I lied.

"You have a good eye, madam."

I moved on to the table of your medals.

"Where are the letters?" I asked.

"I'm not aware of any, madam."

"Not one? Are you certain?" I looked toward the door to The Sex Room. "Closed I presume?"

"No, madam, open. Very much so. *Prosze*." I followed her through a titanium door. A video installation playing on a loop at the end of a dark hall showed a fleshy nude woman on skis, snowplowing down an alpine slope. It was Magda. My former assistant. She was not yet eighteen. I will not attempt to describe the depth of her anguish.

"What does the lady think of the film?" The woman asked.

"I think she is leaning too far forward," I said.

A case of stilettos not in my size, a cup-less bra, crotch-less tights, an appliqué ball gown I never would have worn, ridiculous lambskin restraints, the requisite girls' boarding school uniform, the requisite rubber nurse's costume and enema bag, the remote control vibrators, the anal beads and horseshoes, the flavored creams and nipple clamps, a brush with black strands of hair. Nothing of me.

"There was a portfolio belonging to a young art student," I said. "It should have been here." I sketched you leaning against the twisted bark of a sweet chestnut tree. You scribbled me reaching for a towel, my expression surprised and ashamed as though a stranger had walked in on me.

"I was aware of some portfolios, madam. But they were sent to the port."

"Tell the gentleman and he had no right," I said, escaping your torture boudoir of a gallery. "And tell the gentleman I wish for the return of the canopic jars. They have spent enough time on loan."

I raced through the building to the exit, my lips twitching, my eyes filling with tears.

"You must sign out," the guard said when I reached the door. He handed me a trick pen. When I pressed it to the paper it squirted ink that dribbled over my fingers.

I limped across the park, angry for having put myself in danger. The smell of kabobs cooking at a kiosk repulsed me. I bent over, folding into my knees. A woman in a kerchief pulling a cart stopped next to me.

"*Co jest kochanie?*" She asked, stroking my back.

"*Nic,*" I said, nothing. "*Jestem...*" I could not remember the word for sick.

Smitty saw me through the window of the You and rushed to help.

"You are hurt," he said.

"I am fine," I said. "I just need to wash."

"We have a guest," Smitty said, nodding toward a man in a tweed cape with a zesty laugh in the audio booth listening to recordings of phone conversations I'd meant to destroy. He was Victor Kozol, the proprietor of The Us Museum over by the port. The newspapers carried photos of him attending parties and arriving at benefit performances of the ballet with magnificent young women on his arm. I attempted to fix my hair as I went to greet him.

He removed the headphones and dried his eyes on his handkerchief.

"Forgive me," he said, "but does anyone ever tell the truth about what he or she is wearing?" He asked. "What he or she is doing to him or herself?"

I'd always flattered myself into believing you did.

"Madam, your collection belongs at the Us." His laughter stopped as soon as he studied my face. "I see you've been to the Me." He offered his handkerchief. I wiped the ink on my hand and the mascara I'd cried out under my eyes. "Your wounds are superficial, my dear. You'll see. I would visit a doctor, though, if the feelings persist."

"Who needs a doctor when I have you?" I said uncharacteristically but he was impossible not to flirt with.

He shook his finger and looked me over. I was too old. "I should tell you why I'm here."

"I know why, Mr. Kozol," I said.

"My son..."

"He was here."

"How can I make amends for such insolence?" He asked.

"You've come to buy me out."

"I'd like to move into town," he said. "There's limited foot traffic but I have a following."

He walked the length of the letter cases.

"I wouldn't be able to take all of these," he said. "There is much to admire but I need more standalone artifacts. It's a crowded marketplace, old letters. This one with the tear mark." He took a magnifying glass from the inside of his cape. "I can see by the heft of the stain that it's male. And the double tearstain... you could retire with what that's worth. Assuming it's for sale." I said that everything was for sale. He then stopped at the only letter I'd ever written in pencil. I'd assumed it would bring in thousands, the editing and indecisiveness, the eraser-rage that made the paper practically transparent where once there'd been an accusation, covered over by some non-provocative thought in order to seem unaffected by whatever injury I felt you had inflicted. "Meaningful to me, Madam," he said. "But to my patrons? And I'm sure you could have guessed that replicas would mean little at the Us."

"But this is the suite at the Balmoral Hotel." I swept my hand across the replica of the bed where I had put my knees over your shoulders. "Everything in its place." I opened the drawer to the bedside table to show the condom and the bible.

"People want real things nowadays," he said. "The Gare de l'est platform?"

"On loan," I said.

"Too bad. I recommend you auction the jewels. You'll get more for them. Though I know a young lady who might appreciate the clarity of the pink diamond."

"Would you have a place for Smitty?" I whispered.

"I don't need a guard. If someone steals or defames at the Us it's not a sacrilege, it's gossip."

"As an installation?" He thought a moment, and then seemed to like the idea. "Could you please not let him know?" I asked. "Let him come to work and believe he's guarding?"

"You have my word."

At the door he leaned to kiss my hand.

"My lawyers will send papers. Not as much as you'd hoped but at least you can see I'm a fan."

Not that having a fan was worth a cup of coffee and a cabbage roll at a roadside kiosk.

It was at the time of my closing, as the replicas were dismantled, the letters stacked, a shroud thrown over the cyclo, my red dress, your dress whites, packed into boxes and driven to the port, that you came into the museum. "I suppose you put the blame on me," you said, "when really it was you." You said you understood my putting your letters under glass, sealing up the jewels, and returning the weavings to their rightful country. "Perhaps I deserved it. But," you said, stopping at the windshield with the hole where your wife's head struck, "it was unfair to expose her." And again, after so many years we began to quarrel, accusing one another of infidelities and perceived slights, betrayed confidences, and the unending absences and withholdings, until at last we reached our limits.

"I've been looking for these," you said as you came upon the brass cufflinks you'd had in the navy. I saw the tremor in your hand and a tear I wish I'd captured. "You knew they were mine."

Zephaniah Sole

Infighting

No one in my gym knew what he was fighting. But he was religious in the undertaking of his pugilistic practice, or fantasy, maybe both. I could accurately set an atomic clock every Tuesday, or Thursday, at six p.m. when he stepped into my gym, donned his sporting goods store-bought sixteen-ounce gloves, no hand-wraps, and got to work on one of my long hundred-fifty-pound heavy bags, the kind the mixed martial artists like to kick. He never kicked. He was a purist. But he was good. Flurries and combos in unexpected irregular intervals like a Stravinsky composition exploded out of him in three-minute bars of time. And he understood angles better than any pro I'd ever seen—I'd have a small fortune if I picked up every dime he spun on.

He never sparred. And he never joined the classes, seemingly sniffing when he saw the yuppie millennials throw basic jabs and hooks and uppercuts to the steady good-natured barking of Kent, a twenty-something year old pretty-boy, whose twinkling eyes, and facial shadow that managed to stay at five o'clock no matter what the actual time of day was, helped bring in my main money-making target demographic—young women who wanted to feel like they were kicking ass without having to actually kick any ass.

He always practiced while Kent ran the Tuesday five-thirty to six-thirty Basic Skills Course. One day he was especially warmed up, and though clearly pushing forty, he was dancing like some prospect half that age—pivoting angles and side-stepping imagined counterstrikes and feinting with hips and knees and ankles in a study of fluid aggression. I smiled. I watched. I thought, he must be in love. He was buzzing with an underlying vibration that burned out into the ether. The ladies in Kent's class picked up on it like antennae as their session winded down, giving him side glances, staring at him without staring at him.

Kent picked up on it too. So, when his class ended, Kent walked over and stood at the man's side, watching silently for thirty-seconds or so. The man ignored Kent, continuing his bag work, until Kent finally said, "You should turn your fist when you jab."

The man stopped and took a breath, looking at Kent with a cocked eyebrow. Kent smiled, confident. "You're not twisting the jab. You gotta turn it. So your palm's facing the floor." Kent shoved out his own jab and froze it in place as it connected with the heavy bag. "See? Now you're catching your guy with the knuckles."

The man took another breath. Deliberated. Responded. "That is one way to do it."

"I'm just saying. You're taking the effectiveness out of your jab."

The man nodded, polite. "Depends on what I'm effectively trying to accomplish."

"Jab's a jab, man," Kent smiled.

"OK," the man said, and turned back to the heavy bag.

"Just trying to help."

"Thank you."

"We should spar sometime. You know. Friendly spar."

"Yeah. Sometime."

The man got back to working the bag. Kent strode away. What most would have seen from that interaction was a clashing of antlers, a butting of horns. What I saw was, not only was the man in love, but it was a love that would not last. The fire in his eyes said it all. He had to expend too much energy avoiding the rolling coming of conflict with Kent. And there was a manic quality to the buzz around him. That comes from crazy love. Love that's enveloped by the intense temporality of its own flimsiness. Love that happens when some pre-established condition exists that should rationally destroy the hope of its lasting: she has to go back to her college, or her country, or her husband. Or, she just doesn't give a shit about you.

Kent put on his own gloves and got to work on another heavy bag, slapping leather against leather, and grunting with the effort of digging a power left hook into the bag over and over and over again. The man looked over at Kent and cocked that eyebrow. I laughed to myself, his facial expression communicating his internal monologue: that hook was heavy, but agonizingly slow. A lot of sound. Not too much fury.

I don't believe in the facts of a situation inasmuch as I have access to observable probabilities. When the man came into my gym the following week's Thursday, I did not know, as fact, that something was wrong. My gut simply drew a conclusion based on what my eyes drank in. The skin of his face, taut, pulled his ears back like a pit bull on alert. But his ribs and belly were sagged, his posture too loose. Upstairs, a man in fight or flight. Downstairs, a man already defeated.

This was clear to any who took the time to look. Kent took the time to look as the man fell into his bag work sloppily. Disheveled footwork. Overthinking every strike. And then there went Kent, his Thursday class already complete, heading toward the man to again be a distraction of the unwelcome sort.

The man stopped hitting the bag and faced Kent. I wasn't close enough to hear what the two said, but Kent smiled and strode off to the locker room. The man took off his gloves and put them in his gym bag. He picked up the gym bag. He walked over to the ring. He crouched at ring side. He reached into his bag. Pulled out a mouthpiece. Put it in his mouth. Pulled out headgear. Put it on his head. Adjusted the chin strap. Pulled his gloves back out. Put them on. Grabbed the top rope. Leaned. Stepped between the ropes. Entered the ring.

I don't know what words were exchanged between those two. I'm sure they were very polite. I'm not sure if their politeness concealed Kent's desire to catch the man when he was not in top form, or if they concealed the man's desire to work through some internal demon externally manifesting itself as a younger, prettier competitor. Either way, the man only had to wait thirty seconds before Kent bounded out of the locker room, fully donned in gloves and gear, and joined him in the ring.

Less than two minutes later Kent was laid out on the canvas nursing a broken jaw. I had to help Kent gingerly unstrap his headgear. I took out his mouthpiece, awash in spit and mucus and blood and hoped he wasn't infected with any pathogens from the copious amounts of intimate connections I'm sure he was getting those days. The man and another one of my trainers helped Kent to his feet and out of the ring. My other trainer escorted Kent out of the gym to take him to the ER. The man watched them walk out the door, with a look not dissimilar to that of someone who had just lost his best friend. I went to the bathroom. Wrapped Kent's mouthpiece in toilet paper. A lot. Soaped and scrubbed my hands. Hard. Picked up the paper swaddled mouthpiece, left the bathroom, and tossed the mouthpiece in a drawer in my front desk by the entrance where I normally sit. I walked back to the man who sat by ringside staring at the backs of his hands vacantly.

I approached him with caution. "Don't feel bad," I said. "I always tell Kent he never keeps his hands high enough. Know what he says? I mean, every time. I go, 'you're gonna get hit in the head, in the face, in the jaw.' Every time. He goes, 'yeah, but I can take it.'" I shook my head. "OK man, yeah. 'Til you get hit by someone who can hit."

"I should have held back better," the man said.

"Not your fault you can hit. I saw that. Different than your bag work, when you're sparring. I saw that. On the bag you explode. In the ring? 'Gainst a man? You implode. You know how to breathe."

I tossed out a jab without turning my palm. "And you hit him with the punch he was giving you shit for the other day." I stifled a laugh.

The man fought back a smile and looked at his shoes. That was the most I'd ever spoken with him after he initially signed up for a membership. Encouraged by the gleam of mirth in his eyes, I decided to take a risk, go a little deeper, and test the accuracy of my prior assessment.

"So what's her name?" I said.

The man locked eyes with me, apparently unsurprised by the specificity of my insight. I looked back, unsurprised by his lack of surprise.

"Who says it's a her?" he said.

"Yeah. So what's his name?"

"It's a her."

"Figured. I don't mean disrespect or anything. You don't..."

"Doesn't matter. What her name was."

I took a deep breath. "Dating? Something more?"

"Dating."

"Contact sport."

"It's not. It's not a sport."

"It is. You lose, you get back..."

"Nah," the man said and shoved his gloves and headgear into his gym bag. "Nah. Woman much wiser than me. She said—"

"We're all wiser than you, Chief."

He looked up at the ceiling and closed his eyes. "She said, boxing's not a sport. You play football. You play basketball. Handball. Whatever."

"You don't play boxing," I said, knowing the literary reference all too well. "You think the same thought process applies to dating."

"I think the same thought process applies to anything that involves people's feelings."

He picked up his bag, gave me a polite but tight smile and walked out of my gym. I watched as he left, concerned by my belief, based on observable probability, that I had just spoken with a man broken by that perennial last straw.

He didn't come back the next week. Or the next. Or the next. I wasn't worried. I'm sure things were not easy on his end. I'm sure he was in a place God knows I've been in too many times. A place where you realize the cold wind echoing through the canyons of desert night are nothing more than your own pleading screams, pathetically begging for the answer to a question you're furious you even need to ask: I'm a good person, so why am I alone?

But I wasn't worried. I'm sure he sobbed and shouted into his pillow at night. I'm sure he considered the practical logistics of his self-destruction. I don't know these things as facts. I know them as occurrences of high probability based on the thoughts I've watched run through my own brain in times of trial and need. I could be totally off. But I knew one thing. I knew he was a fighter. That's why I wasn't worried. Whether he was sitting in an empty room somewhere with the barrel of a gun resting between his teeth, or whether he was plowing his body through some other lost and broken soul with whom he was not on a middle-name basis, I knew he'd find his way back to himself. I knew he'd listen to the screaming in his chest and breathe through the panic. Breathe through the pain. Breathe. If you breathe you are here. If you are here, you can fight. Breathe. Because that's what fighters do. Breathe.

A few months later, the door to my gym opened and the world shifted.

She was carrying a plain black gym bag. Plain. Black. Not some designer shit with pink trimming. She was wearing sweatpants. Gray. Sweatpants. Baggy. Not yoga pants. Not skin-tight, form-fitting, cut-out, patterned, honeycomb, mesh leggings or capris. Sweatpants. Gray. With a matching hooded sweatshirt. She wore no make-up. She had a thick scar above her left eyebrow. Her hair was clearly blonde in her youth, but her youth at that point was nothing more than a memory or a summonable state of mind, and so her hair's color had receded to a plain light brown with streaks of further gray. Her deep-set steel blue eyes, her forehead, her mouth, were creased with the lifelines of a woman who had lived a life and then some. There was no botox there. No facelifts. No skin rejuvenation therapy. There was only her. Raw.

She approached me at my front desk and shyly said, "Hi."

"Hey," I said, and tried to gauge two things from her polite smile. One, would she be interested in me? Two, could I get away with cheating on my wife?

"I was thinking about a membership," she said.

I appraised her from head to toe. I could tell there was more going on beneath the grayness of her presentation. I could tell she was in shape. I could tell, not so much because I was a woman, who's been with a lot of women, looking at another woman, but because I was a fighter, who's fought a lot of fighters, looking at another fighter.

"How'd you hear about us?" I asked.

"Online. I wanted a real gym. Something genuine."

I noted the thickness of her traps and hips and legs. "Jujutsu?" I asked.

"Many years," she said, surprised by my trademark precision.

"You want to learn how to punch."

She blinked, stared off into the distance, brought her left hand up to the scar above her eyebrow, then caught herself, and awkwardly moved a few strands of hair from her face. "Ground game is uh... it's not so good when the ground's concrete."

Her voice shook a bit and the look in her eyes begged me not to press further. So, I didn't. "Seventy bucks a month covers your membership and unlimited access to our classes." I lied. It was a hundred a month. "You pay six months upfront it's ten percent off. A year, twenty."

"That's great," she said and reached into the side pocket of her gym bag. "You take card?"

"I take all forms of currency that are not virtual." I winked.

She laughed and took out her credit card. "Six months then."

I took her card and swiped it through the reader connected to my tablet. "I think you should start with Kent's class. Schedule's online. Next one's tomorrow. That'll get you turned on to the basics. Do that a few months, then we'll put you in a more advanced group. Maybe you can join the one I run." I lied again. I wasn't running any group at that point. But I figured it wasn't a bad time to start.

She put her credit card back in her bag, brought her arms to her sides, and gave a slight bow. I brought my fists together and bowed back.

"Thank you," she said.

"Of course. See you soon?"

"Absolutely." She raised her hand as if she were about to wave, but didn't, then turned and went for the door.

"Oh, hey," I called out.

"Yeah?" she turned back.

"With Kent? No matter what he says. Keep your hands higher than he tells you."

I kept an eye on her over the next few months while she worked out in Kent's Tuesday and Thursday classes. I'd also speak with her on her way out or in and this was how I learned more about her and her life. She was a quick study. She kept her hands up like I told her to. She knew how to listen. She twisted her hip with her jab instead of stepping into it, a habit likely formed from her body's trained disposition for throwing and grappling, but I knew I could fix that. She also didn't quite comprehend the mechanics of the uppercut, dropping her arms instead of her legs to throw the punch, but that too was a perfectly correctable beginner's error. If Kent had paid more attention to her, he could have fixed those mistakes himself. But she wasn't one of the girls in a cropped-up tank top that said, "please take notice of my womb," so that wasn't going to happen.

One Tuesday. Six p.m. On the dot. Halfway through Kent's class. The door to my gym opened and the world shifted again.

When he came in, my brain didn't process any event of extraordinariness. Like I said, I was never worried. But Kent? I chuckled as Kent stepped away from his class and ran up to the man. They gripped each other's hands and exchanged a brief hug and a long shoulder bump. The man touched Kent's jaw and Kent laughed and shook his head and gently touched his fist to the man's chest. I'd never seen Kent's face beam so much. Fighters, we're a strange breed. We fall in love with the people who can fuck us up.

They bumped fists again and Kent went back to his class and the man approached my front desk.

"Well look at you," I said.

The man looked down and smiled. He looked good. He looked calm. "Was hoping I could start my membership up again."

"I don't know man. You disappear again, might break Kent's heart. Can't have my guys all emotionally compromised."

The man laughed. "I'm glad he's OK."

"He's fine. Dues are same as before."

"What if I can... what if I want to join the classes too?"

I opened my mouth in mock incredulity. "Someone wake up on the outgoing sociable side of the bed this morning?"

"I'm trying."

"I'm glad. For you? Dues are the same. Take any class you want."

"You don't have to... I can..."

"Same as before. Take any class you want."

He pulled out his wallet, took out four bills and handed them to me. Three twenties and a ten. "Thank you," he said.

At that moment, I wasn't sure why I said what I said next. We waste so much time trying to figure out the motivations of others when we barely understand the motivations of our selves.

"Kent's class is a little basic for you," I said, "but I'd jump in. Some nice people in there. Just saying."

"OK," he said, and looked at Kent's class in progress. "I'll get here earlier, jump in next time."

"Jump in now. No day like today."

"All right," the man nodded. "Yeah. I'll do that."

He walked briskly to the locker room, came out a few minutes later, caught Kent's eye as he approached the class, and pointed toward the group with a question mark on his face. Kent, pacing, barking, smiled and gave the man a thumb's up. The man joined the group, easily falling into their cadence of punches and crunches and burpee box jumps. Between sets, the woman with the scar over her eyebrow stole glances like a pickpocket, inconspicuous and smooth. Staring at him without staring at him.

Marija Stajic

Golden-Grip Gun

The gun had magical powers. No one could ever part from it. No one ever wanted to part from it. Death was the only thing that parted people from that gun. Death was how Mira became its owner, or its servant. And until yesterday, Mira thought that she would be buried with it. Or leave it to Ana, to protect her when Mira couldn't anymore. But now they both had to part with it. It was the price of getting her daughter back. Her daughter, she could tell, recently had been crying, and didn't want to tell Mira over the phone why she wanted to come back to Serbia. But Mira knew. Ana was not happy.

Mira decided to say farewell to her gun, before wrapping it back in the scarf and putting it into her tote bag.

She placed it on her lap. She ran her fingers over the golden handle, over the Old Slavonic letters. She recalled their meaning: *Death is just the beginning.* She imagined her great grandfather, whose old, faded photo she saw once decades ago, fighting with this gun, dying next to it, his commander having to break his death-grip on it in order to send it to his widow along with a medal for bravery and a condolence letter. She imagined her great-grandmother receiving the gun, holding it up and laughing, laughing and dancing with it around her kitchen, finally released from the tyrant, with a war-pension and the respect of a war widow.

Mira caressed the long, steel barrel, calling out to her ancestors' spirits and asking for permission, for forgiveness. She listened to the gun's whispers, what it was saying to her, as well as what was carved on it, its eternal message to everyone whose life it took or saved.

She whispered "Farewell" and "I'm sorry" and wrapped it back in the red silk. It was a price worth paying. She hoped her ancestors would agree. Then she placed it on the bottom of her bag along with all the jewelry she hadn't sold during the bombings, a few 14-karat gold bracelets and pendants, and her wedding ring.

She looked around her house one more time, wondering if she could sell something else instead of the gun. She had sold her husband's car when he died to pay his debts. She sold her late brother's apartment too, and used that money to provide for herself when she became a widow. Even if she wanted to sell the house and all the furniture in it, it would take months. Everybody was in debt. Everybody was selling stuff, only a few buying. No one to borrow from either.

She placed the bag with the gun and jewelry on her shoulder and went into the biggest jewelry store in town.

She shielded her eyes from the glare of the gold, the silver, and the cubic zirconias, sapphires and emeralds in the glass displays. She had heard that this store was the only one in town that had real diamonds, but she couldn't tell the difference between a fake one and a real one.

"I'd like to sell this jewelry." She pulled a plastic jewelry box from the bottom of her purse, carefully, so that she wouldn't disturb the gun sleeping inside the silk scarf, and placed it in front of a smiling man.

He put his glasses on and took out a magnifying glass. He examined the square pendant of the Virgin Mary, the golden cross, the wedding ring, and the two braided bracelets so thin one would think they were made out of golden spider web. Then he pulled a calculator from the drawer below the lighted glass display and began adding.

"The most I could give you for all of this is one hundred euros," he said.

"For all of it? Only one hundred?"

"Yes, I'm sorry," he said, pushing his glasses halfway down his nose. "We can't resell it, it's too old. We have to melt it. That's all it's worth, unfortunately, as raw 14-carat gold. You could try other stores, but we sell and buy the most in town."

"But I need more money, urgently. That's not even going to make a dent," she said, grabbing her head with both of her hands, shaking it in disbelief.

"I could maybe do one hundred and ten, but I'm afraid that would be it," he said.

She looked up. He seemed trustworthy, kind of an honest, middle-aged, workingman. His hands were rough and thick. He had deep crows' feet framing his small brown eyes. He wore a wedding ring on his right ring finger and the flesh around it was swollen.

"My great grandfather left me a gun. It's golden. Would you buy that?"

He looked at Mira as if waiting for her to finish the sentence.

"Could I see it?"

She looked around. There was nobody else in the store or at the door. People passed by but nobody lingered long enough to worry her.

She pulled the red silk sachet out. The gun out-glistened the diamonds.

"May I?" The salesman took it in his hands, turned it around, touched it, weighed it. He took out his magnifying glass again and examined its body, the carvings.

"How old, you say?" He lifted his nose off the gun, his forehead wrinkled in folds.

"World War I."

"Whew. I wish I could buy this. For myself. Why would you want to sell it? It's magnificent! Never seen anything like it!"

"Long story. How much is it worth?"

"Well, I'm not a gun expert, but from what I can tell, the weight, the gold, the antique value, probably ten thousand. Easily."

Mira looked at him. He still looked at the gun, ran his fingers over it, mesmerized.

"Do you know someone who could give me what it's worth for it, today?"

He looked up at Mira. He smiled. He could probably read the desperation lodged in the gap between her eyebrows. Then he took a piece of paper from the drawer. There was a number on it. And a name. Marko. No last name.

"He might be. But be careful. He's not...how should I put this...a typical businessman."

He placed the gun back into the scarf and wrapped it himself, then handed it to Mira.

As she rushed toward the door, he yelled, "Ma'am, your jewelry!" She turned around and quickly shoveled it all with one swoop of her hand into the bag.

Mira called the number on that piece of paper before she took her shoes off at home. The hoarse voice of a man in his late twenties or early thirties picked up.

"Yo," he said.

"Is that Marko?"

"Who's this?"

"My name is Mira."

"Who gave you this number?"

"I'm selling a valuable gun."

Silence.

"How valuable?"

"Very. World War I. Golden handle. Old Slavonic carvings. It's worth... a lot."

Silence. She heard him inhaling then exhaling, as if he were smoking. She also heard fingers tapping on some sort of a keyboard.

"Tito's café. Today. 11pm. Don't be late."

"I will only take cash!" she said in a determined "take it or leave it" voice, as if that would make her sale more plausible.

"Madam, I only deal in cash," he laughed.

"How do I recognize you?"

"I'll recognize you, don't you worry. Bring the gun. And any old bullets if you have them?"

"No bullets. Just the gun."

"Bring it. No photos or crap like that. Ciao."

Mira hung up, took the sachet out of her bag, and unwrapped a silk scarf. There it was. Swaddled like a baby. Her golden-grip gun.

Mira would be lying if she said she wasn't nervous and that she wouldn't mourn the gun. But she had no choice. She didn't have money to buy that ticket. Ana obviously didn't either, otherwise she wouldn't call and ask for Mira to get her back. And Mira needed to walk into a tourist agency the day after and buy that one-way Washington, DC-Belgrade ticket for the day after that. She knew that could probably be up to two or three thousand dollars. Maybe more. Those were a lot of Dinars. But Marko wouldn't pay her in Dinars. Men like him dealt only in Euros. And Nis was famous for being full of men like him.

Then there was the location of her meeting. She didn't even want to walk by *Tito's*. It was the place where her brother killed himself and his lover. She had been avoiding its neighborhood ever since that night. But she didn't want to argue with Marko. It was too important. God knew if Marko would even want to meet her any other place. Those men dealt only in certain locations. Men who bought expensive guns. Men who only worked with cash. Men who could pull three thousand dollars out of their asses anytime. Men in expensive sweat suits and Nike sneakers, with thick-golden chains and crosses, stolen Rolex watches and tattoos of Radovan Karadzic and Ratko Mladic.

She would have to take a mild sedative and meet Marko at *Tito's*, that damned place. And be done with it all. The gun, the past, the curse, the family. And move on with her daughter, who, she hoped, would be able to finally settle down somewhere, have a normal life. As normal as one could have in this God-forsaken country, Mira thought. She had actually hoped that her beautiful Ana would meet a nice American boy so she wouldn't marry a Serbian man, so she would be the first Petrovic woman to break the spell. But it hadn't happened for her. And maybe it was Mira's fault. She had let Ana see how cruel, uncaring, and unreliable men were for most of her life, and it probably left Ana scarred and untrusting. Which was fine by Mira. Better untrusting and safe than too trusting and hurt, like Mira and all of the women in her family before her. Someone had to break the chain. Why not Ana? She was smart enough, she was strong enough. She was the prototype of a new Serbian woman, one who commands her man, not the other way around. One who takes charge. One who cares about her career more than about her husband and children. One who waits for the man who would serve her, not the other way around. Self-sufficient, independent, fierce. One who had the blood of all of her female ancestors in her veins to learn from. To be immune to their mistakes and the turmoil they always led to. Always.

Mira would never let any man hurt Ana. She would rather gouge their eyes out and cut their testicles with her own teeth and gladly rot in prison than let them hurt her only daughter. And she was actually glad Ana was coming back to this shitty country. They could deal with everything together. Maybe they would sell the house and everything in it, just the two of them, and move to Australia or some faraway place like that where they could start from the beginning.

Maybe. Sweet dreams.

The bullets. She had actually bought some bullets after she buried her husband. No one was to mess with her again. The gun was reachable and unlocked. There was one bullet in it, locked and ready to go in the gun's barrel, and no one but Mira knew about it. If a stranger looked at the gun he wouldn't be able to see any bullets in it. He would think it was empty, and Mira found that comforting, as if she and the gun had a secret.

There were more bullets in the small, white box next to it, wrapped in a linen tablecloth she inherited from her grandmother Dika.

She'll leave that bullet already inside the gun. Just in case.

Mira went about the house, absently doing housework, and looked at the clock every five minutes. The plastic handles on the clock moved so slowly she had to check a few times to see if the clock was working properly, if the batteries in it were new, charged and in the right position. Every sound from outside made her jumpy, and she wouldn't answer her phone.

At quarter till 11pm, she placed the silk-wrapped gun in her bag and the bag on her shoulder, holding it tightly with her elbow against her ribs. She walked out onto the quiet streets of Nis and walked slowly but deliberately toward *Tito*'s. As she walked she was aware of the gun's presence, the way it bounced when she stepped from the sidewalk onto the street. It seemed to be vibrating slightly like a phone, but that was impossible, Mira knew. It was just her imagination, her guilty conscience. It was just an item, a thing, an object, something a blacksmith created almost a hundred years ago, just some steel and gold hammered together, Mira tried to convince herself, to no avail. She knew it had always been much more than that. But aren't we all made to sacrifice everything for our children? Even our ancestors' legacies?

She was really close, so close to *Tito*'s she could see young people getting in and out of it, and smell the cigarette smoke, and the alcohol spilled and tracked out on people's shoes. She stood across the street watching them, her stomach twisting and churning, her blood pressure rising into her temples, her palms itchy and hot. She glanced at Ana's photo to remind herself of why she was about to walk into the last place she ever wanted to be.

She put the photo back in the valet and took a deep breath, as if she were about to dive into river where people routinely drowned.

There was a bouncer at the door. A cliché of a bouncer, a tall body-builder with a bald head. Mira expected him to laugh at her, or ask her what the hell was she doing in the café at her age, but he didn't. He just opened the door for her. She smiled courteously and with slight relief, then stooped back and asked: "Do you know Marko?"

He looked at her with a significant stare.

"Marko? I know many Markos. It's a popular name."

"I'm supposed to meet Marko here at 11pm," she said, "but I don't know what he looks like."

The bouncer looked around. There was no one else around them at that moment.

"Red baseball hat. I never told you that, got it?" he said, and pointed his hand in.

She nodded.

The café was as smoky as if it were a lab where they tested cigarette smoke's effects on animals. The folk music was so loud that the speakers hanging from the four corners of the room's ceiling bounced. Red leather booths framed what was supposed to be a dance floor in the middle of the room, but nobody danced.

It was probably too early for that, Mira thought.

When she walked in, people whose faces she could barely see through the smoke all turned their bodies toward her. Mira decided to walk to the bar and wait there. She didn't see anybody with a red baseball hat. She could barely see anything. She began coughing. She felt as if she had picked up and broken a jalapeno pepper, then rubbed her eyes. There was a disco ball above the improvised dance floor, and she hadn't seen one since she briefly dated her now-late husband in the seventies. Then she remembered. If she could kill her husband, make it look like an accident, and get away with it, then she could certainly do this. Deal with this man who was holding the keys to Ana's return to her.

"What would you like to drink, Ma'am?" the girl behind the bar asked. She was about Ana's age, mid-twenties, and, for some reason, that realization made Mira shiver. Is this what Ana would be forced to do if she were to live here again? Serving these illiterate people in this oxygen-deprived room for, what, a hundred Euros a month? No, they would have to move. She needed more money, more money for the gun. Maybe they could open a B&B in Greece? Run it together. Swim in the sea at dusk.

As she looked at the shiny, colorful bottles behind the bar, and at the young waitress with blonde hair burned from repetitive bleaching so she could look like one of the turbo-folk starlets, she felt throbbing pain up and down her spine.

"She with me, Vera." Mira heard the same hoarse voice from the phone behind her. Marko.

He was young, very young. Again, about Ana's age.

Vera nodded and disappeared, and Marko sat next to Mira on a stool. "We can't do this here. Let's go to my booth." He got up and walked toward the dark back corner of the spacious, one-level café. Mira followed slowly, searing her bag into her ribs, looking around.

He walked to the last booth and sat down, pointing to the other side of it. Mira slid in.

"Let me see it," he said.

She procrastinated for a second, still glancing around. She couldn't shake that "I shouldn't be doing this" feeling she had. She dipped her hand, felt the silk, unwrapped it inside her bag and pulled the gun out by its golden handle. She gently placed it on the table, the barrel staring at Marko.

He looked at it, then at Mira, and smiled. He grabbed it by the barrel, pulled it toward him, then grabbed the handle with his other hand.

"Fuck me," he said. "I have never seen anything like it. Where did you get it, Mom?"

Mira swallowed with difficulty.

"It has been in my family for four generations. And I'm not your Mom," she said.

Marko laughed.

"You cool," he said. "I definitely want it. How much for it?"

"Ten thousand. Euros," she said, and pulled her stomach in as if she were getting ready for a blow.

"Too much," Marko said, in a serious tone. "It's not worth that much. I can give you three."

Should she take three? She looked at the gun, at Marko's sparkly eyes, at the way he was groping her gun, *her* gun, her precious gun.

"Then please give me my gun back," she said.

"Hey, grandma, what do you think this is, an open market where you can bargain with the rednecks? I said I want the gun, you said you wanna sell it, there's no backing out now. You know ten thousand is too much, so unless you want me to pay you nothing for it, I suggest you take the four I'm generously offering right now, because you're old, and go back tending to your garden, or whatever else you do in life. Any bullets in it?" he asked, without even waiting for her to answer to his proposal.

"No," Mira said quietly. "It's empty."

"Do you have any bullets with you, old bullets, I mean."

"I told you No over the phone," she said.

He didn't even really listen to her. He began playing around with the gun as if he were a kid playing cowboys and Indians, twirling it in the air, as if it was a new toy that now belonged to him.

"Be careful," Mira said. "It's not a toy. It certainly isn't your toy."

His face got serious, and he pulled his shirt up. She could see another gun, a simple, silver-colored gun on his belt. It looked just like the gun in the photo the police showed her, the gun her brother killed himself with. In this very place. Maybe the same booth. She looked around for traces of blood on the table, leather, floor.

"I'll give you the money tomorrow," he said.

Mira felt as if she were beginning to drown. "I need the money now," she said in a high-pitched voice. "It's urgent."

"Don't give a damn. Tomorrow," he said.

"Then I'll take the gun and bring it to you tomorrow," she said, her voice shaky.

"Why? You don't trust me, Mom?" he said, his face serious, threatening. Then he laughed, laughed like a lunatic, which scared Mira even more than his gun. He continued playing with the golden-grip gun, aiming at the wall, looking at the barrel, caressing the gold and letters, smelling the steel.

"We're done. See you tomorrow, here, the same time. I'll have an envelope ready. Nighty-night," he said, waving his fingers at her, as if she were a dismissed child.

Fear lodged in her chest, and it was hard for her to get up and out of that booth. The leather underneath her was wet from her sweat and her arms got sticky and stuck onto the booth. As she pulled herself off, dragging her tote-bag over the leather seat, staring at her gun for the last time with a strong urge to cry and scream, Marko said: "What does this mean?"

"What?" she asked, standing by the table.

He pushed the gun toward her. "That, those weird letters, what kind of a demented language is that?"

The gun was now in front of her, just inches away from her hand, the handle glistening in the neon lights around her, the barrel dark, ominous, and staring at Marko once again. She leaned in and slowly touched the handle, as if she didn't know what he was talking about and was about to try to decipher the message. She touched the carvings, letter by letter, as if she were blind and it was Braille. She was buying time to think, but all she could hear in her ears was the gun speaking to her, calling out to her, forbidding her to leave it behind, to buy her daughter's return with it.

She leaned in even farther, wrapped her fingers around the handle, put her index finger on the trigger. The gun still lay on that sturdy plastic and metal rectangular table.

"So, what does it say, grandma?" Marko asked again, impatience in his voice. "Come on, I don't have the whole night."

Mira grabbed the handle and lifted it off the table, then slowly sat back onto the edge of the seat.

"Ten thousand now, or I'm walking away, sonny," she said, her hand shaking, her whole body shaking, even her words.

Marko laughed. He laughed. How dumb this young man was, Mira thought.

"You want to know what it says?" she asked.

"I'm dying to find out," he said, without an inkling of fear in his eyes. Mira saw him moving his hand slowly toward his waist. The DJ had increased the volume of the latest turbo-folk hit, *Ceca's*. The screechy music screamed. She could hear people behind her dancing, singing loudly.

"Death is just the beginning," she said, and pulled the trigger.

Kate Tooley

The End of the World Is the Original Femme Fatale

The Blue Dahlia

There's a woman in the shadows. Music rolls out with the piped in fog: a howl of sound, heavy on the saxophone, Adolph Deutsch's genius wailing against the rain wet sidewalk. She's slipping backwards into the alley, the light from a seedy bar streaks down her leg, the sheen off her stockings would attract a magpie,* I shouldn't follow her, obviously—but obviously I will.

I don't crave destruction, but I've fallen in love with the idea of choosing mine, have become a compulsive collector of little deaths.** Just for practice. Whatever bed or scheme she'll lure me into is irrelevant. This has never been about the passion-adrenaline I find with her hand up my skirt or around the pearl handled revolver she slips me in the ally. It is about becoming the ending, being inhabited by her, by it.***

I have a dozen world endings in my birds' nest and so I know that they do not bang and do not whimper. They make a sound like Marlene Dietrich singing: off key, full of pain, and always, always laughing at herself.

* In the slang of noir "bird" is just another word for woman, which makes me both a bird and an ornithophile.

** Orgasms.

*** I am investing in chaos, but with this soundtrack it feels easy.

Gilda

1946, in a Buenos Aires that never existed I learned not to fear destruction.

Ballin Mundson, impeccably calm, says:

"Now then, ... I believe we were about to drink a toast. So: disaster to the wench who did wrong by our Johnny." You couldn't cut that pause with a hatchet. He looks at his new wife who is staring at her lap, "No, Gilda? You won't drink to that?"

She shears her eyes up, half a smile:*

"Why not? Disaster to the wench!" and she drinks for a long time.

Dear reader, she is the wench.**

Dark Passage

1947, a San Francisco that might have been real: A man escapes from prison and hides in my car, says he's been accused of murder but is innocent. He needs a place to stay while he gets a new face, literally.

I put him on the couch.***

At no point is this a good idea, but I have my reasons. To be in proximity to that kind of death is... seductive. Afterward, I wonder if I fell in love with her or with the idea that if everything we are is gone, then the world has ended too.

Maybe I meet the man with a new face in a warm country where the law can't follow us, maybe I stay in San Francisco and see how many kinds of death I can lay down on my couch. The world is my oyster: I'm not Lauren Bacall, my face has always been forgettable.

---

* I have spent years dragging women who smile like this into bathroom stalls and bedrooms.

** And I should have feared destruction.

*** This is what Lauren Bacall does, most of us have a very slim chance of meeting Humphrey Bogart on the side of the road. It's not a bad metaphor for this mess, though given I am not subject to the Hayes code, I never made her sleep on the couch.

Touch of Evil

Legend tells us that when things get too bad, they become unfixable, too heavy, too complicated—Ragnarök, Sodom, whatever. The moral is always to burn it down. But the end of the world doesn't mean everything ends—it just means everything changes.* And since no one has ever figured how to tell a story about nothingness, the end keeps being absorbed and reborn as the beginning. In Noir, someone always walks into the fog.** I thought I'd be the one left for dead, but here we are and now what the hell am I going to do for gas money not to mention the rest of my life.

The police captain confronts the fortuneteller who maybe used to be his lover, says: "Come on, read my future for me."

She replies, tired of it in the way only Marlene Dietrich can be tired of things, "You haven't got any."

Is he afraid yet? It's hard to tell, he only asks her what she means by that.

"Your future's all used up." He didn't know you could spend a future quicker than you could live it. In the movie, he'll fight, but in the end, she finds him dead in a wastewater ditch, killed by a cop who loved him, but not enough to let things get messy.***

(She gets the last real word of the movie because, let's be honest, no one knows more about the end of the world than Orson Welles.)

"He was some kind of a man... What does it matter what you say about people?" It is a happy ending for everyone but her. She's a fortuneteller, she knows too much about endings and how they don't exist.

---

* And it would have been great if someone told me that before I wound up halfway to Arizona, feet kicked out the car window snuggling a bottle of mezcal.

** Future.

*** You can find the words "passion" and "fire" in the same thesaurus entry and I believe this is what has led to such confusion on my part. Or maybe I've just never loved something enough to not burn it down.

Tom Whalen

The Professor

1.

Medieval town, Bamberg, a UNESCO site, his good colleagues had told him, for they were good colleagues, in every sense of the word *good*, of the word *colleague. What must we write*? his students in the hallway wanted to know as he made his way to his office, still bundled in his overcoat and scarves. *What is an "argument"?* He walked along the sidewalks, head down, the cold inside his bones. Christmas market, carols. The prostitutes near Zentral. Some evenings upstairs in candy-colored Müller he flipped through every DVD, from Z to A, without seeing anything that interested him. The hotel in the evening remained eerie with no staff, the entrance, the elevator, the hallways empty. Once he saw a woman in the corridor on his floor just standing there, stiff as a statue.

2.

Another missed connection. He spent an extra two hours in the Nuremberg station reading from a novel about a menopausal wife and her two unmarried friends in their fifties on vacation at a wellness hotel on the North Sea. Once he spent an entire sleepless night in the hotel watching on his tablet interviews with Italian actresses in Italian without subtitles and wondering how these women became more beautiful as they aged. Dreams tainted by what he heard through the earphones, foreign languages, castle walls. His retirement pension would be minuscule. Would he have to move?

3.

Lately, back home in Stuttgart, he had been taking his coffee at a small café in the neighborhood. Here, sitting on one of the café's five stools, he would drink sometimes as many as three cappuccini and eat one or two of the shop's croissants and a brioche, though he knew this was not good for his heart. By his count he was at least ten kilos overweight, but, for what it was worth, the doctor told him his prostate was sound, though his teeth, what was left of them, weren't good. January flu, February, the classrooms awash in viruses. He worried about whether his body would survive the winter. The students sneezed uninhibitedly. His colleagues offered their unwashed hands to shake. Back in Stuttgart, unable to sleep, he trembled from cold one moment, and the next sweated profusely beneath the blanket.

4.

In the morning class no one had read the week's assignment. For minutes at a time he stared out the classroom window and said nothing. Another day he missed his train because a button on his coat got caught in the bus seat, he couldn't get out; at first, he didn't know what was holding him, why he couldn't get out of the seat, until he saw that a button on his coat had snagged on a metal bar. By the time he realized he had to take off his coat before he could extract it, the doors had closed; oncoming passengers pushed him back; the bus drove on. At the next stop he got out and walked back to the station, weighted down by his back pack, the cold, the thought of the hours now he would be delayed in getting home. Wind and sleet raked his face as he hurried back to the station. The next train was delayed. The train was not coming. Then the train came five minutes after the cancellation announcement. Still, he missed his next connection and ended up taking a crowded regional that got him back to Stuttgart three hours late, exhausted, his senses pummeled by the noise and smells of the train, the cell phone calls of his fellow passengers, the old couple who sat across from him in their evening concert dress disdaining his disheveled appearance.

5.

After six in the evening Hotel Central was empty of staff. One used a key to enter the building. The reception desk was shuttered. One machine filled with drinks, no coffee, no snacks, no staff. For several seconds as he waited for the doors to close he observed himself observing himself in the mirror on the wall opposite the elevator.

6.

The morning class passed in a fog of incomprehension on both the professor's and the students' parts, followed an hour later by his Melville and Poe course, *brilliant madmen*, he muttered over and over to himself, though he knew better than to say this to the students who, he was certain, already thought him mad, or at the least *non compos mentis*. After dinner at a student café he drifted toward the bridge over the Regnitz where the students gathered, though he never talked to them, stood alone at the rail looking down at the water or at the half-timbered houses of Little Venice. One evening the walk up to the Dom had been treacherous with ice; he slipped and suddenly saw himself collapse to the pavement like a puppet. Then a man with a small dog under one arm reached down, pulled him back on his feet, hurried off again to escape the cold. The professor spat warm, bitter blood onto the snow.

7.

He battened himself within himself, down to his Russian-doll core, while the wind whipped through Hasengasse. Down the long corridor his students clung to the walls, afraid to approach him. Between classes and his office hour he drank coffee with Bamberg pensioners in a café on Langestrasse. The waitresses were as perfect in their service as he in his, for he thought himself in every way as much at their service as they were his. At these times, surrounded by the café's incomprehensible symphony, with the romance novel beside his cinnamon-dashed cappuccino, the elderly Germans busy with their newspapers and chatter, he felt quite at ease in the playlet going on around him, staged in a mirror-lined chamber. In a basket at the front desk of the hotel connected to the café, a stack of winter apples.

8.

Whenever possible he sat at the same table near the breakfast display and always chose the same meal—pumpkin-seed roll, ham slices, scrambled eggs, black coffee—and read slowly and intently from popular romance novels by German authoresses. Sometimes he would help guests new to the breakfast room orient themselves, but he went out of his way to avoid conversation. He was almost always the first guest in the breakfast room. A half hour later, when he had finished eating, he swept the crumbs of the roll into his hand and back onto his plate, moved the dishes toward the corner for easy removal, nodded *Danke* to the friendly woman on duty as he departed.

9.

For minutes at a time he looked through the classroom's windows seeing nothing, only the winter sky that closed down over the medieval town, and he wondered about dinner or what he would do when the semester ended, if he would stay in Germany. And then someone would sneeze or groan or ask him a question. He didn't want to turn back to the class. He preferred to look out the window or at the blackboard or over the students' heads rather than into their faces, some of them tilted down to their digital devices, like bees imbibing nectar. Sometimes in the student cafés the waitresses were ex-students, though seldom did he remember from which course. They nodded and smiled, took his order. Never did he or they mention his classes. Sometimes on his way back to Hotel Central after dinner, he was stopped near the central bus station by a streetwalker, often from Russia or the Ukraine, whose German was no better than his and who in her high heels comfortably towered above him. Most evenings he would walk for half an hour around town, along the river or to the old city hall or up to Domplatz where he would stare down upon the small city. He batted his gloved hands against his chest to keep them warm, the roofs thick with the snow that continued to fall from darkness.

10.

Always the female anchors on CNN looked as if they hadn't aged in two decades, some even appeared younger. He checked his email, turned off the light, but couldn't sleep, never could he sleep in Hotel Central, though the room was dark, no traffic noise because they placed him at the back of the hotel, the room beside him always empty. He lay awake for hours unable to sleep. Sometimes he read, though never the books for his courses. For them he had prepared enough. He had to maintain a balance, he told himself over and over, rather than trying to think of nothing or of sheep, but not about the classes, no, not them. Eventually the professor's thoughts would drift, brief forays into the tide of sleep, and suddenly he was wide awake again. Had he not created enough bad will from students over the years not to have to suffer them in nightmares?

11.

In his Poe seminar a student asked why he mentioned sex regarding "Ligeia." Where does most of the story take place, he asked her, then included the rest of the class, "Anyone?" Some of the students whispered to their neighbors, others manipulated their phones. He gazed down the corridors of Poe's renovated abbey in a remote area of England, then quoted, "But in death only, was I fully impressed with the strength of her affection." He shook his head back and forth, face down. "Kleist," he said, but the name triggered only blank looks and one audible groan. For Kleist, he had been about to inform them, it wouldn't have been "one of the wildest and least frequented portions of fair England," but *the* wildest and least frequented. "The will to madness," the professor said, then repeated it two times, but didn't elaborate on what he took to be the obvious. "A bridal chamber, to answer my own question, that's where most of the story takes place," he said finally, for those listening. The students stared at him as if *he* were the madman, not Poe, when in every sense Poe had by far the greater claim to madness—and Kleist the greatest. Why was the professor still in Germany? Perched cross-legged on a table, he rocked back and forth, as if adrift on the sea of their dismay or anger. "And the bridal chamber becomes ...?" The eyes of a young woman on the front row, blond hair lit by the glow of her tablet, suddenly teared, as if he had personally insulted her. For a moment, like one of Poe's neurasthenic narrators, he wanted to bow down to her in his abjectness, but instead said, "A chamber of death and resurrection, of morbidity and madness."

12.

After class he ate in student cafes, always the oldest diner in the room. He ordered no wine, and while eating read in the dim light a few lines from contemporary German romance novels.

13.

During his final semester of teaching he lived alone in Stuttgart and commuted to Bamberg once a week. He visited no one, saw his colleagues only at work, otherwise just his fellow travelers. By the middle of the term he had already missed so many classes due to train delays and cancellations, that both he and the students stopped caring whether they met or not. When he did make the first class of the week on Tuesday evenings, few had their course books in hand, fewer still had read them. Hours on the station platform, in the cold, wrapped up in his overcoat, stocking cap, gloves and scarf, freezing without and within. The train was late. A child in its father's arms coughed in his ear. Arrival time unknown. The air was metal cold and seemed to hold only loosely the gray shapes of the station. The train was not coming. The incoherent loud speakers told him nothing. He followed the crowd into the snow toward the buses which would take them only as far as Craisheim or Erlangen. In the bus, with the passengers standing shoulder to shoulder, a deformed child, no older than twelve, screamed at what seemed regular intervals. Beside him a woman twice his size embraced and mumbled to her curry-soaked bag of groceries in a language that at times sounded Swabian, at times Turkish, more often a language neither he nor perhaps anyone, other than the woman herself, understood. Long winter delays, shuffling from bus to S-bahn, S-bahn to bus, then again the wait for the regional that never came.

Kathy Wilson

The Overlook

He met her at the overlook. He arrived in the van he uses for work, got out, looked around the parking lot at the parked cars and then up to the trail behind the viewpoint. He put his sunglasses on. Good call, I thought. No one's going to recognize you now, Stan. He walked over to a silver Buick, looked around once more and got in, the door shutting firmly behind him. A moment later he was leaning into the blonde for an eager kiss. I took a picture.

She had been sitting there longer than the few minutes I had been at the overlook. She was playing a game on her phone, looking up periodically, clearly waiting for someone. Now and then she touched up her lipstick in the rearview mirror, flicked an errant strand of hair back into respectable place. She was off work early and didn't have to be home for hours. Yeah. No one is going to see you in such a public spot right on the highway, Lynn. I took a picture.

This had been going on a while. The kids would be home soon, the spouses back from a long day. They all knew something was up. They all knew the marriages were over. They just didn't know who'd be screwed over the most in the divorces. I got paid either way and this was an easy gig. One day to follow her, three days to get his ATM records, six phone calls to find the motel they used, fifty dollars for the desk clerk to admit she knew him, another fifty dollars to get the days he'd stayed. You can pay for a hotel room in cash, but you have to hold it with a card and they always keep that info on file. Skulduggery ain't what it used to be, Stan.

I pulled into the hotel parking lot five minutes after them. I love it when they stick to a routine. I had plenty of time to get a burger and I sat there scanning the lot for her car while I ate it. There it was, silver Buick right near the dumpster. Gotta love irony. I took a picture. I waited. They never took too long. Seems to me wrecking the lives of three kids, two adults, and a shaggy mutt named Doug ought to take longer than that but what do I know. Right on time, they came out. I took note of the time and room, his hand on her ass over the disarranged skirt and took a picture. I'd taken around twenty pictures of various meetings and couldn't imagine why the spouse wanted more. The first three were enough to bury them. Whatever. I get paid either way.

We all headed back to the overlook. One last furtive and enthusiastic kiss and Stan went back to his company car. She watched him go, then left in the opposite direction. I gazed out at the ocean, the sun turning the water into molten silver. An eagle flashed down from a tree on the cliff winging somewhere wild and clean. I took a picture.

***Fran Abrams**'s poems have been published online and in print, including in *Cathexis-Northwest Press*, Alan Squire Publishing, *Winter 2021 Bulletin*, *The Ravens Perch*, and *Bourgeon Online*. Her poems appear in eight anthologies, including the 2021 collection *This is What America Looks Like* from Washington Writers Publishing House. In 2019, she was a juried poet at Houston Poetry Fest and a featured reader at DiVerse Gaithersburg (MD) Poetry Reading Series. Please visit franabramspoetry.com

***Renée Adams** is an emerging aging poet who has been quietly writing poems for years. Her poems have appeared on her city's buses, in her local art gallery, *The Typescript*, *The Zebra*, and *The Alexandria Gazette*. Articles about her poetry fence have appeared in *The Washington Post*, *The Alexandria Times*, *The Alexandria Gazette Packet*, *Alexandria Woman*, *the Del Ray Patch*, and *The Zebra*. Her PechaKucha Alexandria presentation on her poetry fence can be found online.

Kelli Allen's work has appeared in numerous journals and anthologies in the US and internationally. Allen is the Co-Founding Editor of *Book of Matches* literary journal. Her collections include, *Otherwise*, *Soft White Ash*, (2012), *Imagine Not Drowning*, (C&R Press 2017), *Banjo's Inside Coyote* (C&R Press 2019). Allen's latest book is *Leaving the Skin on the Bear*, C&R Press, 2022. She currently teaches writing and literature in North Carolina. www.kelli-allen.com

Roberta Allen is a conceptual artist and fiction writer. Her interest in language is the bridge that connects these separate pursuits. Works have included drawings, artist books, photo/text works, installations, digital prints and sculpture. Her books include *The Traveling Woman*, *The Daughter*, *Certain People*, *Amazon Dream*, *Fast Fiction*, *The Playful Way to Serious Writing*, *The Playful to Knowing Yourself*, *The Dreaming Girl* and *The Princess of Herself* (Pelekinesis Press, 2017).

Robert R Angell (he/him) writes literary fiction and science fiction and fantasy. His work appears in magazines such as *The Baltimore Review*, *Broadkill Review*, *Chelsea Station*, *Interzone*, and *Asimov's Science Fiction*, and in many anthologies. His first novel, *Best Game Ever*, came out in May 2019 and was featured in the June 2020 LGBTQ Pride Bundle. More at https://rrangell.com.

***Daniel Abbott Armstrong**, aka Dag N'Abbott (among others), is an actor/singer/shaman/bard/busboy/ system analyst/limo driver and customer service rep (among many others) who has written creatively for over forty years and has performed at and/or hosted poetry readings for the last twenty+. Daniel lives in Frederick, Maryland, and has a girlfriend and many sons. To know him is to know he loves you and he thanks you for knowing him.

Cynthia Atkins is the author of *Psyche's Weathers*, *In the Event of Full Disclosure* (CW Books) and *Still-Life With God* (Saint Julian Press, 2020), and a collaborative chapbook (Harbor Editions, 2022). Her work has appeared in numerous journals, including *Alaska Quarterly Review*, *BOMB*, *Diode*, *Florida Review*, *Green Mountains Review*, *Indianapolis Review*, *Rust + Moth*, *North American Review*, *Seneca Review*, *SWWIM*, *Thrush*, *Tinderbox*, and *Verse Daily*. Atkins lives on the Maury River of Rockbridge County, Virginia, with artist, Phillip Welch, and their family. www.cynthiaatkins.com

A Washington, DC, resident since 1997, **Naomi Ayala** is the author of three books of poetry—*Wild Animals on the Moon* (Curbstone Press), *This Side of Early* (Curbstone Imprint, Northwestern University Press), and *Calling Home: Praise Songs & Incantations* (Bilingual Press). She's the translator of *La sombra de la muerte/*

Asterisk (*) indicates first time published in Gargoyle.

Death's Shadow, a novel by His Excellency José Tomás Pérez, Dominican Republic Ambassador to the U.S., and of Luis Alberto Ambroggio's *La arqueología del viento/The Wind's Archeology.*

A multimedia artist living near San Antonio, ***Jeff Bagato** produces poetry and prose as well as electronic music and glitch video. He has published nineteen books, all available through the usual online markets, including *And the Trillions* (poetry) and *The Toothpick Fairy* (fiction). A blog about his writing and publishing efforts can be found at http://jeffbagato.com.

Tom Ball has published novels, novellas, short stories and flash in *Green Wall, Down in the Dirt* magazine, *Defenestrationmag.net, Conceit Magazine* and its imprints, *Gargoyle Magazine,* Spillwords Press, *PBW* magazine, *Fleas on the Dog Online, Sparrow's Trumpet, TRSFR/ Sip Cup, Poetry Pacific, postcardshorts.ca, The Local Train Magazine, Lone Star Magazine,* and others. Tom is currently a senior editor at *Fleas on the Dog* (fleasonthedog.com).

Jeanne Marie Beaumont is the author of four collections of poetry including *Burning of the Three Fires* and, most recently, *Letters from Limbo* (CavanKerry Press, 2016). Her verse play, *Asylum Song,* had its premiere production at HERE Theater in spring of 2019. Recent poems have appeared or are forthcoming in *Image, The Manhattan Review, Columbia Poetry Review, Southern Poetry Review,* and *Laurel Review.*

Anne Becker, author of three books of poetry, *Human Animal, The Transmutation Notebooks: Poems in the Voices of Charles and Emma Darwin,* and *The Good Body,* is also a teacher, working with poets putting together chapbooks and full-length collections. A paper artist, she has printed her poems on her own hand-made paper, as well as collaborated on an artist book with poems and photographs, *The Body in the World.*

Guy R. Beining was born in 1938 in London and arrived in New York City in the spring of 1940. He currently resides in Great Barrington, Massachusetts, and has published thousands of poems along with hundreds of collages and drawings. Books include: *Inner Insight* (Runaway Spoon Press, 2005), *Measurement of Night* (CC Marimbo, 2002), *Several Steps from the Rope* (Xtant, 2002), *Too Far to Hear*, Chapters XIV-XXVI (Standing Stones Press, 1997), and *Carved Erosion* (Elbow Press, 1995).

Delaware native **Nina Bennett** is the author of *The House of Yearning, Mix Tape,* and *Sound Effects* (Broadkill Press Key Poetry Series). Her poetry has been nominated for the Best of the Net, and has appeared in publications that include *South85, I-70 Review, Gargoyle, Yale Journal for Humanities in Medicine, Philadelphia Stories,* and *The Broadkill Review*. Awards include 2019 finalist Jack Grapes Poetry Prize, and the 2014 Northern Liberties Review Poetry Prize.

***Susan Bennett** is a ritualist and poet, leading women's spirit circles in northern Virginia for the last fifteen years. She is a graduate of the University of California, San Diego, and a native New Yorker.

***Joanna Biggar** is a writer, teacher, and traveler by profession, and a Californian by birth and inclination. She has published personal essays, feature articles, poetry, travel stories, fiction and non-fiction for hundreds of publications. She is co-editor of the prize-winning travel series, *Wandering in.... That Paris Year* and *Melanie's Song* are two novels in a trilogy published by Alan Squire Publishing; the third, "To End All Wars," is forthcoming.

Linda Blaskey is the recipient of two Fellowship Grants from Delaware Division of the Arts. She is poetry editor emerita for *Broadkill Review*, coordinator for Dogfish Head Poetry Prize, and editor at *Quartet,* an online poetry journal featuring the work of women fifty and over. She is the author of *Farm* (Bay Oak Publishers), *White Horses* (Mojave River Press), and co-author of *Walking the Sunken Boards* (Pond Road Press).

***Ruth Boggs** is a certified translator and interpreter by profession and writer by passion, with a master's in English and a bachelor's in writing. Her creative nonfiction work has appeared in an anthology, *Turning Points,* and German publications. Having traveled to 45 of the 50 states, if she were to write a professional memoir, the title would be "From the Whore House to the White House" because in her 25+ year career, she's covered it all.

John Bradley's poems have appeared in *Caliban, Diagram, Gargoyle, Hotel Amerika, Lake Effect, Pedestal*, and other journals. His most recent book is *Everything in Motion, Everything at Rest*, Dos Madres Press. He frequently reviews books of poetry for *Rain Taxi*.

Nick Carbó is a Filipino American writer from Legazpi, Albay, Philippines. Carbó writes poetry and essays, and edits magazines and anthologies. His book of poetry *Secret Asian Man* won the Asian American Writers Workshop's Readers Choice Award. He also won the 2005 Calatagan Award from the Philippine American Writers & Artists for his book *Andalusian Dawn*. Through his anthologies *Returning a Borrowed Tongue, Babaylan*, and *Pinoy Poetics*, he consolidates both Filipino and Filipino American experiences.

***Mira Chiruvolu** is an eighteen-year-old, born and raised in California. She loves to write, specifically poetry and short stories. When not writing she enjoys playing basketball and running outside as much as possible. Her writing style leans towards grander themes about life, including courage, bravery, love, loss, etc. Her portfolio is a conglomeration of stories, poems, thoughts, and pieces that she has created over the course of her life.

Joan Colby (1939–2020) liked to say that she worked "anywhere a poem would strike." She was editor of *Illinois Racing News*, a monthly publication focused on the breeding and racing of thoroughbreds in the Midwest for over 35 years. She published over 2,000 poems, plus 22 books of poetry including: *Joyriding to Nightfall, Ribcage, The Wingback Chair, Properties of Matter, How the Sky Begins to Fall, The Boundary Waters*, and *Blue Woman Dancing in the Nerve*.

With poems in *Poetry East, Cloudbank, Boxcar Poetry Review*, and *Gone Lawn*, ***Michael Cole** also has a co-translation of Finnish poet Pentti Saarikoski's long poem *Dances of the Obscure* (Logbridge-Rhodes Pr.) and two poetry chapbooks: *After Uelsmann* (Bottom Dog Pr.) and *Manna for Winter* (Owl Creek Press). After thirty years at Kent State University, he now lives with his artist wife on the shore of Lake Erie.

After growing up in Southern West Virginia, **Kathleen Corcoran** left for Nigeria where she taught English for four years. Now retired after teaching in Maryland, she enjoys long walks through fields and woods with her dog. She is the author of a chapbook, *Bloodroot*, and two of her poetry collections have received awards from the Maryland Arts council. Her poems have appeared in *Tar River Poetry, Paterson Literary Review, Gargoyle, Persimmon Tree, Baltimore Review, Plainsongs*, and others.

Dana Curtis's third full-length collection of poetry, *Wave Particle Duality*, was published by blazeVOX Books in 2017. Her second collection, *Camera Stellata*, was published by CW Books, and her first book, *The Body's Response to Famine*, won the Pavement Saw Press Transcontinental Poetry Prize. She has received grants from the Minnesota State Arts Board and the McKnight Foundation. She is Editor-in-Chief of Elixir Press and lives in Denver Colorado.

Andrew Darlington has walked the magma crust of the Nisyros volcano. James Lowe of the Electric Prunes is his Facebook friend. And Kink Dave Davies answered his Tweet. He writes about music for 'R'N'R' (Rock 'n' Reel), and counterculture for *IT: International Times*. His latest poetry collection is *Tweak Vision: The Word-Play Solution to Modern-Angst Confusion* and his Scientifiction Novel *In the Time of the Breaking* are both from Alien Buddha Press, USA. His writing can be found at *Eight Miles Higher*: http://andrewdarlington.blogspot.co.uk/

William Virgil Davis's most recent book of poetry is *Dismantlements of Silence: Poems Selected and New*. His earlier books are: *The Bones Poems; Landscape and Journey* (New Criterion Poetry Prize and Helen C. Smith Memorial Award for Poetry); *Winter Light; The Dark Hours* (Calliope Press Chapbook Prize); *One*

Way to Reconstruct the Scene (Yale Series of Younger Poets Prize). His poems have appeared in most of the major periodicals worldwide.

James Deahl is the author of twenty-nine literary titles, the three most recent being: *Earth's Signature, Travelling the Lost Highway*, and *Red Haws to Light the Field*. He lives in Sarnia with the writer Norma West Linder.

***Shona Deahl,** like her mother Gilda Mekler, is a student of French. She has worked as a secretary/paralegal assistant. With her father she is translating a selected poems of Émile Nelligan.

Kiki Denis, originally from Greece, has lived in the U.S. since 1990. She holds a BA from Mount Holyoke College and a Master's from Exeter University, England. Her first novel, *The Last Day of Paradise*, won the 2006 Gival Novel Award and her second, *Life Is Big*, won the 2020-Reader's Favorite Award. She lives in New York City with her husband and three kids.

***Dennis Desmond** has previously published adult short stories, including "Camp Jesus," *Broad River Review* (vol. 47, 2015); "Geronimo's Secret," *Mysterical-e* (Fall 2016); "Club Royale," *The Ignatian Literary Magazine* (vol. 28, 2016); and "Dinner Is Served," *The World of Myth Magazine* (March 2020). He is a graduate of the University of Massachusetts (BA 1977) and the Antioch School of Law (JD 1980), and lives in the Washington, DC, area with his wife and daughter.

RC deWinter's poetry is anthologized, notably in *New York City Haiku* (NY Times, 2/2017), *Now We Heal: An Anthology of Hope* (Wellworth Publishing, 12/2020) in print: *2River, Event, Gargoyle Magazine, the minnesota review, Plainsongs, Prairie Schooner, Southword, The Ogham Stone, Twelve Mile Review, York Literary Review* among many others and appears in numerous online literary journals. She is also one of the winners of the 2021 Connecticut Shakespeare Festival Sonnet Contest, anthology publication forthcoming.

Born in 1988, ***Lyudmyla Diadchenko** earned advanced degrees in Literary Creation and Literary Theory from National Taras Shevchenko University in Kyiv, Ukraine. A Vice President of the Ukrainian Writers Association, she has presented her work internationally, in person and in print. *Fee for Access* (2011) was followed by *A Hen for the Turkish Man* (2017), named one the Ten Best Books of the Year in Ukrainian. *Kadem,* her third book, was released this summer.

A native of Jones County, Miss., **Buck Downs** was raised in south Florida and moved to Washington, DC, in 1988. He has led or contributed to many poetry and publishing ventures, including the *Washington Review, Pink Line*, and the DC Arts Center. Books include: *Marijuana Softdrink* and *Unintended Empire: 1989-2012*. Buck is best known for his poetry postcards, which have gone out to a list of about 200 friends and fellow poets since the mid-90s.

Barbara Drake grew up in Coos Bay, Oregon. A retired professor of English, she lives with her husband and assorted critters on a small farm in Yamhill County, Oregon. Her books include creative nonfiction, *Peace at Heart* and *Morning Light*, published by OSU Press, and poetry, most recently *The Road to Lilac Hill*, Windfall Press. She is currently editing a collection of her father's mid-twentieth-century aerial photographs of the southern Oregon coast.

Novelist **Patricia Eakins** is the author of *The Marvelous Adventures of Pierre Baptiste* (NYU Press, 1999) and of *The Hungry Girls and Other Stories*. Her fiction has also appeared in many literary journals, including *The Iowa Review, Parnassus, Storia, Conjunctions, Fiction International, American Letters & Commentary, third bed, Cahiers Charles V*, and *The Paris Review*, which awarded her the Aga Khan Prize for Fiction.

***Dylan Emmons** teaches reading and writing at the college level and works with institutes of higher education to better serve autistic and neurodivergent students. His memoir, *Living in Two Worlds,* was released by Jessica Kingsley Publishers in 2016.

***Michael Estabrook** has been publishing his poetry in the small press since the 1980s. He has published over 20 collections, a recent one being *The Poet's Curse, A Miscellany* (The Poetry Box, 2019). He lives in Acton, Massachusetts.

Born in Washington, DC, **Dyane Fancey** lived most of her life in Baltimore. Graduating with honors from Towson University, Dyane was beloved on the Baltimore poetry scene for decades, a popular server at Baltimore's Great American Melting Pot, or simply Gampy's, and a creative writing teacher at Western High School for gifted and talented girls. *The Origami Swan* is a posthumous collection of mostly unpublished poetry edited by the late poet's husband Reed Hessler.

***Joel Ferdon**'s chapbook, *Elegy for My Father's Bones,* was published by Louisiana Literature Press in 2016, and his poems have appeared in *Verse Daily, Asheville Poetry Review, Flyway,* and *The Southern Quarterly*. Joel is the recipient of an Artist Support Grant through the NC Arts Council and serves as the Director of Library Services at Stanly Community College in Albemarle, NC. He lives with his wife, son, and three black labs in Charlotte.

***Darlene Fife** was born August 23, 1940. She graduated from Penn State University with a BS in physics and an MA in English. Studied at University College Dublin and with Robert Head returned to the US in 1966 to stop the war in Vietnam. She and Robert Head edited *NOLA Express* from 1968 to 1974. She presently lives in West Virginia.

Richard Flynn is Professor Emeritus of English at Georgia Southern University, where he taught children's literature and modern and contemporary poetry for 30 years. He is the author of *Randall Jarrell and the Lost World of Childhood*, a collection of poems *The Age of Reason*, and many articles about poets including Elizabeth Bishop, June Jordan, Gwendolyn Brooks, Muriel Rukeyser, Jacqueline Woodson, and Marilyn Nelson.

***Marc Frazier** has widely published poetry in journals including *The Spoon River Poetry Review, ACM, f(r) iction, The Gay and Lesbian Review, Slant, Permafrost, Plainsongs,* and *Poet Lore.* Marc, a Chicago-area, LGBTQ+ writer is the recipient of an Illinois Arts Council Award for poetry and has been nominated for a Pushcart Prize and a "best of the net." He has appeared in the anthology *New Poets from the Midwest.* Marc's three poetry collections are available online.

DJ Gaskin has published poetry in *The Comstock Review, Iodine Poetry Journal, Gargoyle* (58), *SLAB, DeepWater Literary Review, Ars Medica,* and others. DJ's chapbook, *Of Crows and Superstitions*, is available through Main Street Rag Publishing. DJ is also a visual artist and lives in the mountains of North Carolina with two literate cats named after favorite poets.

***Jason Gebhardt**'s poems have appeared or are forthcoming in the *The Southern Review*, *Poet Lore*, *Tinderbox Poetry Journal*, *Tar River Poetry*, among others. His chapbook *Good Housekeeping* won the 2016 Cathy Smith Bowers Prize. He lives in Washington, DC, and is the recipient of multiple artist fellowships awarded by the DC Commission on the Arts and Humanities.

***Katherine Gekker** is the author of *In Search of Warm Breathing Things* (Glass Lyre Press). Her poems have been nominated for Pushcart Prizes and Best of the Net. Two composers have set her poems to music: "...to Cast a Shadow Again" by Eric Ewazen, and "Chasing the Moon Down" by Carson Cooman. Gekker was born in Washington, DC. She founded a commercial printing company in 1974 and sold it thirty-one years later.

Stephen Gibson is the author of a collection of poetry, *City of Midnight Skies*, and editor of the erratically published magazine, *Mobile City,* that started in the 1990s as a messenger zine. His poems and drawings have appeared in places like the *Boston Review*, *Poetry Northwest*, *Ploughshares*, and *Chain* and his artwork is part of Transformer Gallery's FlatFile. He lives in Washington, DC, the city where he was born.

Robert L. Giron, author of five collections of poetry and editor of three anthologies, has poetry and fiction in national and international anthologies, among other publications. He currently is an associate editor for *Potomac Review*, the editor-in-chief of *ArLiJo,* and the founder/publisher of Gival Press.

Bilingual German-American poet and painter **Gabriele Glang** published her German poetry debut, *Göttertage,* fictional monologues of German Expressionist painter Paula Modersohn-Becker, with Klöpfer & Meyer (Tübingen, 2017). A screenwriter and film translator, she received script funding from Baden-Württemberg's media board, as well as working grants from the society for the advancement of writers in Baden-Württemberg. Until last year, she taught creative writing in English at the University of Applied Sciences at Esslingen, Germany. www.gabrieleglang.de

Jesse Glass grew up near Westminster, Maryland, and has resided in Japan with his wife and family for over thirty years. He is the author of seven books of poetry and plays, including *Lexical Obelisk, The Passion of Phineas Gage & Selected Poems, Lost Poet, Gaha Noas Zorge,* and *Black Out in My Left Eye*. He has over thirty painted books of poetry in Tate Britain's Artist's Book Collection.

***Sharon Goldberg** is a Seattle writer whose work has appeared/is forthcoming in *The Gettysburg Review, New Letters, The Louisville Review, Cold Mountain Review, River Teeth, Chicago Quarterly Review, The Antigonish Review, The Green Mountains Review*, four anthologies, and elsewhere. Sharon won second place in the On the Premises 2012 Humor Contest and Fiction Attic Press's 2013 Flash in the Attic Contest. She is an avid but cautious skier and enthusiastic world traveler

***Sarah Golkar** is a native Texan who lives in Washington, DC. She holds a BA from the University of Texas at Austin and an MA from Tufts University. "Flight from Your Old New York" is her first publication and it was also selected as a finalist in the Eastern Shore Writers Association's 2020 Crossroads Writing Contest.

Regan Good attended the Iowa Writers' Workshop and has published two books of poems: *The Atlantic House* (2011) and *The Needle* (2020). She currently teaches writing at the Pratt School of Architecture.

Pamela Gordon lives in the Bronx, NY, where she is a writer and a high school instructional coach. Her publications include *salon.com; Poets & Writers; New Times; More;* and *The New York Times.*

Susan Gubernat's most recent poetry collection, *The Zoo at Night*, won the Prairie Schooner book award and was published by the University of Nebraska Press. An opera librettist as well as a poet, she is Professor Emerita of English at California State University, East Bay. Born and raised in Newark, New Jersey, she now lives in San Francisco.

***Karen Guzman** is a fiction writer and essayist. Her novel, *Arborview,* was published in 2021 by The Wild Rose Press. Her debut novel, *Homing Instincts,* was published by Fiction Attic Press. Karen's short fiction has appeared in a number of literary magazines. She is the recipient of a 2021 writing fellowship from the Collegeville Institute. You can learn more about Karen's work at www.karenguzman.com

A former high school English teacher, ***Jessica Claire Haney** is a Northern Virginia–based writer, editor, and tutor. Her work has appeared in *The Huffington Post, The Washington Post, Scary Mommy, Beltway Poetry Review, Porcupine Literary, Court Green, Earth's Daughters,* two of the Grace & Gravity DC Women Writers anthologies, and *Written in Arlington*. "Under Construction" is adapted from her first novel. Instagram @jessicaclairehaney & Twitter @crunchychewy. JessicaClaireHaney.com.

Robert Head was born January 7, 1942. His early years were spent in Mississippi and New Orleans. Attended Tulane University and University College Dublin where he studied Old English. Returned to New Orleans in

1966 with the purpose of ending the war in Vietnam and from 1968 to 1974 he co-edited *NOLA Express*. Moved to the woods of West Virginia in 1974. He now owns and operates a bookstore in Lewisburg, West Virginia.

***Victoria Heartwood** is a Pushcart Prize–nominated writer whose short stories and poetry have been published (under the name Victoria Forester) by *Washington Square Review, Spectrum, Belletrist, Funicular Magazine, The Worcester Review, 580 Split, Moonchild Magazine*, and more. She holds a master's degree in fiction and a doctorate of higher education with a focus on embodied learning. Stay in touch with Victoria on Twitter @DoveVictoria, Instagram @victoria.heartwood, and www.victoriaheartwood.com

***Ditta Baron Hoeber** is an artist and a poet. She has published recently in *The American Journal of Poetry, Juxtaprose, Pank, Burningword Literary Review,* and the *American Poetry Review*. Her work has been nominated for a Pushcart Prize. Her first book, "Without You: A Poem and A Preface" is forthcoming in 2022. Hoeber's photographs, drawings, and book works have been exhibited nationally and have been acquired by several collections here and in the UK.

***Shane Holohan** lives and writes in Stoneybatter, Dublin, Ireland. Shane's words have been published in *The Stinging Fly, The Pickled Body, Channel, Flare* and *The Irish Times.*

Joyce L. Huff is an associate professor of English at Ball State University in Indiana. Her poem, "The Hymn of a Fat Woman," which originally appeared in *Gargoyle* 44, was reprinted on the Library of Congress's *Poetry 180* website. Her academic essays focus on fat and disability in Victorian British literature. She has also co-edited the collection, *A Cultural History of Disability in the Long Nineteenth Century* from Bloomsbury Press.

***Tom C. Hunley** directs the MFA Creative Writing program at Western Kentucky University, where he has taught since 2003. He won the 2020 Rattle Chapbook Prize for Adjusting to the Lights, and in 2021 C&R Press released *What Feels Like Love: New and Selected Poems*.

Poet and songwriter ***Paul Ilechko** is the author of three chapbooks, most recently *Pain Sections* (Alien Buddha Press). His work has appeared in a variety of journals, including *The Night Heron Barks, Rogue Agent, Ethel, Lullwater Review,* and *Book of Matches*. He lives with his partner in Lambertville, NJ.

Esther Iverem is a multidisciplinary writer, artist and independent journalist. Her diverse body of social justice work includes four books, two digital media projects, several visual art exhibits and the podcast and show on Pacifica Radio, *On the Ground: Voices of Resistance from the Nation's Capital*. Her latest book, *Olokun of the Galaxy*, uses poetry and images to tell a story of Olokun, an African spirit for the deepest ocean. Her online home is www.estheriverem.net

***Paul Jaskunas** is the author of the novel *Hidden* (Free Press, 2004), winner of the Friends of American Writers Award, and founding editor of *Full Bleed*, an annual art journal published by the Maryland Institute College of Art, where he teaches literature and writing. His work has been featured by a variety of publications, including *The New York Times, America, The Cortland Review, Atticus Review, Panel*, and *The Museum of Americana.*

Originally from the hilly corner of Ohio, **Mark Allen Jenkins**'s poetry has appeared in *Gargoyle, minnesota review, San Pedro River Review, South Dakota Review, Every River on Earth: Writing from Appalachian Ohio,* and *Still: The Journal*. He completed a PhD in humanities from the University of Texas at Dallas and currently teaches in Houston.

Lane Jennings has lived since 1978 in Columbia, Maryland. For many years he worked as an editor and writer for the World Future Society in Bethesda. Several of his poems have appeared in earlier issues of *Gargoyle*

as well as *Bogg, Antietam Review,* and other magazines. He has two published collections of poems: *Virtual Futures* (1996), and *Fabrications* (1998); and his novel *Satisfaction* came out in 2016.

Dennis Jones's work has appeared in *Gargoyle, Georgetown Review, The Crescent Review,* and *Stress City: A Big Book of Fiction by 51 DC Guys*. He lives in Charleston, South Carolina.

Beth Baruch Joselow is the author of more than a dozen books and chapbooks of poems. Her chapbook, *Excontemporary*, was reissued in 2020 by Red Hen Press. For many years she was an associate professor of liberal arts at The Corcoran College of Art + Design in Washington, DC, and also led numerous writing workshops at The Writers Center in Bethesda, MD. She now lives in Lewes, Delaware where she practices psychotherapy.

***Ken Kakareka** grew up in Philadelphia, PA where he studied Literature & Writing at Saint Joe's University, then worked as an ESL teacher in South Korea. He lives in California with his wife. Ken is the author of *Late to Bed, Late to Rise* (Black Rose Writing, 2013). His words have been published or are on their way in *Lost Lake Folk Opera Magazine, HASH Journal, Route 7 Review, Bluepepper*, and numerous others. kenkakareka.com

Toshiya Kamei holds an MFA in Literary Translation from the University of Arkansas. His translations have appeared in such venues as *Clarkesworld, The Magazine of Fantasy & Science Fiction*, and *Strange Horizons*.

Christina Kapp teaches at the Writers Circle Workshops in New Jersey and her work has appeared in *Passages North, Hobart, Orange Blossom Review, The MacGuffin, PANK, Pithead Chapel* and elsewhere. Her fiction has been nominated for Best of the Net awards and a Pushcart Prize. She welcomes you to follow her on Twitter @ChristinaKapp and visit her website: www.christinakapp.com

Jesse Lee Kercheval is a poet, writer, and translator. Her recent books include the poetry collection *America that Island off the coast of France*, winner of the Dorset Prize, and her translations include *Love Poems* by Idea Vilariño, which was long listed for the PEN Best Translated Poetry Book Award. Her essays about the pandemic have appeared in *Guernica, The Sewanee Review, Hobart, Five Points, Entropy, Blackbird, Brevity, Waxwing,* and the *New England Review.*

***John Kinsella**'s most recent volumes of poetry include *Drowning in Wheat: Selected Poems 1980-2015* (Picador, 2016), *Firebreaks* (WW Norton, 2016), and *Insomnia* (WW Norton, 2020). He is a Fellow of Churchill College, Cambridge University, an Affiliated Scholar with Kenyon College and Emeritus Professor of Literature and Environment at Curtin University, Western Australia.

***Naveen Kishore** is a theater lighting designer, photographer, publisher Seagull Books. Recipient of the Goethe Medal, the Chevalier Ordre des Arts et des Lettres, and the Ottaway Award for the Promotion of Literature *2021.* Kishore lives, writes poetry, and works in Calcutta.

***JoAnn Koff's** poetry appears in *Black Bough Poetry, The Art of Everyone, Green Ink Poetry*, and *In the Midst: A Covid-19 Anthology*. Her book *Sand, Pebbles, Fossils, and Rocks* was a nominee for the Library of Virginia's Literary Award in Poetry. *Camera Eyes: On Poetry* was her solo gallery show exhibiting twenty-five poems with her corresponding photography. She was voted Best Author of Prince William County in 2021 by *InsideNoVa*.

Roz Kuehn received her BFA from the Corcoran School of Art in Washington, DC. She is the author of a novel, *Various Stages of Undress* (loosely based on six years as an exotic dancer in Washington, DC), which was runner-up for the Faulkner-Wisdom Competition, and a finalist for both the Breadloaf Bakeless Prize and Bellwether Prize. She acted as fiction editor for *The Washington Review* for four years.

Patrick Lawler wasn't exactly sure when things got confusing, but he was convinced it started when he discovered his Diary was being written by someone other than him—and he wasn't a very good speller. He didn't know who wrote in his Dairy, "Cows moo in my sleep." All the complexity and mystification. Morality? Or mortality? Eras? Or errors? It became more and more difficult to determine what was meant. Oar? Or Ore?

Kristian Macaron (she/her) resides in Albuquerque, NM, a land full of treasures, but is often elsewhere. Her poetry chapbook *Storm*, released in 2015 from Swimming with Elephants Publications. Other prose and poetry publications can be found in *Asimov's Science Fiction Magazine, Uncanny Magazine, Luna Luna Magazine, Solstice Literary Magazine, Rust + Moth, Gargoyle Magazine*, and others. She is a co-founding editor of the literary journal, *Manzano Mountain Review.* View her work and updates at Kristianmacaron.com

***Jack Mackey** lives in Rehoboth Beach, Delaware, and holds an MA in English from the University of Maryland. His poetry has appeared in *The Broadkill Review, Anti-Heroin Chic, Mojave River Review, Panoply,* and others. In 2021 he was awarded a fellowship in Poetry from the Delaware Division of the Arts.

***Elaine Vilar Madruga** is a Cuban poet, fiction writer, and playwright. Her most recent book is the novel *Los años del silencio* (2019). Translated by Toshiya Kamei, Elaine's writings have appeared in venues such as *The Magazine of Fantasy & Science Fiction, Star*Line*, and *World Literature Today*.

***Amadeo Mangune Mendoza** is a former literature instructor at the University of Santo Tomas in Manila, Philippines where he obtained an MA in creative writing degree. His poems have been published in the *Philippines Graphic, Manila Bulletin, Likhaan Anthology of Best Filipino Poems*, and in the *Philippine Daily Inquirer*. His twelve short stories have appeared in *Philippines Graphic*.

Willard Manus is a Los Angeles-based novelist, playwright, and journalist. His best-known novel is *MOTT the Hoople*, the book from which the British rock band of the 1970s took its name. Other popular books of his include *The Pigskin Rabbi* and *This Way to Paradise—Dancing on the Tables*, a memoir of the thirty years he spent in the Greek islands.

***Maria Masington** is a poet, author, and spoken word artist from Wilmington, Delaware. Her poetry has appeared in over a dozen publications including *Adanna, Gyroscope, The Broadkill Review, and Earth's Daughters.* She's had seven short stories published in both local and international press. Maria belongs to The Mad Poets Society, is an emcee, and featured poet on the local art scene. Parnilis Media released her first chapbook *Mouth Like a Sailor* this year.

***Mary McCoy** is a writer and environmental artist living beside a tidal river flowing to the Chesapeake Bay. Her work explores the human experience of the natural world in all its wonder and vulnerability. Her writings have appeared in *Orion Magazine's Place Where You Live, Bay to Ocean 2021*, and Salisbury University's *Here/Not Here.* She writes on art for *The Chestertown Spy* and formerly for several magazines and *The Washington Post*. For information, visit marymccoystudio.com

Dora E. McQuaid is an award-winning poet, activist, speaker and teacher whose unique blend of art, emotion and service has earned numerous awards. Her activism addressing sexual and domestic violence led to her portrait replacing that of convicted pedophile and former football coach Jerry Sandusky in the Penn State mural. Dora performs and speaks internationally, works collaboratively with an array of artists and activists and publishes widely. She is the author of the *scorched earth*. www.doramcquaid.com

***Gilda Mekler** (1954-2007) was a professional translator and painter. Her canvases were exhibited at galleries in Toronto and Hamilton.

***Alexandra Melnick** spends her time juggling writing, education, activism, and her job in nonprofit communications. Her work has previously appeared in outlets such as *Rewire, Newsy, The Clarion-Ledger. Dead Mule Society,* and *Litro Magazine*. She's a proud resident of Jackson, Mississippi and a Millsaps College and University of Mississippi alumna.

Nancy Mercado was named one of 200 living individuals who best embody the work and spirit of Frederick Douglass by the Frederick Douglass Family Initiatives and the Antiracist Research and Policy Center at American University. She is the recipient of the 2017 American Book Award for Lifetime Achievement presented by the Before Columbus Foundation. Currently, her critique of the Broadway musical *West Side Story* appears in *Bigotry on Broadway* (Baraka Books). Visit Nancy at: nancy-mercado.com

***Gary Metras**'s new book of poetry is *Vanishing Points* (Dos Madres Press 2021). His *White Storm* (Presa Press 2018), was selected as a Must Read Title in the Massachusetts Books of the Year Program. His poems have appeared in *America, The Common, Poetry, Poetry East,* and *Poetry Salzburg Review.* He lives in Easthampton, Massachusetts, where, in April 2018, he was appointed the city's inaugural Poet Laureate. A retired educator, he fly fishes his local streams and rivers as often as possible.

Michael Milburn teaches English in New Haven, CT. His poems have appeared recently in *Mudlark* and *Slant*, and previously in *Gargoyle Magazine*.

Maryland resident ***Ted R. Miller** is a health economist who has published extensively on the costs of societal ills like substance abuse and violence. A recorded songwriter, he has twice been a finalist in the mid-Atlantic songwriting contest. These are his first published poems.

Gloria Mindock is editor of Cervena Barva Press. She is the author of 6 poetry collections, 3 chapbooks and a children's book. Her poems have been published and translated into eleven languages. Her recent book *Ash*, published by Glass Lyre Press, will be published in Serbian with translation by Milutin Djurickovic out of Belgrade this year. Gloria was the Poet Laureate in Somerville, MA in 2017 & 2018.

***Barbara Marie Minney** is a queer poet, writer, and quiet activist. Her work has appeared in numerous anthologies. Barbara's collection of poetry, *If There's No Heaven,* was the winner of the 2020 Poetry Is Life Book Award and was selected by the *Akron Beacon Journal* as a Best Northeast Ohio Book in 2020. Barbara is a retired attorney and lives in Tallmadge, Ohio, with her wife of forty years. www.barbaramarieminneypoetry.com

***Jane Edna Mohler** is the Poet Laureate of Bucks County, Pennsylvania. Her first book, *Broken Umbrellas*, was published by Kelsay Books in 2019. Her poems appear in many literary journals and anthologies. She is the 2016 winner of Main Street Voices poetry competition, a two-time Pushcart Prize nominee, and a Robert Fraser finalist. She has presented on the craft of poetry at the 2020 and 2021 Bay to Ocean Writers' Conference in Maryland.

***Ofelia Montelongo** is a bilingual writer from Mexico. She has a MA in Latin American Literature. Her work has been published in *Latino Book Review, Los Acentos Review, Rio Grande Review*, and elsewhere. She was the 2019 Writer's Center Undiscovered Voices Fellow. She currently teaches at the University of Maryland and at The George Washington University and was a PEN/Faulkner writer in residence in Washington, D.C. She is a 2021 Mancodista & a PEN America Emerging Voices Fellow. ofeliamontelongo.com

***Mary B. Moore**'s poetry books include *Dear If* (forthcoming, Orison Books), *Flicker* (Dogfish Head Prize, 2016), *The Book of Snow* (Cleveland State UP, 1997), and the prize-winning chapbooks *Amanda and the Man Soul* and *Eating the Light.* Poems have appeared lately in *Poetry, Prairie Schooner, Gettysburg Review, Catamaran, Nelle, Terrain, Birmingham Poetry Review, Georgia Review, 32 Poems, The Nasty Woman Poet anthology, Fire and Rain–Ecopoetry of California,* and more.

Alice Morris, a prize-winning artist and poet/writer has enjoyed creating art throughout her adult life. Producing wood collages, photography, fine art white oak baskets, stained glass, and woodworking are included in her interests. Her art has been published in the *New York Art Review* and in a textbook, *West Virginia Studies Our Heritage.* She is a Pushcart Prize and Best of the Net nominee, published in *Paterson Literary Review*, *Broadkill Review*, *Bared*, and *Gargoyle* among others.

Mary Morris is the author of three books of poetry: *Enter Water, Swimmer*, *Dear October*, and *Late Self-Portraits*, forthcoming from MSU Press (selected by Leila Chatti for the Wheelbarrow Books Prize). Her poems appear in *Poetry, The Massachusetts Review, Prairie Schooner, Los Angeles Review, Poetry Northwest, Arts & Letters, Boulevard*, and *Poetry Daily*. Mary has been invited to read her poems at the Library of Congress, which aired on National Public Radio. www.water400.org

***Mihaela Moscaliuc** is the author of *Cemetery Ink*, *Immigrant Model*, and *Father Dirt*, translator of Liliana Ursu's *Clay and Star* and Carmelia Leonte's *The Hiss of the Viper*, editor of *Insane Devotion: On the Writing of Gerald Stern*, and co-editor of *Border Lines: Poems of Migration*. She is the translation editor for *Plume* and associate professor of English at Monmouth University, NJ.

Fred Muratori's poems and short prose have appeared in *The Iowa Review, Poetry, Boston Review, Poetry Northwest, Barrow Street, Hotel Amerika, New American Writing, Vinyl, Volt*, and others. His three published poetry collections are *Despite Repeated Warnings*, *The Spectra*, and *A Civilization*. He lives and works in Ithaca, NY.

Elisabeth Murawski is the author of *Heiress*, *Zorba's Daughter*, which won the May Swenson Poetry Award, *Moon and Mercury*, and three chapbooks. *Still Life with Timex* won the Robert Phillips Poetry Chapbook Prize and was published this year by Texas Review Press. A native of Chicago, she currently lives in Alexandria, VA.

***Émile Nelligan** was born in Montreal on Christmas Eve, 1879. He's considered to be the finest Québécois poet of the 19th Century. An early follower of Charles Baudelaire and French Symbolism, he published his initial poems at age sixteen. In 1899, Nelligan suffered a major breakdown from which he never recovered. He died on November 18, 1941. *Émile Nelligan: Poésies complètes* was published by TYPO in 1998. It remains the standard text.

***C.D. Nickols** is a fiction and comedy writer, social theorist, and raconteur. Barely invited to Thanksgiving anymore, C.D. comes from a large family of NYC police officers and firefighters and more police; Foxaphiles that haven't read books this millennium. After years abroad (Asia, Europe...California), C.D. accidentally settled in Northern Virginia, where the humidity's stuck at 90%. C.D. has a short story collection that will change your life and is finishing a novel. Reachable at cdnickols@gmail.com.

***Mark Niedzwiedz** is a professional composer and lyricist, which helps bring rhythm and musicality to his poetry. So far, Mark's poems have appeared in poetry journals such as *Grey Sparrow, Oddville Press, Scritura, Wink, Rat's Arse review, Sac, Literary Heist, Harbinger Asylum*, and elsewhere.

***Randon Billings Noble** is an essayist. Her collection *Be with Me Always* was published by the University of Nebraska Press in 2019 and her anthology of lyric essays, *A Harp in the Stars*, was published by Nebraska in 2021. Currently she is the founding editor of the online literary magazine *After the Art* and teaches in West Virginia Wesleyan's Low-Residency MFA Program and Goucher's MFA in Nonfiction Program. You can read more at www.randonbillingsnoble.com

Kathleen Novak, a graduate of the University of Minnesota, is a poet, writer, and the author of the novels *The Autobiography of Corrine Bernard*, *Do Not Find Me*, and *Rare Birds*. Her poems have been published in small literary magazines nationally.

Mary Overton is happily retired in a college town surrounded by farmland. She spends her days reading and writing and experimenting with hypertext fiction at https://www.maryoverton.work.

***Chris Paranicas** is a native of the northeast. He has written and published on technical subjects in the past but outside of that reads fiction almost exclusively. He has benefitted from reading many excellent LGBT+ stories and hopes writers will continue expanding into that space with new voices and perspectives. For "The Arrangement," he thanks Holly, Hildie, Gerry, and Bill for suggestions, Patrick, Joanne, and Larry. He can be reached about this story at chrispar7@gmail.com.

***Che Parker** is the author of four novels, a collection of short stories, and several screenplays. He earned his BA degree in communication studies from the University of Missouri at Kansas City, and his MA degree in writing from Johns Hopkins University. His latest novel, *The Peregrine*, is about a girl from Washington, DC, who uses her gift of telekinesis to seek revenge for her father's murder.

Meg Pokrass is the author of six flash fiction collections, an award-winning collection of prose poetry, two novellas-in-flash and a forthcoming collection of microfiction, *Spinning to Mars* recipient of the Blue Light Book Award in 2020. Her work has appeared in *Electric Literature, Washington Square Review, Waxwing, Smokelong Quarterly*, and *McSweeney's,* and anthologized in *New Micro* and *Flash Fiction International* (both published by W.W. Norton & Co). She is Founding Co-Editor of *Best Microfiction*. megpokrass.com

Born on the same numbered day of the same month the twin towers in New York fell, ***Rebecca Pyle** is a writer and artist, this year her writing in *Festival Review, Posit, Pangyrus, Guesthouse, The Honest Ulsterman, Eclectica;* her artwork, this year, is on covers of *HitchLit Review* and *JuxtaProse,* and in *Grist* and *december* and *Blood Orange Review.* See rebeccapyleartist.com.

Sundress Best of the Net Nominee, ***Suzanne S. Rancourt**, Abenaki/Huron descent, has authored *Billboard in the Clouds*, Northwestern Univ. Press, (received the Native Writers' Circle of the Americas First Book Award,) *murmurs at the gate*, Unsolicited Press, 2019 and *Old Stones, New Roads*, Main Street Rag Publishing, 2021. She is a USMC and Army Veteran with degrees in psychology, writing, and expressive arts therapy. Widely published, please view her website's publication list: www.expressive-arts.com

***Jordan Redd** is a Spring 2020 graduate from American University with a BA in film and media arts and a minor in creative writing. She is an aspiring screenwriter who loves the realm of fantasy and magical realism. You can find her photography and films at jordanreddfilm.com

***Russell Reece**'s poems, stories and essays have appeared in a wide variety of journals and anthologies. Russ has received fellowships in literature from The Delaware Division of the Arts and the Virginia Center for the Creative Arts. He has received Pushcart and Best of the Net nominations, awards from the Delaware Press Association, the Faulkner-Wisdom competition and others. Russ lives near Bethel, Delaware, on the beautiful Broad Creek.

***Tatiana Retivov** is a Russian-American poet and translator residing in Kyiv, Ukraine where she runs a literary salon and publishes books. She holds a BA in English Literature from the University of Montana and an MA in Slavic Languages and Literatures from the University of Michigan, where she received an Avery Hopwood Poetry Award for poetry in 1980. She has translated *Brodsky Through the Eyes of his Contemporaries.* Vol. I (ed. by Valentina Polukhina), and *Mandelstam* by Oleg Lekmanov into English.

Suzanne Rhodenbaugh's third book, *The Girl Who Quit at Leviticus*, is forthcoming from Homestead Lighthouse Press. She has poems forthcoming in *The Hudson* and *Poetry East*. Since leaving Takoma Park in 1984, she's lived north, and west, since 1999 in St. Louis.

Jonathan K. Rice edited and published *Iodine Poetry Journal* for seventeen years. He is the author of two full-length poetry collections, *Killing Time* (2015), *Ukulele and Other Poems* (2006) and a chapbook, *Shooting Pool with a Cellist* (2003), all published by Main Street Rag Publishing. He is also a visual artist. His poetry and art have appeared in numerous publications. Some of his art is currently on exhibit at C3Lab in Charlotte, NC.

Jeff Richards's Red Light" is based on two blues songs, "Love in Vain," by Robert Johnson and "Big Boss Man," a Luther Dixon song performed by everyone from Elvis to Jimmy Reed. Richards has published two novels, *Open Country* (Paycock Press), *Lady Killer*, and a collection of short stories, *Everyone Worth Knowing*. His fiction and essays have appeared in over 27 publications including *Gargoyle* and five anthologies. Richards lives in Takoma Park, Maryland. jeffrichardsauthor.com

***Thierry Sagnier** has been published here and abroad. He wrote *The IFO Report*, *Bike! Motorcycles and the People who Ride Them*, *Washington by Night*, and *The Fortunate Few*. His novel *Thirst* was an Amazon No. 1 bestseller. The sequel, *Dope* was released in February 2020. His short story *"Lunch with the General,"* was nominated for a Pushcart Prize. His novels, *L'Amérique* and *Montparnasse* were published by Apprentice Press. *Montparnasse*, was nominated for a Pulitzer in fiction.

Dennis Saleh (1942–2020) was a poet, graphic designer and novelist. He was editor and publisher of COMMA Books, Inc., 24 Hour Books, and taught poetry writing and English Literature at UC Riverside, UC Santa Cruz, CA State University at Fresno, and CA State University at San Diego. His books include *100 chameleons, science fiction gold, First Z Poems*, and *This Is Not Surrealism*.

***Roberta "Bobby" Santlofer** (1943–2020) was a mother of sons, an avid reader, and a poet. A posthumous collection of her poetry is forthcoming. Santlofer's poems have appeared or are forthcoming in *Amethyst Review, Black Coffee Review, Bluepepper, Chiron Review, Eunoia Review, Gargoyle, Philadelphia Stories, Grey Sparrow Review, North Dakota Quarterly, Red Eft Review, Remington Review, Vita Brevis*, and *Wine Cellar Press*.

***Louisa Schnaithmann** is a poet living in the greater Philadelphia area. Her work has appeared in *Menacing Hedge, Rogue Agent*, and *Voicemail Poems*.

*__Sherry Shahan__'s photos have appeared in the *Los Angeles Times, Christian Science Monitor, Mount Hope, Moon Shadow Press, Harbor Review, December*, and more. She holds an MFA from Vermont College of Fine Arts and taught a creative writing course for UCLA Extension for ten years.

***Lex Shramko** is currently working on a WW2 fairytale braided from memoir and biography, set in both the past and present, about her mother, a war orphan who discovers her existence as an eighty-five-year-old-woman. An erstwhile philosophy lecturer, she can be found traveling, biking, scuba diving, or checking out the latest coffee shop. Preferably one with a resident cat or dog. Publications include *Moonpark Review* and *Broadkill Review*. @LexShramko

***Leonora Simonovis** is the author of *Study of the Raft*, winner of the 2021 Colorado Prize for Poetry. She has been nominated for Best of the Net and her work has appeared in *Diode Poetry Journal, Tinderbox Poetry Journal, The Rumpus, Inverted Syntax*, and *The American Journal of Poetry*, among others. She lives in San Diego, CA, with her family and teaches at the University of San Diego.

Julia Slavin is the writer of *The Woman Who Cut Off Her Leg at the Maidstone Club and Other Stories* and the novel, *Carnivore Diet*. She has had stories published in *Tin House, McSweeney's, GQ, Mississippi Review, Southampton Review, Gulf Coast, The Believer*, and *Best of Tin House*. Her new work is a collection of stories named, *Squatters*, and a novel. She is the winner of a Rona Jaffe Writers' Award and *GQ's* Frederick Exley Prize.

*__Zephaniah Sole__'s writing is published or forthcoming in *Epiphany, Collateral Journal* and *Vestal Review*. His first novel, "Ikigai and the Land of 7,000 Islands," is slated to be published by Black Spring Press in 2022. He is a recipient of a 2021 Author Fellowship from the Martha's Vineyard Institute of Creative Writing and a member of VONA's 'ghost' class of 2021. Follow on Twitter @ZephaniahSole.

Richard Spilman is the author of *In the Night Speaking* and of a chapbook, *Suspension*. He has published in many journals, including *Gargoyle*.

Marija Stajic is a U.S. diplomat born in Serbia. Her short stories have been nominated for a Pushcart Prize, anthologized, and published in *Prairie Schooner, Doctor T. J. Eckleburg Review, South 85, Barely South Review, Gargoyle* etc. She worked for *The New Yorker* and wrote "Translating the Gorilla." She has an MA from American University, and was an actress before writing, appearing in an episode of *30 Rock* opposite Tina Fey. She's represented by Stefanie Rossitto of Tobias Literary Agency and her novel "American Sorceress" is currently on submission.

*__Darius Stewart__'s essay, "Dearest Darky," is from his manuscript "Call Me When You Get This: A Lyric Memoir," and a collection of poetry, *Intimacies in Borrowed Light: poems 2002-2016*, is forthcoming from EastOver Press. He holds MFA degrees in poetry and nonfiction from the Michener Center for Writers and the University of Iowa, where he is currently pursuing a PhD in English Literary Studies. He lives in Iowa City with his dog, Fry.

Todd Swift, born in Montreal, in 1966, has been Visiting Scholar at Pembroke College, Cambridge. He's had twenty collections of his poetry published. Mentored by Al Alvarez, he has a PhD in creative and critical writing from UEA. He has written over 100 hours of television, including for Paramount, and Disney, and was series editor for *Sailor Moon*. He is publishing director of BSPG, including Eyewear's imprint, in London. He has appeared in *Gargoyle* before, happily.

Devin Taylor holds a BA in English and minors in creative writing and psychology from Washington College (Chestertown, MD). His writing can be found in *Gargoyle, Jersey Devil, The Southampton Review Online*, and elsewhere. His two poetry collections ("Major League Gaming" and "Dead Dad Inc.") are possibly forthcoming someday, someway.

Eleanor Ross Taylor (1920–2011) was an American poet who published six collections of verse from 1960 to 2009. She studied with Allen Tate, Caroline Gordon, and Donald Davidson. Her work received little recognition until 1998, but thereafter received several major poetry prizes. Her books include: *Wilderness of Ladies, Welcome Eumenides, Days Going/Days Coming Back, Late Leisure,* and *Captive Voices: New and Selected Poems.* She was married to the fiction writer Peter Taylor.

*__Dmitrou Teplouhov__ was born in the city of Mariupol (Ukraine) in 1994. Alumnus of Taras Shevchenko Kyiv National University, Master of International Communications.

Padma Thornlyre, of Ukrainian Jewish descent on his mother's side, was born in Colorado in 1959 and earned his BA in literature from Coe College. His books of poetry include *Eating Totem* (2008), *Mavka: a poem in 50 Parts* (2011), and *The Anxiety Quartet* (2020, 2021). He was the primary founder of Turkey Buzzard Press, edits the magazine, *Mad Blood,* and is a member of the poets known as the Fire Gigglers.

J. C. Todd's recent books are *Beyond Repair*, an Able Muse Press Award honoree, and *The Damages of Morning* (Moonstone Press), an Eric Hoffer finalist. Honors include the Rita Dove Poetry Prize, Poetry Society of America finalist, and fellowships from the Pew Center, Pennsylvania Council on the Arts, and residency programs. Her poems have appeared in such journals as *Beloit Poetry Journal, Mezzo Cammin, The Paris Review, Prairie Schooner*. She teaches with the Rosemont Writers Studio.

***Kate Tooley** is a queer writer currently living in Brooklyn, but originally from the Atlanta area. She holds an MFA in fiction from The New School, and is an assistant editor at *Uncharted Magazine*. Her writing can be found in journals including *Barren Magazine, Pidgeonholes, Witness Magazine*, and *Longleaf Review*, and has been nominated for *Best Microfiction* and *Best American Essays*.

M. Kaat Toy (Katherine Toy Miller) has published a prose poem chapbook, *In a Cosmic Egg* (Finishing Line Press 2012); a flash fiction book, *Disturbed Sleep* (FutureCycle Press 2013); a short story collection with illustrations *Many Worlds: Some American Odysseys* (Shanti Arts Publishing 2021); and a novel with illustrations *Madness with Grief* (Livingston Press at The University of West Alabama, November 2021). She is completing a book of prose poems with illustrations, *Silences*.

***Pat Valdata** is a poet and novelist. Her poetry book about women aviation pioneers, *Where No Man Can Touch*, won the 2016 Donald Justice Poetry Prize. Her third novel, *Eve's Daughters* (Moonshine Cove, 2020), won first prize from the Delaware Press Association and received an Honorable Mention from the National Federation of Press Women. For more information about Pat and her books, go to www.patvaldata.com.

***Joanne Van Wie** is a mother of seven and a lover of seriously unapologetic sunshine. She's kind of about birds and entranced by the way a hand folds open not knowing yet. Her poetry can be found in *Connections Magazine* of Southern Maryland, *TEXTure* magazine of Annapolis, *PAX* an Anthology of Southern Maryland Poetry, and her own chapbook, *Surfaces, Edges and Openings*, by FootHills Publishing.

Michael Waters's recent books include *Caw* (BOA Editions, 2020) & *The Dean of Discipline* (University of Pittsburgh Press, 2018), as well as a co-edited anthology, *Border Lines: Poems of Migration* (Knopf, 2020). Recipient of five Pushcart Prizes & fellowships from the NEA & the Guggenheim & Fulbright Foundations, he lives without a cell phone in Ocean, NJ which shares its zip code with the much cooler Asbury Park.

Tom Whalen's books include *The President in Her Towers, Elongated Figures, Winter Coat, The Straw That Broke, Dolls*, and most recently his second selection and translation of short prose by Robert Walser, *Little Snow Landscape* (NYRB Classics).

J.T. Whitehead worked on a grounds crew, as a pub cook, and as a delivery man, inspiring four years as a labor lawyer (workers' side). Whitehead is a *Pushcart Prize*-nominated poet and short story author. He won the Margaret Randall Poetry Prize in 2015. His book *The Table of the Elements* (Broadkill River Press) was nominated for the *National Book Award*. Whitehead lives in Indianapolis with his sons, Daniel and Joseph.

In past lives ***Kathy Wilson** has been an editorial assistant in legal publishing, a tech guru, and an analyst in healthcare. Now she lives in the wilderness of Oregon with a reformed cave troll (her father) and a Samoyed who fears thunderstorms. "The Overlook" is her first publication.

Rosemary Winslow is making it through the pandemic with her husband, John, a visual artist, moving between city—Washington, DC—and country—the mountains and lakes of New Hampshire. Her most recent books are *Defying Gravity* (David Roberts Books, 2018) a poetry collection; and *Deep Beauty: Experiencing Wonder When the World Is on Fire* (Woodhall Press, 2020), a collection of essays she edited with Catherine Lee.

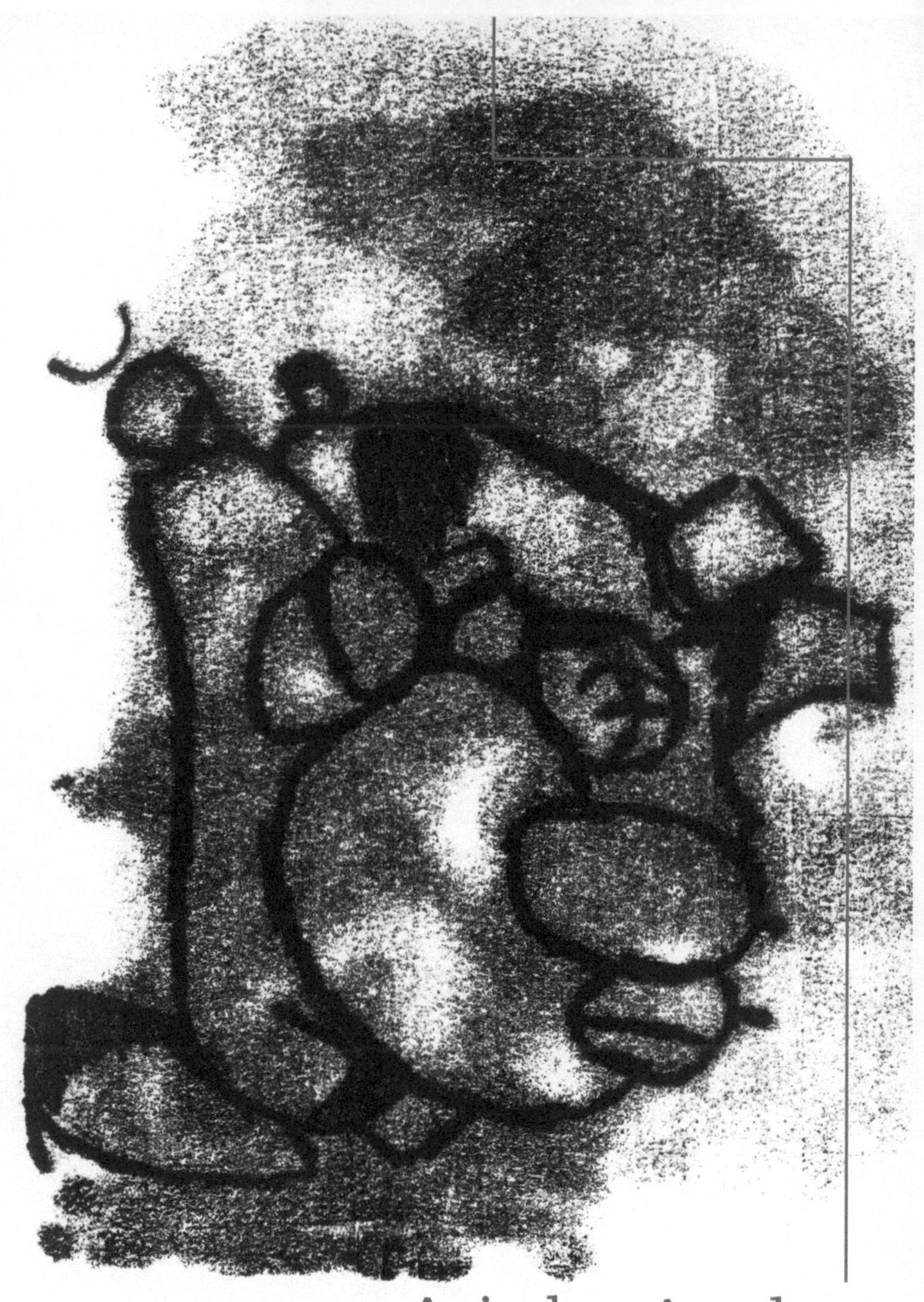

Ariadne Awakens

Instructions for the Labyrinth

Laura Costas

Last Words

"It's okay to not be at your most productive during a fucking global pandemic." —Lesley Jane Seymour

"You don't start out writing good stuff. You start out writing crap and thinking it's good stuff, and then gradually you get better at it. That's why I say one of the most valuable traits is persistence." —Octavia E. Butler

"No one is ever going to see your first draft. Get the story down however you can get it down, then fix it." —Neil Gaiman

"You can always edit a bad page. You can't edit a blank page." —Jodi Picoult

"Don't bend; don't water it down; don't try to make it logical; don't edit your own soul according to the fashion. Rather, follow your most intense obsessions mercilessly." —Franz Kafka

"You don't need a certificate for the creative life, you don't need to apply to do it, you don't even need to ask permission to do it. You just have to claim it—and claim it every day by showing up to do it."—Grant Faulkner

"He is an emancipated thinker who is not afraid to write Foolish things." —Anton Chekhov

"Do not hoard what seems good for a later place in the book, or for Another book; give it, give it all, give it now." —Annie Dillard

"Words, English words, are full of echoes, of memories, of associations—naturally." —Virginia Woolf

"A novel is like a cloud. When you're in the thick of it, it's shape is unknowable. But once you've passed through and gained a little distance, it's much easier to see." —Scott Westerfeld

"Writing is work. Nobody is making you do this: you chose it, so don't whine." —Margaret Atwood

"I write to add my voice to the sum of voices, to be part of the choir. / I write to be one sequin among the shimmering others, hanging by a thread from the evening gown of the world. I write to remember. / I write to forget myself, to be completely immersed in the will of the poem that when I look up from the page I can still smell the smoke from the house burning in my brain." —Dorianne Laux

"And the day came when the risk to remain tight in a bud was more painful than the risk it took to blossom." —Anais Nin

"Life isn't about finding yourself. Life is about creating yourself." —George Bernard Shaw